V

The Russians in Central Asia

SALZWASSER
VERLAG

Valikhanof M. Veniukof

The Russians in Central Asia

Reprint of the original, first published in 1865.

1st Edition 2022 | ISBN: 978-3-75259-048-7

Verlag (Publisher): Salzwasser Verlag GmbH, Zeilweg 44, 60439 Frankfurt, Deutschland
Vertretungsberechtigt (Authorized to represent): E. Roepke, Zeilweg 44, 60439 Frankfurt, Deutschland
Druck (Print): Books on Demand GmbH, In de Tarpen 42, 22848 Norderstedt, Deutschland

THE RUSSIANS IN CENTRAL ASIA:

THEIR OCCUPATION OF

THE KIRGHIZ STEPPE

AND

THE LINE OF THE SYR-DARIA:

THEIR POLITICAL RELATIONS WITH

KHIVA, BOKHARA, AND KOKAN:

ALSO DESCRIPTIONS OF

CHINESE TURKESTAN AND DZUNGARIA.

BY CAPT. VALIKHANOF, M. VENIUKOF

Translated from the Russian

BY JOHN AND ROBERT MICHELL.

LONDON:

1865.

PREFACE.

The valuable contributions to the geography and political history of Central Asia printed from time to time at St. Petersburg are almost entirely lost to this country, owing to their being published in the Russian language. The great interest which Central Asia has lately attracted, in consequence of recent political events in the Khanat of Kokan, and the comparative ignorance which has prevailed in England respecting the true position of Russia in those distant regions, have induced us to make a collection of the most important of the Russian materials relating to the subject, and to present them to the public in an English form. The several chapters composing this volume, on their original appearance at St. Petersburg, excited considerable interest, and their several authors are well-known Russian travellers and geographers, who have made Central Asia their special study.

Among the accounts of journeys and travels in Central Asia here presented to the reader, those of Captain Valikhanof in Dzungaria and Eastern Turkestan occupy a prominent position. Since the days of Marco Polo and the Jesuit Goez, no European, with the exception of A. Schlagintweit, has, to our knowledge, penetrated into those countries. The fear and jealousy of Europeans and the religious fanaticism of the people made that country quite inaccessible to modern explorers, and the mournful fate of the enterprising traveller at Kashgar is an illustration of the danger with which any attempt to reach it is beset. The travels of Valikhanof through Dzungaria and Chinese Turkestan were performed under singularly favourable circumstances. Although an officer in the Russian service and a man of good education, he is the son of a Kirghiz Sultan and a native of the Steppes. He is consequently well acquainted with the language and customs of the people of Central Asia, and could go amongst them without exciting the least suspicion of being connected with Russia. He succeeded in reaching Kashgar in the train of a Kokan caravan, under the assumed character of a Marghilan merchant. His description of Kashgar, and of the political state of Eastern Turkestan, will be acknowledged as an important addition to the scanty information we as yet possess concerning that country.

The chapters descriptive of the political relations of Russia with the different Khanats, and of the manner in which the power of Russia has been consolidated in the Kirghiz Steppe, and on the line of the Syr-Daria or Jaxartes, will, it is hoped, enable the English public to form a correct idea of the present attitude of Russia in Central Asia; and in presenting to our readers these Russian narratives and descriptions, we cannot omit to point out that, as the work of geographers and men of science, it has been executed with impartiality and without any political object.

The recent capture of some Kokan towns and fortresses, and the formation of a new province with the title of Turkestan, have increased the apprehensions that have been entertained by a portion of the English public of hostile intentions against British India. The junction of the line of the Syr-Daria with that of Eastern Siberia has certainly added a considerable piece of territory to the frontier of Russia, on which a distinct military frontier may now be drawn from the Gorbitza mountains on the Amur River to the mouth of the Jaxartes in the Sea of Aral. Before that junction was effected by the capture of Turkestan and Chemkent, the military colonies on the Syr-Daria had no communication with the garrison of Fort Vernoé, the southernmost point on the frontier of Eastern Siberia, except by the circuitous route of Orenburg. The obligation which Russia has incurred of protecting the pastoral Kirghizes under her allegiance against the marauding expeditions of the subjects of the Khan of Kokan, frequently necessitates measures of retaliation and chastisement. It was, therefore, not the gain in territory, but the necessity of establishing a continuity of communication, and a consolidation of power with a view to tranquil possession, that prompted the recent encroachments of Russia on the dominions of the Khan.

There is no doubt that Bokhara and Khiva, as well as Kokan, are entirely at the mercy of Russia, and will probably, in the course of time, become subject to it; but a perusal of this book will afford some evidence of the present uselessness of such conquests to an Empire already too large and unwieldy, thinly peopled at its centre, and just entering upon a long and perhaps troublesome process of political reorganisation. Designs, however, on British India may quite as well be entertained with a force on the Caspian as with an army at Bokhara. The same distance would have to be passed by the invading force before reaching Afghanistan, and the same dangers would have to be encountered by it from a British army rapidly moved on by railways and rivers, and furnished with abundant supplies.

On the other hand, the security and development of the Russian trade with Central Asia must eventually benefit England. Bokhara at present supplies Russia with cotton, dried fruits, and other goods, and imports their value from Russia, half in hardware, wooden boxes, and coarse prints, and half in specie. That specie is all that the Central Asiatics have to offer in return for English manufactured goods, which they highly esteem, but which they cannot buy with their inferior products. As prosperity, coming in the wake of tranquillity, becomes more general in the plains of Turkestan, so will the demand for English manufactures and the means of purchasing them, now almost absent, become available. In the meanwhile, and apart from all political considerations, the continued efforts of Russian men of science to throw light on a region of the world so little known and so highly interesting, cannot but meet with the sympathy of the English public, and merit its warm approval.

The engravings which illustrate the book are from

photographs taken on the spot during General Ignatief's last mission to Khiva and Bokhara, and the accompanying map has been carefully compiled from the most recent Russian sources; while for the introduction we are indebted to the late Mr. Hume Greenfield, formerly Assistant Secretary to the Royal Geographical Society, whose valuable assistance in editing the work and conducting it through the press we cannot sufficiently acknowledge.

J. AND R. MICHELL.

20*th March*, 1865.

CONTENTS.

CHAPTER I.

Introduction.

CHAPTER II.

Abridged Narrative of a Journey to Khiva, with Historical Particulars relating to the Khanat during the Government of Seid-Mohammed Khan, 1856—1860, *by E. Kühlewein.*

CHAPTER III.

General View of Dzungaria, by Captain Valikhanof.

CHAPTER IV.

Travels in Dzungaria, by Captain Valikhanof.

CHAPTER V.

On the Condition of Alty-shahr, or the Six Eastern Towns of the Chinese Province of Nan-lu (Little Bokhara) in 1858—1859.

CHAPTER VI.

Alty-shahr—Historical Review.

CHAPTER VII.

Trans-Ili and Chu Districts, by M. Veniukof. Almaty, or Vernoé.

CHAPTER VIII.

HISTORY OF THE ESTABLISHMENT OF RUSSIAN RULE ON THE SEA OF ARAL AND ON THE RIVER SYR-DARIA (JAXARTES) FROM 1847 TO 1862.

PART I.

CHAPTER X.

PART III.

Events in the Steppe during the Crimean War—Iset-Kutebar, the Knight of the Steppe—Attempt of Perovski to occupy Hodja-Nias—Occupation of Djulek, and Destruction of Yany-Kurgan.

1854—1862.

CHAPTER XI.

Diplomatic Relations between Russia and Bokhara.
By Zalesoff.

1836—1843.

APPENDICES.

APPENDIX I.

APPENDIX II.

APPENDIX III.

APPENDIX IV.

LIST OF PLATES, ETC.

SKETCHES OF TRAVEL

IN VARIOUS REGIONS OF

CENTRAL ASIA.

CHAPTER I.

INTRODUCTION.

Much of the uncertainty attaching to the immense region hitherto known to English readers under the general name of Tartary, is undoubtedly due to the perversity with which each fresh traveller adopts a new spelling for himself, upon some recondite principle of phonography. Every such attempt, moreover, is sure to provoke hostile criticism, and, in so doing, to elicit new views of philology, which tend still further to perplex the student. Another element of difficulty, which seems to have been pretty much overlooked, is that the lune-shaped tract—extending over 52° of longitude, *i. e.* from Orenburg in lat. 51° 48′ N. 55° 12′ E. to Kiakhta, on the meridian of 107° E., and in about the same latitude, the main width of which, however, owing to the physical configuration of the spurs of the Altai, lies between the much lower parallels of 46° and 40°,—forms a sort of debateable land for at least four, if not five, distinct languages—namely, the Persian, the Bokharian, the Thibetan, and the Mongolian, besides the recently intruded Russian. With respect to at least two of these, the first and last-named, the contempt generated by a higher civilization naturally induces a system of nomenclature founded upon the language of the more civilized community, and, in consequence, differing widely from the indigenous appellations by which the more prominent places are known to the natives. In consulting, therefore, the accompanying translations from the Russian of the works of Valikhanof, Veninkof, and others, it is necessary to bear in mind that it is quite possible any given spot has been already visited and described by Europeans, who have contented themselves with the names bestowed by their native guides. A noted instance of this is the perversity with which Russian hydrographers and Russian travellers, when speaking of the region watered by the river Syr-Daria, persistently speak of Fort Perovski, a stronghold on the caravan route from Bokhara to Petropavlovsk (in Siberia, 195 m. W. of Omsk), quite recently constructed to check the audacity of the Kirghiz Cossacks, ignoring that since the close of last century an important native town has existed on the opposite bank, which will be found in all the best maps under the name Ak-Mesjid. There is perhaps a political reason for these attempts to extinguish the native names, since it is notorious that both Persia and Russia have long been endeavouring to feel their way eastward and southward. The exhaustive system of agriculture which travellers have described as characterizing Persia, and which, with advantages hardly equalled, certainly not surpassed, by any Oriental country, still keeps her impoverished and consequently warlike along her frontier line, will readily account for the attempts of that power to subjugate the mountainous region, interspersed with fertile valleys, which forms her Eastern boundary. Hence the permanent feeling of irritation which prevails among the Hill-tribes all along the N.W. frontier of our Indian Empire, and the constant recurrence, every few years, of some miserable squabble about Herat, which, although distant 500 miles of the wildest mountain desert from Attock, it is still the fashion to call "the key of India" in these days, when Bombay is only twenty days distant from London, and when Bombay and Calcutta are themselves on the eve of being brought within three days of each other by the development of our Indian railways.

A cursory glance at the map might, at first sight, seem to give some ground for alarm, when we find that Russia has virtually pushed forward her outposts to within 300 miles of the British frontier on the north. But the barrier here is even more impassable than that to the westward, since there intervenes between the Muscovite and the supposed secret object of all his movements and intrigues in those regions, the mighty barrier of the Hindoo Koosh, and the Kuen Lun, which rise like a wall, 17,000 feet high, with scarcely a crest or depression throughout their entire extent—none certainly practicable for an army with the *matériel* and appliances of war as waged by 19th century civilization. The truth is that, in the interests of science and humanity, Great Britain ought to rejoice that any form of European civilization is penetrating the howling wilderness that lies to the North of the Himalaya, Secure behind that impassable bulwark, still more secure in the gradual elevation in the scale of nations of the vast population which destiny has committed to her charge, she ought to view with feelings of sympathy and interest any policy that will replace the barbarities of such men as Hodja Khan, and the other ruffians that infest the territory conterminous with our own to the N.N.W.

The phantom, however, of a Russian invasion of India has so completely possessed certain classes of *quid nuncs*, that it is possible a succinct sketch of the physical peculiarities of the country may not be out of place, and such a synopsis would at all events be required to enable the reader to comprehend the following pages. Our ignorance of the region in question has long been made a matter of reproach to us, and our knowledge, "chiefly conjectural," has been stigmatized as a disgrace to science, "owing to its wretched state of imperfection." It would perhaps puzzle those who thus readily impeach the energy which has already sacrificed so many valuable lives in this very country, if we were to ask them to devise means for throwing open to Anglo-Saxon enterprise a country where emphatically every man carries his life in his hand. Something more is required to prove con-rage or conduct than to exclaim, "Fool!" or "Coward!" as each succeeding traveller recoils before the hardships and dangers of a journey through Little Bokhara. Round that land of romance, the genius of the West has flung a mantle of refinement, till a sort of notion has got abroad that the virtues of savage life, banished from North America, still survive among the hordes of the Kirghiz Kaisaks, the Kara Kalpaks, the Dzungarians, and the Kashgarians. Every Khan is a Feramorz or Alaris, and among the perennial snows of the Pamir, or the great table-land in which the Indus takes its rise, the imagination delights to picture a state of primeval innocence and Arcadian simplicity, instead of one of constant war, disgraced by more than the atrocities that ordinarily accompany Oriental warfare.

Anything like a physico-geographical and ethnographical sketch of Central Asia must necessarily be a compilation of every authority from the days of Rubruquis 500, and Jenkinson 300 years ago, to the more modern researches of Lesvchine, Abbott, Wood, Burnes, Conolly, Nikoforof, Mouravief, etc. These have been in many instances corrected by the researches since made under the auspices of the Russian Geographical Society, including the experiences of the distinguished authorities whose sketches of travel now make their appearance for the first time in an English translation. Enough, however, remains to enable us to supply a general idea of the entire region, distinguishing the various Khanats, and tracing their general history till within what may be called the historic period, which may be stated as commencing only within the last ten years; in fact, since the Russian Government has begun to enforce some sort of order, partly by the establishment of armed stations and forts, partly by offering to the towns which used to be great entrepôts of trade an outlet for their products through Western Siberia and Russia in Europe.

Western or Independent Tartary, as it was called in the text-books of geography of the last generation, comprises the following main divisions, which, for convenience sake, we shall enumerate *seriatim*, beginning with the river Emba, which, after a Westerly course of 300 miles falls into the Caspian in 47° N. 53° 15′ E.:

I. The country South of the river Emba, Yemba or Jem, consists of a table-land which separates the Caspian and Aral, and rises to an average elevation of 620 feet according to a profile sketch which first appeared in Lesvchine's work on the Kirghiz

Kaisaks, and which we reproduce in the Appendix. This table-land, known as the Ust-Urt, is about 240 miles in length, and extends the whole width, 160 miles, between the two seas. The entire East side of the plateau forms a bold coast line along the Western shores of the Sea of Aral, and at its S.E. corner it turns abruptly to the W.N.W., the angle thus formed at the S.W. corner of the Sea of Aral being known as "the Tchink." The Ust-Urt is, in fact, the S.W. continuation and extremity of the great Steppe of the Kirghiz Kaisaks, this portion forming part of the territory of the Lesser Horde.

II. South of the Ust-Urt, and of the Sea of Aral, is the Khanat of Khiva, including the desert plain of Kharesm, and the oasis of the same name, as also the rich, well-watered plain of Merv, 37° 28′ N., 62° 10′ E. This region, also known in older geographies as Turan, is bounded, according to Captain Abbott, on the S. by an irregular curving line, extending from the river Attreck, which debouches into the S.E. angle of the Caspian, in 37° N., 54° E. nearly to Herat, where it turns N., and becomes the Eastern boundary of the Khanat. The Eastern boundary follows an imaginary line corresponding pretty closely with the 63° meridian, crossing the Oxus, or Amu-Daria, about 90 miles W.

of Bokhara, and is thence prolonged northward till it intercepts the Syr-Daria, or Jaxartes, about 120 miles from its mouth. The area comprised within these boundaries is in round numbers 450,000 square miles, the surface of which is singularly uniform. With the exception of the banks of the Oxus, and the oasis of Merv, the entire country presents an unbroken waste, unrelieved by mountains, rivers, lakes, or forests. The Ust-Urt, last mentioned, is nominally part of the Khanate of Khiva, but the extreme cold of winter, and the intense heat of summer, make it almost uninhabitable. The geological formation of this Khanat is principally red sand-stone on the S., gradually changing into a firm clay resting upon lime-stone. The volume of the various rivers of course depends upon the season, the melting of the snows of the Hindoo Koosh, in which the Oxus rises, causing that river to overflow its banks in many places during the autumn. In some of the older maps, a dried river course is represented as occasionally filled from the Oxus, and finding its way across the desert of the Kharesm, till it reaches the Caspian at Balkan Bay, 39° 40′ N. There is nothing intrinsically improbable in this diversion, as the Sea of Aral itself is known to be 117 feet above the level of the Caspian. The dominant race are Usbec Tartars, to which tribe the latest dynasty of Khans belongs, and the population is variously estimated, by Balbi, at 800,000, by Fraser, at 1,500,000, and by Abbott, at 2,600,000. Khiva, the capital, which, as will be seen, was visited by Kühlewein, is situated on a fertile plain near the Oxus, in 41° 22′ 40″ N., by 60° 2′ 57″ E., and is about half a mile square, containing about 1500 houses, clay built, and arranged in narrow streets, with a population of about 12,000 permanent inhabitants.

III. Immediately to the eastward of the Khanat of Khiva is that of Bokhara, which has acquired a melancholy interest for England by the fate, long wrapped in mystery, of Colonel Stoddart and Captain Conolly, and the heroic enterprise of the late Dr. Wolff, who penetrated as far as Samarcand, only to find confirmation of the bloody fate which rumour had already hinted as having overtaken our adventurous countrymen. The limits of the Khanat of Bokhara are even more difficult to define than those of Khiva, owing to the incessant political fluctuations of this unhappy country. It should seem that when Burnes first visited the country, the Khan claimed the entire territory from the Hindoo-Koosh, including Balkh (the ancient

Bactria) and Andku, or Ankoi, where Moorcroft died, to the basin of the Syr-Daria, or from 35° N. to 45° 30′ N., while the Eastern boundary, in the absence of precise geographical data, has been variously stated at 68° to 70° E. The Eastern frontier is, in fact, conterminous with the Khanat of Kokan, and the Western boundary of what is variously known as Chinese Turkestan, or Little Bokhara, (the scene of Lalla Rookh), of which the capitals are Yarkend and Kashgar. But since 1849, the advance of Russia along the valley of the Syr-Daria and the incursions of the Kirghiz of the Middle Horde on the one hand, and of the Kokanians on the other, have made the basin of the Syr-Daria anything but a desirable acquisition, and it is understood that the reigning Khan of Bokhara does not assert his sovereignty beyond the parallel of 41° N., so that we may estimate the present extent of the Khanat at about 230,000 square miles, with a population estimated by Irving (1809), at 3,600,000, by Burnes at 1,000,000, by Fraser at 2,500,000, and by Balbi (1826), at 1,200,000. Fraser, however, speaks of the city of Bokhara as containing 120,000 houses alone, and doubts if any other Eastern city, except some of the Chinese capitals, contains so large a population;

and as the soil is argillaceous in the plains, and the valleys have long enjoyed in the East a reputation somewhat resembling that of Tempe in Thessaly, it seems probable that the larger estimates are the more likely to be correct. The territory is intersected from S.E. to N.W. by the Oxus, or Amu-Daria, the only other river of importance being its tributary, the Kholiķ, or Sogd, whence the ancient name Sogdiana, given to the district of which Samarcand is the present capital.

The eastern portion of this Khanat is entirely occupied by mountains. Of these the chief are the Kish range, between Kish, 39° N. 67° E., and Samarcand, a spur of the little-known Kara-Dagh chain. In this exceedingly rugged, precipitous system of mountains occurs the celebrated Derbend or Koluga Pass, ("the Iron Gate"), leading from Kish, S.E., and forming the sole means of communication with Hissar and thence to Affghanistan. A still loftier range commences to the N.E. of Bokhara, and runs eastward to the borders of the Khanat of Kokan, where it converges at right angles to the Bolor or Belur Tagh. This is called the Ak-Dagh, or "White Mountains," and seems to mark the Northern boundary of the celebrated high-lying table-land of Pamir, on the West side of which the

Oxus takes its rise. The scene, as described by Lieutenant Wood, who penetrated thither on the 19th February, 1838, in mid-winter, is so striking that we need not apologize for introducing it here. On reaching a spot elevated 14,400 feet above the level of the sea, some of his escort refused to proceed further; upon which Lieutenant Wood determined to push forward with the remainder through deep, new-fallen snow:—"As we neared the head waters of the Oxus, the ice became weak and brittle. After quitting the surface of the river, we travelled about an hour along the right bank, and then ascended a low hill which apparently bounded the valley to the E.; on surmounting this at 5 P.M. of the 19th February, 1838, we stood, to use a native expression, on Bam-i-Dúniah, or 'Roof of the World,' while before us lay stretched a noble frozen sheet of water, from whose Western extremity issued the infant Oxus. This fine lake lies in the form of a crescent, about 14 miles long from E. to W. by one mile in average breadth. On three sides it is bordered by swelling hills about 500 feet high, while along its south bank they rise into mountains 3500 feet above the lake, or 19,000 feet above sea-level, covered with perpetual snow, from which never-failing source the lake is supplied.

From observations made at the W. end, I found the latitude to be 37° 27′ N., 73° 40′ E., and the elevation, as deduced from the boiling point of water, 15,600 feet. The hills and mountains that encircle Lake Sir*-i-Kol give rise to some of the principal rivers in Asia. From the ridge of its East end flows a branch of the Yarkand, one of the largest streams that water Chinese Turkestan, while from the low hills rising on the N. issues the Sir,* or river of Kokan; and from the sunny chain opposite, both forks of the Oxus and a branch of the Kunar are supplied. When the lake is swollen by the molten snows of summer, the size of the river is correspondingly increased, and no great alteration takes place in the level of the lake itself. The aspect of the landscape was wintry in the extreme. Wherever the eye fell, one dazzling sheet of snow covered the ground, while the sky overhead was everywhere of a dark and angry hue. Clouds would have been a relief to the eye, but they were utterly wanting. Not a breath moved along the face of the lake; not a beast, not even a bird was visible."

* Recent authorities since the visit of Lieutenant Wood have, however, established that there is no affluent of the Syr-Daria, which takes its rise so far south as Lake Sir-i-Kol, the immense ranges of the Belur and the Ak-Dagh intervening.

IV. The next region calling for notice is the Khanate of Kokan, which may be succinctly described as comprising almost the entire valley of the Syr-Daria and its various confluents. But the fact that this State has only recently assumed a prominent position in Oriental politics, and that, partly in consequence of the nomad half-savage hordes which form its northern population, partly from its geographical position, it has been among the very earliest to come into direct collision with Russia, makes it necessary to describe with as much accuracy as possible, the exact limits of the territory over which the Khan of Kokan asserts his sovereign rights. In order to this purpose it will be necessary to revert to the north shore of the Sea of Aral, from which extends eastward a series of steppes, inhabited principally by the Kirghiz Kiasaks, who are divided into the Lesser or Western, Middle, and Great Hordes, the latter being the farthest to the east, and extending indeed as far as the great Lake Balkash, and the banks of the Ili, of which mention will be found in the following pages. The pressure, however, of a powerful civilization in the north, and a sudden impetus imparted to the recent history of Kokan, owing to its last Khan having dexterously availed himself of the dissensions long rife among his neighbours, have tended to bring these wandering hordes into a sort of precarious allegiance to one or other of the contending powers. Russia has made her advance it would seem chiefly from the N.E., viz., from the Government of Tomsk, in Siberia. Hence the Greater Horde has been the first to feel the weight of her authority, and, as we shall presently see, it is upon this side that the Russian outposts have been pushed forward to the very foot of the Kuen-Lun to the north. But a not less severe coercion was meanwhile being exercised by the Kokanians, and hence we find the limits of the Khanat are now said to extend as far north as the Ala-Tau, or Algonski range in South-Western Siberia (Lat. 48° North), in which parallel the River Sary-su, which falls into the Teli-Kul Lake, may be said to mark its limits eastwards. From this point the boundary line, at latest accounts, extends to the banks of the Syr-Daria, where the Russians have erected the fort of Perovsky on the right bank, facing the Kokanian town of Ak-Mesjid already alluded to, which is immediately opposite. Although, however, the Russians have pushed forward thus far, it is simply with the view of checking the predatory habits of the Kirghiz, who acknowledge the sovereignty of the Khan of Kokan. The actual boundary line lies farther to the East, and includes the entire Western water-shed of the great Lake of Balkash. From this point it still continues S.E. to the Lake of Issyk-Kul. Here it encounters the immense chain of the Thian Shan, which bounds it abruptly along its S.E. frontier, separating it from Dzungaria and Chinese Turkestan, after passing which we again find ourselves at the table-land of Pamir, which forms a barrier to the South. The Western boundary seems to be rather arbitrary, but it includes a considerable sweep of land yet further west than the city of Khojend; (the Cyropolis or Alexandria Ultima of classical writers). The entire length of this extensive territory may be roughly stated at 950 miles by an average breadth of 360, or about 345,000 square miles; the whole surface being exceedingly mountainous, and forming in part the west buttress of the great central table-land of Asia. The whole region is intersected by immense streams, all flowing towards the Syr-Daria, the majority of which, however, lose themselves in the numerous extensive lakes which here begin to stud the surface of the country, and possess no visible outlet. Kokan, though rather more to the north than Bokhara, is, on the whole, more fertile and of a better soil, but sheep still form, as in past ages, the chief wealth of the community. Kokan includes within its boundaries a number of considerable towns, besides the capital of the same name (a comparatively modern town), Khojend already mentioned, and which still numbers 30,000 inhabitants, Andijan the former capital, a little to the Eastward of the present capital, Tashkend with a population said to amount to 100,000, and others dating from remote times, but doomed to decay beneath the constant warfare which has so long devastated this region. Of the amount of population under the sway of the Khan of Kokan, it is quite impossible to give even an approximate estimate, owing to the uncertainty that prevails as to the Kirghiz and other armed tribes, but Nazarof reckons the standing militia at no fewer than 50,000 horsemen. This may be an exaggeration, but there is every reason to believe that the district watered by the Syr-Daria is at least not less thickly populated than the regions we have already treated of. The time occupied by caravans between Kokan and Bokhara is about six weeks. There is but little communication between Kokan and Little Bokhara, the Thian

Shan interposing an almost insurmountable obstacle.

V. Eastern Turkestan, Chinese Turkestan, or Little Bokhara, is, of all this region, that with which we have hitherto had the least acquaintance. Its Northern, Western, and Southern frontiers are, indeed, tolerably well defined, and as we know that since about the middle of last century, it has nominally belonged to the Chinese Empire, we may assume that its limit Eastward is indefinite, as it will gradually merge in Mongolia, somewhere still further to the East than the great saline basin of the Lob-nor. The Northern boundary is Dzungaria, which forms the subject of a separate chapter. The Western is the Khanat of Kokan already described, including the precipitous Eastern front of the table-land of Pamir, and it is shut off from Little Thibet and Thibet Proper, to the South and South-East, by the Eastern half of the Hindoo-Koosh, and the Western chain of the great Kuen-Lun, over which the most frequented pass is that of Kara-Korum, 18604 feet above sea level, connecting Ladak with Yarkend by the headwaters of the Shayok, which, rising in a glacier not far from the pass itself, falls into the Indus after a Westerly course of 320 miles, just above the town of Iskardo, 35° 10′ N. 75° 28′ E.

The entire territory of Little Bokhara, assuming it to extend as far as the meridian of 90°, thus including the great Lake of Lob, is sterile in the extreme, but relieved by large and fertile oases—a feature common to the continuation of the desert eastward where it becomes the great Desert of Gobi or Shamo. Of the various oases, the most important and best known are those of Kashgar, Yarkend, and Khotan. Of these the first-named lies at the foot of the southern spurs of the Thian-Shan range, and consists of a well-watered tract, on the principal river of which, called by the same name, is the city of Kashgar. This was, for many centuries, the seat of an independent prince; but, since the rebellion of 1826, has been reduced by the Chinese authorities to a secondary position in the district of Ili, of which Yarkend is the capital, and to which Khotan has also been attached. Kashgar city is in 39° 25′ N., and 74° E. (approximative); and the river on which it is situated, after a course of 300 miles, unites with that of Yarkend to form the Tarym, which, after a further course of 250 miles, falls into the great Lake of Lob-nor. Both these streams are famous for the splendid specimens of jasper and jade-stone which are found in their beds. Yarkend is the capital of the Chinese district of Ili, and is situate in 38° 10′ N. and 76° 30′ E. on a river (already mentioned) of the same name. It is walled, but with extensive suburbs, and has a population variously estimated at from 40,000 to 200,000. It has belonged to China since 1757, and is governed by Mahometan and Chinese officials alternately. The environs are highly cultivated, producing wheat, barley, rice, fruits, and silk, and there is extensive pasturage. Yarkend is known to the Chinese by the name of Ja-lo-Kiang.—Khotan lies to the Eastward of Yarkend, and lies in an oasis said by the Chinese to be about 1000 li. or 350 m. in circumference, immediately to the North of the Kara-Korum Pass. It is watered by a great number of streams, almost all of which flow into the Lob-nor. It contains the six cities of Khotan, Yurun-Khash, Kara-Khash, Djira, Keria, and Tak-hubin, each of which is governed by a Hakim, whose united votes constitute what is called the Council of Khotan. It is painful to see the discrepancies into which even the most renowned geographers have fallen as to the true site of this town, which has been variously stated as on any meridian between 75 E. and 84 E. According to the most reliable authorities, the city is situate in 37° N. and 80° 35′ E., a position which very nearly corresponds with the site assigned to it as immediately to the N.E. of the Kara-Korum Pass. It is the Ili-tchi or Ho-taen of the Chinese, and is supposed to contain about 50,000 inhabitants. It was originally a Hindoo colony, supposed to have been founded about the second century; but the magnificent Buddhist Temples and Monasteries were all destroyed by the Mahometan conquerors. The northern portion of Little Bokhara, under the shadow, as it were, of the Ala-Tagh, is the district of Aksu, one of the most fertile of the provinces into which the Chinese have subdivided their acquisitions here after the revolt of 1826. The products are various, consisting chiefly of lentils, wheat, barley, millet, apricots, grapes, and melons, and cotton is also said to grow here of fair quality. The capital, of the same name, is situate in lat. 41° 9′ N., 78° 40′ E., and, according to Timkowski, is the seat of a Chinese ambassador or viceroy. The population of the town is estimated by Moorcroft at about 25,000, and of the entire district at 130,000. The natives of the district are renowned for their taste in dressing hides and manufacturing cotton goods, and it is stated that there are mines of copper and one of rubies in the mmediate neighbourhood.

CHAPTER II.

Abridged Narrative of a Journey to Khiva, with Historical Particulars relating to the Khanat during the Government of Seid-Mohammed Khan, 1856–1860, *by E. Kühlewein.*

THE Mission for Central Asia, organized in 1858 by the Russian Government, under the immediate superintendence of General Ignatief, left Orenburg on the 27th of May of that year, and crossing the rivers Ilek and Emba, passed through the Orenburg Steppe and along the Western shore of the Sea of Aral to Aibugir Lake. At Cape Urga* it was determined to cross in native boats, as the previously selected route, *viâ* Kuhna-Urgendj, was found to be inconvenient in many respects.

From Cape Urga to Aibugir settlement, stretches

* 43° 40′ N., 58° 10′ E. (approximative.)

the South-Eastern Tchink* of the Ust-Urt, which visibly diminishes in elevation as it retires from the Sea of Aral, and in so doing loses its former wild aspect, although it continues to preserve for a long distance its rocky and precipitous characteristics.

Near Cape Urga the Mission was met by four deputies from the Khan of Khiva. These were the Karakalpak Prince Istleu, the Kirghiz Bey Azbergen, Murad Bek, and a son of the Governor of Kungrad. These envoys accompanied us to our camp, which was situated near Aibugir Lake, and close to a four-cornered pyramidal tower, erected by Prince Bekovitch in 1717.†

The passage over Aibugir Lake took three days, owing to the insufficient number of boats, and the tedious transhipment of the heavy baggage of the Mission. Aibugir Lake is about eighty miles long

* L'Oust-Ourt est un plateau qui n'a nulle part plus de six cents pieds de hauteur au-dessus du niveau des mers qu'il sépare. Cette haute plaine se termine en se dessinant circulairement par un rivage escarpé et tout bouleversé, que les Kirghiz, nomment Chink, au bas du quel s'étend, en déclinant, la plaine basse. (Lesvchine, "Description des Kirghiz-Kaizaks:" Paris, Imprimerie Royale, p. 15 Edition, 1840.)

† Prince Bekovitch was despatched by Peter the Great on a mission to Khiva in 1717, in the course of which he was massacred, with all his suite, in the town of Porsu, 66 miles to the North-West of Khiva.

by twenty in breadth at the part where we crossed it. Its chief affluent is the Laudan, a branch of the Amu-Daria (Oxus). The greatest depth in the lake occurs in the Bay of Ak-Cheganak, which is hemmed in by the sterile and precipitous rocks of the Ust-Urt Chink. The banks are overgrown with canes, which cover nearly the whole surface of the lake. The water is brackish, with a muddy bottom.

On the Khivan shore we were met by the above-mentioned deputies and a guard of honour, which was to accompany the Mission as far as Kungrad. On the following day the deputies were accorded a formal reception by the head of the Russian Mission, in a tent specially arranged for the occasion. This audience, however, only lasted half an hour, and the conversation was exclusively confined to ceremonious compliments.

On the 11th July, the Mission, still escorted by Khivans, started for Kungrad. Cultivated patches and small villages bordered this part of the road, and the whole face of the country was intersected by canals, used almost exclusively for irrigating the fields. Nearly the whole of the settled population of the Khanat of Khiva is concentrated on the left bank of the Amu-Daria. Each owner of the soil marks off his allotment with earthen walls, every such enclosure generally containing cornfields, gardens, cattle, and sometimes a little factory; the owner is called a Beg or Hodja.

About half-way to Kungrad we were met by a Custom-House official, who was the bearer of the usual salutations from the Khan, and announced that he had been sent to inquire of what the baggage consisted; a rumour had evidently reached Khiva of the embassy being provided with cannon. It having been explained to him that the baggage of a Mission is never liable to search, he requested to be furnished at least with a list of our effects. Satisfied with an inventory of our heaviest things, he took his departure, after being gratified by a small present. The other Khivan officials also took leave of us here, not omitting to make repeated inquiries during the day respecting the health of the head of the Mission. We encamped for the night near the garden of the Kirghiz Bey, Azbergen, where a repast consisting of mutton, bread, and fruit had been prepared for us.

On the 12th July we found ourselves approaching Kungrad. In a small wood within half a mile of the town, all the members of the Mission put on their uniforms, with the view of making an impos-

Part of the City of Kungrad seen from the River Daria.

ing entrance. As we advanced towards the town, the crowd gradually increased, and greeted us with incessant shouts of "*Urús! Urús!*"

After traversing the narrow streets of Kungrad, we stopped at the gates of the Khan's palace, where we were received by Divan Baba, an official specially appointed to accompany the Mission to Khiva. In this palace apartments were allotted for each member of the Embassy. A tent, in which refreshments had been prepared, was erected in an interior court. The Yesawul Bashi,* governor of the town, did not make his appearance till the evening. He was evidently alarmed at our arrival, and did all he could to induce us to hurry our departure. The motive for this churlish behaviour was clear. He had received orders from the Khan to provide at his own expense for all the wants of the Mission during its stay at Kungrad.

The town of Kungrad extends along the left side of the Khan canal and the river Amu-Daria. Between the right bank of the canal and the river runs a broad earthen wall, about three miles in length, and at a short distance off, between it and

* Chief Master of the Ceremonies. Yesàwul, a Turkish word, means a guard or armed attendant at a court. It has been adopted into Russia, and is there used to denote a major of Cossacks.

the river, is a second wall, both extremities of which abut on the river, thus forming, with the river bank, an oblong square. These two walls constituted at one time the fortifications of Kungrad, which town, so late as the beginning of this century, was independent of Khiva, and governed by its own Uzbek princes. During the reign of Mohammed-Rahim-Khan, in 1814, the whole town and neighbourhood fell under the sway of the Khans of Khiva. The most remarkable building in Kungrad is the palace of the Khan, which was occupied by us during our stay.

On the following day the whole Mission started in seven boats up the Amu-Daria, each boat being towed by four or five Khivans. Our progress was tedious, rarely exceeding ten miles a day. In order to avoid falling in with Turkmen, and sometimes to shorten the journey, our boats were hauled through canals and branches of the river, which had at this season overflowed its banks. These inundations occur twice a year, from May to June, and again from July to August, a sure indication that the sources of the river must lie among the snowy chains of Balkh or Affghanistan. The effect of these inundations upon the canals is various; some are choked with sand, while others are cleaned and deepened by the pressure of the water.

The transport of goods by water is preferable throughout this region to their conveyance by land, not alone on account of the far lower cost, but also because the camel-drivers refuse to follow the course of the river, owing to the swarms of gnats, gad-flies, and other insects, which greatly harass, and even prove fatal occasionally to their cattle, as also to the damp, unwholesome air which induces ague. Almost all the villages and towns were in a deplorable condition, presenting ample evidence of the devastations of the Turkmen. In the ruined "aùls" or camps of the Karakalpaks, we only found old people and infants; the whole of the adult population had been carried away to Khiva, and across the Persian frontier, to be sold as slaves. The towns of Kipchak on the left bank of the Amu-Daria, and Hodjeil, had met with a similar fate. At a distance of twenty miles from the ruins of the ancient town of Giyaùr, and not far from the banks of the river, stands the town of Yany-Urgendj, or New Urgendj, which, after Khiva, is the chief commercial *entrepôt*. Russian merchandise is taken direct to Khiva, but all purchases of native produce are made at Urgendj. All industrial pursuits, moreover, are centred here. Gunpowder is manufactured in the vicinity of the town, but in no great quantities. The principal seat of production of this article is Hazarasp, a little further up the river, S.E. from Urgendj. The Khan had sent Darga, a Khivan dignitary, to Yany-Urgendj with a small suite to receive us. He was a venerable old man, and stood apparently high in the favour of the Khan, as his Cashmere "khalat," or robe of dignity, and jewelled dagger, testified. In his suite were several dancers and musicians.

On the 28th of July we turned out of the Amu-Daria into the Shavat Canal, on emerging from which we passed through the Kazavat and Palvan-Ata Canals, and finally reached the capital by the Ingrik and Chardgeli branches of the two former. The Mission took up its quarters outside the town, in the gardens of Gumgumdan, which the Khan had assigned it. Having no horses, we could not present ourselves before the Khan, and therefore deferred our audience until the 9th of August. On the day of our arrival, at five o'clock, we were visited by the Shawul Bek,* chamberlain to the

* In Bokhara, the Shek-Kawaul is the title of the functionary, a sort of diplomatic chamberlain, charged with the reception and accommodation of Foreign Missions.

court, who, in the name of the Khan, invited the head of the Mission to the palace. Leaving a guard at the door of the embassy, we started for

DARGA, ONE OF THE MINISTERS OF THE KHAN OF KHIVA.

the town. At the gates was drawn up the Khivan infantry, while the body-guard was marshalled in front of the palace. We entered the latter by the lofty principal portals, leaving our escort outside We were first received by the Mehter, one of the chief Ministers of the Khan. It must here be observed that all the officers of state have apartments in the Khan's palace, where they assemble every day to receive his instructions. We remained about a quarter of an hour in the Mehter's chamber, whence we were summoned into the Khan's presence. We found him seated on an elevated divan, with a dagger and pistol lying before him, while behind him floated his state banner. Three ministers, the Kush-Begi, Mehter, and Divan-Begi, stood in front, and the Chamberlain at the door. The Imperial rescript, which the Secretary of the Mission bore on a red cushion, was now delivered by the head of the Mission to the Mehter, who, in his turn, placed it in the hands of the Khan. Having untied the gold cord and taken it out of the case, he examined the seal for some time, and then placed the packet beside him without opening it.

Seid-Mohammed Khan, son of the former Khan Mohammed-Rahim, and brother of the better known Allah-Kuli, was elected in 1856, when he was thirty years old. He succeeded Kutlu-Murad, nephew of Mohammed-Amin, who was killed in 1855 at Saraks, near Merv.* The Turkmen and Karakalpaks, dissatisfied with Kutlu-Murad, respectively chose for their Khans the former, Ata-Murad, and the latter, Jarlyk-Tura.

Intimidated by this energetic form of protest, Kutlu-Murad exhorted his people to rise against the Turkmen, who, on their part, perceiving the weakness of the Khan, determined to take advantage of it, and under the leadership of Niaz Mohammed Bāi, advanced to Khiva. Niaz Bāi, having gained admittance to the Palace under pretence of paying homage to the Khan, murdered him and his seven ministers. This led to an indiscriminate carnage in the unfortunate town; the inhabitants fell on the Turkmen, of whom very few made their escape. Niaz Bāi was there and then seized and executed.

After a short interregnum, Seid-Mohammed was elected Khan. His first act was to punish the rebellious Turkmen and Karakalpaks. A detachment of his troops routed a body of the rebels who were on their way from Kuhna-Urgendj to dispute his

* Merv is a decayed town, situated in an oasis of the same name, about 300 miles S.E. of Khiva. It was once the capital of the Seljuks, and is supposed to occupy the site of Antiochia Morgiana, founded by Alexander the Great. Since 1786, when it was sacked by the Uzbeks, it has gradually dwindled, till its present population does not exceed 3000.

succession. On this occasion Jarlik, the Khan chosen by the Karakalpaks in 1855, was killed, and a portion of that tribe became subject to Bokhara. These dynastic disputes, and the constant wars arising therefrom, produced a famine, which greatly increased the price of all commodities ; bread, in particular, rising to an immoderate figure. During the summer of 1857, Khiva was visited by an epidemic, aggravated if not induced by the famine, and the consequent prostration of strength of the population. It was remarked during the prevalence of this pestilence that the rate of mortality was particularly high among children. From a description of the symptoms of this disorder, it must have been the true Asiatic cholera.

Since the year 1856, Khiva has been on friendly terms with Bokhara. Seid-Mohammed had succeeded in establishing his power so securely, that external aggression and intestine strife were for a time suspended. Thus considering himself firmly established on the throne, he despatched an embassy to Russia in the summer of 1857, conveying an intimation of his succession to the Khanat, his condolence on the death of the Emperor Nicholas, and congratulating His Majesty the Emperor Alexander the Second on his accession to the throne. The head of this mission was Fazyl Hodja, Sheikh-ul-Islam of the Khanat.

During the stay of the Russian mission at Khiva the town enjoyed tranquillity, and the Turkmen tribes, the Yamùds, Igdyrs and others refrained from making depredations; but immediately the mission left, which was on the 12th September, the Kungrad Uzbeks and the Karakalpaks joining in league with the Turkmen Khan, Ata-Murad, assassinated their ruler, Kutlu-Murad, with many of his party. He was succeeded by Mohammed-Fanàa, nephew of Tūra-Sufi, during whose rule Kungrad became, in 1814, subject to Khiva. Mohammed-Fanàa styled himself Khan of the Kharesm, and struck coins bearing his name.

After the lapse of another year the disturbances ceased; Mohammed-Fanàa was killed, and Kungrad again recognized the authority of the Khan of Khiva, Seid-Mohammed.

In 1858 Seid-Mohammed had three legitimate sons, of whom the eldest, Babadjan, was 13 years old; he also adopted the son of his predecessor, Kutlu-Murad, killed in the palace by the Turkmen. The Emir of Bokhara proposed to marry his daughter to this boy, possibly with the view of exercising an indirect influence over the affairs of Khiva by means of such a connection. The Khan was almost entirely under the influence of his eldest brother, Seid-Mahmud, a man of great mental powers and vast wealth, whose advice he often sought, his own intellect being often obscured by immoderate indulgence in opium.

The following are the highest functionaries in Khiva :—The Mehter or Chief Treasurer, who collects the poll-tax in the southern half of the Khanate; he likewise occasionally commands the troops, and, during the absence of the Khan, is charged with the conduct of the government. The second in authority is the Kush-Begi, who receives the poll-tax for the northern division of the Khanat, recruits the army, and superintends the excavation of canals. In 1858 the Kush-Begi, a fierce Uzbek, succeeded in defaming and supplanting the Mehter, whose functions he himself performed during the stay of the Mission. The Divan-Begi is the collector of Customs and Excise dues, and head of the Mint. The high judge and spiritual chief, Kazy,* is responsible for all religious matters. The Darga has charge of the Khan's palace, and the Yesawùl

* In all probability the same as the Arabic cadi. Which is the elder language, or may it not have been introduced with the spread of Mohammedanism?—[Ed.]

Bashi is the military commander-in-chief. Besides these, who are all, as already mentioned, attached to the person of the Khan, there are numerous Mehrems or Courtiers, who wear a knife, a gift of

Son of the Khan of Khiva.

the Khan, which entitles them to free access to the Court.

It may not be superfluous to draw attention to

the condition of the Khanat itself, under the rule of Seid-Mohammed.

LIMITS OF THE KHANAT.—If we are to consider, under the name of the Khanat of Khiva, the cultivated extent of land stretching along both sides of the lower course of the Amu-Daria, its confines may be fixed at the southern shore of Lake Aral at the Kizyl-Kum Steppe and Sheikh-Djeli Hills on the East, the great Turkmen Steppe on the South, and the level plain of the Ust-Urt on the West.

The pretensions, however, of the Khan of Khiva, extend considerably beyond these limits. He maintains that the boundaries of Khiva are the rivers Emba and Yany-Daria, falling into the Sea of Aral, on the North ; a line extending to Kukertli settlement, lat. 40° N., on the Amu-Daria, on the East ; and on the South from Kukertli to the town of Merv, and thence to the Bay of Balkansk on the East shore of the Caspian.

Assuming the former as the actual limits of Khiva, this territory does not contain more than 40,000 square miles.

The population of the Khanat consists of a number of tribes of separate origin, which have not as yet blended into one people. Their number is difficult to determine, as no census has ever been taken.

The principal tribes are: the Sarts, the aboriginal inhabitants, who form the great majority of the settled population.* Previous to Iltezer Khan, who, in the end of the last century, was the first to assume that title, the Sarts suffered much from the oppression of the Uzbeks; but, since the subjection of all the Uzbek "Inaks" or petty rulers of towns, by Iltezer Khan, the Sarts have been admitted to the highest offices of state, from which the Uzbeks were gradually excluded. With the exception of the post of Kush-Begi, all the most honourable positions are occupied by Sarts, who have now become the predominant class among the population. They live principally in the towns, and, in addition to agriculture, are engaged in trade, industrial pursuits, and breeding silk-worms. The Sarts are still distinguishable from the Uzbeks by their type of countenance.

The Uzbeks, the whilom conquering race, who are scattered throughout the whole Khanat, live on farms, and occupy themselves with agriculture, gardening and fishing. They now form, both numerically and politically, the secondary class of the population. The most unruly sept of this tribe,

* The Sarts are Persians in language and sect; Sart in Khivan being equivalent to Taj in Bokharian.

the Uigurs, were exterminated by the Khans for their constant revolts. To the north of the Sea of Aral, the Uzbeks are called Aral-Uzbeks, insular or Arasto-Arals, as the whole portion of the region to the north of the Laudan, an arm of the Amu-Daria, is really an island. The Arals are engaged in cattle-farming principally, as also in fishing. The Kungrad tribe, from which the Khan has sprung, is considered the chief one. The number of Uzbeks and Sarts together is reckoned at 400,000.

The Karakalpaks, numbering 15,000 settlers on the lower course of the Amu-Daria, near the Aral Sea, lead a partially nomadic life. They are burdened with taxes heavier than those imposed on any of the other tribes, the result being to completely impoverish them.

The Kirghizes, under Khivan jurisdiction, are estimated at about 10,000; they roam in the North-Eastern portion of the Khanat, more especially in the vicinity of Lake Dau-Kara.

The Turkmen have for ages been under the dominion of the Khiva Khans. Their type and language are purely Turkish, and many of them have seceded from the Khivans, and are now governed by their own elders; while those still subject to Khiva are engaged in constant wrangles with the Khivans, all arising in the election of a Khan. The Turkmen were desirous to have a Khan of their own tribe, to which the Khivans were opposed; this resulted in the murder of three Khans

A TURKMAN, OR TURCOMAN.

by the Turkmen, within a short space of time. The Khan of their choice, Ata-Murad, usually resides at Kuhna Urgendj. The Turkmen are employed in agriculture, but chiefly in the breeding of horses. Turkmen Argamaks, or steeds intended for complimentary gifts, are famous throughout Central Asia. The women manufacture carpets, which in texture and durability are not inferior to the Persian.

The Kyzyl-Bash, (better known to English readers under the familiar spelling of Kuzzilbash), or Persian prisoners, in slavery, live on the estates of their masters. The Iamshido, or Turk tribe, have returned to their native country in virtue of an agreement between Dost Mahommed and Rahim-Kuli. They were improperly called Affghans.

A small colony of Jews, numbering about ten families, who have immigrated from Bokhara, earn a precarious livelihood by dyeing, and distilling brandy chiefly for their own consumption. There are no Arabs in Khiva.

The Khan of Khiva coins his own money, of which gold, silver, and copper pieces are in circulation. The gold coins, or tilās, are of two denominations: large ducats, worth about twelve shillings, and half-ducats of six shillings. The silver coins are: the tenga, equal to about sevenpence, and the shahi, worth threepence. The pul, or karapul, is a copper coin. The value of money seldcm varies, and during our stay, forty-eight puls formed one tenga. The mint in the town of Khiva was founded, according to Moura-

SARBAZ, OR SOLDIER OF KHIVA.

vief, by Rahim Khan. In official documents, as also on the coins of Khiva, the ancient name of Kharesm is retained.

In Khiva there is a body of about 1,000 infantry, and about 20,000 cavalry, who are commanded by a hundred Min-Bashis.

In time of war the troops receive four times their ordinary pay. Their artillery is in a deplorable condition. Even of the eight or ten pieces of cannon standing in front of the Khan's Palace, some are mounted on carriages, and some not.

The revenue of the Government has materially fallen off. This is partly to be attributed to the migration of the Kirghizes, the secession of the Turkmen, and a general decline of trade—the Customs dues forming at one time a considerable item of revenue. The Mehter has charge of the treasury, and in case of a deficiency, the Khan borrows of the merchants.

The Russian goods usually found within the bazaars, are Russia-leather (Yufta), iron, cast and wrought, steel, copper sheets, needles, and cloth of inferior quality; the English wares brought from Persia are cottons and muslins. Barter-trade is not known, all goods being paid for in ready money.

Land in the Khanat of Khiva is held by families and tribes from time immemorial; that which is not claimed by any one, is given away by the

Khan in the form of rewards. Cultivation is attended with great expense and trouble. The land first requires irrigation, after which it must be covered with clay and black soil, before it can be made productive. The Khan often farms out his grounds, receiving a third of their produce. Industrial and manufacturing pursuits are carried on in the towns, and especially at Yany-Urgendj. A detailed account of the capital is to be found in the works of Danilevski and Basinière, who sojourned at Khiva in 1841. The town since their visit has undergone but little change.

During the stay of the Mission, the position of the town was determined astronomically by Capt. Mojaiski, whose observations were checked by M. Struve. It is as follows:—

41° 22′ 40″ North latitude,
60° 2′ 57″ longitude East of Greenwich.

CHAPTER III.

General View of Dzungaria, by Capt. Valikhanof.

A VEIL of mystery has hitherto hung over Central Asia,—a region pregnant with interest to mankind. Notwithstanding its proximity to the outlying possessions of two great European powers—England and Russia,—the greater portion of this country still remains in many respects inaccessible to Europeans. The learned Russian Geographer, Semenof, in the second volume of his translation of Carl Ritter's "Erdkunde von Asien," arrives at the conclusion that Central Asia has not been explored to a greater extent than the interior of Africa. Indeed the conflicting and contradictory data existing in our geographical literature with regard to Central Asia, render this region, if not altogether a *terra incognita* at all events a difficult scientific puzzle, while at the same time our knowledge of the Central Asiatic races is very confused and incomplete.

Central Asia, in its present stage of social organization, presents a truly mournful spectacle; her present stage of development being, so to speak, a sort of pathological crisis. The whole country, without exaggeration, is nothing but one vast waste, intersected here and there by abandoned aqueducts, canals and wells. The desolate sandy plains, dotted occasionally with ruins and overgrown with ugly prickly shrubs and tamarisks, is wandered over by herds of wild asses, and hardly less shy and timid saigaks. In the midst of this Sahara, along the banks of the rivers occur several small oases, shaded by the poplar, elm, and mulberry; while nothing intervenes to break the monotony of the scene, save here and there badly cultivated rice-fields and plantations of cotton, diversified by occasional vine-yards and orchards, abandoned by the lazy and improvident population to the care of Allah. In the centre of these oases, and constructed above the numerous remains of ancient cities, long since mouldering beneath the soil, stand the miserable mud hovels of a wild and barbarous race, demoralized by Islamism, and reduced almost to idiocy by the political and religious despotism of their native rulers on the one hand, and the arbitrary exactions of the Chinese police on the other.

Ignorance and poverty reign supreme in Mavero-Innahar, the modern Bokhara, Khiva and Kokan, which formed the richest and most enlightened region of the East in the fourteenth and fifteenth centuries. The libraries of Samarkand, Tashkend Ferganah (in the Khanat of Kokan), Khiva and Bokhara, with the observatory at Samarkand, have irrecoverably perished under the merciless hand of Tartar vandalism, which consigned to perdition all knowledge save that of a religious character. Even the monuments of a bygone era of enlightenment and culture, have fallen victims to the fanatical zeal of the Mullahs, who regarded them in the light of Towers of Babel, or as sinful rivalries between mankind and the creative spirit of Allah. The minarets, schools, tombs of Mahometan saints, and the Munar tower, from which criminals were precipitated, have alone survived the general ruin.

Central Asiatic rulers of the present day no longer indite verses and memoirs, nor do they compile astronomical tables as their ancestors did. These pursuits are superseded by solemn daily processions to the mosque, where they hold pious communion with the Mullahs; and, returning home, pass the remainder of the day in the grossest and most grovelling sensuality. Another favourite method of killing time is afforded them at the public arena, where they may witness the spectacle of two infuriated rams, specially trained for the purpose, butting at each other. Here they linger till one of the combatants is disposed of with a fractured skull, at which exciting crisis of the entertainment, and in the thirst for blood it excites, they administer to their generals forty blows on the back and a similar *quantum* on the belly.

The other portion of Central Asia—Little Bokhara—is in a condition hardly less pitiable. Here we find, notwithstanding the prevalence of Islamism, religious toleration, independence of the female sex, and no small development of municipal institutions, a country impoverished and desolated under the yoke of Chinese censorship and military mandarinism. Barbarism, despotism and decay prevail throughout the land. It is natural, therefore, that under such a state of civilization, or rather in the total absence of it, the attempts of Russia and England to become better acquainted with their coy neighbours, should have been attended with so little success hitherto, and occasionally with such mournful results.

In the latter part of 1859, accompanying a caravan in the guise of a Kokan merchant, I succeeded in reaching Kashgar, which, since the visit of the celebrated Marco Polo, in 1272, and that of the Jesuit Goez, in 1603, had only been reached by two Europeans—one a German, an officer in the East India Company's service, whose name is now unknown, and who has left an extremely interesting itinerary and description of his journey;* the other

* In a paper on the Pamir and upper course of the Oxus, read last year before the Russian Geographical Society, by M. Veninkhof, he says:—

"The chaos of our geographical knowledge relating to the Pamir table-land and the Bolor was so great, that the celebrated geographer Zimmerman, working under the superintendence of Ritter, was able to produce only a very confused and utterly incomprehensible map of this region. The connecting link was wanting; it was necessary that some one should carry out the plan conceived by the Russian Government in the beginning of this century, by visiting and describing the country. Fortunately, such an additional source of information has been found—nay, even two, which mutually corroborate and amplify each other, although they have nothing further in common between them.

"I here allude to the 'Travels through Upper Asia, from Kashgar, Tashbalyk, Bolor, Badakshan, Vakhan, Kokan, Turkestan, to the Kirghiz Steppe, and back to Cashmere, through Samarkand and Yarkend,' and to the Chinese Itinerary, translated by Klaproth, in 1821, leading from Kashgar to Yarkend, Northern India, Dairim, Yabtuar, Badakshan, Bolor, Vakhan and Kokan, as far as the Karatau mountains. The enumeration alone of these places must, I should imagine, excite the irresistible curiosity of all who have made the learned and much-lamented Adolphe Schlagintweit. The former was beaten so unmercifully with bamboos at Kashgar, that he could not sit his horse for two days after; the latter had his head struck off and placed on the apex of a pyramid formed of human skulls—a custom which, it should seem, distinguishes the Bokharians equally with their not more savage brethren on the coasts of Africa.

Chinese Kashgar is one of the district towns in the province of Nan-lu (southern country), and may be said to have enjoyed, ever since the days

the geography of Asia their study. These fresh sources of information are truly of the highest importance. As regards the 'Travels,' it is to be inferred from the preface, and from certain observations in the narrative, that the author was a German, an agent of the East India Company; despatched in the beginning of this, or at the latter part of the last century, to purchase horses for the British army. The original account forms a magnificent manuscript work, in the German language, accompanied by forty sketches of the country traversed. The text has also been translated into French in a separate manuscript, and the maps worked into one itinerary in an admirable style. The Christian name of this traveller—George Ludwig Von—appears over the preface; but the surname has been erased. Klaproth's Itinerary is so far valuable as the physical details are extremely circumstantial; almost every mountain is laid down, and care taken to indicate whether it is wooded or snow-capped, while equal care is taken to show whether the inhabitants are nomads or a stationary people. Ruins, bridges, and villages are also intelligibly designated, so that, although the same scale is not preserved throughout, its value, lucidity, and minuteness are not thereby deteriorated."

of the Ptolemies, great repute for caravans, particularly through its extensive tea-trade. Kashgar stands in the same relation to Central Asia that Kiakhta does to Siberia, and Shanghai and Canton to other European nations. This town, moreover, is famed in the East for the glowing charms of its "chaukens,"—young women, with whom the traveller may readily form an alliance for a certain number of years, or for the period of his stay, be it longer or shorter. It also enjoys great celebrity for its musicians, dancers, and "janissary hashish."* Owing to these attractions, Kashgar is the resort of Asiatic merchants from all parts of the continent. Here can be met the Thibetan with the Persian, the Hindoo with the Volga Tartar, Afghans, Armenians, Jews, Gipseys, and runaway Siberian Cossacks.

Of late, the town has obtained a notoriety of a different character. Here human beings have been daily slaughtered like barn-door fowls, the skulls of the victims being disposed in regular layers till they formed towers. In the words of a popular song, "It is difficult to keep a horse in Kashgar when hay is twelve *puls* the bundle—still

* Hashish—an extract made from *Cannabis sativa*, which has at once stupefying and exciting properties.

more difficult is it to keep the head on one's shoulders." The Hodjas, descendants of the former Kashgar rulers, in whose favour several sanguinary insurrections had latterly taken place, do not vent their fury so much on the Chinese, as on their own subjects the Kashgarians. One, for instance, is put to death for having served the Chinese Government, another for yawning in the presence of his ruler, or on similar trivial pretexts. The Chinese, when they succeed in expelling the Hodjas, notwithstanding their military inefficiency, inaugurate their triumphs by fleecing the people, destroying their cornfields, seizing the women and desecrating the mosques and tomb. They then hold a general flogging tribunal, whose operations are conducted with great ceremony and refined cruelty.

When I arrived at Kashgar, I found the Chinese reposing after the infliction of these multifarious tortures. The road leading to the gates of the town was bordered on both sides by a succession of small wicker cages, in which were displayed the heads of the natives who had suffered execution. The town, however, was relapsing into a quiet state. The native authorities, newly established by the Chinese, were riding about in the full dignity of mandarin caps, and castigating the pedestrians who were not sufficiently alert in making way for them. Intercourse was resumed with Kokan; the Kokanian Consul had been residing more than a month in the town, and the Bokharian and Kokanian caravans were rapidly filling the empty caravan-serais. The arrival of our party created a great sensation. Before we reached the town the Kirghizes had spread a rumour of the advance of a Russian caravan, consisting of 500 camels, while in truth it only numbered sixty. They had also declared that it was transporting boxes of destructive projectiles, and gave the name of "board of iron" to the leader, in consequence of his possessing an iron bedstead; to this they added that he was a Russian, and of suspicious character. The Asiatic is the most gullible of human beings—there is no absurdity that he will not swallow, and the more extravagant the rumour, the blinder is his credulity. The Chinese form no exception in this respect to their Semitic brethren of Central Asia, as it proved in our case. Luckily the Kokan Consul knew the leader of our caravan, and also some of the merchants composing it, but it was owing to this circumstance alone that we were permitted to enter the town.

I shall not dwell on the cross-examinations, annoyances, and trials, to which the caravan was subjected on the part of the Chinese Government and local authorities, but shall confine myself to a relation of my travels and stay among the Dikokamenni horde.

The Northern slope of the Thian-Shan has recently been explored from the Russian side, but M. Semenof, a Fellow of the Imperial Russian Geographical Society, succeeded in penetrating only as far as the sources of the River Narym, one of the affluents of the Jaxartes, or Syr-Daria. I crossed the Thian-Shan range in two directions, and examined the neighbourhood of Kashgar and Jengiskehr, or Yany-shahr, to the sandy ridge stretching between the latter town and Yarkend. Political disturbances in Kokan, terminating in the expulsion of the former Khan, and spreading to Kashgar, prevented me from visiting Yarkend, the largest and most populous town in Chinese Turkestan.

My travels may be divided into two periods. The first embraces my route through Dzungaria, that is, the Semiretsk (Seven rivers), and Trans-Ili regions, and so to Lake Issyk-kul. The physical aspect of these localities is already well known from the excellent surveys made by the officers of the Siberian Staff, and they have been scientifically explored by MM. Schrenk, Vlangali, Semenof, and Golubef. The information, however, furnished by these travellers has been limited to the physical geography of the region, without touching at all on its ethnography. My first visit to Dzungaria was in 1856, and I took part in the first expedition organized by Colonel Khomentovski to Lake Issyk-kul, passing subsequently three months in Kuldja. My travels in Dzungaria occupied in all five months, during which time I succeeded in traversing this region throughout its whole breadth and length, from Ala-kul to the Thian-Shan.

I shall only dwell here on what has been omitted or not noticed by travellers who preceded me, giving a short account of the Dzungarian *fauna*, and of the antiquities and inhabitants of the country. The *flora* of Dzungaria is more or less known, Alexander Schrenk having devoted much time to its study, and produced a general account of the vegetation of this country, in an interesting article inserted in Helmerson and Baehr's "Beitrage zur Kenntniss des Russischen Reiches," for 1840.

Mr. Semenof has also directed attention to the vegetation of the Thian-Shan, and has, I believe, a very rich *herbarium* collected on that range. Dr.

Tatarinof compiled a list of plants identified by him when travelling with M. Kovalevski to Kuldja, and which appeared in M. Vlangali's work. With regard, however, to the *fauna* of Dzungaria, not a single article has, so far as I know, been published.

Lakes Ala-kul and Balkhash formed, most probably at no distant period, one common water basin. Even at the present time, during the spring inundations, Ala-kul lake, according to the testimony of the Kirghizes, communicates indirectly with that of Balkhash by a marshy, saline belt of land. This belt forms, in Mr. Semenof's opinion, the natural boundary of the Kirghiz Steppe, beyond which Central Asia commences, together with a new soil and new *flora* and *fauna*.

As far as I can perceive, Dzungaria is not distinguished by any marked peculiarity of vegetation. The *flora* of the plains is the same as that in the Southern portions of the Kirghiz Steppe, while that of the mountains resembles, with a few exceptions, the *flora* of the Altai.

Zoologically, however, certain differences are perceptible.

With regard to the distribution of animals, Dzungaria may be divided into three zones, Alpine, Sub-Alpine, and that of the plains.

In the mountain zone of the Dzungarian Ala-tau, and of the Thian-shan, are to be found mammals indigenous to the mountainous parts of Southern Siberia, and of the Kirghiz Steppe; such as the stag (*Cervus elaphus*), horned goat (*Ibex Sibericus*), arkaz, or mountain sheep (*ovis argali*), the wolf, foxes black and red, the white-breasted martin, &c. &c. Besides these, a reddish-brown wolf is spoken of, very much resembling a dog, and called by the Kirghizes "chi-buri." Of birds of prey the commonest species is the vulture (*Gypaëtus barbatus, vultur fulvus, vultur meleagris*), and sometimes the golden eagle (*Aquila chrysaëtos*), the falcon (*Falco peregrinus*, and *Falco Subbuteo* or Hobby), the hawk (*Astur*); but the ger-falcon (*Falco caudicans*) is never seen here, nor did I come across any nocturnal birds of prey; in confirmation of which I may mention that the Kirghizes assert that they are rarely met with. Of the *gallinaceæ* order, the grey grouse (closely resembling the *tetrao caucasicus*), the partridge (*Perdrix saxatilis*), and the rail are found in the mountains.

In the Sub-Alpine zone we meet with the tiger, panther, wild-boar, antelope, Djeiran (*Antilope gytturosa*, Pall:) porcupine, pheasant, (*Phasianus Colchicus*), bustard (*otis tarda*), turtle-dove,

(*Columba œnas vel turtur*). All these are met with also in the zone of the plain. The woods of the Sub-Alpine zone abound with singing birds, (*Passerini*). The following are some of the varieties I noticed :—*Corvus dauricus; Coracias garrula*, L.; *Merops persica*, Pallas (probably the *Corvus Panderi* of Fish); *Tichodroma muralis*, L.; *Sitta Uralensis; Hirundo Alpestris; Hirundo Lagopoda; Parus Sibericus; Parus cyanus; Fringilla orientalis; Fr. arctus; Turdus Sibericus; Turdus fuscatus; Pyrrhula rhodochlamys; P. pusilla; P. Siberica; Emberiza rustica; E. Pittyornus; E. brumiceps; Coccothraustes speculigerus; Accentor Altaicus; A. atrogularis; A. montanellus; Cinchis leucogaster*. Waterfowl are very scarce both in the mountain and desert zones.

The wide tracts of sand, which extend between Balkash and the mountain zone, are merely continuations of the arenaceous Kirghiz plains of Khara-kush and Khan-tau, and present no characteristic features. They are dotted with the same saline patches which are called "Kaks" in the Kirghiz Steppe; but nevertheless the "Kulans" and "Saigaks,"* which fill the barren

* Saïga. Chèvre Sauvage (que Pallas appelle *cervus pygargus*, et M. Eversman, *antipola Saïga*). Les troupeaux de ces animaux,

waste and sands on the river Chu, never pass to the eastward of the meridian of It-Kechu. Some years ago a cold season forced these animals to migrate to the Trans-Ili region, and seek pasturage high up in the Ili valley; but with the spring, they returned to their native plains. It would, therefore, appear that Dzungaria is the natural boundary, separating the central-Asiatic "Kulan" from the "Djigitai" of the Mongolian Gobi, and the limit of distribution of the Saigak—the antelope of the depressed wastes—as also of the "Djeiran" of the mountain table-lands. The natives have long since observed this. The Kirghizes relate that the

sont singulièrement nombreux dans les Steppes; on compte quelquefois, dit-on, jusqu'à dix mille têtes dans un seul troupeau. . . . Le museau de la Saïga ressemble à un oignon; Ses narines sont larges; son regard n'est pas toujours pur, vu qu'il se forme quelquefois des taies sur les yeux; mais elle a l'odorat le plus fin, aussi sent-elle de loin l'approche d'une bête fauve ou celle de l'homme. Elle n'est guère plus haute de taille que la chèvre domestique; mais son poil est doux, court et ordinairement jaune foncé. Ses cornes sont petites et roides, ses jambes minces et sèches; la rapidité de sa course est faite pour étonner. C'est par cette faculté et par ses hauts bonds renouvelés coup-sur-coup, qu'elle échappe à ses ennemis. Au reste il est fort aisé, si on la prend jeune, de la bien apprivoiser. De touts les herbages dont elle se nourrit, elle préfère l'absinthe blanche et les algues marines. La chair en est succulente, mais quelquefois on trouve des vers dans son épine. Ces vers, l'excès des chaleurs en été et les insectes qui attaquent en foule l'intérieur de ses naseaux, sont cause qu'aux mois de juin et de juillet elle souffre, et ne vît plus que dans un état d'inquiétude visible. . . . Levschine sur les Kirghiz Kazaks. Page 75.

traces of deep pits, which are to be found along the base of the Dzungarian-Alataù, are those of excavations made by Khan Djani-Bek for destroying the "Kulans." A herd of these animals, it is said, enticed among them, a horse, mounted by a young son of the Khan, which resulted in the death of the boy. The Khan, exasperated by the loss, had a trench dug from Tarbagati to Ili, into which all the Dzungarian "Kulans" were driven; a male and female alone escaped beyond Balkash, and left a warning to their posterity against entering the country that had proved so fatal to their species.

Russian Dzungaria, as at present constituted, has exercised quite a classical influence in the historical fate of the Central-Asiatic races. Abul Ghazi says that Abuldjor Khan, son of Japhet, founder of the Turk tribes, roamed along the rivers Talas and Chu, and in the vicinity of Lake Issyk-kul. From Chinese sources, we know that all the tribes who migrated from the High Gobi, were detained and settled down in these parts, until they were expelled by stronger races. Russian Dzungaria presents, in reality, every convenience for a nomad life. The upper mountain valleys served as cool camping grounds during the sultry summer, while the cattle grazed at ease on the rich pasture, unmolested by the gad-fly. On the approach of autumn, the wandering population descended to the lower ravines, where they gathered their corn; while in the winter they sheltered themselves in the caverns of the river banks, or among the hollows of the sandy hillocks of the Balkash steppe. Fuel was likewise found in abundance, the *saksaul* of the plains yielding a constant supply.

Notwithstanding the prevalence of nomad habits among the population, Dzungaria always possessed a certain proportion of settled inhabitants. The first historical record of this mode of life, occurs in Chinese works, relating in particular to the town of Chigu, which, it must be presumed, was situated on the eastern shore of Lake Issyk-kul, and was built by Chinese workmen for the Kunmi of Ussun. In the Middle Ages a settled mode of life prevailed to a great extent in these regions, particularly along the Ili valley. The towns of Almalyk (now a Turkestan village), Khanaka and Kainak (which still exist), and Almaty (where Fort Vernoe now stands), were renowned for the extent of their trade, and were chief stations on the high road traversed by the Genoese traders proceeding to China, as well as by the Kipchak ambassadors on their propitiatory missions to the great Khan.

It is, moreover, worthy of special notice that many Nestorian and monophysitic congregations formerly existed in this part of Asia, and that Syrian Jacobians, according to the evidence afforded by the Catalan map, had a monastery, containing the relics of St. Matthias, in the vicinity of Lake Issyk-kul. Christianity, indeed, was so widely diffused here, that it experienced some persecution; but by the sixteenth century there were several Mussulman settlements at Issyk-kul. These facts strongly interested me; but, unfortunately, I was not able to make any further researches, as the Kirghizes had demolished the last of the buildings that had, up to that period, escaped destruction, mistaking them for Lama temples.

A Chinese, who visited Lake Issyk-kul in 1820, told me that he had seen in those parts a large idol carved out of a block of stone. For my own part, I did not stumble on any traces of antiquities of this description, though I found evidences of the sedentary pursuits of a portion, at least, of the population nearly throughout the whole of Russian Dzungaria, and was enabled to collect some traditions current among the people, confirmatory of these evidences. I likewise obtained some gold coins and ornaments, which were turned up among the ruins of the ancient town of Almalyk. Some remains of "Chud" spears, which I found in the heart of Central Asia, led to the inference that mining was not in those ages exclusively practised by the Finnish race.

Among the different races that inhabited Central Asia during the Han dynasty, Chinese records mention six tribes, which were distinguished by blue eyes and reddish hair, and whom Klaproth, in his "Tableaux Historiques de L'Asie," and Abel Remusat, in his "Recherches sur les Langues Tartares," classed as tribes of Hindo-Gothic extraction. To these, among others, belonged the Hakasis, or modern Kirghizes, who excited the astonishment of the Chinese by their strange types of face, resembling horses more than anything else.

At the present time, Dzungaria is inhabited by two peoples, viz: Buruts, or Kirghizes Proper, and Kirghiz-Kaisaks of the Great Horde, known under the collective appellation of Uisuns. Among these there is a tribe called the Red Uisuns, who assert themselves to be the remnants of a great and powerful nation.

The Buruts and Uisuns, it is to be observed, must not be confounded, as they are two distinct races. The celebrated Asiatic travellers, Meyendorf and Père Hyacinthe, strove hard, in their day, to establish this fact; but up to the present time no attention has been paid to the distinction. Even Von Humboldt and Ritter erred on this subject. They imagined that the Buruts formed the great Kaisak Horde, and that this horde should be distinguished from the Little and Middle Hordes. This, however, was a grave mistake on the part of those revered seers of science. The Great, Middle, and Little Kirghiz-Kaisak hordes form one "Cossack" family, distinct from that branch of the Kirghizes, called Buruts by the Chinese, and Dikokamenni by the Russians. These two family groups differ in language, extraction, and customs.

From the form of the skull, and the type of the features, the Central Asiatic races may be divided into Persians, Mongols, and Turks. The Persians are again subdivided into the mountain "Galcha," and Tadjiks of the plains, both of which must be classed with the Caucasian race. The Tadjiks have dark complexions and hair, while fair people are met with among the "Galcha."

The Kalmyks may be taken as representatives of the Mongolian type in Central Asia; they have dark hair, olive complexions, oblique eyes, flat faces, high cheek-bones, thin lips and flat noses. The remaining races, such as the Mongolo-Turk, and those of Turko-Finnish extraction, present a strange admixture of types and shades of complexion. One remarks among them fair men, with the Mongolian angle of face, and oblique eyes, with a regular Roman nose. Generally speaking, however, in the physical appearance of these tribes, there is observable a mixture of the Caucasian race with the Mongolian.

The second period of my journey finds me in the upper course of the Narym river, the chief affluent of the Syr-Daria, which formed the limit of M. Semenof's travels in this meridian. Before me lay stretched a real *terra incognita,* the mysteries of which had never hitherto been explored by civilized travellers.

Notwithstanding the great risk, I constantly kept a tolerably full diary during my travels, especially whilst staying at Kashgar. The friendly footing on which I stood with the natives, the learned, and the officials, and the frequent excursions I made in the neighbourhood, enabled me to form an accurate estimate of this remarkable region. Through my acquaintance with merchants of different tribes and from various countries, I procured a collection of itineraries with statistical, ethnographical and commercial notes relating to the neighbouring countries. Mixing, moreover, continually with merchants, and living in the caravanserai, I became accurately acquainted with the commerce of Central Asia, the articles forming the caravan trade, and in particular with the commodities most in demand at Kashgar.

The information collected during my journey consists firstly, of my own personal observations; secondly, of oral narratives by individuals on whose trustworthiness I can confidently rely; and lastly, of written accounts received from merchants and officials, and of extracts from local official documents and books.

The *Uigur* (sometimes called Ugrian) language, as spoken at Kashgar, is altogether unknown to European *savans*, who are only acquainted with the written tongue which resembles the Djagatai. A kind of official dialect has sprung into existence in Little Bokhara, owing to the prevalence of Chinese forms.

The history of Little Bokhara is scantily known. We are more or less acquainted with it up to the time of Timur Beg or Tamerlane from Chinese records, and subsequent to that period from Mussulman sources, which, however, glance but cursorily at it.

The excellent history of this reign, written in the middle of the sixteenth century by Mirza Muhammed Haidar Kurekan, vizier of Abdul Rashid, Khan of Kashgar, and called "Tarikhi Rashidi" in his honour, remains almost entirely unknown, and is certainly never consulted at the present time. A Turkish translation of this work is to be found in the Academy of Sciences of St. Petersburg, and an original copy in Persian in the library of the St. Petersburg University. Unfortunately, the translation is incomplete, and the University copy abounds with mistakes, having evidently been transcribed by a person ignorant of the Persian language. The "Tarikhi Rashidi" is divided into two parts, the first containing a history of the Kashgar Khans, from the time of Tomuk Temir to the reign of Rashid, A.D. 1554. The second partakes of the character of a series of memoirs, in which the author describes his personal adventures, and communicates much useful geographical and ethnographical information respecting the Bolor, Thibetan, Thian-Shan, and Kuen-Lun ranges. The writer was a scion of the celebrated Duglat family, which played the same part in the "Mogul-

Ulus" or "Tchete,"* as the *Maires du Palais* in the households of the Merovingian dynasty in the eighth and ninth centuries.

It has been already mentioned that the history written by Haidar terminates with the year 1554, and that it is the only historical work relating to this country known in Europe, where, however, it is known only by name.

I was fortunate enough while at Kashgar, to obtain possession of a manuscript called the "Tiaz-kirai Hodjaghian," which is, a history of the Hodja dynasty.† This remarkable composition terminates with the capture of Yarkend by the Chinese in 1758. This history of the Hodjas thus forms a continuation of the Tarikhi Rashidi.

The following are some of the more notable books I procured at Kashgar:—

1. Tazkiarai - Sultan - Sultuk - Bugra - Khan - Gazy," Biography of Khan, Sultan Bugra

* "Mogul Ulus" or "Tchete" was the eastern division of the Djagatai country; its Khans camped during the summer in Dzungaria, and resided at Aksu, Kashgar or Yarkend in the winter. The Tchete Moguls are not to be confounded with the Mongols, as they were Mussulmen and spoke Turkish.

† The Hodjas are the descendants of Mahomet; they form an hereditary priesthood, and are much reverenced.

of the Ilek Dynasty, who first embraced Islamism, and introduced it in Kashgar.

2. "Tazkirai - Tugluk - Timur - Khan," Biography of Tugluk Timur Khan of the Djagatai Dynasty, who was the first of the "Mogul-Ulus" Khans to embrace Islamism.
3. "Rishakhat," or Information respecting the Asiatic Law Teachers and Saints.
4. "Abu Muslim Murazi," a heroic novel, remarkable on account of the many local historical traditions which are introduced in it.

CHAPTER IV.

Sketches of Travels in Dzungaria, by Capt. Valikhanof.

MY travels in Dzungaria commenced on the 28th of May, 1856, when I joined a trading caravan which was then encamped in the settlement of Karamul, at a distance of twenty miles from the town of Kopal. This caravan had come from Semipalatinsk, and belonged to Kokan and Bokhara merchants. It consisted of eight travelling tents, one hundred camels, sixty-five horses, thirty-four attendants, and merchandise to the value of £3,000. I was known to the party by the name of Alimbai, and passed for a relative of the caravan-Bashi, the worthy Mussabai.

We did not, however, set out till the following day. The weather was fine, and favoured our journey, the first part of which lay along the picket road to the out-post of Altyn-Emel, through the beautiful valleys nestling among the lower spurs of the Ala-Tau. After traversing a distance of seventeen miles daily, the caravan usually came to a halt in the cool of the evening, and pitched its tents under the shade of a high poplar or silver-leaved wild olive (Djigda), on the brink of some brawling rivulet. A lively party formed at each halting-place round the blazing fire, while the Bokharians smoked their *kalian,* and beguiled the time by reciting passages from Hafiz.

The Kirghizes, encamped in the vicinity, would likewise make their appearance with sheep, which they offered for sale, while their more distinguished chiefs approached with the view of receiving a "bazarlyk," or present. They would approach the caravan with great ceremony, accompanied by a numerous suite, making the inquiry, "Who is the richest?" On this, each owner of a tent, in his turn, usually treated the dignitaries of the horde to tea, biscuits, and dried fruit, which the Kirghizes stowed away about their persons, and, after soliciting a present, would speedily withdraw. The caravan was once honoured with the presence of the Sultan Djungazy, ruler of the Djalair tribe, and his *adlatus* or resident, who is attached to his person in the capacity of Mentor by the Russian authorities, on account of the Sultan's imbecility. Djungazy surprised us by the eccentricity of his conduct. He entered the tent, used by the Kirghizes only on extreme official occasions, with the gait of a fat goose, took the seat of honour, and assumed an expression of profound meditation, everybody observing the strictest silence. Then, suddenly lifting his head, and casting a penetrating glance around, he exclaimed in rhyme, "The Djalairs have many sheep, Djangazy has many thoughts." He had spoken, and again resumed his Buddhistic immobility. In the meantime, the Sultan's *adlatus* and other Kirghizes opened a conversation with us. They described all the particulars relating to the Governor-General's visit to Fort Vernoe, repeated the words he addressed to the Kirghiz people, and imitated the gestures with which he accompanied them. They entreated us to instruct them as to their legal duties and their legal rights, saying, "Our bullocks and horses are taken for picket-labour, and rarely returned; the Cossacks know the laws, and persecute and rob us with impunity. We cannot resist them by force, as the Cossacks are servants of the Tsar, and for any complaint against them we should be sent off to the perforated mountains (mines.) A great stir was once made about three of them, who disappeared mysteriously; two officials lived a whole winter in Karatal, calling on us to confess to the murder of the Cossacks. God forbid that we should! We never saw them. Even now the Governor says, 'Find me the guilty ones, or I will twist you all into the shape of a goat's horn. I,' says he, 'am thunder and lightning.'" The Sultan, meanwhile, rolled his eyes about in a curious manner, giving occasional utterance to rhymes in couplets. After partaking of the customary pilaff, our guests retired, leaving a strange scent of almonds behind them.

Crossing the Ala-tau by the Djaksy Altyn-Emel Pass, which is swept in autumn by strong north-easterly winds, called locally "ébé," similar to those prevalent on the shore of Lake Ala-Kul, the caravan entered upon a bare siliceous tract, intersected by a valley, from the ridge of which the Ili was occasionally visible in the distance. We proceeded in the direction of the ferry, kept by Kirghizes, over this river, and passed the night at a spring in a valley of the Kalkan hills, which literally swarmed with snakes, tarantulæ, scorpions, and other reptiles; for a long time after I could not shake off the recollection of that horrible resting-place. We passed a sleepless night, and resumed our journey at break of day.

The caravan was two days crossing the river Ili on crazy flat-bottomed boats. The wretched, rotten craft was towed across by horses, actually swimming,. and, of course, exercising but little power over the movements of the boat; while the bargemen were busily employed baling out the water with pails! After celebrating the safe transit of the Ili under such disadvantages, the caravan, clearing the Suguty, Taraigir, and Utch-Merke passes, reached the Kar-kara Valley, having made altogether seventeen forced marches. Here we found some Kirghizes of the Aitbuzum tribe, and dispersed ourselves among their "aùls" for barter; but we found the Kirghizes in a state of great agitation. Prior to our arrival a sanguinary struggle had occurred on the banks of the Kar-kara, between the branches of the Kisyl-Burk and Aitbuzum tribes. They were expecting the appearance of a Russian official who had been sent to investigate the affair by demand of the Kisyl-Burk party, and were contemplating a hasty migration in case of an adverse decision.

And so it happened. On the 4th of August the

Kirghizes began to decamp in a hurry, and towards evening not one of them remained on the shores of the Kegen, our own tents alone rearing their heads on the site of the deserted Kirghiz camp. Our position was an awkward one. The caravan-Bashi, and some of our more experienced men, considered that the 900 sheep we had received in barter from the Kirghizes were insufficient, and they, therefore, determined to proceed to the Dikokamenni horde, whose encampment we reached accordingly on the 6th August. We were met by the chief of the Salméké sept, Manap-Karatch, surnamed the Big, who was well-disposed towards the Russian Government, and yearned for the rank of Yesawul of Cossacks. He well merited the epithet (or title, whichever he might consider it), of "the Big," because, without exaggeration, he was as fat as a bullock. Karatch wore a peaked hat of white felt, with the brim slit in two places over the forehead and at the back of his head, besides a wadded "Khalat," or long robe of striped cotton material, ornamented with three green silk cords over the breast. His feet were cased in clumsily-shaped boots of red leather, with large wooden heels. His son was arrayed in a similar manner, only his khalat was of a more brilliant colour, while the collar and sleeves were faced with velvet. The suite was nothing but a ragged regiment of attendants, armed with cudgels and spears. I particularly noticed the costume of one red-haired spear-

A KIRGHIZ.

man, which consisted simply of his nether integuments and a felt mantle; while another, regardless of the hot weather, wore a heavy sheep-skin coat and fur head-piece. The Kirghizes spoke with great rapidity and shrillness, and continually filled their mouths with snuff.

The valley of the Upper Kegen lies very high, and presents excellent pasturages, but the shores of the stream are swampy, forming, in some places, hillocky morasses, called "Saz;" the three contiguous highland valleys of Kegen, Tekes, and Karkara are the only localities in the whole of Dzungaria which have a rich black loam, with luxuriant vegetation.

The "Kibitkas," or tents, of the ninth division of Kalmyks were spread over the great "Saz." These Kalmyks had previously been encamped in the vicinity of a Chinese mine, now abandoned. We next erected our tents on the banks of the Chalkuder. During the night there was a fall of snow, which the wind whirled round and drove in clouds in every direction, just as in the depth of winter; the weather, too, was extremely cold, and the snow-drift continuing for two days, completely cut off, for the time being, all communication with the Kirghizes. On the third day the heads of the Kirghiz tribes arrived at the camping-ground of the caravan, and took us with them to their several aùls. I and my companion, Mamrazyk, fell to the share of the aùl of Bai-Bursuk, chief of the small Kydyk tribe. On gaining the aùl we proceeded to pay a visit to our host, by whom we were received with all due ceremony, and assisted off our horses at the door of the tent, which we were invited to enter. The tent was in a sadly dilapidated state, and begrimed with smoke. Bursuk occupied the seat of honour by the hearth, facing the door-way; his wife and two daughters, with several Kirghiz women, were seated on calf, skins to the right of the entrance. Nearer to the door were placed cauldrons, pails, bowls, platters and other domestic utensils. On the left was a Kirghiz occupied in cobbling boots of red leather; and on the floor were strewed chips, fragments of felt, wool, and gnawed bones. We were seated on a piece of fancifully-stitched felt, which is the ordinary apology for a carpet among the Kirghizes. Our host was extremely civil, though he frequently cursed the tombs of our fathers, apparently only from force of habit. The amiability of his wife would have been equally expressive, had her articulation not been impeded by the snuff that clogged her gums. Bursuk ordered some "kumis" for us, on which our gentle hostess pulled out a small, but well-filled skin of this refreshing beverage, carefully wrapped up in an old khalat, and produced some wooden bowls. These, she and her daughters carefully cleansed of the adhering layers of impurity with their fingers, which they afterwards sucked with unmistakeable relish. Bursuk's children, nine in number, handed us the kumis, and I drank it with the best grace I could. All this was by no means new to me. In 1856 I had been entertained in the tent of the high "manap," and wealthiest Kirghiz, Burambai. On that occasion, although we squatted on the carpet, and our host on a Bokharian blanket, his wife reposed, as the lady did here, on a calf-skin. We drank kumis out of porcelain cups; but the salt tea, in default of another vessel, was boiled in a cast-iron washing-basin, and the general equipment of his establishment was the same in all essentials as that of Bursuk.

Uncleanliness is, in short, elevated into a virtue by the Kirghizes, and hallowed by tradition. They consider it as great a sin to wash their domestic utensils as to spit on the fire, or step over the tether of their mares when being milked To purify their bowls is to invoke misfortune, and scare away abundance. The men are not in the habit of changing their linen, but continue to wear it until it falls off their bodies The hunting for vermin on each other's persons affords them agreeable pastime for their leisure hours, without which they would be at a sad loss for amusement, the ladies, especially, shewing a great predilection for this savoury occupation. The ritual of Kirghiz mourning is very simple, and consists of total abstinence from ablution or change of raiment for a whole year.

The hospitality of the Burut Patriarch was further displayed in the slaughter of a lamb for our entertainment. This was done in our presence, totally regardless of the poor animal's bleatings, after which a fire was kindled, the tripod adjusted, and the cauldron placed over it in due order. The apathetic countenances of the Kirghizes became at once animated; the members of the family bustled around the fire with augmented zeal, so much so as to hinder each other in the culinary operations of the hour, and finally quarrelled among themselves. Hungry dogs with savage keenly-whetted appetites, licked and snuffed at the ground where the lamb had been killed, while troops of Kirghizes, in expectation of a mouthful, gradually filled the tent, and a native artist, accompanying himself on a "balalaika," sang a monotonous ditty, consisting of the constantly recurring word "dait, dait." At last the cauldron was taken off the fire and a large platter placed before us with mutton heaped into a pile, the whole surmounted by the *os sacrum* as the most esteemed morsel. We ate the meat dipping it into the salt broth.

Early on the following day Bursuk appeared to breakfast with us; he came again to dinner and to tea in the evening, while our supper was also graced by his presence. This he did regularly each suceeding day. His children followed his example, and his relatives exhibited such greediness that we were obliged to hide everything eatable from them; one of these gluttons had already devoured all my sealing-wax! Apparently the entertainment of Bursuk and his family was considered by the party most interested a bounden duty on our part. The only food of the Kirghizes consists of milk and fallen cattle. Before this occasion the Kadyks, we remarked, had never had the pleasure of entertaining a caravan among their aúls. This was apparent from the behaviour of Bursuk, who since our arrival, had assumed an air of great importance. "May the mouth of your father be defiled!" would he exclaim to those he wished to impress with his dignity, "I have Sartas (merchants,) living with me," &c. &c. We were likewise visited by matrons and maidens, who brought us boiled mutton and "kumis" or "airan" in pails, with cheese and butter. In return for

A Kirghiz Girl.

this we were obliged, according to local custom, to give them presents. My companion, quite a man of the world and a devoted admirer of the fair sex, was delighted at this opportunity for playing the amiable. He treated them to dried fruit, made them presents of cotton dresses, plush, fowls, &c., and paid them extravagant compliments, which, however, they could not appreciate.

Sometimes of an evening the daughter of our host organized little parties in my companion's tent. On such occasions young men, women, and girls collected there, the men sitting on one side and the women on the other. The games would then commence. One of the girls rising coquettishly from her seat, would choose the swain who found most favour in her eyes, by a wave of her kerchief. The lucky youth was thereupon obliged to perform some dexterous feat or sing a song. If his performance were creditable, his partner would reward him with a hearty kiss; while on the other hand remissness was punished by a severe beating. Singing was generally preferred to physical exercises, though probably not for æsthetical reasons. The process is as follows: the singer sits on one knee and sings in an unnatural tone of voice, his lay being usually of an amorous character. The production of the first note costs the Kirghiz great efforts: his eyes become bloodshot, and his nostrils dilate, and a few hollow sounds escape at first until he pitches the proper key. Central Asiatic wits compare the singing of the Kirghizes, and the first introductory notes, to the bray of a donkey. On finishing his song, the performer gets up and places himself back to back with his partner, then skilfully twisting their necks round they salute each other. The relation between the sexes, among the Kirghizes, is altogether on a very primitive footing; mothers, fathers, and brothers regard any breach of morality with great leniency, and husbands even encourage their friends to close intimacy with their wives. My caravan friends did not I believe neglect this custom, particularly as the Buruts had many attractive women among them. Like the Kirghizes, the Buruts are strangers to jealousy, a feeling so common to the Asiatic. The reason of this is that Islamite notions of chastity have not yet spread among this people. The Buruts call themselves Mussulmen, and yet do not know who Mahomet was. Their weddings and funerals are conducted after Shaman fashion, but if they can secure the services of a scholarly Central Asiatic or Tartar, prayers are read. I can safely assert that throughout the whole country, from Issyk-Kul to Badakhshan, there is not a single individual of this tribe who can read.

The Kirghizes drink a spirit which they distil from Kumis, and with which they intoxicate themselves on every available occasion. The condition of the Russian Kirghizes, or those of the Middle Horde, was the same thirty years ago. The Russian Government, however, proceeded to erect mosques and appointed Tartar Mullahs, under whose influence the Middle Horde Kirghizes do not now yield in fanaticism to the most fanatical Dervishes. They regularly observe the period of prayer and thirty days' fast, while some have even introduced the seclusive system of the harem. It would be difficult to decide which would be more beneficial to the Kirghiz Steppe, the former state of ignorance with perfect religious toleration, or contemporary Tartar civilization with its strong anti-progressive tendencies. The Tartars in Russia constitute a totally separate Eastern world, having nothing in common with the interests of Russian nationality. The great Kirghiz Horde is now in a transition state, and the Tartars who are scattered throughout it are making their influence felt more and more with each succeeding year.

It must be observed that the farther we remove from the Tartars the less fanaticism do we find among the Kirghizes, notwithstanding that they live here under the influence of Central Asiatic rulers, and in a country usually regarded as the very focus of bigotry. The Bokhara Mullahs are, in my opinion, much less to be dreaded than their Tartar brethren.

We passed nearly a month with the Dikokamenni Horde, roaming with it from place to place, and carrying on a constant barter in sheep.

Our host did not, as already stated, belong to the class of "Manaps" (the Kirghiz aristocracy), and therefore took no part in the councils of the tribes; he was, furthermore, very poor. Bursuk, however, was aiming at securing the footing of a hereditary chief, and carried on a constant depredatory warfare, or "Baranta," with all the Kirghiz aristocrats, in order to enrich himself. He was obliged, consequently, to choose the most secure and inaccessible positions for his aúls, at a distance from the general camping grounds. During the whole of our sojourn with him, he kept close in the unapproachable ravines of the Muzart mountains, or among the swamps of the Upper Tekēs. He did not venture from his retreat even when the other tribes, having pitched their tents in the broad valley of the Kegen, made general preparations for solemnly celebrating the nineteenth day after the death of the High Manap, Burambai. My host and his nine sons were during this time engaged in horse stealing. In 1855, Burambai, High Manap of the Begu tribe, with 10,000 of his followers, took the oath of allegiance to Russia. In the spring of the following year, Colonel Khomentovski, with a company of Cossacks, was despatched, by petition of the Kirghizes, for the purpose of becoming better acquainted with them, and for surveying the country they occupied. This first Russian expedition succeeded in the course of two months in surveying the northern part of Issyk-Kul, and constructed a map, on a scale of two versts, of the locality along its northern shore to the River Aksu, and along the southern, to the River Zaũkũ. Accompanying the expedition, I visited Burambai's aúl, where I gathered some remarkable traditions, and drew up a memoir on the Dikokamenni Kirghizes. I subsequently came into contact with Buruts of other tribes, Sarabaguishes and Saltus, and during my present journey explored their camping grounds as far as Kashgar.

The origin and history of the Dikokamenni Kirghizes remain matter of dispute to the present day. The majority of *savans*, who have directed their attention to the elaboration of these questions from Chinese and Eastern historical records, are, however, of opinion that the modern Dikokamenni Buruts are the Kirghizes of the Enisei, deported on the downfall of the Dzungarians in the last century to new camping grounds, and consider them, on the strength of this, to be identical with the Khakasis of the Tau dynasty, and Kelikidzes of the Yuan dynasty. Rashid Eddin, in his history of the Mongols, classes the Kirghizes with the people of the forests of Southern Siberia, who inhabited the region of Barkhudjin-Tukum. The appellation of Kem-Kemjut, which he and Albū-Gazi give the Kirghizes, suggests the Kem (Enisei) and the River Kemchuk, as the locality in which they probably then sojourned. On the conquest of Siberia by the Russians, the latter found Kirghizes on the Abakan and Yuz, and maintained an obstinate warfare with them about the end of the seventeenth and beginning of the eighteenth century. From that time the name of this people suddenly disappears from Siberian annals. Fischer is of opinion that they were removed by the Khan-Taidsis of Dzungaria, and, relying on mere hearsay, considers their new territory must lie on the frontiers of Thibet and the

Hindu Cush. M. Levshin, in his work on the Kirghiz-Kaisaks, remarks that the Swedish officers were the first to note this event in history, and maintains that their migration was the result of a special stipulation on the part of the Russian Government with the Khan-Taidsis. But the Chinese call the Dikokamenni Kirghizes, Buruts, and assert that they migrated to their present encampments from the Kuen-Lun, where they lived under the name of Bulu, or Pulu, during the Tau dynasty. Père Hyacinthe was the first to distinguish the Kirghizes of Southern Siberia from the modern Buruts, assuming the latter to be a Turkish tribe, and calling them K*e*rghizes, in contradistinction from the first. Ritter, in his "Erdkunde von Asien," unwarrantably confounds the Dikokamenni Kirghiz Buruts with the Kirghiz-Kaisaks, and takes them all for Kilidsis or Khakasis, migrated from the Enisei, whom, following Klaproth and A. Remusat, he classes with the Indo-Germanic family—Mahomedanized in consequence of an amalgamation of tribes.

With regard to the deportation of the Kirghizes from Russian-Siberia in the seventeenth century, Ritter says that, harassed by their neighbours, they joined their kindred tribe, the Buruts, in Eastern

Turkestan, and in the Steppe to the south-east of the Irtysh ; he consequently considers the Buruts the original nomads of the country they at present occupy.

Such is the present state of the inquiry regarding the origin of the contemporary Dikokamenni Kirghizes.

In order, if possible, to throw some additional light on the question, I directed my attention to the study of local popular traditions, and found that the people known under the name of "Dikokamenni, Black Kirghizes," call themselves simply Kirghizes, or, as they pronounce it, "Krgyz." The appellation of Buruts, given them by the Kalmyks and Chinese, is altogether unknown to them. I also ascertained that the Kirghizes consider the Adjan mountains as the cradle of their race.

The tradition of a migration from Southern Siberia does not exist among them, although there is one to the effect that in their wanderings from South to North, they extended as far as the Black Irtysh, Altai and Hangai, and eastwards to Urumchi. From this it must be inferred that the Dikokamenni Kirghizes are identical with the Enisei Akazis or Kirghizes, pronounced Khilikizi by the Chinese. A Chinese writer, contemporary with the

Mongols, asserts that Khilikizi, in the language of the natives, signifies forty maidens, from *Kyrk*, forty and *Kyz*, maiden or girl. This etymology is also adopted by the present Kirghizes in explanation of their name. I further imagine that the Kirghizes spread themselves eastwards, to the limits of their present territory, at a very remote period, which conjecture is further borne out by existing popular traditions. Their migrations only ceased when the powerful domination of the Oirats and Dzungarians sprang into existence. The opinion entertained by the learned world, that the deportation of the Kirghizes in the beginning of the eighteenth century, from the Enisei to the Thian-Shan, was entirely effected by the Dzungarians, and, with the approval of the Russian Government, is not quite consistent with the additional facts I have obtained. In the "Tarikhi Rashidi," or History of Kashgar, I found evidence that the Kirghizes (Buruts) so early as the latter part of the fifteenth century, were roaming the mountains near Adjan, while, during the life of the historian, in A.D. 1520, they wandered as far as Lake Issyk-Kul. In the Archives of the Central Office of the Siberian Kirghizes at Omsk, there is a very curious document or "Act," relating to the Khirgiz migration from Siberia in the summer of

1746. In this "Act" it is mentioned that twelve men, with their wives and children, asserting themselves to be Kirghizes, made their appearance at Ust-Kamenogorsk, and declared that they formerly lived in Siberia between the towns of Tomsk and Eniseisk, opposite the town of Krasnoyarsk in the Steppe, and on the river White Yus, under the sway of Tambyn-Batyr-Datji, also paying a tribute in furs into the treasury of His Imperial Majesty. "Fifty years or more ago," said they, "during the life-time of the present Khan, Taishi-Galdan-Cheren, three Kalmyk leaders, named Dunar, Sandyk, and Chinbin, at the head of 500 armed followers, attacked us when numbering three thousand 'smokes' on our camping-grounds, and carried us away with the son of our former Khan-Tambyn-Batyr-Datji-Chainish, to the Züngar territory, ultimately driving us to Urga, where we have remained ever since, paying tribute to Galdan-Cheren." These strangers stated, furthermore, that their kindred and other Kirghiz Kalmyks lived in the Sagai Steppe, and were tributary to His Imperial Majesty. In the following year, viz. 1747, two Kirghiz Kalmyks, who were captured after they had succeeded in effecting their escape from Dzungaria, corroborated the above statement, adding that two leaders, Kharta-Idash and his brother Emgen-Mergen, camped about in the Sagai volost or district. It will appear from this that the Siberian Kirghizes, from their proximity to the Dzungarians and Uriankhaitsis, had become extensively intermingled with the Mongols, and that the Dzungarians did not carry away the whole tribe, but only to the extent of 3,000 kibitkas or tents. These most probably became thoroughly amalgamated with the Dzungarians, and might have formed a Kalmyk tribe of Kirghizes, thus leading Père Hyacinthe to suppose that all the Siberian Kirghizes were of Mongolian origin. The question then arises, what became of these Siberian Kirghizes, a people powerful enough, during a whole century, to have kept the towns of Siberia in a state of constant alarm by their inroads, and to have struggled with such formidable neighbours as the Dzungarians, and Altyn Khan of the Uriankhaitsis? In reply to this, I would surmise that the obliteration of their name might have been produced by the same cause that has reduced the once powerful territory of the Golden Khans, who received tribute from the Kirghizes, to its present insignificance. This formidable State is now known as the duo-tributary State, on account of its paying homage both to Russia and China. It is, besides, well known that the Siberians give separate names to all non-native tribes, and that the remnants of the Siberian Kirghizes follow their nomad instincts on their old grounds, but under new names.

Men of science have long since perceived the importance for Ethnography of a study of such relics of national literature, as most truthfully illustrate national morals, manners, and customs. Now it so happens that profound regard for antiquity and an abundance of traditions forms a marked and characteristic heritage of the nomadic races of Central Asia. These traditions are devoutly preserved by the elders of the tribes, either in the form of ancestral reminiscences and genealogical legends, or in ballads which are perpetuated by a special class of bards. Many words and locutions now obsolete, prove their antiquity. The traditional account of Queen Gulmalika having been the ancestress of Genghis Khan prevails among all the Tartar tribes. Thierry, in his "Histoire d' Attila et de ses Successeurs," quotes this as a legend of Attila and the Huns. The story of the origin of the Dikokamenni Kirghizes from a red grey-hound (kizin-taizan), and a certain queen with her forty handmaidens, is of ancient date. A characteristic feature in Central Asiatic traditions is the derivation of their origin from some animal. According to the testimony of Chinese history, the Goa-Gui (Kao-tsché), otherwise known as the Telé or Chili people, sprang from a wolf and a beautiful Hun princess. One of the Hun princes had two daughters of such uncommon beauty that he determined not to marry them to any ordinary mortals. Building a high tower in an uninhabited wilderness, he left them in it, exclaiming, "I pray Heaven to take them." The youngest princess falling a prey to ennui, encouraged the attentions of an old wolf, who for a whole year, night and day, prowled around the tower, and at last made his lair at the foot of it; till the princess, notwithstanding the entreaties of her eldest sister, married the wolf.

The Tugus (called Dulgasses by Père Hyacinthe), professed to derive their origin from a she-wolf, and the Tufans (Thibetians) from a dog. The Chinese assert that Batachi, hereditary chief of the Mongol Khans, was the son of a blue wolf and white hind, ("Mémoires relatifs a l' Asie," par Klaproth, p. 204). In like manner some of the red-skinned tribes of North America pretend to be descended from beavers, tortoises, &c. It is evident, from these instances, that this kind of tradition in Central Asia, and even in America, is the most ancient, and even seems to be regarded as a descent to be proud of. The out-spoken yet exalted tone of the Kirghiz legends, considered indecent by the present generation of Kirghiz, is a strong proof that they have descended in their original form. The tradition of the origin of the ninety-nine Kipchak branches has been preserved among the Uzbeks and Kaisaks in such an indelicate shape, that it is doubtful whether it will ever be possible to present it to the general reader.

Genealogical traditions form a most important section of their legendary lore. The relation of one tribe to another depends on the degree of affinity which exists between the chiefs. The hereditary superiority of one branch over the other is determined by the right of primogeniture. Traditions of this nature are in so far important, as they represent the extraction of the people, and the composition of society. It appears from the genealogical tables of the Kaisaks, Usbeks, and Nagais, that they are a medley of different Turkish and Mongol tribes, formed after the decline of the Golden and Djagatai Hordes. The genealogy of the Buruts indicates at the same time that the principal portion of the people is composed of the Turkish "Kirghiz" tribe, recruited ultimately by two alien sections.

Of these, the first comprises the Kipchaks, Naimans and Kitais; whose claims to Kirghiz nationality is expressed genealogically by their having had one common chief placed over them, who is stated to have been the son of Kirghiz-Bai. The Tchilik, or second section, though claiming a common ancestor in the son of Kirghiz-Bai, is not acknowledged by the other tribes. A third division is composed of the present Kirghizes, divided into two wings, *On* and *Sol.* In the present generation these are split up into numerous branches, each branch being again and again subdivided.

The third class of tradition is formed of the so-called "tales of olden times," or "Djir" of the Nogais. These are in vogue among the Kaisaks, Uzbeks, Nogais and Kirghizes. It is to be presumed that the Nogais comprehended originally all the nomad tribes of Central Asia, speaking the Tartar language, who were of Turkish and Mongol extraction. The Nogai traditions relate to the fourteenth, fifteenth and sixteenth centuries;

they are of an epic character, sung in rhyme, and should therefore be classed under the head of colloquial literature. These traditions are interesting, as expressions of the tone of the native mind, and of the ideas, customs, morals, and mode of life of those primitive ages, while they are equally remarkable in philosophical respects, and are not devoid of historical interest.

Among the Kaisaks, Uzbeks, and Nogais, who trace their origin from the Golden and Djagatai Horde, are preserved several poetical fables, founded on the exploits of the horde-heroes, Edigei, Ir-Kokcha, Urak, Chor and others. These are all historical personages: Edigei was one of Tamerlane's generals, and is known in history for his victory over Vitort on the Vorskla; Urak, a descendant of Edigei, was, according to tradition, a prisoner in Russia, and married a Russian princess, on which point, however, there is no historical evidence; mention is made of Ir-Kokcha in Nicon's Chronicles in 1423, with reference to Tsar Kuidadada's attack of the town of Odoev, as follows: "They also killed at this time Kokcha, a Tartar hero, of great stature and strength." Tchora was a Tartar prince, who relieved Kazan, and his name occurs in the annals of that town. The manner in which these legends are handed down from age to age proves the tenacity of regard for antiquity among the nomadic tribes of Asia. It must, however, be borne in mind that these poetical traditions, from the proximity of the different roaming grounds to each other, and the dialectic affinity of the tribes occupying them, are easily adopted by all, which renders it difficult to trace them to their true source. M. Hodzko, for instance, heard many episodes out of the *Idichi* from the Turkmen, who must have borrowed them either from the Kaisaks or Nogais; in like manner their classical robber, Kor-Oglu, figures in Kaisak rhapsodies. Asia is rich in wandering traditions, legends, and fables. M. Castrén, while in Lapland, heard narrated the myths concerning Cyclops, Polyphemus of the Odyssey, &c., with some national and local adaptations, current among the Karelians. The same fable is current in the Kirghiz Steppe. Cyclops is there called Alp, a giant ogre, and a Kirghiz giant, Batur-Khan, enacts the part of Ulysses.

The Dikokamenni Kirghizes possess a remarkable epic, "the Manas," relating to the Nogai period.

The "Manas" is an encyclopædical collection of all the Kirghiz mythological tales and traditions, brought down to the present period and grouped round one person—the giant Manas. It is a species of Iliad of the Steppe. The Kirghiz mode of life, their morals, geography, religious and medicinal knowledge, as well as their relations with other tribes, all find illustration in this compendious epopee. This poem has evidently undergone recent modifications and additions, and its concentration into one whole, out of prosaic "Djumuks" (tales), may probably be of very modern date. The "Manas" consists of many separate episodes, having the form of a connected relation. Another *epos*, the "Samyatei," serves as a continuation of the "Manas," and is the Burut Odyssey. The Kirghizes say that three nights are insufficient for the relation of the "Manas," and that as much time is required for the "Samyatei," but this is in all probability an exaggeration.

I am at present engaged in translating the "Manas," and intend to compile a small dictionary, in order to make students of Oriental literature acquainted with a hitherto unknown dialect. The language of the Dikokamenni Kirghizes is Turkish, resembling more closely than any other that spoken in Little Bokhara. In it there are very few, or scarcely any, Arab and Persian words, it being composed principally of Mongolian and primitive Turk terms.

At this point I would fain say a few words on the distribution of the Kirghiz race, its principal tribes, and their present political condition.

The Dikokamenni Kirghiz Horde is divided into two wings, as already mentioned: "On" and "Sol," *i.e.* right and left, corresponding to the Mongolian "Borongar" and "Dzungar." The right wing consists of two divisions, "Adgené," and "Tagai." The latter is the largest, and with it must be classed the kindred but hostile tribes of Sarabaguish and Bugu, Sultu, Sayak, Cherik, Chonbaguish and Bussyz—numbering eight in all. The Bugus, since 1855, have been subject to Russia, and number eight camps. They follow agriculture on the southern shore of Issyk-Kul, and roam in summer about the upper courses of the Kegen and Tekes. The Sarabaguishes, numbering ten tents, wander along the Chu river and eastern part of Issyk-Kul. The Sultu, the most predatory tribe, forming fifteen camps, wander on the Talas and Chu, in the vicinity of the Kokanian fort of Pishpek.*

* This fort was stormed in October, 1862, by a Russian detachment, under Colonel Kolpakovski, when nine guns and 600 men were captured.

The Sayaks occupy the upper parts of the Narym and Djungal; the Cheriks, the highlands of the Thian-Shan, south of Issyk-Kul; the Chon-baguishes skirt the mountains to the North-West of Kashgar. The last two tribes are very poor. The other tribes of the Tagai branch occupy the mountains North of Namangan, in the neighbourhood of Andijan and the upper course of the Djum-gol. The Adgené Kirghizes pursue agriculture in the Ferganah Valley, near the towns of Margilan and Osh, and pass the summer among the hills extending from Osh to Kokan. These Kirghizes enjoy the same rights as the Uzbeks; they serve as soldiers in the Kokanian army, and their chiefs fill important civil and military posts. The present Kokan Vizier, Alim-Beg-Dashkha, is a Kirghiz Bey of this tribe, and with his Kirghizes assisted the ruling Khan Mallya to gain possession of Kokan.

The left wing is formed of three tribes, who frequent the Talas. Their chiefs are related to the Khan of Kokan, who are, on the female side, of Kirghiz extraction. The country, peopled by the wandering camps of the Naimans, Kipchaks and Kitais, tribes which have become incorporated with the Kirghiz, stretches from Osh along the Pamir plateau to Badakshan, and thence to the Kara-Korum range; with them rove likewise the

Itchkiliks and some families of the Adjéné tribe. All the Kirghizes in the neighbourhood of the Kashgar town of Tash-Balyk, with the exception of the Bugu, who are Russian subjects, although under immediate subjection to China, recognize the power of the Khan of Kokan, to whom they pay a tribute of one horse out of every hundred. For governing the Kirghizes, the Kokanians have in the country they roam over, the forts of Pishpek, 44° 10′ N., 74° 50′ E., Mérke, on the Chu, 44° N., 74° 10′ E., Aulie-Ata (the ancient Taraz) on the Talas, 43° 44′ N., 72° 36′ E., Kurtka and Truz, on the Naryn, 41° 38′ N., 76° 54′ E., Ketmen-Tupé and Djungale, on the river of that name, 41° 47′ N., 74° 10′ E., and Tash-Kurgan 46° 17′ F., 70° E.*

In the latter part of August, the Kashgar merchants, having concluded their affairs with the Horde, made preparations for departure. Our Kirghiz friends advised us to join the Kashgarians, the road, according to their account, being unsafe for a small caravan. The banks of the Tekes at Utah-Kapkak Pass were fixed on as the place of rendezvous. Here, by the 27th September, were collected sixty tents, or in caravan parlance, sixty fires. While the route to be chosen (there being

* These latitudes and longitudes it must be distinctly understood are simply approximative, as obtained from the most recent Russian maps.

several), for proceeding to Kashgar was being discussed by the seniors of the caravan, a circumstance occurred which quite upset our original plan. A Kokan Yuz-Bashi (centurion) despatched from Pishpek to collect tribute from the Bugu tribe,* arrived at the caravan with six soldiers, and demanded payment of the customary dues. On being asked what dues, and why they were demanded? the Yuz-Bashi took offence, and forcibly seizing three hundred sheep, drove them up the mountain, where he kept careful guard over them.

The Kashgar men, accustomed to conflicts with the Chinese, forthwith armed themselves with sticks, and fell on the Kokanian soldiers. Unhorsing them with remarkable dexterity, they thrashed the warriors so unmercifully, that one remained insensible on the field of battle. The Kirghizes, fearing to incur the vengeance of the Tashkendians, declared that they would not allow the Kashgarians to depart before the recovery of the wounded soldier. As we did not take any part in the affray, we joined company with some Tartars and Kashgarians, who had also remained

* Although the Bugu, as stated previously, are Russian subjects, they, nevertheless, do not fail on every opportunity to propitiate the Kokanians and Chinese.

neutral, and started at once on our journey; and with all the greater speed, seeing that snow had already commenced to fall in the mountains. Our united caravan consisted of ten fires, and the total number of men was sixty. From the upper course of the Tekes we cleared in two marches the San-tash mountain pass, presenting a level plateau famed for its traditions about Tamerlane, after passing which we crossed the low Kyzylki mountains, and entered the valley of the Djirgalan (happy). From this point our route lay along the level and fertile Terskei valley, in which we observed half-naked Buruts employed in their corn-fields.

At the Djity-Uguz river we fell in with our old friend Bursuk, who had removed thither with his Kadyks, for the purpose of gathering his harvest; also several aùls of the same tribe, subject to Bin-Samsal, and the renowned robber chief Djanet. Taking leave of Bursuk's aùls, and accompanied by himself as a safeguard, we entered on the ninth of March the Zaùkù pass. The presence of Bursuk did not, however, save us from the rapacity of the Kirghizes. On the 11th, as the caravan was ascending the narrow defile which was obstructed by fragments of rock, a deafening shout was suddenly raised, and several small flags were simultaneously displayed. We had hardly time to take up a defensive position, and to fortify ourselves behind the natural barricades, when we were attacked by a band of seventy Kirghizes. My comrades, actuated by the instinct of self-preservation, disappeared under cover of their camels, and did not show themselves again until the fray was over. Our servants, however, owing to the strong position of the caravan and their effective weapons, succeeded in repelling the Buruts and taking prisoner one of their chief leaders. The engagement was limited to a few wounded on both sides, and to an exchange of prisoners. The worthy Bursuk, whom we had taken with us to ensure our safe passage, considering himself compromised, departed secretly without the promised present.

The Zaùkù pass is formed by the rapid course of the Zaùkù, and by the Zaùkùchak, Kashka-ashu, and some Dzungarian* rivulets, which fall intoit, and also form passes. The route thus runs first along the course of the chief river, after which it bifurcates. Beyond the junction of the Dzungarian

* Mr. Semenof was evidently not aware of the existence of this stream, as will appear from his remarks on Ritter's "Asia," p. 16, vol. ii

river, the Zaùkù defile becomes steeper and narrower, forming terraces with two Alpine lakes between. Fragments of rock, in huge, irregular boulders, block up the passage. The defile terminates in a precipitous ledge of about 800 feet in height. The skeletons of beasts of burthen which strew the path, bear witness to the difficulty of the ascent.

The whole of the caravan could not ascend in one day, and, therefore, the advanced portion of it bivouacked on a small marshy plateau, at which the Zaùkù pass terminates, while the other portion remained at the bottom, at the old encampment. The difficulty of the ascent was increased by an abundant fall of snow. The pack-horses, and more especially the camels, often slipped over the wet stones, and on more than one occasion, losing their footing, fell ricochetting, and with a loud crash, into the yawning abyss. Five camels and two horses perished in this way. My companions were quite distracted. Each was occupied with his own beasts. The cries of the drivers, alternating with curses and abuse, and devout appeals to Allah, Baha-ooddeen, Appak-Hodja, and other Mussulman saints, shook the snow accumulated for ages on the surrounding hills with their reverberating echoes.

CHAPTER V.

On the Condition of Alty-shahr, or the Six Eastern Towns of the Chinese Province of Nan-lu (Little Bokhara), in 1858-59.

EASTERN TURKESTAN is enclosed by mountains on three sides: by the Thian-Shan on the Northern, the Bolor on the Western, and Kuen-Lun on the Southern. These mountains belong to the highest ranges of Central Asia, and form the natural limits of the Western portion of the Chinese Empire. The actual boundary, however, runs along the line of pickets stretching through the outlying lower ranges on the Chinese side; beyond this frontier the territory is occupied by roaming Kirghizes, who recognize the authority of the Kokan Khan.

To the Eastward, Eastern Turkestan is bounded by the uninhabited sandy deserts of the Makhai and Kamul Gobi. It occupies consequently a plain between 36° and 43° North latitude, and 70° and 90° West longitude, from the meridian of Paris.

Eastern Turkestan occupies the centre of the table-land of Eastern Asia; but Humboldt, guided by the vegetable productions of these parts, concludes that the plain of Little Bokhara cannot have an absolute elevation of more than 1,200 feet, and calls it the Tarym depression, after the river Tarymgol (otherwise Ergol), whose basin occupies the whole plain of Eastern Turkestan. Little Bokhara does, in fact, present the appearance of a great depressed valley, resembling, in physical features, an open plain; and this general view receives confirmation from a consideration of the course of the river Ergol, whose bed slopes very gradually to the eastwards.

The interior of this country is a sandy desert, the peculiar features of which first become visible in the eastern slopes of an undulating range of hills, of no great width, between Yanyshahr and Yarkend. From this region it gradually widens as it runs to the eastward, where it forms the vast Gobi, devoid of all vegetation, though interspersed with reservoirs of brackish water, and where the sand is heaped in such lofty ridges that the inhabitants give them the name of "Gag" (mountain). If we are to credit native writers, this sand is subject to the same phenomena of drifting and regular locomotion as the famed moving deserts of Africa, and occasionally buries whole cities. The parts that lie at the foot of the mountains have a clayey soil, strewed with small stones, and in some places impregnated with salt. The numerous rivers running from the neighbouring hills afford means for the artificial irrigation of the earth, which would otherwise yield but scanty and poor vegetation, owing to the extreme dryness of the air; and, at best, there are but a few well-watered parts that form fertile oases. These cultivated and peopled patches form a ring round the base of the Thian-shan, Bolor, and Kuen-lun. The water system of the river Tarym, with its tributaries, relieves the interior of this desert, by a narrow strip of fertile land along the various river courses, where the fertility of the soil admits of a rude system of cultivation.

Such is the general character of the territory of the Southern line, which is completely level, and somewhat monotonous in aspect, owing to the absence of any mountain lines of demarcation.

The mountains surrounding Turkestan, on its other frontier, lie beyond the political limits of the country, but are of importance to it as regards roads and passes, and consequent facilities for communication with the rest of the world. The mountain roads generally run through defiles, with many ascents and descents, or wind by paths to a considerable height, or lead along the face of dangerous slopes. With regard to communication, the Thian-shan affords the greatest facilities for access. This mountain chain has three characteristic divisions, from the meridian of Kucha 82° 48′ E., to its intersection with the Bolor. To the East, from the transverse course of the Aksu to Kucha, the celestial mountains rise in a towering ridge, covered with perpetual snows, which feed enormous glaciers, and are therefore called the Muzart, or Icy Mountains.

The rivers rising in these rock and ice-bound fastnesses have a transverse course throughout the entire mountain line. The declivities are covered with coniferous trees, and abound in pasturages; but this district is, nevertheless, all but uninhabited. There is only one pass through the Muzart mountains, which is called by the Chinese the Pass of Glaciers, and by Humboldt "Djeparlé."

Through this pass there is a road leading from Kuldja, 43° 54′ N., 80° 58′ E., to Aksù. Although, according to Chinese accounts, Djeparlé presents very great difficulties, it is nevertheless practicable for camels. The Muzart Pass is closed against foreigners. Its crest lies in about 42° 28′ N., 80° 38′ E.

Westward of the Aksù river, as far as the meridian of Kashgar, the Thian-Shan merges into a broad table-land, called by the Kirghizes "Syrt," about a hundred miles in width, and intersected by transverse valleys considerably elevated above sea-level. The "Syrt" is quite destitute of timber; its soil is utterly incapable of cultivation. It is covered with a short but thick grass, and serves as a summer pasture-ground for the Kirghizes. There are many caravan tracks across the "Syrt," which are all available with camels. To the west of the meridian of Kashgar the Thian-Shan separates into several branches. The mountains of this region are all well wooded; the valleys of the rivers, all of which have deep beds, are fertile; and the ascents become, consequently, steeper at several points. Over this tract there are several horse paths, but only one commercial road, leading from the Ferganah valley to Kashgar, through the Terekty-davan Pass, known to us under the name of the Kashgar defile. A considerable trade was carried on, in the most remote times, along this road, between Asia and China. The Terektin road abounds with fuel and forage. The distance along this road from Kokan to Kashgar is estimated as a caravan journey of eighteen days.

The Bolor mountains, otherwise called Alai by the Andijans, are precipitous and inaccessible on their western face, and form on the east a high, cold plateau, visited only in the summer by the Kirghizes. There is only one caravan road over the Bolor, which passes through Badakshan. This Badakshan road is said to be very fatiguing, and, at best, is not practicable on horseback. The road through Badakshan to Yarkend leads to Khulum, thence to Bokhara, Balkh, and Cabul; caravans requiring sixty-five days to reach Bokhara by this route.

The Pamir is intersected by roads well-trodden by the Kirghizes; all of which lead to the Khanate of Kokan, or to Karategin.

Over the Kuen-Lun one pass is known, that of Kara-Korum, by which Eastern Turkestan communicates with Thibet and India. The road, as far as Thibet, leads through uninhabited places with poor pastures, while from Thibet into India they become so difficult that Indian produce from Bokhara reaches Eastern Turkestan through the Terektin Pass. The distance from Yarkend to Thibet is a journey of forty days, and twelve from Thibet to Cashmere; horses and yaks are the beasts of burthen chiefly employed on this road.

The mountains encircling Little Bokhara generally offer but few approaches; the line of the Thian-Shan, from the Aksù to its point of intersection with the Bolor, alone affording anything resembling facilities for communication.

Of all the routes above named, the Terektin is that most frequented by troops as well as by caravans; it is enlivened by constant commercial traffic, and not a day passes without the passage of a caravan over it.

The rivers of Little Bokhara belong to the river system of Tarimgol, with the exception of a few which, rising in the Kuen-Lun range, fall into lakes or lose themselves in the sands. The chief rivers forming the Tarimgol are the Aksù-Daria, Faizabad-Daria (otherwise called the Kashgar-Daria), Yarkend-Daria, and the Khotan-Daria. The Aksù-Daria is formed by two affluents, viz. the Aksù proper (the higher waters of which are first called the Sary-Djas, then the Kopchagai, but receives the name it is best known by only in its lower course), and the Kakshal river. The Aksù rises in the northern slope of Khan Tangri-ula, on emerging from which it runs parallel to the meridian, bisecting the Thian-Shan, in which it has excavated for itself a deeprocky channel. The Kakshal flows from the hilly elevations on the eastern side of the mountain-lake Tchadyr-kul, and runs due east under the name of Aksai, through an extensive table-land, on quitting which it turns abruptly in a southerly direction, descends the southern slope of the Thian-Shan and falls finally into the Aksu, having a course parallel to the base of the mountains, and a general direction from N.E. to S.W.

The rivers forming the Kashgar-Daria rise in the Thian-Shan and Bolor. The Faizabad-Daria is formed by the two rivers Tümen and Kizyl-Daria; the first takes its rise in the Kok-Tonn mountains, to the North-West of Lake Tchadyr-Kul; the second, the Kizyl, has its source in the Altai mountains, where the Thian-Shan is intersected by the Bolor. The Faizabad-Daria receives on its right the river Usten, or Khan-Aryk (marked Yamaniar-Usten on Russian maps), and the Yangishahr-Usten, and on its left the Artysh. The Artysh rises in the elevation of the Torgat, bordering Lake Tchadyr-kul on the South, and before emerging into the valley is called the Toin. This river receives many affluents in the mountains, of which the most remarkable is the Terekty or Astyn-Artysh, joining it on the right side. The river Usten or Yamaniar, is the outlet of Lake Karakul in the table-land of Pamir. To the Kashgar-Daria system belongs the Yanyshahr-Usten, flowing from the neighbourhood of Lake Sarikol and falling into the Kashgar-Daria on its right bank. The Yarkend-Daria or Yarkend-Usten is formed by the Yarkend-Daria proper which rises out of Lake Sarikol, and the river Tynzap, flowing from the northern slope of the Karakorum Pass in the Kuen-Lun mountains. The Khotan-Daria also takes its rise in the Karakorum hills, and is formed by the junction of two streams; the Kara-Kash and Yulgun-Kash, (pronounced Yurun-Kosh by the Chinese). Below the junction of the Aksù, Kashgar, Yarkend and Khotan Darias, which all unite nearly at the same point, the river takes the name of Tarim-Usten, and Tarimgol or Ergol according to Chinese geography. Among the rivers falling into the Tarim the most note-worthy are the Muzart, Kucha-Daria and Khaidu, descending from the Thian-Shan and falling into the Tarim on its left bank. The Tarim disembogues into Lake Lob-Nor, signifying, in the Mongolian, Starry Lake. This lake, according to Chinese authorities, is 400 lis in length by 200 lis in width. The neighbourhood abounds in turbid springs, which play like fountains.

There are many lakes in Little Bokhara, all lying along the borders of the inner desert, and containing brackish water. There is a tradition current among the inhabitants that their forefathers sprang originally from the bottom of a large inland sea. All the rivers of Eastern Turkestan bear, more or less, the character of mountain torrents in their upper courses, having an inconsiderable depth, but a rapid current over a rocky bed. In July and August the waters swell considerably from the melting snows, but they are fordable at all seasons of the year. They assume a great depth and breadth only on the junction of several streams. Ferries exist over the Kizyl river, between Kashgar and the Chinese fort, as also over the Faizabad-Daria, (at the junction of the Tümen and Kizyl). Although, throughout, the Kashgar-Daria and Yarkend-Daria are navigable when full, and the Tarim at all seasons and along its whole course, yet the natives do not take advantage of these admirable facilities for intercommunication. The rivers of Little Bokhara, viewed either as convenient for communication or in a scientific or agricultural light, are of the utmost importance for this region, inasmuch as they diffuse fertility in the inner deserts, and convert the otherwise inhospitable plains into a country suitable for the abode of man.

The roads in the interior, between the towns of Eastern Turkestan and China, are convenient enough. "Urtengs," or stations, have been built along all of them by the Chinese, each of which is occupied by fifteen or twenty Chinamen under an officer, with as many Turkestan families. Besides these "Urtengs," there are signal houses for the speedy transmission of intelligence in the event of war or insurrections; and, for the accommodation of travellers, forage and provisions for small caravans are also obtainable at these stations.

The city of Aksù is the point of divergence for all the roads of this region. The various routes centring at Aksù lead to China, Ili, and all the towns of Eastern Turkestan.

All the roads leading from the interior of China,

to the Western frontiers, converge at the town of Hun-Chanfoo, whence there is a road to Lian-Djèu, where a large magazine of warlike stores has been established for use in the event of a war in the west. At a distance of 37 versts (24½ miles) from this town, at the western extremity of the great wall, is the fortress of Tzia-yui-Hùan, which commands the road. From this point to Komula extends a sandy steppe, uninhabited, and destitute alike of water, forage, or vegetation. Important granaries have been in like manner established by the Chinese at Komul. Farther on, the road branches off in two directions, one, the "Northern Road," leading to Dzungaria, the other, the "Southern Road," to Eastern Turkestan. The Dzungarian road trends along the eastern lateral depression of the Thian-Shan, through Barkul, Urumchi, and Hurkharasu to Ili. The Southern Road takes a westerly direction through Pidjan to Turfan, which latter town has direct communication with Urumchi by way of Bogdo-ùla. Beyond Turfan, it leads to Kara-Shahr, which in its turn is accessible from Ili by the rivers Julduz and Narat-Davam. Marshy swamps, stretching westward, extend to the south of Kara-Shahr, necessitating an earthern embankment at the town of Buigur, and the road, after passing Kuchi, finally reaches Aksû. The Chinese calculate the distance from Pekin to Aksù at 3844 versts (2546¾ miles). The Southern Road runs through level tracts of country, more or less inhabited; a barren steppe, however, terminating within 34 miles of the Khami oasis, spreads between the barriers of Tzia-yui-Hùan and Khami, for a distance of 750 versts (497 miles). The Chinese have founded settlements along this road, and built stations. The remarkable points along the Southern Road, in military respects, are:—Khamil, 45° 18′ N., 92° 14′ E., where are magazines of grain and arms, and Buigur. This town lies in the middle of impassable marshes, and with a small force is capable of defending the Southern Road. It takes four and a half and five months for caravans and troops to traverse the road from Pekin to Aksù, but the journey is effected in one month by special messengers.

From Aksù to Ili (Kuldja), at which place the military and civil governments of the Western region are concentrated, the distance is reckoned at 615 versts (407½ miles), the road leading through very mountainous localities. The famous Djeparlé, or pass of glaciers, occurs on this road.

A quick journey over this road, completed in fifteen days, is looked upon as a marvel of expeditious travelling, even with all the advantages of numerous "Urtengs" which have been constructed along it. The principal Chinese high road from Aksù goes to Ush-Turfan, 41° N., 76°, 20′ E., and Yarkend. To Ush-Turfan the distance is estimated at eighty miles, and to Yarkend at 247 miles. At a distance of 290 versts (192 miles) from Aksù, on the road to Yarkend, lies the town of Burchuk, garrisoned by a Chinese force, and provided with a ferry. From hence there is a direct road to Kashgar, the distance thither, from this point, being estimated at about 240 versts (159 miles); trading caravans from Aksù always proceed straight to Kashgar along this road. The main road from Yarkend leads to Kashgar, through Yanyshahr on to Kokan. The distance between Yarkend and Yanyshahr, is 113 miles, and fifty-seven miles from the latter place to Kashgar, the length of the journey between Kokan and Yarkend being computed at 270 miles. Chinese troops and Government convoys march to Kashgar and Khotan, through Yarkend.

Besides these roads, there is one direct from Aksù to Khotan, following the course of the Khotan-Daria, (along the banks of which caravans travel for eighteen days, or fifteen days in quick travelling), and two others from Ush-Turfan to Kashgar. One of those between the latter places emerges at the fourth station of the Yarkend route; after joining which it proceeds to Burchuk, and thence to Yarkend and Kashgar, while the other leads straight to Kashgar. This latter road follows up the course of the Kokshal, and, passing the military station of Bokchan, reaches Altyn-Artysh. The distance to Kashgar by this route is calculated at 233½ miles. The road traverses various uninhabited tracts, which, however, abound in forage and fuel. The routes leading from Aksû to Ush, Kashgar, Yarkend, and Khotan pass through populous localities, and the last three follow the course of rivers whose level and fertile banks, hardly rising above the stream, present fine natural meadows, so that the roads winding along between the base of the mountains and the channels of the rivers, pass through densely populated regions.

In former ages the Chinese communicated with the Western region through Hua-Chjeù (133½ miles west of Tzià-yui-Hûan) straight over the sandy steppe to Khotan; at present, however, this road is altogether closed. There is likewise a road from

Turfan to Khotan *viâ* the Lobnor, but like the last named, it is also closed.

Notwithstanding its enormous extent, Eastern Turkestan possesses a remarkably uniform climate, which can only be accounted for by the peculiarities of its geographical position. The circumjacent mountainous districts are subject to climatic conditions, which differ materially from those of the Little Bokharian plain. Even in summer snow storms are of frequent occurrence among the mountains. It is cool, indeed, throughout the whole of the season; in the valleys the snow remains on the ground until the months of May and June, while the mountain summits are covered with perpetual snows. Winter commences in October; at all events, a caravan which left Kashgar on our arrival at that place (13th October), was compelled to return on account of the Terektin defile having been blocked up with snow.

We shall now speak of the climate of the Plains, dwelling chiefly, indeed almost exclusively, upon that of the "territory of the six towns." Beginning then with our own observations: on the 9th October, when we entered on the southern slope of the Thian-Shan chain, into the Terekty defile, the shores of the Terekty river were clothed with luxuriant trees and picturesque clumps of bushes. The thermometer indicated 81° .5 Fahr.; and on entering Kashgar, our caravan passed through fruit gardens where women and children were cutting down the remaining vine branches, after gathering the season's vintage, and the pomegranates were still on the trees. The rice and cotton crops had not all been got in. Fresh greens and fruit of various sorts, such as apples, quinces, pears, peaches, and figs were exposed for sale at the bazaar. The weather from the 9th October till towards the end of November was uniformly warm and clear. The heat rose to 81° .75 Fahr.; about the 22nd November the nights grew colder, and the leaves began to fall, while the water in the canals was covered with a thin crust of ice, and on the 26th November the water was stopped at the "aryks," or aqueducts. The first snow fell on the 31st December, and continued falling until the middle of the following day; the second fall of snow was on the 19th January, when it snowed all day and half the night, and again on the 24th January until the morning of the 26th. The thermometer generally stood at 32° Fahr., and upwards, falling only twice below the freezing point. On the 31st December it indicated 14° Fahr., and on the 28th January 4° Fahr. The rivers Kizyl and Tumen did not freeze during the whole winter, but the ponds in the town were covered with ice eight inches thick. After the Chinese new year, from which the natives reckon the commencement of spring, the weather actually became warmer. On the 26th February water appeared in the canals, and nature began speedily to revive. In the beginning of March, pies filled with the first shoots of vegetables were offered for sale as "delicacies of the season," and on the 21st, several trees in the court yard of our abode were already in full leaf. During the whole time, until the departure of the caravan from the open country, on the 29th March, the weather was bright and warm. On the 26th and 27th of this month a warm N.E. wind prevailed. Fogs and rain were, generally speaking, of rare occurrence, usually lasting two days only, after which, at intervals, it rained slightly. During the middle of February, the weather was frequently windy, west and N.W. winds predominating. Relying on these facts, and on the strength of the testimony of the inhabitants, it is certain that spring commences here in the middle of February, and somewhat later in the neighbouring Ferganah valley. The summer, it is said, is distinguished by great heat, and the air becomes insufferably oppressive from the heavy clouds of dust, the more so by reason of the great scarcity of rain in these parts. The inhabitants of Eastern Turkestan are particularly afraid of thunderstorms. When the horizon is clouded, all the "ahunds" with their pupils walk out on the terraces of the Mosques and read a prayer or "knut" in a loud voice; and it is a fact that they ascribe to these prayers a power of propitiating the threatening heavens. The cause of this intense apprehension of an ordinary phenomenon, is to be ascribed to the circumstance that the earth, after a fall of rain, becomes covered with salt, which destroys the harvest, and also to their houses being built of mud, with flat roofs, so that in the event of a heavy fall of rain, the towns of Little Bokhara would be entirely destroyed.

The winter, according all accounts, has generally much the same character that it bore during our stay, *i. e.* the snow remains on the ground not longer than three or four days, and the rivers do not freeze at all. When the rivers are frozen along the shores, the winter is considered a severe one. Intense colds prevail at the end of the twelfth month of Chinese computation, that is, in January, and spring commences from the Chinese holiday of the new year, which the Turkestans call by its name in Mongolian, Chagan. This gradual transition from summer to autumn, and the abrupt change from winter to spring, form climatic peculiarities almost exclusively confined to this country. The change of the seasons is accompanied by the following variation in the vegetation. The apricot-tree blooms in the middle of March, when other trees commence budding; cultivated meadows become covered with fresh blades of thick "musu-yu" and grass, tulips, and anemones then make their appearance in the fields. In April the apricot-tree begins to bear, and towards the end of May the mulberry, apricot, and the "zamuch" melon, arrive at maturity. At this time barley is reaped, and onions, turnips, and other kitchen vegetables are planted over it. Peaches and apples ripen between June and August, while other cereals and fruit are gathered in August. Hempseed, sesame, rice, "djugara," (Javary), maize and cotton are not harvested until September and October.

The prevailing winds here are Westerly and North-Westerly, which blow principally during the spring, and raise dust and dense clouds of sand. Yanyshar, Yarkend and Khotan are under nearly the same climatic conditions as Kashgar; at Khotan the winter is yet milder. In Turfan, Aksù, and more especially in Bāi and Sairam, lying nearer to the mountains and more to the north, no great heat prevails in summer, and the winter is severer. The rivers become frozen, but snow first falls towards the end of January, melting immediately; this does not, however, retard the growth of pomegranates, figs, and cotton at Aksù. If we are to believe the concurrent testimony of the Emperor Kan-Si, and Père Gerbillon, relative to the cultivation of orange trees, Khamil must enjoy a more genial climate. In the Eastern towns, it is said, the winters are cold, and summers exceedingly hot. Yet Turfan and Khamil are famous for their vegetable productions, the latter in particular for its melons, which are eaten at the Imperial Court.

The climate of Eastern Turkestan, judging by the health of its inhabitants as well as by its beneficial influence on strangers, must be very salubrious. Epidemics and pestilential diseases are altogether unknown to the Turkestani, with one important exception, however, the small-pox, which in former times swept away whole settlements, and drove the panic-stricken inhabitants into the mountains. The ravages of this disease are now stopped by the introduction of vaccination. Notwithstanding the great consumption of fruit, and the universal custom of smoking hashish, which is known to have a most injurious effect on the human organization, very few of the Turkestani ever suffer from sickness. Venereal diseases, notwithstanding the great depravity of the natives, have not spread hither. Throughout the town of Kashgar, we only saw two persons who were disfigured by them. The males are well built and strong, yet they seldom attain a great age. The women are of weak form, and, owing to early marriage (at twelve, and even ten years of age), become subject to various chronic complaints. At fifty, the Kashgar women are as withered as our own at seventy or eighty. Goitre is very frequently met with at Yarkend, the natives of which attribute its prevalence to the property of the water; and it is also met with in Kokan.

Passing now to the natural riches of Little Bokhara, we shall first point to the characteristic productive features of this region. The mineral wealth of Little Bokhara is very little explored. Gold is washed out at the Karja settlements in such large quantities that the inhabitants pay their dues in this metal, and dispose of it to private individuals. Eighty "Lans" of this gold are annually sent to the Court of Pekin from Khotan. Copper is obtained at Aksù, Sairam, and Kuchi. The copper of Aksù is known for its malleability, and contains, according to local accounts, a considerable admixture of the precious metals, the method of extracting which, however, is not known to the natives.

Eastern Turkestan affords in abundance sulphur, sal-ammoniac, alum and saltpetre. The volcanic soil around the town of Kuchi is particularly rich in these materials. Sulphur is obtained at Ush-Turfan, in the Yarkend district, and saltpetre at Ush-Turfan, and at Sairam, 110 miles further east. Salt mines are worked in the Yan-chi-Shan mountains, east of Aksù. Among the more remarkable mineral productions of Turkestan must be included the oriental jasper, Nephrite, or Jade stone, which is highly esteemed in China under the name of "Yer." The Nephrite found here is of two kinds: that from the mountains, called by the natives "Loucha," or "bish-bargan," which is found in the mountains of Mirdjai and Sutash, 74 miles from Yarkend, and the second obtained in the river Ulgunkash (pronounced Yurunkash by the Chinese), under the special supervision of a Chinese officer. About ten "gins" of the mountain nephrite, and the whole of the quantity got out of the Yurunkash river, are annually despatched to Pekin; where its sale and disposal is one of the most rigidly enforced monopolies of the Chinese Government. We are not aware of silver, iron and coal having been discovered in the "territory of the six towns,"—at all events no such mines have been worked in Little Bokhara. Mention of silver mines in the vicinity of Khamil is made in Chinese chronicles, but to what extent this is true we cannot say.

Two smelting works, one for copper the other for lead, which occur on the route from Kashgar to Kokan are not now in operation, owing to political causes. As the greater part of the mineral wealth of this region goes in tribute to China, and all the copper is despatched to the mint at Aksù, the requirements of the inhabitants in these products, fall very far short of being satisfied. Iron, cast and wrought, lead, copper, and latten are received from Kokan, to which place they are brought, either in a natural or manufactured state, from Russia. The very limited acquaintance of the Turkestani with metallurgy, and their ignorance of the simplest forms of mining, prevent them from deriving any benefit from the mineral wealth which the bowels of the mountains surrounding Little Bokhara must yield in abundance.

The Kokanians, it is said, obtain a considerable quantity of gold by washing, in the upper course of the Syr, which takes its rise in the Thian-Shan; and lead mixed with silver is also procured in the hills to the east of Andijan. The Bolor is particularly rich in minerals. Gold in nuggets forms the staple of trade betwen Karategin and Kokan, and slaves (*Lapis Lazuli*), turquoises and rubies constitute that between Badakshan and Yarkend. The Pamir Kirghizes bring rock-crystals, jasper in various forms, and gold nuggets to Yarkend and Kashgar. Huen-tsang, a Chinese traveller of the eighth century, states that the Pomola (Pamir) country yields gold of a fiery colour. No mineralogical investigations have as yet been made in the Kuen-Lun range, but it may be taken for granted there is no absence of rich metallic lodes in it. The river Karia, which is worked for gold, rises out of these mountains, and the name of Zar-Afshan (auriferous), which some rivers flowing out of it bear, together with the tradition throughout Central Asia to the effect that the ruler of the Gildits keeps concealed in his cavern bars of gold, tends to strengthen the foregoing inferences.

The natural vegetation of Little Bokhara is poor and undiversified. The character of the flora of these parts bears a general resemblance to the steppe vegetation of the Ili valley. The northern slope of the Thian-Shan, impending over the valley of the Issyk-kul, has a rich alpine flora, and presents luxuriant meadows of thick grass diversified by flowers of bright colours; the declivities of the mountains are covered with the Siberian silver-fir, mountain ash and dwarf medlar (*Cotoneaster multiflora*), while along the banks of rivers are found the barberry, honeysuckle, alpine currant, brier, &c. Above the coniferous zone, the juniper (*Juniperus sabina*), and "Chiliga," or wild southern wood (*Caragana jubata*) are met with. The southern slope of the Celestial mountains, descending to the plain of Little Bokhara, west of the meridian of Aksù, consists of argillaceous schist and conglomerate, while the less lofty auxiliary ranges in front are formed of layers of laminated clay The exposed rocks of the Southern slope are either dotted here and there with isolated patches of rank grass, or where this is not the case, are perfectly bare. Among these the Kirghiz goats and sheep with difficulty find food for themselves in the autumn. Eastward of Aksù the mountains are covered with coniferous trees (silver-fir), and present rich mountain pastures. The table-land of the Syrt, excepting the valleys of the rivers Atbash, Arpa, and Naryn, is not suited for cultivation, through free from timber, and covered with fine thick grass. On the plains of the Atbash and Arpa, the Kirghizes sow wheat, barley, and millet. These plains are also devoid of trees and bushes, being covered with fine grasses, such as the feathergrass and wormwood. The deepened course of the Naryn forms a fertile valley, whose elevation is equal to that of the Issyk-kul. The banks of the Naryn are bordered with the "Oblepikha" *(Hipophæ rhamonoides)*, willow, poplar, and varieties of the "Chiliga" or wild southern wood *(Caragana jubata)*, while the mountain slopes are clad with dense forests of coniferous trees and plants natural to the alpine zones of the northern slope. That part of the Thian-Shan which abuts on the Bolor is typified by spiræa, the juniper, and dwarf medlar *(Cotoneaster multiflora)*. The latter plant, as well as different liliaceous types, such as tulips and a species of wild garlic, form the chief characteristics of the Bolor flora, which, it is said, also abounds in rich pasturages. The Kuen-Lun, according to Thompson's evidence, has but a poor and limited flora; its crags are clothed with prickly plants, amongst which the astragal is the most common. The landscape and the vegetation of the plain of Little Bokhara are still more dreary and sterile-looking. The interior of the country is one vast desert steppe, consisting either of sandy dunes with the inevitable "Saksaul" (*Anabasis saxaul*), or of bare illimitable wastes impregnated with salt. The most fertile spots are considered to lie between the sandy plains and the base of the mountains. When we arrived at Kashgar, in the month of October, we perceived that the vegetation in the neighbourhood was very scanty; the characteristic plants were the "Yantak" (camelthorn), tamarisk, *artemisia*, and different *gramineæ* peculiar to a sandy-argillaceous soil, such as the "Chi" and *Iris augustifolia.* In consequence of the extreme dryness of the atmosphere, and the nature of the soil, vegetation is entirely confined to well-watered localities. The courses of the rivers are marked by two narrow parallel belts of verdure and forest, consisting of different species of bushes and trees. The native inhabitants call these littoral woods "Djengels." River-side clumps of this description are called "Uremis" in Siberia and throughout the Orenburg region. The jungles of Little Bokhara have a character of their own; in the upper courses of the various rivers in the low bushes of the *Hipophæ rhamonoides*, by tamarisks in the Thian-Shan, and by copses of dwarf medlar in the Bolor. Wherever a river about mid-course enters upon a plain at the base of the lowest lateral spurs running down from a mountain range, the jungle becomes more diversified, and the poplar, willow, barberry tree bearing red and black fruit, sweetbriar, wild rose, yellow caragan *(Caragana frutescens)*, and other papilionaceous bushes *(Halimodendron argenteum)* appear in this portion of its course; the elsewhere abundant dwarf-medlar ceases to be found, and the *Hipophæ rhamonoides* attains a lofty growth. In the lower part of its course, from the increasing pressure of the water, each river becomes broader and forms moist meadows and cane-brakes all along its banks, while the jungles border the shores in a dense and broad belt, in which new forms, such as the hawthorn and wild olive (*Elæagnus-augustifolia*) are found in abundance. After the confluence of the Little Bokharian rivers with the Tarym, the jungle disappears, and the banks of the main stream are formed into broad and marshy swamps thickly overgrown with reeds and cane.

Owing to careful irrigation and the long cultivation which the soil has undergone, the agricultural productions of Little Bokhara are sufficiently diversified. The outskirts of the towns and villages are surrounded with shady gardens, producing figs and pomegranates. Plantations of cotton and artificial meadows cover extensive areas of land, and the moist parts are sown with rice. The vegetable productions of Little Bokhara are the following cereals:—Wheat, barley, rice, javary, red and black lentil, and, to a small extent, millet; oats are not grown at all. Of plants for dyeing and manufacturing purposes, Eastern Turkestan produces—cotton (belonging to the graminaceous variety, viz., *Gossypium herbaceum*), hempseed, sesamum (*Sesamum orientale*), madder, and tobacco. Several varieties of melons and water-melons, of exquisite flavour, are likewise grown, as also carrots, radishes, beet-root, onions, mint, peas (*cicer Arietinum*), poppies, and saffron. Cucumbers are only occasionally to be found, and belong to the kind called Chinese. The various gardens are planted with the willow, poplar (*Populus pruinosa*), pyramidal silver-leaved poplar, mulberry, wild olive (*Elæagnus hortensis*), and "chiliani;" the two latter yield fruit which tastes like the date, and a glue is extracted from the first. The fruit-trees are apple, pear, bergamot, peach, apricot, quince, pomegranate, and fig. Grapes are grown principally of two sorts: "Khuseini," a white, elongated variety, of delicious flavour; and "Sakhibi," of a round form and dark colour. The foregoing trees and plants are common to the whole of the Little Bokharian valley, with the exception of those grown on the hills; peaches, pomegranates, and figs, for instance, do not grow in Sairam and Bai, while grapes and cotton are successfully cultivated there. Prunes, cherries, and walnuts are grown in Yarkend. The inhabitants of the village of Kargalyk, in the Yarkend district, occupy themselves exclusively with growing nuts, which form the staple of the trade of this place. From this it will be seen that the vegetation of Little Bokhara is very poor, and that agriculture is in a state of decline. Without taking into account European countries under the same latitudes, and which are characterized by the richness and variety of the semi-tropical zone, the flora of Little Bokhara is even poorer than that of Central Asiatic countries under the same parallel of latitude. The vegetation of the mountains of the Dzungaro-Kirghiz Steppe presents a much greater variety of natural forms. In the neighbourhood of Fort Vernöe, five degrees further north, apricots and apples grow wild, and the leafy trees are distinguished for their size; while the grass vegetation is remarkably rich, notwithstanding the severity of the winter and great depth of snow. The neighbouring Ferganah valley is considered the most fertile part of all Central Asia. Its mountains are covered with coniferous trees, walnut groves and pistachio bushes; and agriculture and the cultivation of fruit trees contribute no small portion to the trade of this region. In addition to the fruit grown in Little Bokhara, the gardens of Ferganah yield almonds and plums. Bokhara, although it presents the appearance of a fertile island amidst an ocean of sand, has more cultivated vegetable forms than Little Bokhara.

Eastern Turkestan is characterized by the absence of meadow-land, by bad agriculture, scarcity of wood and the sterility of the surrounding mountains. The cause of this paucity of vegetation must not be attributed to the elevated nature of the region, as vegetation in this zone can flourish at a considerable altitude—as evidenced by the ripening of grapes and peaches on the shores of the Issyk-kul—but to the character of the soil, which is never moistened by rain, and to the insufficient tillage of the land. With regard to the vegetable productions of this country, we must state, in conclusion, that the sugar-cane referred to in the Chinese chronicles of the first century of our era, and to which Ritter would have particular attention drawn, does not grow anywhere in the vicinity of Kashgar. We should imagine that the Chinese historian comprehended under this name either the sweet "sorgho" or the javary, the stalks of which contain a sweet juice much esteemed by the native children.

The animal kingdom has several characteristic varieties; in the mountains there are multitudes of wolves, foxes, jackals, lynxes, bears, and white-breasted martens; also mountain goats (*Capra Tartarica*) and sheep (*Ovis argali*), which frequent the mountain summits. The deer hide in the forests. Alpine marmots burrow in the south-western slopes of all the high table-lands of the Thian-Shan, and rats are plentiful in the marshes about the sources of rivers. It is said that herds of wild asses (*Equus onager*), and "djeirans" (*Antelope subgutturosa*), roam over the sandy Steppes. Chinese works very often speak of wild camel hunts, which formed one of the amusements of the rulers of these cities in past ages. Notwithstanding that the chronicles in our possession corroborate this remarkable fact, the natives could not give us any information regarding it; and we are, therefore, driven to conjecture that these wild camels must be entirely annihilated, or have been scared away to the inaccessible wilds of the Sahara of Little Bokhara. The wild animals indigenous to the plains are the Caragan fox (*Canis Melanotus*) and Corsac fox (*Canis Corsac*). Tigers, wild boars, and grey hares, abound in the jungles. Birds of prey are found in the mountains, of which those best known to us are, the lammergeayer (*Gypætos barbatus*), attaining, according to Chinese accounts, the size of a camel; the condor (*Vultur fulvus*), eagle (*Aquila nobilis*), falcon, hawk, and others. The eagle is the only bird employed by the native nobility in hunting the fox and mountain goat, for which purpose it is chiefly got from Khotan. Falcons and hawks are procured from the thick forests of *coniferæ* in the Aksù district, and are trained for the chase by the Kokanians. Of the *gallinaceæ* found on the mountains are the "ular," of the size of the capercailzie, of an ashy grey plumage, and with red circles round the eyes; and the "kiklik," about the size of a partridge, also of a grey colour, but with black marks over the eyes, and black and red stripes over the breast. These birds are also indigenous to the other mountainous regions of Asia. The flesh of the "ular" is tender, delicate, and highly esteemed by the Kokanians, and the flesh of the "kilkik" is equally palatable. A more curious and less justifiable purpose for which the latter bird is in request, is to train it for fighting, as was the custom with gamecocks in England in bygone days. Pheasants and quails are found in considerable abundance in the jungles. Pigeons of the Steppe (*Syrrhaptes paradoxus*, Illig.)* fly in vast flocks over the plains; while crows, rooks, magpies, sparrows, starlings, &c., affect the streets of the towns. In the better populated localities and on the mountain lakes the rarer water-fowl are singularly scarce, though ducks and geese are common, more especially in the lower course of the Tarym, and on Lake Lobnor, where swans, geese, ducks, and other water-fowl are so numerous, according to native and Chinese accounts, that the inhabitants manufacture the down into clothes, and sleep on feather beds. It is remarkable that Eastern Turkestan is not visited by the stork,

* *Tetras paradoxus*, Pall.

which in Western Turkestan builds its nest on the mosques, and struts in the streets in common with other domestic animals.

The rivers of Little Bokhara, and those debouching into Lake Lobnor, contain an abundance of fish. The Chinese relate that the Lobnorians when coming to Korlo (a settlement in the Kuchi district) on business, always carry with them a supply of fish for their consumption, because they cannot eat any other food; other Turkestans almost wholly abstain from it. Judging by the general character of the natural productions of this region, the fish here will, in all probability, be found to be the same as those which naturalists have already discovered in the rivers of the Balkhash system.

The fissures of the sandy-clay soil of Little Bokhara shelter numerous venomous insects of the spider family, such as scorpions, phalangia, and tarantulæ; and there is more especially a great variety of lizards. We did not see any snakes; but it is said they are rarely encountered, and cases of persons being bitten by them have scarcely been known to occur. In summer there are many gadflies, gnats, and moths, particularly in marshy places, overgrown with reeds. Of useful members of the lowest division of the animal kingdom, there is, in Little Bokhara, but the silk-worm, reared only in Khotan and its vicinity. It is said that near this city the silk-worm is found in its natural form.

The domestic animals of Little Bokhara are of the same species with those bred in neighbouring countries. The horses, which are of the Kirghiz breed, are obtained from the Great and Diko-kamenni Hordes. It is only the rich, and those engaged in the transport of goods, who have large studs, as, owing to the scarcity of grass, the animals must be fed the whole year round on dry provender. In imitation of the Chinese, the native nobles prefer the Kirghiz steeds. Hence Turkmen horses are not numerous, and being kept only by the Khotanians for the saddle, they are either of pure blood—"topchaks," or mixed—"karabairs." The Begs, following the Chinese fashion, employ mules in harness, which in other Mussulman countries are regarded as unclean animals, breeding them being considered in the light of a grievous sin. The camels are of the breed so extensively diffused throughout Mongolia, and the Chinese employ them in transporting Government stores; they are also used by the tea caravans, and occasionally by the Khotanians. The Turkestani occupy themselves merely in rearing sheep, yaks, and asses.

In order to avoid repetition when treating of the topography of the towns and settlements of Eastern Turkestan, we shall here indicate their general features.

The external aspect of the towns is monotonous and dull. The mosques in Little Bokhara being universally built without minarets (in Yarkend alone there is a tower over the ancient Registan mosque), and the houses being low, with flat roofs, the traveller approaching a town sees only the mud walls, which are of the same colour as the ground, usually relieved somewhat by small barred towers, of Chinese architecture, at their angles. All the towns of Eastern Turkestan are encircled by a wall diminishing in breadth towards the top, about eight fathoms thick, and reaching sometimes eight and more fathoms in height. Counter-forts are erected at the gates and angles.

The gates are made of planks, and are generally threefold. Moats of three and more fathoms in depth are dug round the walls, with bridges thrown over them. The houses are likewise built of mud, not even excepting the palaces of the rulers; they are flat roofed, and each is surrounded by a wall. The interior usually embraces an open square, with a water basin in the centre, shaded by a few trees, the domicile itself, a stable. and occasionally a garden. There are both large and small apartments; the former being, for the most part, open at the top. Inside these a continuous bench of common clay, overhung with drapery, runs round the walls, and serves in lieu of furniture. The inner rooms have a roof of slender branches, with apertures for the light. Fires are kindled in stoves, but in winter charcoal is burnt in braziers in the rooms. The rich have the inner walls of their houses stuccoed, and the niches ornamented with arabesques, while many paper their windows *à la Chinoise.* The walls of a house closely adjoin those of its neighbours on either side; but from the street walls and doors are alone visible. It is only the mosques, medréseh (colleges), and other public buildings, that have a façade to the street, the exterior of which is ornamented with coloured glazed tiles. The streets are irregular and very narrow, even the two-wheeled araba being only able to pass through the principal ones. The stalls, refreshment houses, and barber-shops, are situated on both sides of the larger streets leading from the gates to the market-place, in the centre of the town. Some of these streets are covered in at the top with mats. The centre of the town is generally near the chief mechet, "Registan" or "Aitga," adjoining which is the market-place, called "Charsu." One or two canals, filled from several ponds and lined with avenues of trees, pass through the town. In winter, when the water freezes in the canals and the supply is stopped, the natives draw it either from the ponds or river.

The Chinese fortresses, manchens, or "gulbai," are armed like the Mussulman towns. If the manchens occur close to a native town, the space between them is converted into a street, on both sides of which are Chinese houses of refreshment and shops. Such streets are called "Hai-Chan." The "Hai-Chan" at Yarkend and Khotan serves as a weekly bazaar. Turkestani settlements or villages consist of scattered habitations standing apart from each other. Each house is closed in by a wall, and surrounded by gardens and corn-fields, and several such connected by avenues of mulberry and olive trees, form a settlement. In more thickly-populated villages, the houses are grouped closer, but have no walls. The Chinese call the large settlements towns, but the natives term them "Yasy," or villages. With respect to the local administration of the six Western towns of Eastern Turkestan, they form departments or districts, independent of each other; and as the Chinese do not exercise any immediate influence in their government, we shall here adopt the native division.

1. *Kashgar District.*—Kashgar is one of the largest towns of Eastern Turkestan; it contains 16,000 houses, is situated between the rivers Kizyl and Tümen, surrounded by a clay wall six fathoms high, about ten arshines thick at its foundation, and five at the top, and about eight miles (twelve versts) in circumference. It is defended by six towers. The town has two gates, on the Eastern and South-Western sides; the first is called "Suv-Davsa," the second "Kum-Davsa" (sandy). Owing to the constant dryness of the atmosphere, the streets are clean, but irregular and narrow; two-wheeled arabas can pass only through the two principal ones. The houses are built of clay, excepting four religious colleges ("medresé"), and one sepulchral chapel, which are externally coated

with glazed tiles, after the Chinese fashion. The town is divided into two almost equal parts; the old town, or "Kuné-Shahr," and the new, or "Yany-Kurgan," founded by the ruler Zurund-Beg in 1838. The old town is situated on an eminence, while the new one occupies a much lower position. The centre of the town is a plain, with the chief mosque in front of the palace of the Hakim-Beg; while the market-place, "Aitga," is close by. The old town is divided into two quarters, "Charsu". and "Ambar-ichi;" and the new one into four—"Urda-aldy," "Ustan-bui," "Yumalak-shahr," and "Andijan-kucha."

In Kashgar, there are seventeen "medreseh" or religious seminaries, seventy schools ("mekteb"), eight caravansarais, and two other market places ("Aitga" and "Charsu"); the first-named of which is in front of the chief mosque, the second in the old town. Two principal streets lined with butcher, cook, and barber-shops and artificers' stalls, lead from the two gates to the centre square or Aitga. The road from Aitga Square to Charsu is covered in by an awning, and constitutes a mart or bazaar. Foreign merchants occupy the shops in the Sarai, of which the more famous are,—1, *Andijan*-Sarai, the largest, situated in the central square, and in which the Kokan custom-house is established for the clearance of foreign goods; 2, *Kunak*-Sarai, within a short distance of the former, in the street leading from the Sand-Gates to Aitga; it is principally occupied by Margilans, merchants from the town of Shakhrizebza and Afghans. Of other Sarais, all situated in the above streets, the best known are the "*Urtü-tin*"-Sarai, occupied by Bokharians and Urtü-tin Tadjiks, the *Yarkend*, *Aksù*, and *Jewish* Sarais; besides all which there are constant bazaars held near the "Sand-Gate," one for the sale of cotton, called "Pakhta" bazaar, and "Gundan" for the wholesale disposal of "Daba." Cattle are sold at the "Gaichan," outside the walls at the Sand-Gates.

There is a "Tynsa," "Dynsa," or police station, and a jail in the town, as also a further evidence of civilization, in the shape of a barrier, or toll-gate at the "Gundan," at which the tax on Daba is collected. Besides these public buildings and places of resort, there are two ponds and a canal (Usten) running through the whole town. One pond lies opposite to the house of the Hakim-Beg, and the other in the Djen-Molak-Shahr quarter. Every Friday a bazaar is held, at which the natives of the surrounding villages and the townspeople exhibit the fruits of their weekly labour. Of the settlements pertaining to the Kashgar district, the following lie along the system of the river Artysh :—

1. A group of settlements called *Ustün-Artysh* (Upper Artysh), at 17 miles N. of Kasghar; *Aryn*, a small settlement, 63 miles (190 lis) N.E. of Kashgar; *Saaran*, on the Termechuk rivulet; *Astyn-Artysh* (Lower Artysh), otherwise Altyn-Artysh (golden), 40 miles N.E. of Kashgar, distinguished for its tomb and mosque erected over the grave of Sultan Sutuk-Bagrakham-Hasi, whither devout Mussulmen repair on a pilgrimage; *Kol-Tailak* at the confluence of the Artysh and Faizabad-Daria, 38 miles E. of Kashgar; *Bishkerim*, 8 miles N.E. of the same town, between the Artysh and Tûmen rivers. Along the banks of the Tûmen lie the settlements, *Mushi*, 47 miles N.W. of Kashgar; *Samen* and *Toguztash*, or Dchan-Yan-Kurgan, faubourgs around Kashgar, the first on the N.W. the second on the W. side; *Djinchke* and *Abbat*, 8 miles E. of Kashgar, on the left bank of the Tûmen; *Shaptan*, on the right bank of the Faizabad-Daria, below the junction of the Tûmen with the Kizyl, 28 miles E. of Kasghar, where there is a ferry; *Faizabad*, a large settlement at a distance of 35 miles, on the S. bank of the Faizabad-Daria; *Yanshbat*, on

the S. bank of the same river, opposite *Koitoalaka*, 10 miles below *Faizabad.* The settlements along the Kizyl, are: *Tuguzak* at 17 miles; *Tuzgum*, on the right bank of the same river, 6 miles S. of Kashgar. The Khan-Aryk settlement is the abode of the Aléne-Akhund, who is considered the head of the Black-Mountaineer party, 27 miles S.E. of Kashgar, on the river Ussen (Khanaryk, or Yamanyar). The settlements of *Burakhatai*, *Ufal*, and *Tashmalyk* lie at the foot of the mountains, W. of Kashgar. To *Tashmalyk*, the distance is estimated at 120 miles and to *Burakhatai* 40 miles.

Of all the settlements in the district of Kashgar, the most extensive are: *Faizabad*, containing 2,000 houses; *Khan-Aryk* the same number; *Ustün-Artysh* 1,000 houses. They are all governed by Hakims (rulers), and have their own Aléne-Ahunds or Spiritual Chiefs.

A bazaar is held at Faizabad once a week, on Mondays; at Khan-Aryk twice a week, on Sundays and Tuesdays.

In the neighbourhood of Kashgar there are several tombs of saints, much reverenced by the natives and other Asiatics. The tomb of Appak-Hodja is the best building throughout the whole of the Kashgar district; it is situated at 4 miles N.E. of the town, on the left bank of the Tûmen; it is built of burnt brick and decorated externally and internally with coloured tiles; the cornices are composed of the horns of the mountain sheep, goat, and deer brought as sacrifices, while flags and standards decorate the entrance and the crypt itself. A large mosque, with spheroidal cupola of handsome proportions, has been erected close to the tomb by one of the sons of the Hodja.

The tomb of Ak-Mazar and Pojakhom-Hodja lies on the road to Artysh, at seven miles from Kashgar. In the town itself is the tomb of Abrazyk-Kazi-Hodja, among many others, but those we have mentioned are the most conspicuous. The Chinese Manchen lies 4½ miles S. of Kashgar, on the right bank of the Kizyl river, surrounded by a wall like that of Kashgar, with two gates on the N. and S. sides. Its garrison numbers 5,500 men.

2. *Yanyshahr District.*—Yanyshahr numbers 8000 houses, and lies at about forty-seven miles to the south of Kashgar. It is surrounded by a stone wall, has two gates, and two caravan-sarais. The main street runs from the Yarkend gates to the house of the Governor, facing which is a pond and

canal. All the shops, the places of public enter. tainment, and the two sarais are in this street. The weekly bazaar is held on Sundays, outside the town, in front of the Kashgar gates. The most notable villages of this district are:—*Laba,* at a distance of ten miles from *Yanyshar* to the South, and *Terektek,* celebrated for the hashish it produces. The notable holy places in the neighbourhood of *Yanyshahr* are, *Chilan-lyk* in the South-East, at a distance of ten miles, and *Mazar-bygim* at the same distance, and in the same direction. On the road to Yarkend there is a garden belonging to *Mazar-Bygim,* with a pond in which the lotus grows. The Chinese town lies at about a mile to the Westward, and its garrison, it is said, amounts to 2000 men,

3. *Yarkend District.*—Yarkend, the largest town of Eastern Turkestan, formerly the residence, first of the Khans, and then of the Hodjas, stands between the branches of the river Yarkend-Daria, which flows out of the Sarikul. The chief superintent of the Southern road—the Amban-He-be, resides in the Chinese fortress commanding the town. Yarkend has 32,000 houses. The town is surrounded by a wall eight fathoms in height and

seventeen miles in circumference, with four gates. It has four sarais, seventy medreehs, or religious seminaries, and one *Tynsa* (police station) near the great Registan Mosque. All the shops, taverns, sarais, and the Charsu market-place are situated in the chief street leading from the gates of Altyn-davsha to those of Kabagat. The most noted quarters of the town are those of "Urda-Aldy-Soka-Kul," the place of residence of the Cashmerians and Hindoos, and the "Aksakal," or quarter inhabited by the Badakhshans and Andianis. The most remarkable buildings are the Palace of Hakim-Beg, near the Khotan gate, and the Registan, an ancient mosque with a minaret. A bazaar is held every evening at seven o'clock, in the street that runs from the Registan to the pond of Nas-Hodja-Kul. The weekly bazaar, on Fridays, takes place between the Chinese citadel and the town. Quite a street has lately sprung up between the Altyn gates and those of the Chinese citadel, where houses of refreshment have been established; and indeed all the commercial activity of the place may be said to be concentrated in this single quarter.

The foreigners who reside in this town are chiefly Badakshanis, who have their own elder, and carry on a trade in Cashmere slaves. Amongst the inhabitants there are besides many Baltis from Little Thibet, a class who hire themselves out to labour, and comprise nearly all the drivers and water-carriers.

The neighbourhood of Yarkend is infested by many liberated slaves of the mountain Tajek tribes of Chitral and Vakhan, who are known here under the general appellation of "*Rofiz.*" The most important villages or settlements lying on the Northern boundary of the Yarkend district are :—

Burchuk, at two hundred and fifty-seven miles from Yarkend, at the confluence of the Yarkend-Daria with the Tarim ; and *Maral-Bashi*, peopled by Dolons, who are governed by their own Hakim-Beg, with a Chinese garrison of 300 men. To the West of Yarkend lies the village of *Sarikal*, near Lake Sarikul. The elevated nature of this district, and the cool atmosphere which always prevails here, are favourable to the successful breeding of Thibet cows. To the South, at the base of the Kuen-Lun, near the point of which the Tyznab issues from among the mountains, is the settlement of *Yangi Chunpak*. On the road from Khotan to Yarkend is situated the well-known trading settlement of *Guma*, at one hundred and thirty-three miles from Yarkend. It numbers two hundred houses, and has a bazaar every Saturday. In the lower ranges of the Kuen-Lun mountains are the village *Sanchja* and *Kilyan,* in high repute for their extensive breeding establishments of Mongolian cows. The settlements occurring along the Tyznabu river are :—*Tagbui*, *Kukyar, Yularyk*, and *Kargalyk,* all of which have their own Hakim-Begs. Of these villages, Kargalyk, or Kargally, has three hundred and fifty houses, and grows a great quantity of walnuts, a thousand of which may be purchased for about one shilling English. There are several tombs round Yarkend; among others, that of Hodja Mahomed-Shirif Pir, Altyn-Mazaz, and the temple of the holy hair (Mui-Mubarak), together with the highly venerated sanctuary of Aftu-Moódan, situated inside the town.

The Chinese fortress lies to the West, at about one mile and a half from the Mahomedan town; it is surrounded by a wall, which is both thicker and higher than that of Kashgar. The garrison consists of 2,200 men.

4 *Khotan District.*—Khotan, or "Iltsa," according to the Chinese, lies between the Karakash

and Yurunkash rivers; it is surrounded by a low wall, and has eight sarais, of which three are occupied by foreign merchants, the others being used by traders from Ilchi, Karakash, and Yurunkash. The number of houses is computed at 18,000. The Chinese town lies at 1⅓ miles to the West of it, with a garrison of 1,400 men. The neighbourhood of the town is embellished with gardens, and the space between Khotan and the Chinese town is very thickly peopled. A road in which, like that at Yarkend, all the trade is concentrated, leads from the one to the other. Khotan is famous for rearing silkworms, for its manufactures of thin felts, carpets, a semi-silked material called "mashru," fine "biazi," and a silk stuff called "darai." A species of nephrite, considered the best, is obtained in the river Yurunkash, and despatched thence to Pekin. The most remarkable settlements are: *Ilchi*, adjoining the Eastern extremity of the district; *Karakash*, *Yurunkash*, and others. These settlements have a considerable population, and are well-known as places of commerce.

5 *Aksù District.*—The town of Aksù contains 12,000 houses; and is situated at the confluence

of the Aksù and Kokshal. It is surrounded by a wall considerably smaller in circumference than that of Kashgar, but has four gates.

In Aksù there are six caravansarais. The "Charsu" Square forms the centre of the town, whence the chief streets, lined with shops and houses of refreshment, lead Westwards to the Temurchi gates, and Eastwards to the Aksù gates. There are five medreséh in the town. A bazaar is held twice a week, on Thursdays and Fridays. Aksù is noted as being the centre point of the Chinese trade, and is no less important in military respects, as the main roads from Central China and Ili meet within its walls. Besides these general claims, Aksù is well known for its production of "Daba" of a good quality, called "Shisha," and leather, both of which are exported to Khotan, Yarkend, and Kashgar. To the Aksù district belongs the settlement of *Bai* (in Chinese, "Pai"), 137 miles distant to the North-East, famous for its sheep-farming and manufacture of felts; it has 500 houses. Twenty-seven miles East of *Bai*, on the frontier of the Kuchi district, lies *Sairam*, garrisoned by Chinese. Of the settlements nearest to Aksù, the most important are, *Kum-Bash* and *Aikul*.

A Chinese fortress, with four gates, is situated at about two-thirds of a mile West of Aksù. A great many Chinese merchants from the province of Shansi live at Aksù, besides camel-drivers, who are for the most part Chinese Mussulmen. The garrison consists of 600 men.

6. *Ush-Turfan District.*—Ush-Turfan, a small town, or properly settlement, consists of scattered habitations ; possessing neither walls nor fortresses. It is said to have forty Yuz-Begis, or centurion chiefs, consequently about 4000 houses ; but according to other sources 6000. A bazaar is held on Sundays. It has neither mosques nor medresehs. Ush-Turfan is known for its trade in cattle, and for the excellent tobacco it produces, which is exported to the Kirghiz Hordes. In historical respects, this town has acquired a celebrity from the fact, that in 1765, during an insurrection, all the inhabitants were murdered, and 500 families from various native towns settled in it, who were compelled to become agricultural labourers (*toronchi*). A Chinese citadel occupies the centre of the Mussulman settlement ; it has four gates, and its walls on the North side abut on a rock ; it is considered strongly fortified, and is garrisoned by 800 men.

CHAPTER VI.

Altyshahr.—Historical Review.

The natural features of Eastern Turkestan, exposed, as we have just seen, on the East and hemmed in by colossal mountain ranges on the West, have materially influenced the historial march of events, and given a distinct character to Turkestan nationality.

From remote times, as far back as the period of the Tan dynasty, which flourished in China two centuries before the Christian era, when Djan-Tsian, or Djan-Kian, discovered the Western region, up to the present time, Eastern Turkestan has been under continual subjection either to China, or to one or the other of the wandering Hordes who were for the time being dominant in Mongolia.

On the other hand it never succumbed to the political influence of its Western neighbours,—not even to the celebrated conqueror of Asia,—Tamerlane, who, although he marched victoriously through the country, did not succeed in subjugating it.

Eastern Turkestan adopted the rudiments of religious worship, first from the South and afterwards from the West. The date of the introduction of Buddhism into this country cannot be definitely fixed ; according to the evidence of Chinese writers it already existed there during the Kau dynasty. In A.D. 140 the towns of Eastern Turkestan formed independent states and professed Buddhism. Huen-Chan, who visited them during the Tan dynasty, A.D. 629, found that religion generally prevalent there, and propounded in temples by priests and "Arans," or holy hermits. It continued to hold its own until the ninth century, when it was driven out by Islamism, which spread from Mavero-Innahar through the Bolor and Thian-Shan. The social institutions of Eastern Turkestan became naturally imbued with the spirit of Islam laws, but owing to the force of counteracting causes, these institutions did not assume an exclusively religious character. Islamism has nevertheless exercised considerable influence over the political fate of the country. It is only by closely studying its introduction and development, that a proper appreciation of the spirit, organisation, and signification of the present political factions of Turkestan can be obtained, and a true cause assigned for the moral influence of the Hodjas, who, even in exile, retain their political weight.

It was only natural that after so long a predominance of Buddhism, the doctrines of Mahomet should not speedily take root. They penetrated into Eastern Turkestan during the eighth century, when Arabian merchants first began to visit this region, but it is a notable fact in the history of this particular religious movement that the Arabs encountered great opposition in the towns, and that their first converts were among the nomad population.

The Chinese make mention of a sanguinary war carried on by the Arabs in Eastern Turkestan during the eighth century. Mussulman historians also assert that Shamar, the first Arab ruler of Mavero-Innahar, was killed in a war with the Chinese.

In the ninth century several Mussulmen preachers, or religious propagandists, among the most renowned of whom were, Sheikh-Hassan-Bosri and Abunassart-Samani, succeeded in converting to Islamism the Khans of the wandering Hordes, then in possession of the towns of Eastern Turkestan, and who had not long before overthrown the dominion of the Samanides.

These converts, animated with all the enthusiasm of new believers, commenced by inculcating sword in hand the teaching of Mahomet. The tombs of the Turkestan rulers of that period still preserve the title of "Hazi," or Warrior for the Faith. One of these, Sutuk-Bukhra-Khan, who died in the year 429 of the Hegira, A.D. 1051, carried the Hazat, or religious war, into Turfan and Komul. The extensive grounds near Khotan, used exclusively for putting to death the professors of the old religion, as also those between Yarkend and Yanyshar, locally called "Shaidan," or resting places of the happy, bear mournful testimony to the fact that, here as everywhere else, the establishment of Islamism was accompanied with the most merciless carnage. Nevertheless its domination was long confined to the Western towns. According to the evidence of Marco Polo, the inhabitants were idolators in the eighth century. About the same period, an independent state was founded in Eastern Turkestan, under the sway of Mongolian

Khans of the Djegatai dynasty, under whom the Pagan element again lifted up its head.

Although Tugluk-Timur-Khan, a descendant of Ghenghiz-Khan, who possessed the country from Ili to the Bolor and Kuen-Lun, embraced Islamism at the hands of Seid-Rasheddin,* anno 754 of the Hegira, or A.D. 1376, and induced many Mongolian and Uigur Emirs to follow his example, Buddhism was still the prevailing form of religion, during the succeeding century, in all the Eastern towns. The embassy sent by Shah-Rok a son of Tamerlane, to China in 1420, found in Khamil a heathen temple adjoining a magnificent mosque. It was not before the sixteenth century that Mohammedism finally succeeded in expelling Buddhism from the confines of Eastern Turkestan.

The Mussulman religion must be considered to have been predominant in the Western part of this region since the fourteenth century. The successors of Tugluk-Timur-Khan were zealous Mussulmen, and granted to the descendants of Rasheddin special honours and privileges, bestowing on them likewise tracts of rich land.

The fourteenth and fifteenth centuries became important, in the history of Central Asiatic Is-

* Seid-Sheik, a descendant of Mahomet.

lamism, by the appearance of many teachers who acquired the reputation of saints, or workers of miracles. Samarkand and Bokhara were the centres of the religious learning of the East, and the casuistry that sprang up there at last reached Kashgar. One of the Seids, descendants of Mahomet, Hodja-Makhturmi-Aziam, gained great celebrity, in Bokhara, as a theologian. On arriving at Kashgar, he was received with great enthusiasm, and was presented with rich estates by the Kashgar Khans. After his death, his sons, Imam-Kalian and Hodja-Isaac-Vali, enjoyed the same respect, and became the religious heads of the Mussulmen of Eastern Turkestan.

From this time the Hodjas commenced to grow in the estimation of the people. They received honours from the Khans, and were profoundly respected by the natives. Each of the two sons of Hodja-Makhturmi-Aziam was surrounded by a crowd of disciples, as well as by numerous fanatical Suffis (Naibs), Duvans (Dervishes), and pupils. In this way two parties were gradually formed, differing not so much on doctrinal points, as in the character and qualities of their respective heads. The followers of Imam-Kalian were called *Ishkias*, and those of Isaac-Vali styled themselves

Isakias. Subsequently the first appropriated to themselves the name of Mont-Albanians, or White Mountaineers; and the second, Montenegrins, or Black Mountaineers, which distinctions have survived to the present day.

Soon after the formation of these parties, inimical feelings sprang up between them, which at first partook of a religious character; but when the adherents of both parties increased in numbers, and all the population split into two rival camps, to religious dissensions there naturally was speedily added a struggle for political power. This rivalry openly declared itself when Hodja Appak, head of the Mont-Albanian party, assisted by the Dzungarians, acquired supreme secular power, and thereby ultimately deprived Eastern Turkestan of its independence.

The Dzungarians and Chinese, taking advantage of the dissensions of the contending parties, adopted the policy of supporting one against the other, and thus eventually succeeded in subjugating the whole country.

Appak-Hodja was much esteemed by the people; the high reputation of the teacher and saint attracted to Kashgar the Mussulman youth of the East, who were eager to follow his footsteps in the path of sanctity; and many rulers of Mavero-Innahar even were numbered among his scholars. His tomb at Kashgar to this day attracts many pilgrims from various Mussulman countries; and the Eastern Turkestani, who regard him as their own peculiar patron, call upon his name in moments of peril.

The Kashgar Khan Ismail, a zealous supporter of the Black Mountaineer party, drove Appak from his native country; the Hodja retired to Cashmere, whence he proceeded into Thibet, where he so ingratiated himself with the Dalai-Lama, that the latter despatched him with a letter to Galdan of Dzungaria, requesting the latter to re-establish the authority of Appak in Kashgar and Yarkend.

Galdan, seizing this opportunity, conquered Little Bokhara in 1678, and appointed Appak his viceroy, with Yarkend for his capital. The family of the Kashgar Khan was carried by Galdan into captivity in the Ili region, and settled in the Mussulman town of Kuldja.

The Dalai-Lama was so satisfied with the obedience of Galdan, that he conferred on him the title of *Boshektu* (Blessed).

From this time Little Bokhara, until its conquest by the Chinese, was ruled by the Dzungarians, who did not interfere with the internal administration of the country, but limited themselves to receiving a tribute of 400,000 tiangas per month. The government, from a remote period, was carried on by the same heirarchy as at present; each town had its *Hakim* or ruler, with an *Ishkaga* or assistant, Shanbegis, Haznotchis, &c. The internal strife and dissensions of parties still continued, with the result that, although the Black Mountaineer Hodjas were very rich and powerful, they were nevertheless obliged to leave Yarkend, and take up their abode temporarily in Cashmere.

Hodja-Appak, in order to reinstate himself in the good opinion of the Mussulmen, who now regarded him as the betrayer of his country, had to renounce his secular power. He summoned his brother, Khan-Ismail-Muhamed-Emil, from Ush-Turfan, proclaimed him Khan, and prevailed on him to attack the Dzungarians. Muhamed-Emil fell on the Kalmyk "ulusses" or camps, and returned with 30,000 prisoners of both sexes, and a great quantity of cattle and booty; but was afterwards so frightened at his own intrepidity, that he fled to the mountains, where he was killed by one of his own guides.

Appak then resumed the temporal power. On his death, his widow, Khanym-Padsha, a woman of determined and ambitious character, wishing to secure the supreme authority for her favourite son, Mekhdi, enlisted in her cause some fanatical dervishes, and killed Appak's eldest son, Hodja Yakhia; whose infant son, Ahmed-Padsha, sought refuge in the mountains. Khanym-Padsha herself was murdered shortly after by the dervishes.

Taking advantage of the discord in the family of Appak, Akbash—another brother of the late Hodja—made himself Khan of Yarkend, and recalled the Black Mountaineer, Hodja Daniel, from Khodjend, where he resided. The Kashgarians, who were firm adherents to the White Mountaineer cause, invited Ahmed-Hodja among them, and proclaimed him Khan.

An obstinate and sanguinary struggle now broke out between Kashgar and Yarkend. The Kashgarians, assisted by the Dikokamenni Kirghizes, besieged Yarkend, with the object of seizing Daniel Hodja. Ashem-Khan, of Yarkend, a Kirghiz Sultan by origin, totally defeated them; but was himself soon afterwards forced to withdraw to his Steppe, in consequence of the intrigues of the Hodjas. The secular government of the towns of

Yarkend and Khotan then fell into the hands of Daniel-Hodja.

At this time the Kalmyks, who had not been able until then to resent the inroads of the Kashgarians, arrived at Yarkend with a large force. Daniel, with the view of gaining the favour of the Dzungarians, joined their troops, with all his Yarkendians, and the united forces forthwith marched upon Kashgar. After several encounters, the Kashgarians were obliged to open their gates. The Kalmyks appointed a Hakim-Beg, chosen by the people, and led away the Kashgar Hodja Ahmed, their own ally, Daniel-Hodja, and the families of both, prisoners to the Ili.

In 1720, Tzaban-Raptan restored Daniel to his native country, and made him ruler over the six towns. On his arrival at Yarkend the Hodja appointed governors over the towns entrusted to him, and fixed his own revenue at the modest rate of 100,000 tiangas, that of Appak having been 1000 tiangas from every hundred of his subjects. His eldest son, Djagan, was a hostage with the Dzungarian Khans, and Daniel himself paid occasional visits to Ili.

Galdan-Chirin, on succeeding to the throne, confirmed the Hodja Daniel in the enjoyment of his former privileges. The immediate sway over Little Bokhara was, therefore, as the next result of these changes, transferred to the descendants of Hodja Isaac; or, in other words, the Black Mountaineer party.

After the death of Daniel, Galdan-Chirin—with the view of dividing the government of Little Bokhara, issued sealed patents to his children, apportioning Yarkend to the eldest, Hodja-Djagan; Kashgar to the second, Yusuf; Aksù to the third, Ayub; and Khotan to the youngest, Abdullah. The most celebrated of these was Yusuf, ruler of Kashgar, whose mother was the daughter of a Kalmyk Noyon, with whom Yusuf spent his childhood, in Dzungaria, and thereby acquired a thorough mastery over the Kalmyk language, which he spoke and wrote with much facility.

Yusuf, who had been compelled by the Khan Davatsi to reside in the province of Ili, seeing the dissensions that at that period convulsed Dzungaria, determined to take advantage of the weakness of his oppressors, and to liberate his country. Under the pretence that Kashgar was threatened by the Dikokamenni Kirghizes, he obtained the Khan Davatsi's permission to return to his native place. Here he put forth all his energies for the purpose, first, of fortifying the town; and secondly, of raising and organizing an army with all possible speed. This was in 1754, when Amursana applied to the Bogd-Khan for troops, to subdue the Dzungarians. The Kalmyks had latterly appointed Hakim Begs, on whose fidelity they could rely, and who were bound to them by the tie of common ambition. Two of these, Abdul-Vakhab, of Aksù, and Khodja Sybek, of Ush-Turfan, acquainted the Kalmyks with the real cause of the warlike preparations at Kashgar. They also incited Hudoyar-Beg, *ishkaga* of Kashgar, and Absatar-Beg, of Artosh, to fall upon the Hodja, and put him to death, while at his devotions in the Mechet; but this plot was discovered, and its chief instrument, Hudoyar-Beg, executed. Absatar and the son of Hudoyar made their escape to Ili; and, appearing before Davatsi, declared that the inhabitants of Kashgar and Yarkend had thrown off the Dzungarian yoke, and that the Hodja had put the Ishkaga to death for his fidelity to the Dzungarians. The Kalmyks had not at that time a force at their disposal, and Davatsi therefore determined to send an emissary to ascertain the true position of affairs.

The design formed by the Kalmyks, of seizing the Hodja in Kashgar, was thus frustrated; but at

Yarkend, assisted by the Hakim, Hazi-Beg, they succeeded in arresting the Hodja Djagan, after having enticed him into the Hakim's house.

This intelligence was received with a violent outburst of indignation at Kashgar. Yusuf assembled the people and informed them that the time had now arrived for shaking off the thraldom of the unbelievers, and represented to them the hopeless condition of Dzungaria. This appeal was received with enthusiasm. Timbrels were sounded over the gates of the town, and the Kashgarians swore to remain true to their determination of reconquering the lost liberties of their country. The Hodja Yussuf, as an ardent Mussulman, proposed to the people that they should convert three hundred Kalmyk merchants, who lay encamped in the vicinity of the town, to Islamism, and ordered them to be slaughtered in case they refused to adopt it. A small number of Olots, who acted as police officers or "kazakans" in the towns of Little Bokhara, were sent back to their country to acquaint the Khan of Dzungaria with what had occurred. Yusuf then despatched one thousand men to Burchuk, to attack the Kalmuk envoy, in case he should attempt to carry off the Hodja Djagan to Ili, and also made preparations for sending a large force to Yarkend. Hodja Sadyk, son of Djagan, who had eluded capture, gathered together 7000 men in two days, at Khotan; and, joined by a body of Kirghizes, marched against Yarkend. He carried with him the family of Hazi-Beg in chains, intending to put every individual of it to torture and death should harm befal his father. Hazi-Beg, learning their fate, and the decided steps taken by Yusuf, was thoroughly distracted; and his position was all the more critical that the Yarkendians openly exhibited their discontent at his conduct. His only alternative was, therefore, to ask pardon of Hodja Djagan, an extremely kind and weak man. With tears in his eyes and the Koran on his head, he appeared before him, and easily obtained forgiveness. Hazi then informed Djagan of the events that had transpired at Kashgar, and asked permission to kill the Dzungarian envoy and his retinue, and to raise the standard of Islam. The Hodja answered that an unbeliever could only be killed in battle, and ordered the Kalmyks to be escorted out of the town under a strong guard, warning them never to visit the country again.

Yusuf in the meanwhile sent ambassadors to Kokan and Bokhara, to acquaint those cities of their emancipation from the Dzungarian yoke, and to request assistance. He likewise appealed to the Chiefs of the Andijan Kirghizes, at the head of whom was Kibat-Mirza.

The independence, however, of the three towns was not of long duration. Events occurred at this time in Dzungaria, which exercised an important, indeed decisive influence over Little Bokhara.

In 1775, Amursana appeared in Dzungaria, at the head of Chinese troops, before whom Davatsi, unable to offer effectual resistance, fled with three hundred men through the Muzart pass to Ush-Turfan. The governor of that town, Hodjam-Beg, delivered him up to the Chinese, for which service he was created a prince.

In this manner Dzungaria, after having been for so long a time the terror of the neighbouring States, as well as a source of danger to the Chinese, was subdued by them without any opposition.

The troops of the Celestial Empire returned after the first campaign, leaving behind at Ili, their General, Bandi, with five hundred Manchurs, to organize a new system of government with the co-operation of Amursana. Amursana, having established himself at Ili, thought of again subjugating the emancipated towns of Kashgar

Yarkend, and Khotan, but as he was not able to send against them a large body of troops, the ruler of Aksù, Abdul-Vahab, and Hodja Sybek of Ush-Turfan, suggested that the children of Ahmet-Hodja of Kashgar, who were then at Ili, should be employed for this purpose. They said that if one of Ahmed's children were sent with a small detachment, and with the promise that they should be made rulers, Kashgar would be taken without resistance, that the other towns would likewise surrender, as the Kashgarians were particularly attached to these Hodjas, and that their adherents in the other towns were numerous.

With the consent of the Chinese General, Bandi, the sons of Ahmed, Burhaneddin and Khan-Hodja, who subsequently obtained a melancholy notoriety in Chinese history, were summoned to Kuldja from Iren-Habargan, where they lived in exile. The eldest of these, Burhaneddin, marched with an army consisting of Olots, Turkestani, and a small number of Chinese, to Aksù; while the youngest, Khan-Hodja, remained as hostage at Ili. Burhaneddin reinforced his army at Aksù, and proceeded to Ush, where he was joyfully received by the inhabitants.

The news of the military preparations that were being made by the Black Mountaineer Hodjas, so frightened Burhaneddin and his confederates, that they delayed their farther advance. Their force consisted of 5000 Musselmen from Kucha, Aksû, Turfan, and Dolon; 1000 Dsungarians, commanded by the Zaisan Dan-Chin, and of 400 Chinese, headed by Turuntaî-Dajen. These were not sufficient to combat the numerous armed bands of Yarkend, Kashgar, Khotan, and Yanyshahr, which were strengthened by the neighbouring Kirghiz Hordes.

In the meantime the news reached Yarkend of the arrival of the troops at Aksù. The inhabitants of the former town thereupon resolved to despatch a strong force against them. Yusuf-Hodja, of Kashgar, had abdicated his power, and lived then in Yarkend. He strenuously endeavoured to dissuade the Yarkendians from their intention, urging that Burhaneddin would not attempt to proceed farther, and that in case the expedition were defeated, which, seeing the Mont-Albanians might prove false, and the Kirghizes could not be relied on, was very far from improbable,—the enemy would be encouraged to attempt more daring and important enterprises. The Yarkendians, however, stimulated by a love for their Hodjas, burned with impatience to march to Aksù, seize the town, and to stifle the machinations of the White Mountaineer Hodjas in the bud. A numerous force of Khotanians, Yarkendians, and Kirghizes, commanded by Hodja-Ahi, the eldest son of Djagan Huda-Berdy, as also Shanbegi of Yarkend, and the Kargalyk ruler, Mirgus-Beg, accordingly directed its march towards Yanyshahr, and being joined there by further reinforcements, proceeded through Artysh along the route to Ush.

The death of Yusuf Hodja occurred in the meantime. Hodja Abdulla was chosen to succeed him as ruler of Kashgar, under the title of Pasha-Hodja, after having been lifted on a carpet, according to the custom of the country, and at once proceeded to despatch Kashgar troops under the command of his brother, Hodja-Mulin, to the assistance of the Yarkendians.

The united forces of Kashgar, Yanyshahr, Yarkend, and Khotan, passing through Aksù and Kakshal, reached Ush-Turfan and beseiged that town. The Black Mountaineer Hodjas sent a deputation to the besieged, calling on them in the name of the Koran, and of their common ancestors, to forget all animosity, join the common cause, and march altogether to Ili. To Burhaneddin they promised to yield possession of Kashgar, Aksù, and Turfan; and the Begs were offered hereditary rights. The deputation found Burhaneddin surrounded by Chinese, Kalmyks, and by Begs, whom native writers have stigmatised as 'impious' men. He told the deputies to advise the Black Mountaineer Hodjas to repair to Ili and seek forgiveness of the viceroy of the Emperor of China, and of Amursana. There were many of the White Mountaineer party in the camp of the besiegers, particularly among the officers. While negotiations were being carried on, these latter entered into secret communication with Burhaneddin. The Kirghizes, in the first action that was fought, went over in a body to the enemy, and were shortly afterwards followed by the majority of the Begs with the troops under their command. Ultimately it was with great difficulty that the leaders alone of the expedition escaped capture; they were pursued by the Kirghizes to the very gates of Kashgar. Burhaneddin, encouraged by the completeness of this unexpected success, pressed forward to Kashgar. The inhabitants of that town issued out in crowds to meet him, and refused to obey the Black Mountaineer Hodjas, to crown whose misfortune, the Andijan Kirghizes, summoned under the leadership of Kabat-Mirza to defend the town, declared that they would not fight againt Burhaneddin.

Under these circumstances, the Montenegrin Hodjas were obliged to evacuate Kashgar; on leaving which they hastened to Yarkend, while Hosh-Kaifiak, Hakim-Beg of Kashgar, and a partisan of the Black Mountaineer cause, emigrated to Kokan. The Mont-Albanian Hodja was thus admitted into Kashgar without oppposition and greeted with the joyful cries of the populace, who, in honour of the event, sounded drums and trumpets over the city gates. Burhaneddin then advanced to Yarkend, having first appointed the Kirghiz Kabada, Hakim-Beg of Kashgar. His army consisted only of 600 Kalmyks, and 200 Chinese. The Montenegrin Hodjas, perceiving all the danger of their situation, resolved to quit their country, and, under pretence of a pilgrimage to Mecca, made preparations for departing with their families.

Hodja Djagan was a benevolent and an upright man, and encouraged learning. His reign is compared by a contemporary writer to that of Mirza-Hussein. The Yarkendians were nearly all of the Black Mountain faction, and the private virtues of this ruler endeared him to them more strongly. When he declared his intention of leaving the country, the people besought him with tears in their eyes not to abandon them at such a critical juncture, and swore to defend themselves to the last against the infidels and the impious Mont-Albanians. They only asked for the dismissal of Hazi-Beg, the Hakim, and of Niazi the "Ishkaga," as the former had already proved himself untrustworthy, while the latter was an avowed partizan of the enemy. Djagan consented to remain, but from facility of temper and softness of character, allowed Hazi-Beg and Niazi to retain their posts.

The Mont-Albanian Hodja, appearing under the walls of Yarkend, sent a deputation to the town composed of several Begs, a Chinese Mandarin, and a Kalmyk Zaisan. They were presented to the Hodja Djagan, having been first obliged to go through the degrading ceremony of licking the threshold of the palace. To Burhaneddin's summons, in the name of the Bogdo-Khan and that of Amursana, to surrender and place himself under the protection of China, he answered that, as an independent Mussulman prince, he would listen to no terms, but would wage against them a "Hazat" or religious war. The letter which conveyed the terms of Burhaneddin he ordered to be torn and thrown into the fire.

The city was thereupon invested, and during the seige which ensued, the beseiged were always successful in their sallies, and maintained their vantage-ground until the Ishkaga Niaz—allured by the offer of the governorship of Yarkend, and Hazi-Beg, chief of the Hodja's courtiers, formed a daring and dangerous conspiracy, which, notwithstanding its discovery and the indignation of the people, was allowed to fall through without leading to their arrest, owing to the Hodja's infatuated clemency.

The defence was maintained for some time longer; but Ynayat, one of the Hodja's sons, being killed in a sortie, the Governor, Hazi-Beg, at last resolvėd to carry out his long-cherished scheme of traitorously delivering the town into the hands of the enemy. He entered into secret negotiations with Burhaneddin, and received from him a promise that he should be made hereditary Beg in Yarkend. The traitor urged on the Hodja the necessity of making a general sortie, on the ground that the townspeople were suffering severely from a want of provisions. The Hodja, who did not penetrate the designs of the Beg, called on all the inhabitants, both young and old, to arm in the cause of the Hazat. In answer to this appeal, 40,000 Yarkendians issued out of the town and drove the enemy from their position. Hazi, at this critical moment, dropped his standard, and took to flight, producing general consternation among his followers, ending in a complete rout. The Kirghizes, led by Kaborda, who had remained in reserve, fell on the retreating Yarkendians with these fresh troops, and the latter, who were crowded at the gates, fell almost to a man under the spears of the Buruts. The remaining inhabitants of the town lost heart after this disaster, while Hazi-Beg still continued his intrigues. The Hodja Djagan had now to choose between putting him to death or quitting the town himself: he preferred the latter. During the night, all the Hodja families left Yarkend by the Mahazar gates, and proceeded along the Kargalyk road to the mountains, on their way to India.

On the following day, the Yarkendians, finding that the Hodjas had fled, opened the gates, and Hazi-Beg, exulting in his treachery, led Burhaneddin in triumph into the town. The new Hodja immediately despatched a body of 500 men after the fugitives, who were overtaken just as they were preparing to cross the river Zarafshan. The Hodjas defended themselves desperately, and one of them, Erke, son of Yusuf Hodja, was killed in the conflict.

At length they effected their passage over the river, but in so exhausted a condition that they were unable to prosecute their journey. Only one young prince of this family, Nazar, reached India with two companions; the remainder surrendered. The Kirghizes, after plundering them of everything they had, brought them to Yarkend, where they were all put to death a few days after their arrival.

Such were the sanguinary means by which the Mont-Albanians once more acquired the ascendency. Subsequently, in 1758, Burhaneddin, assisted by his brother, Khan-Hodja, rose in insurrection, of which all the circumstances are to be gleaned from Chinese historians. After an obstinate struggle, which lasted three years, Burhaneddin and the Hodja Djagan, defeated by Chaokh, the Tzian-Tziun of Ili, fled to Badakshan, where they were slain by order of Sultan-Shah, ruler of that place, and their heads sent to the Chinese camp.

Of all the family of Appak, only one son of Burhaneddin,—Sarym-Sak, or Saali-Hodja, escaped, —four were killed in battle, and two taken prisoners by the Chinese and sent to Pekin.

From this time Little Bokhara has continued a province of the Chinese Empire. The Chinese, in order to consolidate their conquests in the Western region, founded in 1764 the town of Hoi-Yuan-Cheu, on the river Ili. Dzungaria having been depopulated by the massacre of half a million of Olots, was settled by Chinese from the province of Khan-su, and to increase the population, was converted into a place of exile for criminals. For the protection of the country, Manchur soldiers of the green banner were also transferred thither, and colonies established, of Sibos, Solons, and Daurs, in the Ili district. Seven thousand Mussulman families were forcibly converted into agriculturists, and the remnant of the extirpated Dzungarians were allotted a certain extent of country to roam in. The Government of the country was confided to a Tzian-Tziun, with three lieutenants; the residence of one being at Tarbagatai, and that of another in Little Bokhara. The Chinese showed great caution in the treatment of the country, as its population had fought with great determination in the attempt to assert their independence. The internal government was left on the same footing, and it was only for maintaining the peace of the country that Chinese garrisons were stationed in the most important towns. Pickets were also posted in such localities as were best suited to guard the frontier, and stations were established for ensuring rapidity in travelling.

This successful subjugation of Dzungaria and Little Bokharia infused into the Chinese a military spirit and thirst for conquest. During the Government of Tzian-Lun they apparently desired to re-enact the scenes of the *Tan* dynasty. In the years 1756, 1758, and 1760, bodies of Chinese troops entered the territories of the Middle Horde. The fall of Dzungaria, once so powerful as to be a perpetual menace to every country adjacent, and the conquest of Little Bokhara, caused a panic throughout the whole of Asia, and strengthened a curious Mussulman superstition, that the Chinese would one day conquer the whole globe, when there would be an end to the world. The immediate result of the general uneasiness was that Ablai, the head of the Middle Horde, Nurali of the Little Horde, and the Burut chiefs hastened to negotiate with the Celestial conqueror. Ablai, in 1766, acknowledged himself a vassal of the Bogdo-Khan, and received the title of prince. Nurali sent an embassy to Pekin. The ruler of Kokan, Edenia-Bi, in 1758, and after him his successor, Narbuta-Bi, likewise recognized the protectorate of the Son of Heaven.

Notwithstanding this apparent submission, the Asiatics were in a state of chronic agitation. The general dissatisfaction reached its height, when in 1762, some Chinese mandarins, at the head of 130 men, presented themselves before Sultan Ablai and Abdul-Mahmet-Khan, of the Middle Horde, for the purpose of acquainting them that Tzian-Lun intended in the ensuing spring to send an army to Turkestan and Samarcand, and had therefore sent requisitions for men, horses, oxen and sheep for the troops.

Erdenia-Baty, who had then seized possession of Tashkend, the ruler of Khodjend, Fazyl-Bi, and the independent Kirghiz Sultans, despatched a letter to Ahmet-Shah of Affghan, the greatest potentate of the East, imploring him to save the Mussulman world from the invading infidels. The son of Burhaneddin and the Kashgar emigrants travelled through all the Mussulman States, asking for similar assistance. The fear inspired by the Chinese was indeed so great, that the Central Asiatic rulers buried their mutual animosity, and formed a common league, at the head of which was Ahmet, ruler of Candahar, the founder of the Turan dynasty.

Affghan troops arrived in 1763, and were

stationed between Kokan and Tashkend. Emissaries were despatched by Ahmet to the Mussulman States, calling on all true believers to join the "Hazat," or fight for the faith. All commercial intercourse between the Central-Asiatics and Chinese was broken off, and the Kirghizes were pressed to follow this example. The embassy sent by Ahmet to demand the restitution of Eastern Turkestan, was badly received at Pekin. The Turkestani yearning for freedom, solemnly avowed to attempt their own liberation. The inhabitants of Ush-Turfan, calculating on Mussulman assistance, rose in 1765 in open insurrection, and the town in consequence of this was completely destroyed. The Affghan Shah was unfortunately engaged at this period in a war with the Sikhs; and the other Asiatic rulers, unless supported by him, dared not openly resist the Chinese.

The league, though unattended by any practical results, had, however, the effect of deterring the Chinese from attempting further conquests. Badakshan, alone, consigned to the curses of all Mussulmen, for the murder there of the Hodjas, incurred the wrath of the faithful. An Affghan detachment, consisting of 15,000 men, devastated this territory, and its ruler, Sultan Shah, was executed in retaliation. His previous treatment of the Hodjas brought on all the misfortunes that weigh over the country even to the present day.

The extension of Chinese dominion to the Westward was limited by the natural boundaries of Eastern Turkestan, and was further kept in check by a jealous confederation of the native rulers. On the North-West, the Chinese frontier adjoined the camping-grounds of the Kirghizes and Buruts, and presented but few natural barriers. The less fanatical inhabitants on the North-Western confines voluntarily sought the protection of the Bogdo Khan. Somewhat later, viz. in 1763, on the demand of the Kirghizes, the Bogdo Khan gave them formal licence to roam over the lands formerly occupied by the Dzungarians, namely, the Steppes between Lake Balkash and the Dzungarian Alatau range. The Chinese, in return, demanded of the Kirghizes one out of every hundred head of horses and cattle, and one sheep out of every thousand. Detachments were annually sent to collect this tribute; two from Ili, and one from Tarbagatai and Kashgar respectively. One of the Ili detachments marched through Karatal to Ayaguz, where it joined that from Tarbagatai; the second, passing over the Santash, proceeded along the Northern shore of

Lake Issyk-Kul, turned its Western extremity, and then traversing the Zaûkū pass, ascended the course of the Naryn to the place where it receives on its left bank the river Shar-Krat-ma, where a bridge existed.

The Kashgar detachment, after clearing the Terekty pass, ascended the Aksai plateau, emerged through the Bish-Bilchir mountains on the river Atbash, and then gained the Naryn by way of the pass formed by the course of the Shar-Krat-ma. These were accompanied throughout almost their entire campaign by Chinese merchants, who bartered their goods for cattle. The Chinese opened a trade with the Kirghizes at Kuldja and Chuguchak, and the Bogdo Khan used to confirm the Kirghiz Khans in their authority by special patents. The Tian-Tziun bore the title of Commander-in-Chief of the generation of foreign Khans; and in the Chinese regulations respecting foreign relations, a paragraph was added, determining the order of sending Kirghizes and Buruts to Court, and pronouncing the penalty of death against all nomads creating disturbances.

After the frightful vengeance taken for the insurrection at Ush, Eastern Turkestan was obliged to submit to the Chinese, and to bear the imposts exacted from it. This state of things continued until 1825, when the authority of the Chinese simultaneously began to be weakened in Little Bokhara and among the Buruts and Kirghizes. The appearance of Russian troops on the seven rivers and on the Bogu camping-grounds, destroyed their influence over the Kirghizes and Buruts, and the insurrection of Djengir Hodja, a descendant of Sarym-Sak, in Little Bokharia, sufficiently proved to the Central Asiatics that the Chinese were not so formidable as they had previously been supposed to be.

From the foregoing sketch it will be perceived that the towns of Eastern Turkestan, situated to the Eastward of Kuchi, did not take part in any of the political disturbances that agitated this country, especially during the dominion of the Hodjas. In consequence of their close proximity to China, they were exposed to the immediate pressure of that Empire. Chinese military settlements existed there during the Han dynasty, and subsequently a Turkman state, called Oi-Hor, was created in Turfan and Khamil, under the dominion of China. During the Yuan dynasty, Khamil and Turfan fell to the share of Hubelai, while the other towns of Little Bokhara passed to the children of Djegaiat.

Afterwards, when Little Bokhara enjoyed an independent government, the Eastern portion of this country was still under subjection to the house of Min; it was only towards the close of this dynasty that it was abandoned to its own resources and became subject to the Dzungarians. During the first years of the Government of the Manchur dynasty, the Beg of Khamil acknowledged the supremacy of China, and the Emperor Kan-si visited that town in person. The inhabitants of Turfan, with their Beg, Amil-Hodja, despoiled by the Dzungarians, threw themselves under the protection of the Emperor Yun-Chen, who deported them to the towns of Ansi-Chéu and Sha-Chéu, in the vicinity of the Chinese wall, and it was only in 1755 that they were allowed to return again to their own country. The influence of the Hodjas had not extended to these parts, and it was for this reason, therefore, that the Chinese always showed a preference for the Turkestani of the Eastern towns, to the extent even of granting them exclusive privileges. The rulers of Ush-Turfan and Khamil received the hereditary titles of Tziun-Vans (princes), and the Emperor Tzian-Lun, with the view of acquiring fresh claims on the allegiance of the natives, married a Khamil princess.

Although this policy on the part of the Chinese was attended with success in the Eastern portion of Eastern Turkestan, the Western towns, having formerly enjoyed greater liberties, could not adapt themselves to Chinese thraldom. Inspired by a love of freedom familiar with warfare, and imbued with religious fanaticism, the inhabitants bore a deep-seated hatred towards the Chinese. The Ush rebellion proved to China its insecure tenure of these towns in which peace could only be preserved by constant intimidation, and by stringent enforcement of the most merciless police regulations. Distrusting the population of the Six Towns, the Chinese appointed natives of Khamil and Turfan, on whom they could rely, to the highest local posts, and began to maintain powerful garrisons in the country. The terror inspired by the massacre of the inhabitants of Ush-Turfan and a wide-spread belief in the invincibility of the Chinese, deterred the population of the Six Towns from rising in open revolt against their oppressors, whose severity and extortion tried their patience severely. In this deplorable state of affairs the people regarded the exiled Hodjas with particular veneration. These were still enabled to maintain some sort of correspondence with their native land, as the Chinese, although introducing with their rule a system of exclusiveness, were nevertheless obliged to throw open the six frontier towns of Little Bokhara for the purpose of trading with the Buruts and inhabitants of the other Central Asiatic States. The privileges accorded to foreign traders prove that the Chinese were aware of the advantages, and alive to the necessity of commercial intercourse. The Chinese tariff was so framed that *one-thirtieth* of the cattle brought by foreigners was exacted in kind, while the Turkestani and nomad subjects of China paid *one-twentieth*.

The right of free trade was not extended to Khamil, Turfan, Karashahr, and Kuchi, an invidious distinction which only seemed to bind their population more effectually to the exiled Hodjas.

Affairs continued in this state up to the year 1825. The Turkestani veiled their strong discontent, and patiently bore their fate. It was not until 1816 that their dissatisfaction was openly displayed. In that year Ziaveddin, Ahund of the Montenegrin party, who lived in the settlement of Tashmalyk, one hundred and twenty miles from Kashgar, raised the standard of revolt, and retreating into the mountains, made repeated raids against the Chinese, in which he was assisted by the Kirghizes. Notwithstanding his capture and execution, the insurrection was carried on by his son Ashriab-Beg, who being likewise made prisoner, ere long experienced the same fate. Subuheddin, the infant son of Ziaveddin, was sent to Pekin, and put to death on attaining full age. This rising was not attended with any important results, as it had not been headed by a Hodja; it is only remarkable as having been the last outbreak of the Black Mountaineer faction, who then represented the patriotic party, but subsequently attached themselves to the Chinese on the appearance of the White Mountaineer Hodjas as claimants for the throne of Kashgar. The Black Mountaineers, although they hate the Chinese, regard the White Mountaineers with still greater animosity and aversion, as is the custom among more civilized people and nations. The Hodja Sarym-Sak, after wandering for many years through the different territories of Central Asia, settled towards the end of his life in Kokan, in order to be nearer to Kashgar, whence he derived his revenue. The Montenegrins then commenced to emigrate to Kokan, and Central Asia was gradually overrun by Kashgarians. They gave exaggerated descriptions of the misfortunes of their country, and of the injustice and oppression of the Chinese, and complained that the infidels carried off their wives and daughters, and prohibited the free observance of their religious rites.

The unfortunate and sanguinary fate of the two Hodjas of Kashgar, had always excited the sympathies of the Asiatics. In the beginning of the year 1820 the question of independence was again agitated throughout Central Asia. The Kashgarians became the objects of universal respect, and their emissaries proceeded from town to town collecting contributions for the projected "Hazat," or holy war. The description of the fate of their country produced the desired effect; it drew tears, increased the amount of the offerings, and placed the Kashgarians in the light of martyrs in the eyes of the Mussulman population. Public recitation from the book of Abu-Musmil, in which that Sovereign relates his exploits against the unbelievers, was forbidden at Bokhara, because it so excited the youthful generation that it induced many to make forays into Persia for attaining the pious distinction of a "Hazi," or meeting a meritorious death as "Sheids," who, according to the Koran, are transported straight to Paradise. Bokhara was then at peace with Persia, but this infatuation threatened to produce a rupture.

The re-conquest of Badakshan by Murat-Beg, the Emir of Kunduz, who deported the inhabitants of this beautiful country to his own morasses, was undertaken, as the Asiatics affirm, out of respect for the memory of the Hodjas, as Murat-Beg was related to Sarym-Sak. Sarym-Sak had three sons: Myat-Yusuf-Hodja, Pahaveddin-Hodja, and Djengir-Hodja, of whom the eldest resided at Bokhara.

After the migration of the Hodjas to Kokan, the Chinese, in 1813, opened negotiations with its Khan. By means of rich gifts, the emissaries of the Celestial empire induced him to maintain a strict watch over the Hodjas, for which service they engaged themselves to pay an annual subsidy of 200 yambs (£3660?)

Djengir-Hodja was born in 1783. He was a man of energy and sense. Aware of the weakness of the Chinese, and knowing the devotion of the native population to his family, he determined to rise in arms. Profiting by the death of Omar Khan, in 1822, Djengir escaped from Kokan to the camping grounds of the Dikokamenni Kirghizes, and made preparations for a campaign against Kashgar. Djengir thus laid the foundation for those constant disturbances that distract the country to the present day. They are regarded as rebellions by the Chinese, while by the Asiatics they are termed "Hazat," or holy wars. While out hawking near Kokan, Djengir first formed the resolution of attacking Kashgar, and proceeding straight to the Dikokamenni Kirghizes, prevailed on them to assist him in the attempt. Suranchi, head of the Kirghiz tribe of Chon-Bagysh, marched to the town, where he plundered the adjacent villages, but was speedily forced to beat a retreat. After the miscarriage of this enterprise, Djengir wandered in the mountain territories of the Bolor, and among the Kirghiz "Ulusses," until he fell in with the Kirghizes of the Sayak tribe. Its influential chiefs, Atantai and Tailak, became his ardent supporters. The upper course of the Naryn, the place of gathering of the Kirghiz camps, became the permanent place of residence of the Hodja, and he succeeded in gaining, among the nomads, the reputation of an inspired saint. The Kirghizes of the Thian-Shan have always taken a lively interest in the affairs of Kashgar, and acquired from its inhabitants a respect for the Hodjas; they are mostly adherents of the Mont-Albanian party.

Djengir, with his marauding partisans, made several forays on Kashgar, but they all proved unsuccessful. One event, however, encouraged him to make further attempts, and increased the number of his followers.

The Chinese, with a view of putting a stop to his inroad at one blow, despatched a body of 500 Solons and Sibos, under the command of an Amban, to make a sudden attack on Atantia's camp, and above all to secure Djengir. The plan was designed with great craft. Kirghiz guides led the detachment up the river Toin, across Chadyr-Kul, to the banks of the Naryn, somewhat below Fort Kurtki, where lay the encampment of Atantia. The Chinese marched only by night, so that their approach was not discovered. Djengir was then fortunately absent from the camp, and the Chinese, after plundering everything they could, marched back. On learning what had occurred on his return, Djengir, at the head of the Kirghizes, who had been away with him, pursued the retreating Chinese, and overtook them in a narrow defile. Bi-Chebyldy, of the Basyz branch, attacked them with such vigour, that only one Chinese succeeded in making his escape; the others were slaughtered with their General on the spot. This victory was regarded as a miracle, and Djengir began to adopt more decisive measures. He hastened to acquaint the Khan of Kokan and other rulers of his success, and sent emissaries to the different camping grounds of the Uzbek, Kaisak, and Burut tribes. The whole year of 1825 was passed in hostile preparations. Kashgar emigrants, Kokan Sepoys, Uzbeks, Kipchaks, Turks, and other Mussulmen warriors, and mountain Tadjiks in their picturesque black garbs, hastened to range themselves under the banner of the Appaks, while many Kokanians, even including officials, left their posts to take part in the "Hazat."

In the Spring of 1856, Djengir with his troops, commanded by Isa-Dakhta, formerly military governor of Andijan, encamped at the village of Bishkirim. His army having been reinforced by the inhabitants of the Kashgar villages, he attacked the Chinese who had marched to meet him under the leadership of the Ili Tian-Tziun, and entirely routed them on the plain of Davlet-Bakh, on the right bank of the river Tümen.

In this engagement the mountain Tadjiks fought with uncommon bravery; their black rather scanty clothing gave rise to the rumour that Englishmen had been present. The Chinese shut themselves up in their citadel, and the Hodja entered Kashgar amidst the joyful plaudits of the populace. He assumed the title of Seid-Djengir-Sultan, and appointed civil and military officers similar to those of Kokan. Isa-Dakhta was raised to the rank of Min-Bashi, and all the Kashgar Begs were suffered to retain their posts; but the Chinese caps with the ball and feathers were substituted for the turban. The Governor of Kashgar, Miat-Seid-Vaun, a native of Khamil, was condemned to death by a council of Ahunds for having circulated defamatory reports affecting the Hodja, and for his oppression of the people. The towns of Yarkend, Yanyshahr, and Khotan next rose against the Chinese, cut the garrisons to pieces, razed their fortresses to the ground, and organized armed contingents for the service of the Hodja.

In the month of June, the Khan of Kokan, thirsting for glory and wishing to take an active part in the struggle, arrived with 15,000 men. For some unknown reason Djengir received him very discourteously, and the Khan, thrown on his own resources, after making several attempts against the Chinese fortress of Kashgar, before which he lost 1000 of his soldiers in twelve days, returned to his own dominions and there contented himself with striking off coins on which he styled himself "Hazi" or holy warrior.

Djengir in the meantime continued the siege of the fortress, which the Chinese, deprived of water and provisions, were compelled to surrender on the seventieth day. The mandarins committed suicide, and the rest of the garrison, after escaping in the night-time, were overtaken in the mountains and put to the sword, with the exception of 400 Tungens and Chinese who adopted Islamism. One account states the Chinese garrison to have consisted of 10,000, and another of 8000 men, under the command of I-Ya, Tian-Tziun of Ili. The Hodja, after this success, sent agents to Kokan while the 400 converted Tungens and Chinese were distributed between Bokhara, Kunduz, Balkh, Khiva and the wandering tribes. These emissaries even reached the Great Horde. Expecting further assistance from the Mussulmen of Central Asia, Djengir did not take advantage of his success, and by this fatal temporising policy gave the Chinese time for collecting their forces. Had Djengir marched direct to Aksû after the capture of the fortress, the whole of Eastern Turkestan would, to a certainty, have fallen into his hands, and even Kuldja would most probably have submitted to him.

By his lenient and moderate policy, however, Djengir won over the staunchest adherents of the Chinese government, and many of the Begs, from a sentiment of devotion to his person, subsequently shared his misfortunes; and with the people, he was and continued to be a universal favourite. He at the same time courted the good will of the Montenegrins by conferring offices on them. The Kalmyks, it is said, became so disaffected that the Chinese ceased to employ them against the Hodja, as they deserted to him in large bodies. The Mussulmen population of the towns still held by the Chinese, and even that of Kuldja, also began to entertain thoughts of emancipating themselves from the Chinese yoke.

Numerous conspiracies were brought to light, and the plotters exiled to the Southern Governments of China, whilst on the other hand the intrigues of the Khan of Kokan occasioned disturbances among the troops of the Hodja, which resulted in obliging the latter to deprive Isa-Dakhta of the rank of Min-Bashi. The continued inactivity of the Hodja rendered his former successes completely nugatory. The Chinese had time to recover themselves, and began to concentrate their forces at Kuldja for a fresh campaign.

Djengir's army numbered 200,000 men, imperfectly armed, with a few pieces of artillery captured from the Chinese, and some "zemburaks," or guns mounted on camels. Flying detachments of Kirghizes were employed in intercepting the Chinese convoys of provisions and forage. Atantai, who commanded these detachments, was a man of great influence in the Council of the Hodja, who conferred on him in marriage a daughter of the former Hakim-Beg.

In the month of September, 70,000 Chinese arrived at Aksù, commanded by Djun-Tan, one of the highest Chinese dignitaries. They remained stationary there until February, and it was only after their new year that they advanced to Kashgar. They were encountered by the formidable contingents of the towns of Kashgar, Yarkend, and Khotan, by a mixed body of volunteers, by the Dikokamenni Kirghizes, and by the auxiliary forces of Kunduzes, Uryatups, and Tadjiks. The Chinese advanced in regular order, and met the enemy with a discharge from their artillery. The troops of the Si-Chuen province, wearing turbans and long "khalats" or robes, got intermixed with Djengir's militia, occasioning great disorder among them. The Kokanians, panic-stricken, were the first to fly, whereupon the whole body of the army retired in confusion. The Hodja with difficulty escaped to the mountains, surrendering his power, after a rule of nine months.

The Chinese, elated with success, despatched a strong force in pursuit of Djengir, which, on approaching the town of Ush, reminded the Kokanians of the end of the world. The Khan assembled his army, and all the inhabitants were seized with a fanatical terror. Djengir meanwhile gathered a large force of Dikokamenni Kirghizes, and, engaging the Chinese in another action, signally defeated them.

Issak-Van, a wily native of Ush-Turfan, and a devoted supporter of the Chinese, had been appointed Governor of Kashgar. By distributing money among the Dikokamenni Kirghizes, he brought some of them over to his side, and assured Djengir, through his agents, of his loyalty and of his readiness to deliver up Kashgar. With the assistance of a Chon-Bagysh Bi, Issak-Van succeeded in treacherously securing Djengir, whom he delivered up to the Chinese. Djengir was sent to Pekin, and after a few years was barbarously put to death as a rebel.

Djengir's rebellion, which terminated in 1828,

although it lasted only nine months, was of great importance in its results. He gave his attempts the lawful colouring of those of a Sovereign ruler endeavouring to regain his hereditary rights, and, by calling the insurrection a "Hazat," or holy war, he awakened the sympathies of the fanatical Mussulmen of Central Asia. After the insurrection had been crushed, all the impotence of the Chinese, who had hitherto been considered invincible by the Asiatics, became glaringly apparent. The Kashgar patriots rallied the broken spirits of the natives by inspiring them with fresh hopes of a return of the independence of their country. Naturally, therefore, the people of Eastern Turkestan, who had suffered so patiently under the oppression of the Chinese officials and of their own Begs, looked up to the Hodjas as their protectors, ever ready with arms in their hands to defend them against the infidels.

It was at this time that the Kokanians obtained that political influence which they enjoy even to the present day. Noyan-Chen, the Chinese plenipotentiary, entrusted with the pacification of the Western region, adopted stringent precautions against the recurrence of similar outbreaks. All the weight of these repressive measures fell on the poor natives, who were put to death, their houses demolished, and their entire property confiscated. Aware of the traitorous conduct of the Khan of Kokan, and to chastise him for his participation in the late rebellion, the plenipotentiary ordered the arrest of all Kokanian merchants as rebels, and the cessation of all communication with Kokan. Among other exaggerated notions of their own importance, the Chinese are convinced that the welfare of all nations whomsoever depends on their having commercial relations with China. Noyan-Chen, therefore, considered that by depriving the Kokanians of these advantages he would be punishing them most severely. With this view, he erected custom-house barriers at the villages of Tuguzak, within fourteen miles of Kashgar, and at Liangar, twenty-seven miles from Yarkend. On the approach of a caravan to the military picket, it was met by a party of Chinese soldiers under an officer, who took a note of the number of people accompanying it, the quantity of goods brought, &c., and conducted it to the caravansarai; here another official was stationed, under whose superintendence the goods were sold. During the sale, the merchants who attended it were strictly watched; and, on the termination of the barter, the caravan was escorted beyond the Chinese lines, under guard of the same officer and men who had met it on its arrival. To make these rigorous measures still more keenly felt, the Chinese invited the Bokharians and Kunduzes to trade with them; but these merchants, on responding to the invitation, found themselves subjected to the same inconveniences as the Kokanians. Although the Dikokamenni Kirghizes deserved the same punishment as the Kokanians, the Chinese were obliged to show them clemency, owing to the scarcity of cattle in the region of "the Six Towns," to which they even despatched envoys to beg them for their herds. A Russian merchant relates that, during the struggle with Djengir, prices ruled so high at Aksù, that the Chinese paid a yamb (£18. 6*s.*) for two sheep, for which they paid but £4. 17*s.* at Kashgar. The Chinese scheme had the anticipated effect of increasing their trade and suppressing that of the natives. All Central Asia and Afghanistan were supplied with tea, which found its way through Kashgar and Kokan.

In 1829 their exclusive system of commerce became so insupportable, that the Kokanians resolved to open a trade for themselves by force of arms.

At the head of this enterprise was Madali, Khan of Kokan. Notwithstanding his youth, and luxurious and sensual habits, he had the good sense to choose most able confederates, such as the Min-Bashi, Hak-Kuli, an Uzbek of the Yuz tribe; and the Kush-Begi, Liashkar, originally a Persian bondsman, raised by Madali-Khan to the highest offices, and afterwards appointed Governor of Tashkend. With the assistance of these two viziers, Madali subdued the petty mountain states of Karategin, Darvaz, and Kuliab, and extended his power over all the Burut races, over the Great Horde, and even to some extent over the Kirghizes of the Middle Horde. The first half of the reign of this Khan was the most brilliant period in the history of Kokan, and his successes induced him to make preparations for a war with China.

Anticipating opposition to his schemes on the part of the Central Asiatics, who were then generally indisposed towards the Kokanians, and to secure, if possible, their assistance, Madali-Kahn secretly prevailed on Djengir's elder brother, Med-Yusuf, to leave Bokhara, where he permanently resided, and to join him at Kokan. The Khan next issued a general proclamation to the inhabitants of the Khanat, in which he set forth that, as a Mussulman ruler, he could not remain a passive spectator of the tyranny of the infidels, who imposed unjust taxes, and violated the chastity of the wives and daughters of Mussulmen. For the stronger enlistment of their sympathies, he further added the fact, improvised for the occasion, that the Chinese desecrated the Mussulman sanctuaries, and prevented the performance of the ceremonies of their religious faith. Lending an ear, therefore, to the lamentations of the faithful Kashgarians, whom he wished to liberate from bondage, he declared his intention of seating Hodja Med-Yusuf on the throne of his ancestors.

In September, 1830, Med-Yusuf-Hodja took the field with an army of 20,000 Kokanians, 15,000 Tashkendians, and 2000 mountaineers from Karategin, making a total force of 40,000 men, including about 3000 Kashgar emigrants. His artillery consisted of ten "Zemburaks," mounted on camels. The whole force was commanded by the Min-Bashi Hak-Kuli, brother-in-law of the Khan; by Miad-Sharif Liashkar, and the Kush-Begi of Tashkend. The Chinese, hearing of the warlike preparations of the Kokanians, marched to attack them with 3000 men, but were completely defeated near the little village of Min-Yul. Hak-Kuli, discomfiting the Chinese afterwards in another action, took Kashgar, and placed the government in the hands of Med-Yusuf-Hodja. Kush-Begi Liashkar then gained possession of Yanyshahr, Yarkend, and Khotan, crossed the Aksù, putting to the sword all who opposed him, and scoured the country as far as the Muzart pass. The Chinese troops were concentrated at Karashahr, and delayed their advance. In Kuldja, the camels of the Kalmyks were forcibly taken by the Chinese, and the Torgouts were compelled to furnish 2000 men, who marched very unwillingly under the oppressor's command.

In the meantime, the hostile attitude of the Emir of Bokhara obliged the Khan of Kokan to recall Hak-Kuli, who was besieging the Chinese citadel of Kashgar, and in November the Kokanian troops returned home. Med-Yusuf, perceiving that he could not hold his ground without support, and being of a peaceful disposition, also returned to Kokan, his rule having endured just ninety days. During this war 70,000 Kashgarians migrated to Kokan, where they settled on the river Syr-Daria, below Khodjend, in the village of Dalvas; and in Tashkend, where they founded another settlement named Yanyshahr. All these Kashgarians received a ten years' immunity from all taxes. The Kokanians in this war seized 500 Chinese, a large collection of arms, and a considerable quantity of tea and silver.

Western China in this year was in an embarrassed state. An insurrection broke out in the province of Shan-Si, and the insurgents operated with success. Barkul was taken by the Mahommedan rebels, and its inhabitants were killed. It was not before January that the Chinese began to concentrate their forces in Ili, at the time when the Kokanians evacuated Kashgar.

In the spring of 1831, the Kokanians commenced a war with the Dikokamenni Kirghizes. Hak-Kuli, with 7,000 sepoys, scattered the "Ulusses," or camps of the Sayaks, on the Upper Naryn, took their chiefs, Atantai and Tailak, prisoners, and returned with many captives and much valuable booty. The Kushi-Beg of Tashkend, at the same time, pursued the Bogus, and pushed beyond the boundaries of the Ili district to the military settlement of Sibo.

These events forced the Chinese to alter their line of policy. In the spring of 1831, four Chinese envoys arrived with proposals of peace. The Khan of Kokan detained three of them, and sent back the fourth with an agent of his own to Pekin. The Kokan plenipotentiary was Alim-Patcha, a merchant, who secured for his Sovereign the following rights and privileges :—1. That the dues on merchandise brought by foreigners to the Six Towns of Eastern Turkestan, Aksù, Ush-Turfan, Kashgar, Yanyshahr, Yarkend, and Khotan should be appropriated by the Kokanians. 2. That for the collection of these dues, the Kokanians should have in each of these towns an "Aksakal," or commercial agent, under the authority of a Kashgar inspector, and who would also be the political representative of his country. 3. All foreigners arriving in the above towns should in every respect be amenable to the Kokan agents.

The Kokanians, on their part, bound themselves to watch the Hodjas, in order to prevent their leaving the territories in which they dwelt, and to imprison them in case they attempted to do so.

In 1832, the same Alim was appointed Aksakal of Kashgar, receiving this office on lease, as is the custom in Kokan.

In this way, commercial and political relations between Kokan and Western China were established. The influence of the Kokanians once more extended, and taking advantage of the amicable policy of the Chinese, they gradually appropriated to themselves different privileges. As a people ignorant of the laws that should regulate national intercourse, their conduct is marked by a brutal audacity, which the Chinese bear with astonishing patience.

The insurrections of Eastern Turkestan in 1825 and 1830, were severe blows to the prestige of the Chinese Empire, which it has not recovered to the present day. The military frontier has not been visited by them since 1825, and a new route has been chosen for the passage of their troops over the Muzart pass. The Kokanians, after subjugating the Dikokamenni Kirghizes, threw out their frontiers so as to include Khotan itself, and founded there, in 1832, the fortress of Kurtka on the Naryn, and, a little later, another on the Pamir Plateau, called Tash-Kurgan.

The Kokanians are no less powerful in the towns of Eastern Turkestan, as nearly one-fourth of the population is under their rule. Kokan having acquired such political weight, its interest lay in preventing the outbreaks of the Hodjas, who were accordingly kept under strict surveillance. Until the year 1846, Eastern Turkestan enjoyed perfect peace under the Hakim-Beg, Zurdun, who proved himself a just ruler, and protected the interests of the inhabitants against the Chinese officials.* He favoured trade, and was well disposed towards the Russian Tartars, whom he encouraged to establish direct relations with Kashgar. It is to Zurdun-Beg that Kashgar is indebted for the construction of its walls and of the new quarters of the town.

In the year 1845 fresh disturbances, which were reflected in Kashgar, broke out in Kokan, on the elevation of the youthful Hudoyar to the Khanship; under the protectorate of the all-powerful courtier, Mussulman-Kul. The Aksakals were being constantly changed, and even one of these, Abdul-Afur, recalled to Kokan, was summarily hanged. The Dikokamenni Kirghizes continually broke through the Chinese frontier-pickets in large parties, and the Aksakals of Kokan, while promising to stop them from doing so, accepted bribes for shutting their eyes to these constant infractions of the treaty.

* In 1830, Zurdun-Beg had removed to Kokan, whence he made his way to Petropaulovsk on the Siberian frontier, and thence to Kazan, and returning through Semipalatinsk to Kuldja, presented himself before the Tian-Tziun. Zurdan said that he had escaped from imprisonment in Kokan, and on the strength of this statement received the office of "Ishkaga" of Kashgar, and ultimately that of Hakim-Beg.

The Hodjas also profited by these disorders, and with a small force, composed principally of Kashgar emigrants and Dikokamenni Kirghizes, appeared under the walls of Kashgar in the autumn of 1847. The governor of the town, Kasim-Beg, resolved to hold out until the Hodjas had taken the Chinese fortress. In one sally from their stronghold, the Chinese were beaten, and flying before the Hodjas who pursued them, were all drowned in the river Kizyl. The Hodjas apprised the town of their victory by sounding trumpets; but the Begs would not surrender, and forced the inhabitants to man the walls. Named-Khan, a Tashkend merchant, succeeded in communicating with the Hodjas outside, through a subterranean passage, and by his treachery, the gates of Kashgar were opened to the besiegers early one morning in the second week. Hakim-Beg, Kasim, and the other Begs escaped to the Chinese "Manchen" or citadel.

This event is known as the insurrection of the seven Begs, from the circumstance that it was carried out by seven members of the Appak family. The eldest, Ishan-Khan-Türia, better known as Katta-Khan, was proclaimed ruler, and the other Hodjas were appointed governors of the surrounding settlements.

Vali-Khan-Turia, the same who headed the insurrection of 1857, was governor of the town of Yanishahr, where he signalized his administration by unexampled ferocity. The rule of the seven Hodjas commenced with the pillage of the Begs' houses, and with the establishment of a large harem. Educated at Kokan they avoided the observance of the customs of their countrymen, and surrounded themselves with Andijans.

Named-Khan, the Aksakal of Kokan, was raised to the rank of Min-Bashi. Katta-Khan, generally speaking, did not secure the affections of his people, nor yet did he inspire them with fear. The only able man in this insurrection was Tavekel-Hodja, also a descendant of Mahomet. This active and very brave man, had commanded the army when besieging Kashgar, with the rank of Batyr-Bashi, and was afterwards sent to Aksù.

At Kuldja, preparations were being made for war, and immediately on receipt of the news of the insurrection, a force was despatched to suppress it, but the departure of these troops seriously weakening the garrison of the town, they were recalled before they had reached their destination. An army intended to operate against Kashgar was expected from Urumchi and Lan-cheu; upon the arrival of which in November, it was at once ordered to advance. It was composed of several hundred Manchurs, soldiers of the Green Dragon, of Sibos and Solons, and re-inforced by one thousand Torguts, and three thousand Chashpans, *i. e.* criminals transported from the Southern Governments, who, before leaving Kuldja, attested the justice of their sentence, by pillaging the shops and private houses. This army was commanded by the Tian-Tziun Jo, and entered into winter quarters at Maral-Bashi.

Before the arrival of the Chinese, the Hodja Katta-Khan made a move against Yarkend, which city he was bent on securing. The Chinese jail-birds, disobeying the orders given them, fell on the advanced divisions of the Khan's forces, and utterly routed them. Katta-Khan then hurried to Kashgar, but the inhabitants of that place, dissatisfied with the preference he had shown for the Andijans, and enraged at the heavy taxes which he had imposed on them, closed their gates. After a few more desultory engagements with the Chinese, the Hodja fled to Kokan, and the enemy occupied Kashgar without any opposition. The Chinese forces amounted, it is said, to 64,000 men, and it was affirmed that further reinforcements were advancing on Kuldja. The above figure is exaggerated, probably, and it is more likely that another account, estimating the troops from Urumchi at 4000, from Lian-Cheu, 20,000, and those of Kuldja at 6000, is nearer the truth. On the occupation of Kashgar by the Chinese troops, 20,000 individuals of both sexes fled from the town, the majority of whom perished from exposure to severe frosts, in the Terekty mountains, where their bleaching bones still strew the pass.

In the same year, on the proposition of the Chinese, political and commercial relations were again renewed with the country on the former footing. The Kokanians, now thoroughly acquainted with the weakness of the Chinese, and feeling their own superior strength, besides having a firm hold on all the Hodjas, treated the government of the Bogdo Khan with very little ceremony. Named-Khan, who had delivered Kashgar to the Hodjas, and was Min-Bashi to the Khan of Kokan, again became Aksakal of Kashgar. All the Kokanians who had been faithful to the Hodjas in the last rising, remained unmolested and enjoyed his protection at Kashgar.

The Kokanians now accorded greater liberty to the Hodjas, as they did not thereby endanger their relations, but on the contrary increased their influence in the country. In 1855 and 1856, Kichik-Khan-Turé and Vali-Khan-Türia attempted several inroads, but owing to the numerical weakness of their troops, they did not succeed in penetrating through the frontier pickets.

The last insurrection occurred in 1857. In the spring of that year, on the day after the termination of the Ramadàn fast, Hodja Vali-Khan-Türia fled from Kokan in company with seven Kashgar emigrants. They arrived during the night at the Kokan fort of Oksalur, situated on the road from Ush to Kashgar, the garrison of which, after killing the commander, the Hodja persuaded to join himself. He likewise succeeded in gaining over several soldiers who had been sent by Nar-Mat-Datha, Aksakal of Kashgar, to collect the "Ziaket" or tribute from the Kirghizes of the Chon-Bagysh tribe, at that time encamped in the vicinity of the fort. He further stationed guards and scouts along all the roads leading to Kashgar, to prevent Kirghizes from giving the alarm, and despatched emissaries to raise an armed Kirghiz force. Several Kashgar Begs, sent by the Chinese in the direction of Ush to collect information respecting the Hodjas, were taken prisoners and brought before Vali-Khan, who immediately cut off their heads with his own hand. Having passed the night at the ford over the Kizyl, he reached, on the next, an outlying Chinese picket. There were no sentinels on the walls, and one of his followers having scaled them, opened the gates. Vali-Khan-Trüia entered, sword in hand, with his retainers, and put to death all the Chinese soldiers who were peaceably reclining and smoking opium in their barracks. Some Kashgarians who chanced to be at the picket at the moment, shared the same fate. Having thus effectually silenced the picket, the Hodja at four in the morning appeared before the South-Western gates of Kashgar. All was still in the town. The Hodja's followers collected the wood that had been brought for sale and left outside the walls, and kindled a large fire; with the powder they had captured at the picket they endeavoured to blow open the gates. The peace of the town, however, was not disturbed by these proceedings, and none of the inhabitants were aware of what was occurring. When at last the gates fell in, one of the Hodja's band galloped through the streets of the town exclaiming—"All hail to Buzruk-Khan-Türia!" *

* Buzruk-Khan is the only son of Djengir. This Hodja has not yet ventured on a "Hazat." He is much beloved by the Kashgarians, who expect him as a deliverer. Vali-Khan made use of his name to gain the sympathy of the inhabitants.

The effect was magical. The inhabitants rose tumultuously to arms, massacred all the Chinese, and "looted" their houses and shops. The Hodja, welcomed at the gates by the Kokanian Aksakal, entered the town in triumphal procession. The palace of the Hakim-Beg, who effected his escape through another of the city gates to the Chinese town, was hurriedly got ready, and Vali-Khan-Turia installed himself in it to the sound of trumpets and gongs. All those Begs who had not succeeded in escaping, were seized by the loyal inhabitants and brought before the Hodja, who indulged his savage nature by hacking several of them to pieces with his own hand. On the following day, the inhabitants of the Artysh and Bishkarim settlements, headed by a powerful Mont-Albanian, Sheikh-Ahund and his two Begs, Halyk and Tair, joined the successful Vali-Khan.

All the Begs who had entered the Chinese service, and had not fled to the Chinese citadel, were murdered, together with their children, while their wives and daughters became the prey of the soldiers of the Hodja. But the two above-named Begs, from the Artysh settlement, although they had also accepted office under the Chinese, presented themselves fearlessly before Vali-Khan because they had been at the same time in constant secret communications with the Hodjas, and furnished them with large sums of money for the support of a "Hazat."

Vali-Khan-Türia immediately conferred the rank of Min-Bashi on Nor-Named, Aksakal of Kokan, while returned fugitives from Kokan received different posts at court.

The insurrection spread so rapidly that the Hodja found himself in a short time at the head of 70,000 mounted horsemen, and 4000 sarbazes or foot soldiers; and he had, furthermore, a large force of volunteers, raised in the surrounding towns and villages. These troops were dressed in uniform, and arms were provided by the Hodja, who divided them into banners, with 500 men under each, commanded by Pansads. The inhabitants proceeded daily with spades and shovels to dam up the river Kizyl in order to divert its course against the walls of the Chinese fortress. The foreign merchants were also armed and forced to take part in the siege works.

The Hodja proceeded actively with the work of organizing his troops, and employed all the artizans of Kashgar in manufacturing arms. Horses were impressed from the natives, and foreign merchants compelled to serve in person as well as furnish forth requisitions for the army. Fresh taxes were daily imposed. The Hodja also formed a park of artillery of eighteen guns, which, however, did but little execution. The guns were cast at Kashgar under the superintendence of an Afghan. According to the testimony of an eye-witness, the troops of Vali-Khan were much better armed and organized than those of the Emir of Bokhara, whose army serves as a model for the whole of Central Asia. The Chinese attempted in several sorties to stop the progress of the siege, but were on every occasion repulsed with loss. They at last confined themselves to firing at the assailants from their guns and matchlocks, while the Solons and Sibos galled the besieging army with showers of arrows from the lofty walls.

The town of Yanyshahr was soon after taken by the Hodja. He next despatched his favourite, Tilya-Khan, son of a Yanyshahr emigrant, to invest Yarkend, who, to further the success of the enterprise, was falsely given out as a Hodja. The siege of Yarkend was formally commenced in the month of June. The Chinese, who had marched out of their "Mancheu," or citadel, at that town, to meet Tilya-Khan, were defeated. Notwithstanding this reverse, the inhabitants of the town still resolved to defend themselves. The local Begs, the Bokharians, Badakshanis, and Balts, urged the people who were favourable to the Hodjas, not to participate in the insurrection, assuring them that Tilya-Khan did not belong to the order of Hodjas, but was the son of a Yanyshahr butcher. Ismail-Van, Hakim-Beg of Yarkend, made a speech to the inhabitants, in which, regardless of the presence of the Chinese, he declared that, should the real Hodja arrive, he, Ismail-Van, would not presume to oppose him.

Notwithstanding the material forces that supported the authority of the Hodja, it also required a great amount of patience and devotion on the part of the Kashgarians to suffer the cruelty and injustice of the tyrant. From the continual smoking of hashish, Vali-Khan-Türia was reduced to a state of savage frenzy, in the paroxysms of which he gave full scope to his brutal passions. His mania was a thirst for blood, and not a day passed without several men being slaughtered in cold blood, either by himself or in his presence. On the banks of the Kizyl, he erected a pyramid of human skulls, and anxiously watched the gradual rise of a monument so worthy of him. The heads of fallen

Chinese and Mussulmen were collected from all parts, and added to the pyramid. Many men of influence fell victims to his ferocity. Among those executed by him without any cause were Named-Khan, who had several times occupied the post of Aksakal of Kashgar, and who had fled from Kokan to enter the service of the Hodja; the Halyk-Beg of Artysh, one of his bravest supporters; and, lastly, an European traveller. This latter was making his way to Kokan, and, wishing to present himself before the Hodja, desired a friend of the author, Naman-Bai, who is related to the Hodja, to procure some Indian gold brocade and Cashmere shawls as gifts for Vali-Khan. It is said that this European gave himself out to be an English agent, sent from Bombay to the Khan of Kokan. The Hodja demanded his papers, but the traveller told him that he could only deliver them to the person to whom they were addressed. This answer was sufficient to seal the doom of the poor Feringhee. Judging from the date of the occurrence and the intelligence received subsequently in Europe, it may safely be assumed that the European executed at Kashgar in 1857 was no other than the learned Prussian traveller, Adolphe Schlagintweit. The Hindoo servant who accompanied him, still resides at Yarkend.

The ferocity of this Hodja may further be illustrated by the following story:—A Kashgarian who had made some sword-blades, brought them to the Khan, accompanied by his son. Taking one of the swords into his hand, the Hodja inquired whether it was sharp, to which the maker answered in the affirmative. "Let us see," said the Hodja, and with one blow he struck off the head of the boy. "Yes, it is a good blade," he said, "give this man a 'Khlat' (robe) of honour!"

It is also related of Vali-Khan-Türia that, on one occasion, he invited to his palace the most respectable personages of Kashgar, together with several Andijan merchants, and according to Kashgar custom called in some musicians. During the entertainment the stentorian voice of the Hodja was heard to cry out, "Executioner!" His trembling guests sat stupefied and aghast. The executioner entered, and the Hodja pointed with his finger to one of the musicians who had imprudently yawned. His head was severed from his body before the eyes of the horror-stricken guests and taken away to be placed on the pyramid.

Men as well as women, Montenegrins, Montalbanians, adherents of the White and Black Mountaneer parties, soldiers and mullahs alike fell victims to the sanguinary predilections of the Hodja. The prisons were crowded, till at length Kashgar from one end to the other presented the appearance of a vast slaughter-house strewed with corpses. The national customs of Kashgar, differing from those of Kokan, were distasteful to the Hodja, and persecuted by him. The national costume was prohibited; the women were ordered, in imitation of the Andijans, to cover their hair with a white kerchief and not to venture out unveiled. They were also forbidden to plait their hair, and this was strictly enforced by the police. For the infraction of this regulation the fair offenders were shorn of their tresses.

The males from the age of six were obliged to wear a turban and to frequent the mosques regularly, to which the Kashgarians were not accustomed.

It may easily be imagined, after all this, why the intelligence of the advance of a numerous body of Chinese from Ili was hailed with universal delight. Speedy release from such an all-paralysing terror was anxiously and impatiently awaited, and moreover the Kashgarians felt aggrieved in the appointment of Andijans to all the highest ranks in the army and at court. Nor-Mohammed, former Aksakal of Kokan, was now Min-Bashi; Mohammed-Rahim was Mehter; Med-Karim-Kari was Hasnatch; Satykul, a Kipchak, was chief of the court functionaries; and Mussa Pansat, a Kashgar emigrant, was general of the body guard; the office of Kurshi was filled by Essaul-Tokhtar, a native of Kokan. The different divisions of the army were respectively commanded by Abdulla-Khan-Hodja, a Sheikh, and by a former mehrem of Tillia-Khan; the forces sent to Aksù and Khotan were under Chalgurt-Tokhta-Manju, a notorious robber and adventurer, and an obscure Margilan butcher, who in his expedition to Khotan succeeded in taking possession of the large settlement of Puma on the road from Yarkend to Khotan. Tokhta-Manju had once been transported to the Southern governments of the Chinese Empire for the murder of a Chinaman, but made his escape thence to Kashgar in the disguise of a Manchur officer, where he served as a common soldier under the Aksakal of that town. Among the Kashgarians near the person of the Hodja, who still occupied prominent posts, was a certain Sheikh-Ahund from the settlement of Altyn-Artysh. He was the wealthiest and only influential man of the White Mountain party in all

Kashgar, his daughter being also married to Vali-khan-Türia. There were many Kashgarians and Chalgurts in the army holding the rank of Colonel or "Pansad," but none of these possessed the confidence of the Hodja, or had access to him.

This invidious preference for Andijans, who were originally common soldiers of the Aksakal of Kokan, excited the jealousy of the Kashgarian patriots even from the very outset.

But by way of illustration of his first joyful reception in Kashgar, an Ahund describes that on the day after the taking of Kashgar, the Bishkarim and Artysh militia, under the command of the Sheikh-Ahund and two Begs, waving their banners, and sounding their timbrels, approached his palace with shouts of joy, demanding to see the Hodja and to kiss his hands. The sight of the Kokanians, who surrounded the palace and refused to admit them, raised a loud murmur of discontent. "If we may not call upon the Hodja after sacrificing our lives and property in his cause, what claims have the Andijans to his favour?" cried the militia. Here Mussa-Pansad issued from the palace and told them laconically: "If your heads are not too heavy for your shoulders, then in the name of Allah himself hold your peace." After this the Kashgarians dispersed silent, and thoroughly disenchanted.

The resources of the country were soon exhausted, and the cessation of trade as well as of every branch of industry, became painfully felt. The horses and donkeys were impressed for the army; copper kettles, dishes, and other utensils were seized for casting cannon. During one hundred days the whole population was occupied in siege works. In addition to all this, the suspicions and cruelty of the Hodja passed all limits. Named-Khan, while superintending the siege works, was seized and executed, and the civil and military officers were coninually being fined; the Min-Bashi was several times imprisoned, and had to pay a heavy sum to save his life. The lives of all were in constant peril. An Uidacha of the Hodja relates that every moment he expected death. Such a state of excitement could not last long. The people, exhausted by the siege works, prayed for the surrender of the Chinese fort, the walls of which daily threatened to give way under the pressure of the accumulating waters of the Kizyl river. A Chinese force suddenly arrived, and all rejoiced. The Min-Bashi, who had been sentenced to death, speedily retired with his army, and fled to Kokan.

The Andijan merchants, after having laboured during one hundred and fifteen days in conducting the siege of the Chinese fort, followed on the heels of the Min-Bashi. Vali-Khan, left alone with a few persons who still remained faithful to him, among whom it must be observed there was not a single Kokanian, fled to the mountain territory of Darvaz, the ruler of which, Ismail-Shah,—first robbed him of all he brought with him from Kashgar, then, at the request of the Khan of Kokan, delivered him up to his enemies.

During this period, 15,000 individuals voluntarily emigrated from Kashgar to Kokan. The Chinese now occupying Kashgar, were guilty of excesses no less violent than those of Vali-Khan. The surrounding villagers especially suffered from the exactions and cruelties of the Chinese, who seized their corn, hay, cattle, etc. The windows, doors, and other wooden appurtenances of the mosques and tombs of the Hodjas were, to the great grief of the Mussulmen, broken up for fuel. The Kalmyks stabled their horses in the temples, maltreated the natives, and violated the women. But the Chinese soon appointed Kattu-Beg to the post of Hokim-Beg of Kashgar, a clever and energetic man; who in a short time restored the peace of the town, expelled the Kalmyks from Kashgar, and put an effectual stop to all lawless proceedings. By this Beg's advice, all those who had taken part in the insurrection were seized and executed, as a warning to others. The Sheikh-Ahund, who has been so often mentioned in this sketch, and his eldest son, Kyzy-Ahund, after undergoing torture and imprisonment, were both beheaded; his two other sons effected their escape to Kurtka, whence they ultimately reached Kokan.

The other persons who were sacrificed to the rage of Vali-Khan, were of no note; they were executed in fits of fury, and their heads, placed in separate cages, still line the road leading to the gates of Kashgar.

The houses of the Andijans were occupied by Kuldja and Yarkend Begs, who had arrived at Kashgar with the Chinese troops. The military executions of the Chinese lasted till the month of August, 1858, so that for nearly two entire years Kashgar was the scene of torture and executions.

Trade during this time gradually languished till it became utterly stagnant. The insecurity of life repressed native industry and pursuits, and the fruits of former labour were plundered by the Kalmyks. The corn-fields were trampled under foot, and Kalmyk studs grazed in the gardens and enclosures. Vali-Khan, on his being brought to

Kokan, was imprisoned by the Khan of that place, and the "ulems" (judges), were requested to decide on the punishment that should be inflicted on him for the murder of so many innocent Mussulmen. The relatives of the murdered Named-Khan demanded reparation, and they were joined by other applicants for justice on the fallen despot. In consequence of these complaints, many Kokanians who had served Vali-Khan, were deprived of their offices; among these was Nar-Mahomet, Aksakal of Kashgar. The case of Vali-Khan-Türia, however, notwithstanding the demand of Hudoyar that he should be executed, took a favourable turn for him in consequence of his cause being espoused by all the Seids. The members of the Sahib-Zadde family, whoenjoyed the fanatical respect of the whole population of Turkestan, advocated the interests of Vali-Khan so skilfully, that he not only escaped all punishment, but his accusers were in their turn prosecuted and compelled to pay very heavy fines. The case of the Hodja affected the whole privileged class of Seids, descendants of Mahomet, who are exempted from execution and corporal punishment. Possessing the general confidence and respect of the people, and assured of their own personal safety, they boldly reproach the Khan for any misdeeds, thus acting as a sort of check upon an otherwise unlimited despotism.

After this it will be understood why Hudoyar-Khan was so strongly opposed by all the members of the Sahib-Zaddé family, and by the Hodjas. The right of punishment, if enforced in the case of Vali-Khan-Türia might in future be applied also to the other Seids or Hodjas. Hudoyar, however, placed all the latter under close surveillance, and gave orders at the frontier towns for every Hodja who passed the barriers more than ten times to be brought under a guard to Kokan.

In the spring of 1858 a Kokanian ambassador was sent to Kashgar to renew the former relations with that town, and to inform the Chinese officials that the Khan was extremely concerned at the former flight of the Hodja, and that the rebel who had produced all the disorders at Kashgar was then in irons. This the Chinese believed, or at least pretended to do so. The negotiation was entrusted to Nasyr-Eddin, ruler of Shabrikhan, who had been sent as envoy in 1847, shortly after the rebellion of the seven Hodjas. Matters were speedily arranged, and the Kokanians received permission to have their own Aksakal, and to trade on the same terms as formerly. The post of Aksakal was conferred on this same Nasyr-Eddin, with the title of Datha. The Kokan Aksakal arrived at Kashgar in the month of August, with a small caravan, and accompanied by 5000 Kashgarians of both sexes. A new Hakim-Beg, Alych, was appointed about this time at Kashgar. He was a man of advanced years, but notwithstanding his age, indulged in every sensual vice without restraint. The Ishkaga-Beg, his assistant, is Sypergu-Beg, a native of Yarkend. The Hakim-Beg has a red ball, and the title of Tiadzi, and the Sybergu-Beg wears a light blue ball, and ranks in the fifth class. Kutlu-Beg, who formerly filled the post of Hakim-Beg, was made governor of the settlement of Faizabad, but has subsequently been named Hakim-Beg of Ush-Turfan.

Mid-day Halt on a Kirghiz Steppe.

CHAPTER VII.

Trans-Ili and Chu Districts.—By Veninkof.— Almaty or Vernoè.

Fort Vernoe was founded in 1854, when the Russians first occupied the Trans-Ili region. Ranging along the foot of the Alàtaù chain, the small but picturesque Almatynka rivulet, issuing out of the mountains, branches out into several small streams, that irrigate this military-agricultural colony, the population of which consists of between five and six thousand inhabitants. The Russian military and civil administrations being centred here, the place wears an animated appearance. Unfortunately, notwithstanding the abundance of stone in these parts, and in spite of the great scarcity of timber, which only grows in the mountains, Almaty is entirely built of wood. As yet the houses have a clean and cheerful exterior, but they will soon become dingy. The preference generally shewn by the Slavonic race for hasty and perishable constructions will then have to be regretted. The greater part of the inhabitants of Almaty are engaged in agriculture, which yields a fair remuneration for the labour bestowed on it, and the Government buys up all the surplus grain at good prices. It lies in 43° 16′ N.

Almaty, we are entitled to suppose, will soon become a place of no small commercial importance to all Central Asia. The small Tartar village with a mosque, now forming the southern part of the settlement, gives promise of being developed in time into a large trading town. The geographical position of Almaty, which is mid-way between Kuldja and Kokan, and on the road from Kashgar to Semipalatinsk, justifies us in anticipating that many merchants from the three neighbouring countries will transfer their activity to this point of convergence of the various routes of Central Asiatic commerce. Accordingly we find that the commercial importance of Vernoé is increasing annually. Trading caravans, which so late as 1856 usually passed by without stopping, now always halt here for traffic, although as yet supplying only local wants. Large purchases of cattle are also made each year in the vicinity for Kuldja, Tashkend, and Petropavlovsk, which latter place is distant upwards of 800 miles from Vernoé.

The agricultural conditions of the Almaty colony are extremely favourable. Its height above the level of the sea is about 2500 feet, and the mean moisture of the air in spring, after mid-day, is 0·52. This hygrometric range clearly shows that the parching air of the Steppe does not affect a sub-mountainous region; but is, on the contrary, counteracted by the proximity of perpetual snows. The humidity of the atmosphere, however, prevails only within a narrow zone bordering the mountains, at a certain distance from which it rapidly decreases, upon which the vegetation, thus deprived of moisture, becomes entirely scorched towards the commencement of June. The latitude of Vernoé (43° 16′) is almost identical with that of Marseilles. But the influence of a far inland climate, combined with the greater elevation of the former, produces a marked difference between these two places, for, while the hot summer of Almaty favours the successful cultivation of grapes, pears and melons, plants requiring a mild winter, cannot be reared. The range of temperature during the year is as much as 106° Fahr.; the heat in summer rising as high as 97°, and the cold in winter falling to 9° Fahr.

The Kirghizes in Vernoé.—The Sultan Ali.—Vernoé is the metropolis of the Kirghizes of the Great Horde, and as such, presented many interesting features to me on my first arrival. The hospitality of its inhabitants facilitated my observations of local life, with which I soon became familiar. I was particularly struck by the Kirghizes, who rode through the streets of Almaty with the same patriarchal dignity and ease that they exhibit in the Steppe. The camel, the cow, the long-necked "arghamak" or Turkoman horse, and the Steppe trotter, low, but exceedingly active, are seen bestridden by these gaily dressed cavaliers. A real Djigit, or affluent Kirghiz, however, will never mount any other animal but a thorough-bred horse. Oxen and camels are exclusively owned by shepherds and husbandmen, or "eginitches," while the arghamak is only found in possession of the wealthy and distinguished, and even by them is used but seldom.

Sultan Ali is the head of the largest division of the Horde, *i. e.* of those known as Dulat Kirghizes. This old man has seen a great deal of adventure in his day, and having at various times been subject to three States, he has learned to adapt himself to the customs of different countries.

In many instances his natural cunning and ready wit were remarkable. I had been informed of his intention of paying me a visit, and was told at the same time to regard it as a special honour, seeing that the descendant of Ablai-Khan was not at all given to visiting. Although he received an allowance of 350 rubles silver, or about £52. 10*s*., from the Russian Government, when required to attend at Vernoé on official business, it was no easy matter to ensure his presence The Russian military head of the district introduced me to Ali, and the interview took place at my own quarters, in order that the dignity of a Russian officer, sent as they supposed direct from the Emperor, should not be compromised in the eyes of the Kirghizes. I exerted myself to please the old man, assuring him that he held a high place in my estimation on account of the lofty position he held in the Horde, and that I appreciated the honour he was paying me by his visit. Ali was equally polite, and paid me the usual extravagant Asiatic compliments. "I do not doubt, Sultan," I said to him, "that your people are happy in having you for their ruler. Your fame had reached me even at St. Petersburg, and now I see that it represented only half your merits."

"Do not say so," answered the old man; "I govern my people according to the decrees of the Padishah—may Heaven protect him!—and his deputy, the Pristav. As you must know, a piece of timber is a rude block at first, but becomes seemly and serviceable as this arm-chair, under the skilful hands of the joiner. I and my people are the block, the deputy is the joiner. Were it not for him and the Padishah, we should always remain blocks."

"You are too modest, Sultan. Can he thus speak whose wit is as sharp as the well-stropped razor, and whose will, inclined to good, is as hard as steel? All of us certainly fulfil the wishes of the Emperor, and every one in Vernoe should obey the Pristav; but you, Sultan, are yourself of high degree in the Horde. The allegiance of your people to the Padishah depends on you."

"My people cannot but be faithful to the Padishah and obedient to those he sets over us. We live together here as two hands. You Russians are the right-hand, we the left, and the Pristav is the head" (he here joined his hands, making the fingers of one fit between those of the other).

"It were indeed bad if the left hand disobeyed the right, and if both did not fulfil the orders of the head."

Ali, as already mentioned, has been a subject of three rulers. In his youth he went to Pekin, to be presented at the Court of the Bogdo-Khan Iziatsin; but about this visit he is not fond of conversing. For a long time after the whole of his tribe acknowledged the power of Kokan, although deputies from the Horde had previously sworn allegiance to Russia. On one occasion, the Sultan and his Bis, perceiving that the Kokanians were bent on abolishing, at any cost, even the nominal dependence of the Horde to Russia, determined to oppose their machinations by force, and planned an attack on Kopal, which belonged to Kokan. Ali, who with his tribe was then roaming along the Koksu, was chosen by them to commence the outbreak. But the artful politician, after calculating the probabilities of success, held aloof. Enraged at this, the Sultans and Bis reproached him with cowardice. "Most worthy Sultans and Bis," Ali wrote, "the serpent, when on its way to its nest, winds and trails along slowly; it is only at the entrance that it erects itself and quickly glides in." This answer disarmed their wrath, and delayed the enterprise, which was ultimately abandoned.

The Great Horde.—On the 24th May, 1859, I joined an expeditionary detachment, which moved to the West from Vernoé, and on the next day crossed the Kes-Kelen. This river contains a considerable body of water, and is bordered by rich meadows and land. The road at its source leads across a path into the Kebin valley. The Kes-Kelen defile forms the limit of forests to the west of Vernoé; beyond that, to the It-Kichu, we did not observe a single tree, only the barberry, briar, and some other bushes. It may be observed, as a general rule, that the forests of Central Asia occur only on the slopes of mountains, whose summits are covered with snow, which supply the soil with moisture. In the absence of this necessary condition, the atmosphere of the Steppe exhausts the young trees as soon as they commence to bud. The totally woodless character of the southern slopes of the mountains is readily explained by this dryness of the air.

In the sultry valley of the Chu, near the mouth of the Karakanus, we observed a few trees growing close to the bed of the rivulet, but these consisted of the mulberry and peach.

Between the Keskelen and Kestek, as we gradually left Vernoé behind us, our detachment was joined by a band of Kirghizes, who volunteered to escort it in the hopes of receiving some remuneration. Amongst them were some of the most renowned men of the Horde, distinguished either for their valour or high birth. It was gratifying to observe in these men some symptoms of civilization, for which they are exclusively indebted to the Russians. Some of the Sultans and Bis, in conversing with me, expressed a desire to have their sons educated in some of the Russian military schools, and loudly inveighed against their wives and relatives who opposed the scheme, through dread, lest the children, after leaving their native aùls, would forsake their religion, and early mode of life.

Other Kirghizes whom we encountered here were to a certain degree self-educated, and had acquired a few European habits. It must, however, be confessed that the result of their contact with the Russians is also but too frequently displayed in a development of vicious habits, many having become inveterate drunkards.

The Great Horde gives fairer promise of civilization than either of the others, first, on account of the more favourable geographical conditions of the

Steppe it occupies, and secondly, owing to the special attention paid by the Russian Government to its organization. The internal government of the Horde, and the administration of justice by its own Bis, have been retained without any change, thus offering good guarantees for a steady and natural development of the people. The judgments of the Bis, or esteemed elders, are prompt, and based on the known and universally recognised customs of the Kirghizes, and produce consequently the happiest results. The only objection to this system is, that the judge takes presents from both sides. In this way the most influential Sultans and Bis accumulate considerable wealth. In addition to these gifts, the elder Sultans yearly receive a sheep from each of their respective aùls, on which they feed the applicants who seek their counsel and judgments. This is in accordance with the national custom, which requires the judge to shelter and feed all those who entrust to him the defence of their interests. The superior Sultans decide more important matters than those referred to the Bis; but cases of a still more serious nature, such as barantas and murders, are settled in a council of both Sultans and Bis.

In Mr. Levchin's work on the Kirghiz Steppes,

there is very little information concerning the Great Horde, which between the years 1820-30 was scarcely accessible. A brief account of its composition will therefore not be unacceptable in this place.

Three principal divisions of this Horde roam within Russian territory—the Djalairs, the Atbans, which include the Suvans, and the Dulats, with various branches, some of which wander beyond the Chu to the Talas and Boraldai mountains. These last amalgamate with the Uisuns. The most numerous division is that of the Dulats.* They occupy the whole region to the North-East of the Chu and Alatau range, as far as the southern extremity of Lake Balkhash and the Altyn-Imel pass, and thence eastward to the River Turgen. Still further eastward it extends along the Chiliu and Charyn, and along the right banks of the Ili, as far as the Koksu; this region is occupied by the Atbans, a part of whom wander in the Chinese dominions, where they pay tribute for their pasturages.

* The following is the composition of the principal sub-divisions of the Dulats :—The Seikym branch numbers about 795 aùls ; the Djanys, consisting of the Djailymys, Bals, Kybrai, Kashkaran, and other tribes, 1090 aùls ; the Butpai, with the Chogai, Kudaigul, and Isenbai tribes, 785 aùls ; Chemir, 1770 aùls ; Sary-Usium, 300 aùls ; and Itsy, 300. The latter camp on the island of Komaú, and roam along the lower course of the Ili.

The Djalairs are diffused throughout the belt to the extreme North of the Great Horde along the river Karatal and its small affluents.

These form the largest group of the three divisions of the Horde, and the numbers may be estimated at 25,000. The Atbans (including the Suvans) are inferior to them in numbers, and embrace not more than 20,000. These figures, however, it should be understood are mere approximations, the obstacles in the way of forming a correct estimate being almost insuperable; and this is still more especially the case with the Great Horde, the Kirghizes of which are not subjected to any regular taxes. The figures given above are founded on statements of certain Bis as to the number of aùls and yurts occupied by the two divisions. In the same way it may be computed that the number of Dulats and Uisuns amounts at the lowest to 70,000; so that the whole population of the Great Horde must reach somewhere about 115,000, which figure differs but very slightly from that originally given by Keppen.

The Kirghizes had retired to the mountains when our corps left Vernoé.

Numerous aùls of the various Dulat tribes were scattered over the sub-mountainous region of the

Alatàu, and along some of the rivulets where rich grass grows on the banks even at a considerable distance from the hills.

In the month of May, the Steppes generally offer rich pasturages, but the Kirghizes are obliged to protect themselves from the swarms of flies in the low grounds by retiring into the mountains. These flies are a great scourge to the cattle, and by their incessant persecution fairly exhaust the unfortunate animals. It is only in the month of July that the Kirghizes descend to the plains, and then with but a small portion of their cattle, leaving the rest just below the snow-line until the beginning of autumn.*

Zoology of the Steppe.—FAUNA.—To the West of Almaty the Alatau mountains gradually lose their elevation, till at the upper course of the Kastek river, they barely attain a height of 7500 feet. But immediately beyond this stream the conical-

* Towards the end of July, on my return from the river Chu, after ascending the Talgar, I fell in with some large herds of well-fed horses and colts at an elevation of at least 9000 feet above the level of the sea, and perhaps higher. The one disadvantage of these mountain sojourns is that the herds are very frequently driven away by marauding parties of Dikokamenni Kirghizes, especially of the Slaty and Sary-bagysh tribes.

shaped Suok-Tiubé (peak) mountain rears its rounded summit to a height of nearly 10,000 feet. In the fissures of its slopes the snow remains until July. A defile or depression in the ridge to the East of Suok-Tiube offers a strange phenomenon. Sometimes after still weather a strong Southerly wind blows through it for more than two hours. If the atmosphere has been previously disturbed, this wind increases in force towards the evening, and assumes a Northerly direction from behind Suok-Tiube. Hence it might be inferred that the cold mountain air descends at such times, while the heated atmosphere of the plains lying to the North of the chain ascends to the top; but this surmise requires to be confirmed by more accurate observation.*

What are the animals which occupy the Steppe in the neighbourhood of the snowy mountains, where the climate varies as we ascend? This question may seriously engage the attention of the zoologist;

* A somewhat similar phenomenon is familiar to Alpine travellers in Northern Italy, where, as for instance, on the Lakes of Como, Lugano, Iseo, and Garda, a strong wind springs up pretty regularly towards sunset, and lasts two or three hours. It is less conspicuous on Lago Maggiore, and is unknown on the northern side of the chain, unless the somewhat similar, but more capricious atmospheric disturbance known as the Föhn be presumed to be analogous.—[Ed.]

but it is not void of interest for any and all persons traversing the Steppes of Central Asia. In the barren, woodless tracts, every evidence of organic existence involuntarily arrests the attention of the traveller.

Beyond those animals bred for man's use, the number of mammals in the Steppe is, generally speaking, not great. The most numerous are the wolves. These follow the droves of the Kirghizes, and create panics among the shepherds and in the aùls. The loud barking of the dogs on such occasions is distinctly heard throughout the neighbourhood.

The next in numerical abundance are:—the fox, marten, and marmot, many of which are found in the valleys of the mountain streams. Besides these there are in the mountains and forests, bears, antelopes (saiga), red deer, arkharas, and a few tigers. At the numerous points where the waters of the rivulets running from the Alatau are choked with reeds, wild boars abound in great numbers. These are sometimes hunted by the Kirghizes, who organise *battues* for the amusement this sport affords them. A wild-boar hunt is always a gala time for the Cossacks when on the march, because they then feed well and make up for their usual scanty fare, humorously replying to over inquisitive strangers that their commissariat cattle hide in the reeds or swim in the Issyk-kul Lake or river Chu.

In the winter the inhabitants of the stations around Almaty occasionally catch porcupines. The shrew mouse and Siberian jerboa (alactaga) are also frequently found in the fields, but these animals do no great damage to the crops.

Birds are far more abundant in the Steppes of the Great Horde, if not in actual quantity, at least in variety of species. The most common of these are, the black grouse and the starling (*Sturmus Roseus*, Pall.), which collect in large flocks, and are seen both running upon the Steppe and flying. Eagles are seen in the mountains, and pheasants are frequently found in the valleys. The latter are shot by the inhabitants of Almaty, and sent for sale as far even as Omsk. The peewit frequents the stone tombs of the Kirghizes, and allows itself to be easily caught. It is so tame indeed that it does not attempt to escape even when placed upon the pommel of the saddle.

The most numerous reptiles of the Steppe are, lizards and serpents; and some species of insects are also common, such as the *phalangium*, the *karakurt*, the *scutiger arenarius*, the cricket, and the chafer (*cicada*). The latter does no small damage to the young corn before it is scorched by the sun. On the other hand, the venomous *phalangium* and *karakurt* are especially dangerous to man. The *phalangium* of these parts is a large spider, often more than an inch long, which burrows in the earth. Where the soil is sandy clay, the naturalist will rarely fail to fall in with this venomous insect. Those who are obliged to lie on the bare ground should, above all, take precautions against it. The least movement, or so much as an involuntary contraction of the muscles during sleep, is sufficient to occasion a bite, because the insect immediately grasps at the object from which it anticipates danger. The *phalangium* will, however, creep harmlessly over a motionless body. At the moment of the bite the pain is inconsiderable, something resembling that attending the sting of the gnat, but the results are dreadful. The pain spreads quickly over the whole frame, accompanied with fever, and total exhaustion rapidly follows. The only remedy before the poison has circulated through the veins, is cupping; but this is not always practicable, because it is difficult to discover the bitten part. More than fifteen of our men suffered from the bite of this insect, and two of them most severely, as they had been bitten during the night, and discovered it only after some time had elapsed, when the effects of the poison began to show themselves. One man who was bitten had very fortunately caught the *phalangium* while still on his body, upon which he was at once cupped, and thus directly relieved of the consequences of the bite.

The bite of the *karakurt* (earth spider) is still more dangerous than that of the *phalangium*, or even that of the scorpion or *tarantula.* In all instances ammonia is administered internally with success.

Serpents and lizards are plentiful about the Steppe, especially in the neighbourhood of reeds and water, while the prevalence of venomous insects is confined to dry localities. The Kirghizes eagerly exterminate the serpents, in apprehension of danger to their cattle. It may be here observed that serpents are very numerous on the Northern slopes of the Alatàu, while the Southern declivities of the range, and more especially the Chu Valley, teem with *phalangia.* The latter crawl from the sandy shores of the Ili over the arid Steppe, to the West from Kastek to Kurdai and Dala-Kailar, and thence spread Westwards over the desert Steppe of Betpak-dala, as well as Eastwards to the Kebin river. There are no *phalangea* either in the mountains, where, owing to the moisture in the atmosphere the grass does not wither in the sun, or in the valleys, where the same conditions are preserved by irrigation; halts for the night should therefore be made, if possible, in such places.

Passage over the Alataŭ-Chu—Unsuccessful Reconnoissance.—From the Kastek rivulet, on the banks of which we halted for about a week, several roads lead to the Chu, across the Alataŭ Mountains. The first and most difficult is that through the Suok-Tiubé pass, which winds through wild and rocky defiles up the Kastek rivulet, after which it branches off in two directions. One, a narrow bridle-path, leads to the Kara-Bulak, and the other to the Kara-Kupus streams. This latter route is frequented by caravans, when, from the accumulation of water in the Chu, they are obliged to cross the river above Tokmak. Another route, presenting greater facilities for travellers, leads along the Bish-Mailak stream, across the upper course of the Djamanty, which likewise afterwards emerges on the Kara-Kunus, opposite Tokmak. It was along this latter that we determined to proceed.

The detachment moved rapidly up the ascent of twelve miles to the summit of the mountains and crossed the ridge on the 7th of June. I measured the mountain rising near the source of the Djamanty, and found its height to be 7450 feet above the level of the sea.

The view from this point is one of surpassing grandeur, and produces a lasting impression on the mind. In the foreground extends the broken outline of the craggy chain of the Kirghiz Alataù, beyond the Eastern extremity of which, at a distance of no less than one hundred miles, are visible the clearly-defined summits of the Celestial Mountains, overhanging Lake Issyk-Kul. Below, under the very feet of the wondering traveller, spreads the Valley of the Chu, through which the river, whose borders are fringed with green waving reeds, winds in a silvery line. The little fortress of Tokmak* bears from a distance the appearance of a small cottage in the midst of the mountain Steppe. Through the clear blue sky, the snowy peaks of the Kirghiz-Alataù glimmer in the western horizon, and the Chu Valley gradually widens in that direction.

When, after a journey of eighteen miles along a narrow and very hilly pathway, we descended

* This was in 1859; the fortress is now no longer in existence.

into this valley, we found it of a dismal and barren aspect. The grass was everywhere scorched by the sun, and it was necessary to drive the cattle into the defiles in search of pasture, so that they should recover from the fatiguing journey. No aùls or herds were visible; occasionally a solitary armed horseman, watching the movements of our corps, would appear in the distance, and, for a moment, dispel the solitude of the scene. I carefully examined the neighbourhood, which had been previously visited but by few Europeans, and discovered that we stood close to the spot where Kenisar Kasimof, celebrated in the annals of the Steppe, was killed by the Kirghizes. This turbulant marauder long incited the Russian Kirghizes to revolt during the years 1840-50; but at last lost his head on the banks of the Chu, near the mouth of the Kara-Kunus. The following are the sole recorded particulars of this event:—After having been driven by the Russian troops to the extreme Southern part of the Steppe, he here encountered new opponents in the Kara-Kirghizes. The treachery and continual depredations of Kenisar at last so exasperated the long-suffering Dikokamenni Kirghizes, that they flayed him alive and boiled his body in a cauldron, and his head, after being struck off, was exhibited at Kopal and Tashkend. The Russian Government rewarded the Manap Urman, who had been the most active in the pursuit of the rebel, by conferring on him the rank of lieutenant-colonel; and gave twelve gold medals to the chiefs who had taken part in the battle at Kiklik-Sengir, in which Kenisar was taken. In 1847, soon after this event, the topographer Nifantief visited the Alataù country, and constructed the first map of it. This was the commencement of our knowledge of the regions adjoining Kokan and the Celestial Mountains.

Our halt at the Kara-kunus was marked by an untoward occurrence. The Kirghizes who accompanied us, hearing that a party of the Dikokamenni, after having paid a depredatory visit to their aùls, were on their way back, and would cross the Chu at Kiklik-Sengir, determined at all hazards to intercept the robbers. Our Kirghizes, being inferior in number to the Dikokamenni, who were about 500 strong, it was necessary to reinforce them with 50 Cossacks. But the impatience of the Asiatics had resulted in a disastrous termination of the affair before the Cossacks had time to reach the scene of action. A Sultan, a Batyr, and three Djigits were taken prisoners by the Dikokamenni

Kirghizes, and a Kirghiz of the assailing party was wounded in the chest by a spear, the point of which entering his back, pierced the lungs, and broke one of his ribs, which protruded through the skin. This man, strange to say, not only remained alive, but two days after returned to his aùl, about 53 miles distant, and was again on horseback in less than a month, as if nothing had happened!!

Whether this facility of recovery from wounds is attributable to the moderate diet of the Asiatics when on the march, or whether it is owing to the skilful surgical treatment of the native doctors, I am not prepared to say.

Geographical particulars relating to the Chu and its Valley.—As the new Russian fort of Kastek is situated in latitude 43° 3′, and the embouchure of the great Kebin, into the Chu, lies in 42° 4′, it would seem that the breadth of the Alataù in the meridian of this fort is about 30 miles. The southern slope of this latter ridge is abrupt, poor in vegetation, and affords no convenience, even for nomad life. The northern slope is richer in grasses and more plentifully irrigated. They both descend on plains, which extend high above the level of the sea. Barometrical observations, though made during a short period of time, gave the height of Kastek at 3200 feet, and 3600 feet for the bed of the Chu near the former Tokmak fort. When we consider the low level of the Syr-Daria Steppes, about Telekul-tat, Saumal-kul, Babystyn-kul, and other lakes, it is easy to account for the rapid current of the Chu. It is a turbid stream, running apparently along a horizontal plain, but watering in reality a Steppe, rising at a pretty rapid inclination. The reeds protect the banks from being washed away by the swift current, but, though they are thus defended, the water is still very muddy.

The Chu emerges from the Celestial mountains under the name of the Koshkar, and runs first in a North-Easterly direction to the lake Issyk-Kul. Its high valley contracts here in some parts into narrow ravines. After breaking through the rocky Kizyl-Ompol ridge, the Koshkar issues suddenly into the basin of a neighbouring lake, pursues its course for three miles farther, and throwing off on the East a small branch, the Kutemaldy, disappears again with the whole body of its waters into the mountains. The wild gorge through which it rushes bears the name of Boam. In order to form an idea of its rapidity at this part, it is sufficient to say that from Issyk-Kul to the old Tokmak fort, a distance of 47 miles, it has a fall of 1600 feet, which is much greater than that of the Volga over its whole course of 2067 miles, from its source to Astrakhan. Even 20 miles after it emerges from the mountains, the swiftness of its current is not less than 10 feet per second.

The valley of the Chu, which commences at the mouth of the Kebin and Djel-aryk, rapidly widens towards the West. Already at Pishpek it is no less than 11 miles across from North to South; farther to the West, near It-Kichu, the distance between the mountains on the right and left bank, becomes still greater. There are few places on the surface of the earth where the dryness of the atmosphere reaches such an extreme point, as it did here on the 10th June, the humidity of the atmosphere on that day being expressed at 0.12! This figure is the lowest hitherto obtained in any country. Humboldt, Ehrenberg, and Rose made observations on the dryness of the air in the Steppes bordering the Irtysh, when they got 0.16 as a result. Even the Khorassan expedition of 1858 did not find it lower than 0.14 in Northern Persia. The effect of this dryness appears in the monotony and paucity of the vegetable kingdom of the Chu valley, and in its little adaptability for settlements. The majestic power of nature presents itself here in striking contrast to the impotence of man, and it can be safely asserted that until the Caspian is connected with the Black Sea, its waters reduced to the same level as those of the ocean, and their surface spread over a portion of the Volga, Turkmen, and Orenburg Steppes, so long will the greater part of Central Asia remain incapable of development.

As the valley of the Chu gradually widens, its resemblance to a desert becomes stronger. Only along the Southern borders of the plain, a zone, well-watered, and consequently marked with verdure and groves of apricot and other trees, extends along the base of the Alataù mountains. On the North bank of the Chu its tributaries terminate with the Dali-Kaipar rivulet, beyond which, farther to the West, spreads a barren waste. It is strange that, notwithstanding the melancholy and inhospitable nature of this region, it was visited and described much earlier than even the Trans-Ili region. Information respecting it is contained in the works of Pospelof, Burnashef, Teliatnikof, and Potanin. Additional particulars were gathered by Colonel Schultz, who was sent to the Chu in 1852 from Siberia, to explore the surrounding country with a view to its military capabilities and prospect of agricultural development. "At ordinary times," says that officer, "the depth of water in the Chu, from the Tulu tomb to Sauman-kul Lake, is not less than two feet, which increases to a fathom and a half at full water during spring, when the depressed banks become submerged. At this period, caravans are unable to ford the river, and must therefore construct rafts of reeds, bound together by ropes of camel hair, on which they transport their goods across, forcing the cattle to swim the river. As the waters subside the river becomes fordable in many places, the most frequented fords being those at Kazangan, Tasty, Toi-tiubé, Bish-kurgan, and Kara-utkul. Fish are pretty plentiful in the river, particularly in the adjoining lake of Beger-kul. Venomous insects are less numerous in the lower valley of the Chu than in the upper part of its course. Gnats and moths on the other hand are a positive scourge to man and beast alike. The abundance of these insects is owing to the great quantity of reeds, which, it should be observed, line both banks of the Chu from Tokmak. The height of these reeds is sometimes three fathoms, and innumerable boars, and even tigers, find shelter in these jungle-like recesses.

"The tiger is common in the Steppe, throughout

Central Asia, particularly in the reeds and copses along the banks of the rivers. In the Trans-Ili region this animal prowls in the mountains, and has even been shot near Vernoé. Beyond the Ili, however, tigers are generally not so numerous as on the Syr-Daria (Jaxartes) about Fort Perofski. Northwards, in the heart of the Steppe, the range of this animal extends as far as Kopal, *i. e.*, to 45° latitude; and isolated individuals have been encountered farther North than this comparatively high parallel. Towards the East, in Manchjuria, the large wild cat is found much farther North, in fact up to the 49th and even 50th parallel. Owing to the abundance of food, the latter attains, in these regions, a great size."

As a pendent to these purely geographical observations on the Chu region, I must add a few words relative to the Barren Desert. They will serve to explain why our knowledge of these parts must necessarily be limited to a dry enumeration of local objects, without touching on the people who only stray into these wilds by chance. "The Betpak-dala," say Pospelof and Burnashef, "is covered with thorns and wormwood; owing to the scarcity of water it is uninhabited, and the wells, which are few in number, often contain bad water.

Although in the spring, caravans may obtain a supply of this element from the thawing snows, in the summer they are obliged at their night halts to dig wells two fathoms below the surface. The whole breadth of the Steppe, from North to South, along the road from Semipalatinsk to Tashkend, is one hundred and twenty miles. On its Southern side, or more properly in its depressed valley, salt marshes are numerous; these overflow in spring when the snows dissolve, but become completely dry during the hot weather. A fine acrid dust is carried off from their surface by the wind, which blows frequently and with great violence from the East. On the South of the Chu, the appearance of the Steppe changes; the salt marshes and half-exposed clayey tracts of country are replaced by dry sands, on which here and there grow the Saksaul, Djuzgun, Djeralchik, and other plants of the prickly species. On the journey from the banks of the Chu to Lake Kara-kul, a distance of thirty-three miles, there is not a single well in this arid desert. Caravans are therefore obliged to supply themselves with water at their halting-places for the night, and carry it in leathern bags, as is the custom in Nubia, Arabia, and the Sahara.

Brief Account of the Country lying South of the Chu.—The immense hollow occupied by Lake Issyk-Kul and the Chu valley, limits the mountainous country of the Dikokamenni Kirghizes, and the Khanat of Kokan on the North. A line of Kokanian towns and fortified settlements, extends Southward from the Chu, along the route from Tokmak to Fort Perovski. The Western portion of this country is occupied by the Kara-taù ridge, which, commencing at about ninety miles from Akmechet, stretches in an E.S.E. direction, and forms a rugged chain, whose Northern declivities have a very steep inclination, while those on the South slope gently to the plain. At the very base of the mountains, on the North side, are two Kokanian forts, Suzak and Cholok-kurgan, which have each small outlying settlements. The roads from Tashkend to Petropavlovsk and Troitsk lead past these forts. The passage over the Kara-taù mountains on these routes to Turkestan and Tashkend is effected through three mountain passes — Suùndyk, Karagyr, and Saùskandyk. The first of these is the most easily traversed, and occurs on the road between Suzak and Turkestan. Caravans proceeding this way to Petropavlovsk, journey three days from the foot of the mountains to the River Chu, at about thirty miles from the point at which it falls into Lake Saùman-kul. The passage over the sandy Steppe in this direction presents greater facilities than that from Cholok-kurgan to Kazangan-utkul. In some places whole forests of the Saksaul are met with. The grass is throughout good, and the water in the wells sweet. The barren Steppe again commences on reaching the Northern side of the Chu, and the route by way of Uvanas-kuduk is as tedious as that to Tius-Bulak, a settlement in the Betpak-Dala Steppe, on the road from Kazangan-Utkul. The Kara-taù mountains, I may here remark, are at present occupied by the descendants of Kenisar, and the remnants of his horde. They are the most fierce plunderers on the whole route from Tashkend to the Siberian line.

East of the meridian of Cholok-Kurgan, the only objects of attention are the Karakul lakes, overgrown with masses of reeds, and the Boroldai mountain range. These localities have apparently been visited by but one European, namely, Müller, in 1739.

On the authority of Potanin's "Itinerary," I have altered the configuration of Lake Karakul from that ordinarily given it on maps. With regard to the Talas, we are more acquainted with this river at its middle course, near Aulie-Ata, than at its lower portion. In the list of astronomical points fixed by the Jesuit missionaries, who were employed by the Emperor Tsian-Lun, we find one point selected on this river, in latitude 42° 30°, and longitude 91° 37′ east of Ferro (73° 42′ 48″ E. of Greenwich); but whether this is the determination of Aulie-Ata or another point, in the absence of more recent data, it is difficult to ascertain. Generally speaking, the observations of latitude made by the Jesuits are reliable, which is not the case with those of longitude. I am of opinion that the labours of Reguip, Bouvé, Gerbillon, Ferbiste, &c., in the reign of Han, in China Proper, in Manchjuria and Mongolia, are more accurate than those of Hallerstein, Arochi and Espigny, in Turkestan and Dzungaria.

The accompanying Itinerary (v. Appendix 1 F) gives some particulars of the route between Cholok-Kurgan and Aulie-Ata, along the northern slopes of the Boroldai range. The Talas river, like the Chu, has no good pasturage on its banks, which, with its valley, are both overgrown with reeds. The river is pretty abundantly supplied with water where it first issues from the mountain, at Aulie-Ata, although fordable at this point. Lower down it becomes gradually narrower, till nothing but a small stream of water debouches into Lake Kara-kul. Above Aulie-Ata it flows through a narrow valley, and its sources lie in the vicinity of the Kashgar basin, almost on the same meridian as Pishpek.

A real *terra incognita* extends beyond the Talas, as far as Ferganah. In this classification, I comprehend the country between the parallels of Aulie-Ata and Namangan, before reaching the more remote table-lands of Central Asia. On the strength of information I obtained on my journey, and according to the accounts of a few travellers who have visited the South-Western part of the Khanat of Kokan, two main chains appear to extend here; one on the Northern side of Chirchik, terminating with the Kyzyrkurt mountains, rather farther to the North than Tashkend; the other, stretching Southwards from Chirchik, its South-Western extremity being formed by the Kendyr-taù range. We are acquainted with two routes which cross these mountains, or skirt their base; one running Eastwards from Aulie-Ata to Namangan; the other from Turkestan to Kokan, approaching the Kyzyrkurt range, and then crossing the Kendyr-tàu.

The Dikokamenni Horde.—With the great Kirghiz Horde and its subdivisions, of which I have given a short account in the preceding pages, we are more or less acquainted from Levchin's work on this subject, as well as from other sources. But our information respecting the Kara-Kirghizes, otherwise Buruts, or Dikokamenni Kirghizes, is exceedingly limited. The earliest reliable particulars respecting them, (and even these must be received with caution), have been strung together from Chinese sources by Klaproth and Père Hyacinthe, and a few desultory remarks respecting this Horde are to be found in the works of Wood, Khanikof, and Veliaminof-Zernof. A more systematic description was drawn up in 1851, by MM. Nifantief and Voronin, and presented to the Russian Geographical Society. An examination of all these materials will show that the ethnography of the Buruts is still very imperfect.

For the following details regarding the Dikokamenni Horde, and particularly for those bearing on the tribes whose haunts lie close to the Russian frontiers, we are indebted to Mr. Bardashef, the intelligent interpreter attached to the chief of the Alataù district:

" 'Dikokamenni' is the name given by the Russians to the people who chiefly frequent the mountains about Lake Issyk-Kul, and call themselves Kirghizes, in contradistinction to the Kaisaks (or more properly, Koisaks). The former race has no distinct history, and may hardly be considered to belong to the aboriginal population of the country, in which the Nogais (or Kalmyks) were formerly dominant. One portion of them, it is certain, migrated to the Thian-Shan mountains from the upper part of the Yenisei, where, so early as the seventeenth century, they were engaged in hostilities against the Russians. But the Kara-Kirghizes usually claim to be of Western origin, and profess to have once inhabited countries occupied even to the present time by Turkish tribes. This, it must be allowed, is borne out by their language, which is the Uigur dialect of the Turkish, with an admixture of foreign words. The imagination of the people has surrounded with romance the cradle of their race, as having lain in the mountains bordering on the Naryn and the Southern margin of Lake Issyk-Kul. The following is one of the legends to this effect, which, however, has but little to recommend it in point of fancy, and does not convey a very favourable idea of the æsthetic condition of the Kirghiz :—

"'The daughter of a certain Khan was in the habit of taking long walks, accompanied by forty maidens. Returning home after one of these promenades, she found her aùl completely pillaged;

but one living animal having been left in it—a red dog (Kyzyl-Taigan). By this untoward sire, all the forty handmaidens,' says the tradition, 'became pregnant, and, in memory of them, their descendants assumed the name of Kirghizes (Kryk-Kys, forty maidens).' This legend is occasionally given with additions and variations. Another version says, that the princess and her attendants were miraculously fecundated after having tasted the foam of the lake when agitated, and were in consequence expelled from their homes by their relatives. They wandered about in the desert for a long time. The forty maidens, regarding the princess as the cause of their misfortunes, at last rebelled against her, and drove her beyond the Chu. Here the poor daughter of the Khan was found by the progenitor of the Kirghizes, who installed her as one of his wives, and whom she speedily presented with a goodly son, named Kyrgyz-Beg. This personage is considered the true founder of the Dikokamenni race. He was persecuted by his other brothers on account of his dubious origin, and portioned off on the death of his father; ultimately, however, he triumphed over his brothers, having succeeded in stealing from his mother's 'yurt,' the Kumis stick and bridle, which are symbols of priority of birth."

From Kyrgyz-Beg, the traditions become more distinct, and lose their imaginative character. The proper names of the Kara-Kirghiz chief ancestors are, nevertheless, very doubtful.

Kyrgyz-Beg had two grand-sons: Abl and Kovl. The latter was the founder of the Kokche, Soru, Mundus, and Kytai tribes, which are conjointly designated Sol—*i. e.* Left (Western Buruts of Klaproth). From Abl there sprang ten tribes, forming the On, or Right division (Eastern Buruts). The tribes forming it are: the Bogu, Sary-Baguiche, Sultu, Cherik, Sayak, Adyginé, Baguiche, Monandyr, Djadygyr, and Tungatar. All these petty roaming mountain tribes occupy the country between Badakshan and Kungei-Alataù, from the Tekes and Muzart passes to Kokan and Samarkand. The tribes with which we are best acquainted are the Dikokamenni, Sary-Baguiche, Sultu, and Bogu. The first-named at present wander along the upper course of the Chu, as far as the Western extremity of Issyk-Kul. They number about 10,000 yurts, or not less than 40,000 individuals. They are a warlike race, and their most celebrated chiefs at present are Umbet-Ali, Turegildy, Ruskul-Beg, Adil, and Djantai. Eastward of the Sary-Baguiches, along the Tiubé, Karkara, and Tekes, roam the

Bogus, whose late high chief, Buram-bai, was the first of the Kara-Kirghizes who swore fealty to Russia. At the present time, the Bogus have no influential chiefs, and the tribe being split up into numerous sub-divisions, has lost its former weight, particularly from its strife with the Sary-Baguiches. After these two sub-hordes, the nearest to the Russian boundaries is the Sultys, a small tribe numbering 6000 yurts, but the most warlike in the whole Dikokamenni Horde. The Sultys inhabit the Kirghiz-Alataù mountains, from Tokmak to Aulie-Ata, and their camping-grounds are conterminous on the East with those of the Sary-Baguiches. Their most influential chief is Djan-Karatch. On the South, the Sultys spread only as far as the valley of the Talas, beyond which they are succeeded by various tribes of the right and left divisions of the Horde.

The Sayaks roam on the Southern side of the Celestial mountains, along the upper course of the Naryn; to the Eastward of them, as far as Aksù and Nuan to Kucha, are the camping-grounds of the Cheriks. These tribes, with their neighbours, the Baguiches, descend in winter from the slopes of the Thian-Shan into the valley of the Tarym, and thence push forward as far as Kashgar,

Yarkend, and even Khotan. The geographical distribution of the other branches of the Horde is difficult to determine; it is certain, however, that they occupy the whole system of the Bolor, Badakshan, Karatigen, and Vokhan chains, and frequent the neighbourhoods of Ush, Andijan, Kokan, and even Tashkend, to the N.W., and Samarkand to the S.W. The influence of these tribes in the Khanat of Kokan is very great; the first minister of the Khan, Alym-Beg is a scion from the Andygine tribe, while to that of Karatigen belongs the well-known leader of the Kokan army, who in 1860 attacked Kastek.

The political condition of the Dikokamenni Kirghizes is at once varied, uncertain, and ill-defined. Some of them, as for instance, the Bogus, and part of the Sary-Baguiches, profess to be subject to Russia, although internally they are not governed by that country, and only occasionally appeal to the Russian authorities for the settlement of their own intestine disputes. Other tribes, such as the Sultu, Adygine, Kytai, &c., of the Sol or Left division, own allegiance to Kokan, and pay tribute to that Khanat. A third portion, composed of the Cheriks and Baguiches, pay the Chinese a land-tax, although they govern themselves. Lastly, the tribes on the extreme South, occupying the Bolor mountains, Karatigen, and Badakshan, are, partly independent, and partly subject to Bokhara, Kunduz, or Kokan, with which States they are, nevertheless, often at enmity. Respecting the inhabitants of these highlands of Asia, we have scarcely any information. Burnes, in his "Travels to Bokhara," only casually observes that the Kirghizes, natives of the Pamir whom he met, have flat faces, and resemble the Turkmen. In other places he mentions that their food consists of meat and milk, and that flour is not known to them. But neither Burnes nor Wood touches on the moral condition of these mountaineers.

Among the Dikokamenni Kirghizes upon the outskirts of Russia, there are no aristocratic races like the Sultan families in the Kaisak Hordes. The people consequently form one equal mass, differing only according to their sub-division in branches. The Kara-Kirghizes are governed by Manaps, or elders, who at one time received their titles by election, though these have now become hereditary. The word Manap literally means a tyrant, in the ancient Greek sense. It was at first the proper name of an elder distinguished for his cruelty and unrelenting spirit; from him the appellation became general to all Kirghiz rulers. In addition to the Manaps, who, as already observed, are not of aristocratic lineage, the Kirghizes have Bis, who settle their differences. These Bis found their judgments on the customs of the people, but it is scarcely necessary to say that they are far from being impartial. Truth, throughout Central Asia, is subservient to the powerful, and the ruler who governs leniently commands but little respect.

The name of Kara-Kirghiz, or Black Kirghiz, may be traced to the undistinguished origin of their chiefs, the Manaps, who, according to Kirghiz phraseology, do not spring from the "white bone" of the Sultans. It must be remarked that although the organization of the people is democratic, its elders enjoy great power. The influence of a Manap is particularly strong, when he is likewise a Batyr—*i. e.* a brave and dashing leader of marauding expeditions. Burambai, the ruler of the Bogus, was a chief of this description. In general, the Manaps do not derive any regular income from the people, but receive voluntary contributions, and impose fines on those they find guilty of misdemeanours. I need not point out the evils that arise from such a state of things, or the facilities which the Manaps and Bis enjoy for satisfying at once their ambition and cupidity.

Life and Condition of the Kara-Kirghizes.—The Kara-Kirghizes, like the nomads of the neighbouring Steppe, derive all their wealth from cattle breeding; but the Dikokamenni are generally not so well off as the Kirghizes of the Great and Middle Hordes. Very few amongst them possess as many as two thousand horses or three thousand sheep. They likewise keep fewer camels, but on the other hand, they have an excellent breed of oxen, which are employed for traversing the mountains. The camels are the ordinary double-humped or Bactrian camel of classical writers, and the single-humped, or dromedary, which latter is universally preferred. Although the cows belonging to the Dikokamenni are of a large size, they yield but little milk, and then only when with calf. Yàks are kept instead of cows by the Kara-Kirghizes, by whom they are called "Kudos." From these more milk is obtained than from ordinary cattle. Their sheep are of the Kirghiz breed, but have finer fleeces. The horses are small, but being hardy, are well adapted for the mountainous country. The cattle are never subject to epidemics; the only disease that attacks them is the Sarpa, a sort of dry rot, by which they generally lose their hoofs. Until quite recently the Bogus were the largest cattle breeders ; now, however, the flocks and herds of the Sary-Baguiches are fully as large. Both these tribes are richer than any of the rest. The Dikokamenni Kirghizes are generally employed in agriculture. Although the soil is mostly clayey, and becomes dreadfully parched by the sun, yet by an ingenious system of artificial irrigation, it yields good harvests, millet yielding seventy and wheat eighty fold. The richest land lies at the Eastern extremity of Lake Issyk-Kul, along the Tiub and Djirgalan, the Zaŭkŭ, and in the neighbourhood of Tokmak and Pishpek; along the Northern and Southern shores of Issyk-Kul, the soil is stony and therefore but little cultivated. The Kara-Kirghizes sow principally millet, wheat, barley (for horses), and kupock, a smaller kind of millet, from which they distil a spirit.

The chase is not, as with most semi-barbarous races, a special pursuit, by the Kara-Kirghizes, although the mountains abound with game. Occasionally, however, they hunt the wild sheep, antelope, and goat for pastime. The deer is killed for its horns alone, which when containing blood, are highly prized by the Chinese as a medicine, and sold at from £8 to £25 per pair, according to their quality. Besides the eagle, the Dikokamenni kill foxes and martens, whose skins they dispose of to Tartar merchants, though not in great quantities. They likewise hunt bears and wolves, but do not know how to prepare the skins, which the rich Kara-Kirghizes accordingly use undressed as carpets for their tents.

The Dikokamenni Kirghizes are not fond of fish, and catch but little, notwithstanding that Lake Issyk-Kul might yield the man abundant supply of this delicious food. Carp, in particular, are very plentiful in its waters.

The chief staple of industry among the Kara-Kirghizes is the preparation of felts, which are in great demand on account of their durability. The Dikokamenni who range along the Talas manufacture the best. The Kara-Kirghiz felt hats, conical in shape, with a turned-up brim, are much esteemed throughout all the Hordes. The women weave a rough material of camel's hair, called "Armiachina" by the Russians. The dress of a Dikokamenni Kirghiz consists of a Khalat, or long robe, with wide pantaloons, or "Chembars." A shirt is also sometimes worn, but this article of clothing is not taken off, but is suffered to fall to pieces on the person of the wearer.

The Dikokamenni Kirghizes, with the exception of those in the vicinity of towns, do not traffic directly in any of their own productions. They even do not drive horses to Kokan, Kashgar, or Kuldja. All the trade in their country is carried on by Tashkend, Kokan and Kashgar caravans, and partly by Russian merchants. These supply the Kara-Kirghizes, with all their requirements, and sometimes remain a whole year among their aùls. From Kashgar the Dikokamenni are supplied with cotton stuffs, khalats, biaz, printed cottons, dried fruit, &c. These goods the merchants exchange with great profit for sheep. Russian goods are brought hither by Tartars, who find a sale for the inferior articles which they cannot dispose of in the more civilized parts of the Russian empire. They thus sell cheap cotton prints, nankeen, calico, leather, ironware, small looking-glasses, ear-rings, &c. Metallic productions and leather are in very great demand. Oxen, sheep, fox, and marten skins are procured in exchange. The profits of the merchants are very great, as a yard of red cloth worth about three shillings is exchanged for three sheep;

a hide of "yufta" for seven and eight sheep; while cast-iron and iron wares are sold at still higher prices. The camping grounds of the Kara-Kirghizes are besides yearly visited by Chinese from Kuldja, under pretence of verifying the boundaries, and supply the Horde with tea, rice, tobacco, and silks, at moderate rates; or in exchange for sheep. Coloured silks are obtained from Kokan and Tashkend, though in small quantities, and chiefly for the rich Manaps and their wives.

As already mentioned, those Kara-Kirghizes, who are subject to Kokan, pay a yearly tribute to that Khanat. This tribute is called a Ziaket, and consists of the following imposts, viz.—The Tunluk-Ziaket, or smoke tax, amounting to a sheep from each tent. Koi-Ziaket, or sheep tax; one sheep out of every fifty, forty, or twenty, according to circumstances. Harazela, an impost on agricultural products; one sheep from each corn-barn. Besides these taxes, the Dikokamenni Kirghizes contribute three sheep from each tent towards the maintenance of troops. The Sultys and a portion of the Sary-Baguiches annually supply the Kokanian troops with 5500 puds—about forty-four quarters—of wheat and millet. They are also obliged to entertain the Ziaketches (tax-gatherers), who make their circuits in large parties, at their own cost. It is certain that the pressure of these taxes does not produce continual disturbances, only because the Kokanians profess the same creed as the Kara-Kirghizes. In those parts where the Dikokamenni pay tribute to China, they stand in quite different relations to the predominating population, with whom they are constantly at war, as exemplified by their driving away the cattle of the Chinese as well as those of the Kalmyks.

The Dikokamenni are in fact more addicted to cattle stealing, than any of the other Kirghiz tribes, and their "Barantas" or marauding expeditions are by no means conducted in that chivalrous spirit that characterizes those undertaken by the Kirghizes of the Hordes subject to Russia. The Barantas of the Kara-Kirghizes are organized on a military plan, but with the avowed object of robbing some neighbour both of his life as well as his property. The attacks of the Sary-Baguiche on the aùls of the Bogus, between whom there exists a deadly feud, are, in particular, attended with great bloodshed. However, the valour of the wandering mountaineers is mostly limited to cattle lifting and pursuing a flying enemy; as soon as there is a prospect of a fair stand-up encounter, a Kirghiz, after galloping half a mile after his foe, will discreetly turn his horse's head, and retreat without engaging him. In their relations with the Russian Kirghizes of the Great Horde, the Dikokamenni exhibit the darker side of their character; prowling across the mountains in small parties, they steal the cattle of their neighbours, by two or three head at a time. The Russian Kirghizes mercilessly hunt down these petty thieves. Thus, Suranchi, a Kirghiz-Batyr, or warrior-chief, whom I knew, was in the habit of sending out his "Djigits" nightly in the summer to intercept these plunderers in the mountains with their booty. When caught, they were bound in fetters, and only regained their liberty when ransomed by their tribe. Suranchi on one occasion offered me one of these prisoners as a present. The unhappy wretch was brought forward with his hands tied and a heavy chain round his neck; at my request he was liberated and made to understand that the Russians did not require slaves, but wished all to live in freedom and amity. "Kulduk, thank him, dog," said Suranchi, as he struck the Dikokamenni, who had remained silent, on the head with his whip. Nevertheless these unfriendly relations do not prevent the Russian Kirghizes from intermarrying with the Dikokamenni, and during my stay, while the tribes were at open variance, many of our own Kirghizes visited the aùls of the Dikokamenni with the object of seeing their brides, cousins, &c.

The spiritual condition of the Buruts is on the same low level as their social state of development. In justice they must be viewed as children of nature, in the most mournful sense of the term. All their conceptions and ideas of morality are founded upon the rudest beliefs and prejudices. Before the arrival of the Russians at Lake Issyk-Kul, the only sources of learning in the Horde were wandering Tashkendians who taught the children to spell through the first chapter of the Koran, but without explaining its meaning. Since the appearance of the Russian Tartars the number of those who can read and write has somewhat increased, and the want of education is beginning to be more felt, so much so that many Dikokamenni Kirghizes, not having the means of instruction among themselves, send their children to their friends in the Great Horde, in whose aùls Tartar teachers are almost always to be found. But even at present there is hardly one Kara-Kirghiz among a thousand who can read and write, and the majority of their Manaps are as ignorant as the mass of the people themselves. I was myself a witness to the amusing astonishment of one Manap, when he was shown a document bearing his own seal, in which he had confessed to a "Baranta;" he little thought that in affixing his seal to this piece of paper, his enemy had made him confirm a deposition of his own guilt.

The religion of the Dikokamenni Kirghizes is Islamism; their Mahomedanism, however, is very superficial, particularly among the tribes adjacent to China. Some Kara-Kirghizes are not alone unacquainted with the ninety-nine names of Allah, but do not even know the name of their prophet! Drunkenness, which is strictly forbidden by the Koran, is not regarded as a sin by the Dikokamennis. Mendé, a venèrable Manap of threescore years, after drinking about two quarts of brandy during the day, boasted that he could gallop any distance in the evening without losing his saddle. In many other things they openly violate the prescribed rules of the Koran through ignorance. Strangely enough, some customs of Shamanism are still retained by the people. According to Mr. Bardashef, the Kara-Kirghizes worship fire, and celebrate this religious rite on the night of Thursday. Grease is thrown over the flames, round which nine lamps are placed. Prayers are also read if a literate person be present, during which the worshippers remain prostrate.

The Kara-Kirghizes likewise reverence the remaining monuments of an ancient race which formerly inhabited the country. Near Tokmak there is a high brick column held in great veneration, in which, according to popular tradition, a certain Khan built up his daughter after her death, in order to preserve her body from venomous insects!

The old relics of their own people are yet more highly reverenced. The tombs of their ancestors are held sacred, and they are generally surrounded by stone walls. To remove the remains or any appurtenance belonging to the dead is considered a crime. Public games, or Baigas, as among the other Kirghizes, are instituted in commemoration of deceased persons, and these sports are celebrated on a larger scale, if the departed had been wealthy and powerful. Races, however, constitute the chief attraction of these Baigas. As the Dikokamenni are poorer than other Kirghiz tribes, the prizes given away are not so valuable as those of the Middle and Great Hordes. There, as many as nine nines, or 81 head of cattle, and even slaves occasionally, fall to the winner. Although the prizes of the Buruts, on such occasions, likewise usually consist of male and female slaves, they are not so profuse in awarding cattle. Wrestling is also practised at these Baigas; and another coarser form of amusement is to seize a coin with the mouth out of a vessel filled with sour milk. This, as is usual with a rude, ignorant population, is the favourite game, and excites great amusement. The use of the hands is not allowed, and the dexterity of the venturesome Kirghiz must be confined to his mouth. His exertions to catch the coin are sometimes so severe, that blood flows from the nose and ears; at this stage the place of the player is taken by another thirsty Kirghiz, avaricious for the money.

In 1860, a Sara-Baguiche poet or rhapsodist was attached to the Russian expeditionary column. He every evening attracted round him a crowd of gaping admirers, who greedily listened to his stories and songs. His imagination was remarkably fertile in creating feats for his hero—the son of some Khan—and took most daring flights into the regions of marvel. The greater part of his rapturous recitation was improvised by him as he proceeded, the subject alone being borrowed usually from some tradition. His wonderfully correct intonation, which enabled every one who even did not understand the words, to guess their meaning, and the pathos and fire which he skilfully imparted to his strain, showed that he was justly entitled to the admiration of the Kirghizes as their chief bard. When the chief of the expedition gave an entertainment to the Kirghizes on the Kutemaldy, this poet loudly and eloquently extolled the virtues of the giver of the feast—probably with a view to a noble largesse, while his fellow countrymen seemed to appreciate the song of their bard fully as much as the pillau that they had been treated with, though to do them justice, they brought to the latter an excellent and by no means fastidious appetite.

CHAPTER VIII.

History of the Establishment of Russian Rule on the Sea of Aral and on the River Syr-Daria (Jaxartes) from 1847 to 1862.

I.

General Review of the Orenburg Region and its Future Importance.—First Appearance of the Russians in these Parts.—The Sea of Aral and the Syr-Daria.—Establishment of Russian Rule in the Steppe since 1833.—Erection of Forts in the Steppe and on the Shores of the Sea of Aral.—The Aral Flotilla.

1847—1852.

In an administrative sense, there is comprehended under the Orenburg region a vast extent of country, reaching on the North to the river Kama, on the

West to the Volga, on the South to the Caspian and Aral Seas and river Syr-Daria, and on the East to the Sary-Su river and Ulu-Táu mountains. Besides the governments of Orenburg and Samara, and the lands of the Orenburg and Ural Cossacks, this region contains within itself extensive Steppes, occupied by roaming Kirghizes. Notwithstanding the thinness of its population, and the barren and desert Steppes, which separate the commercial points on the Caspian from the fertile oases that occur along the course of the rivers Syr and Amu-Darias, and, in spite of the difficulty of communication between the Eastern provinces of Russia and the countries of Central Asia, this region is of great importance to Russia. And although its present condition is capable of great improvement, there is not the slightest doubt but that a brilliant future awaits it—that it will become the great highway of trade between Central Asia and Western Europe, and that Russian productions will eventually be exchanged in its markets for Asiatic goods.

A detailed and systematic account of the gradual advance of Russia in this region, and of her relations with Central Asia, will be subsequently presented to the reader. For the present, in order to make him familiar with the more recent events on the Syr-Daria, we shall confine ourselves to a sketch of the progress of Russia here during the last fifteen years, alluding but briefly to the occurrences prior to that period.

The spread of Russia beyond the Volga and Ural commenced in the sixteenth century, with the fall of the kingdom of Kazan and Astrakhan. But neither the internal condition of Russia, nor the political circumstances of the period, imparted any significance to this movement Eastward. On the accession of Mikhail Fedorovitch to the throne, the Don Cossacks, who had settled in the sixteenth century on the Yaika, or river Ural, swore fealty to the Tsardom of Moscow, and the advance of Russia on the East commences from this river.

In 1574, the original inhabitants of the Orenburg region—the Bashkirs, voluntarily petitioned for the construction of a Russian town in their country. With the foundation of Ufa, 49° 40′ N., 50° 20′ E, Samara, 49° 30′ N. 53° E, and other towns, Bashkiria became permanently attached to Russia, and all the insurrections that took place after that period terminated with a cruel punishment of the rebellious Bashkirs.

Peter the Great was the first Russian Sovereign who, with characteristic penetration, perceived the importance and significance for Russia of the Trans-Volga region. In 1722, when in Astrakhan, he thus expressed himself on this subject:—"Although these Kirghizes are a roaming and fickle people, their Steppe is the key and gates to all the countries of Central Asia."

Five years after the death of Peter the Great, Abdul-Hair, Khan of the smaller Kirghiz Horde, oppressed by the Dzungarians and harassed by the Bashkirs and Kalmyks, sought the protection of Russia, and swore allegiance to the Empress Anne in 1732. In order that his subjection should involve practical results, it was necessary to remove the Russian military boundary much farther southwards. In this manner, owing to the exertions of the first Russian governors of the region—Kirilov, Tatischef and Nepluyef—the towns of Omsk and Uralsk, between which, up to 1730, there existed only the one small town of Sakmarek, became connected together by a line of settlements along the shores of the rivers Ural and Uya. Dating from this period, neither the constant rebellions of the Bashkirs, the inroads of the Kirghizes, nor even the insurrection of Pugachef, could weaken the power of Russia in this region; and a hundred years after the submission of the Kirghizes and Karakalpaks,

Russia had established herself firmly on the Sea of Aral and along the lower branches of the Syr-Daria; respecting which latter occupation a few particulars must here be given.

The Greeks, speaking of the Jaxartes and Oxus, unanimously and positively assert that both these rivers disembogued into the Caspian. From this an opinion has been entertained, that the Sea of Aral formed, in ancient times, a part of the Caspian. Humboldt, however, does not admit this, and holds, in spite of the recent formations of the Ust-Urt, (the isthmus between the two seas), that the connection could never have existed. The first allusions to the existence of the Sea of Aral, are made by European travellers in the sixteenth century. The Russians, however, had long been aware of the existence of the "Blue" sea, as they called it, and into which the river Syr discharged itself on the East,* but having no close intercourse with Western Europe, they could not communicate their knowledge. It was only with the subjection of the Kirghiz Steppes, after 1840, that reliable accounts were received respecting the Sea of Aral, which covers an area of about 23,000 square geographical miles. From

* From the "Book of the Bolchago Cherteja," a kind of Russian Doomsday Book.

the large body of water discharged into it by the Amu-Daria (Oxus) and Syr-Daria (Jaxartes), the lake, although brackish, is not so salt as the waters of the ocean. The fish that are found in it, are small sturgeons, dog-fish, carp, and a peculiar herring. Seals, which are very common in the Caspian, do not exist in the Aral. There are no shoals in the centre of the sea, and they only occur near the sandy and depressed coasts. This sea belongs to the stormy and troubled class of waters. The wind freshens suddenly, raising high waves, and leaving, on subsiding, a heavy swell, which renders tacking impossible. Even winds, blowing continuously for several days, are extremely rare; there is either a complete lull in the atmosphere, or heavy winds, and frequently severe gales. The vessels best suited for navigating this sea are iron steamers drawing little water; and good anchorage grounds, protected from all winds, hardly exist. The shores of the sea present the appearance of a desert. In summer, with the exception of some parts on the South-West and South, they are altogether uninhabited. In winter, Kirghiz encampments occur along the Northern and Eastern shores, as also on the adjoining islands. The Northern coast is low and sandy, and being very sinuous, forms many bays, peninsulas, and capes. The "Bolchie" and Malie Barksuki sands abut on this part of the sea. The Western shore is bordered by the precipitous sides of the Ust-Urt plateau. The Southern is low, and consists of reeds, which cover the drift mud brought down by the Amu-Daria, and of sand thrown up by the waves. The Eastern shore, adjacent to which are the Kyzyl-kum sands, is, in general, depressed, sandy, and overgrown with bushes and reeds.

The Syr-Daria takes its source in several streams in the snowy Belur-Tag (Bolor-Dagh of Indian authorities) mountain range, extending on the Western confines of Chinese Turkestan.

The sources of geographical information respecting the river Syr-Darya, are exclusively Russian. Almost to the commencement of the present century we had no certain accounts of the river, while in Russia, we find already in the Book of the *Bolchago-Cherteja,* sufficiently accurate descriptions of the "Blue" or Aral Sea, the Kara-Kum sands, the rivers Syr-Daria and Sary-Su, and of the Kara-taù mountains, and since the extension of the protection of Russia to the Karakalpaks in 1732, our knowledge of this region has gradually increased.

The River Syr, after passing the Kara-taù range, pursues its course first in a North-Westerly direction, and then Westerly to the Sea of Aral, and divides into a considerable number of branches and irrigating canals, without receiving into itself a single rivulet. Part of the Syr, from its source to the Kara-Uziak branch, is called the Djaman-Daria (bad river), probably on account of its being very tortuous along that part of its course, and not so broad, deep and rapid as at other parts. Its breadth is not uniform. In the Kokanian dominions, by the evidence of natives, it attains 400 fathoms; in Russian territory, both above and below Kara-Uziak, it is from 50 to 100, and even 250 fathoms broad. In the Djaman-Daria, however, it is considerably smaller than at other parts, not exceeding in some places 30 fathoms. The contraction of the river towards its mouth, and particularly in the Djaman-Daria, must be attributed to the uncompensated loss of a large body of water which is diverted from the main bed into innumerable branches, expansions, and irrigation canals. The observations made by Captain Ivaschinsov show that the current of this river is unequal at different parts and at different periods of the year and day. In summer, at full water, the flow above Kara-Uziak is from two and a half to four knots; in the Djaman-Daria from one to two, and below Kara-Uziak from one and a quarter to two and a half knots, increasing in rapidity at the bends to three and even five knots. During the autumnal season, when there is less water in the river, the current is considerably slower. It was besides remarked during the expedition of 1853, at the landing place of Fort Aralsk, 46°2′ N., 61° 50′ E., that the current changed during the day. It flows more rapidly in the morning at about ten or eleven o'clock, becoming weaker at about two in the afternoon, and towards evening sometimes attains its matinal rapidity. Its water, owing to this rapidity of current, and its flowing over a sandy-mud bottom, is always turbid. It quickly clears, however, when drawn for use, is perfectly sweet, and is salubrious, not only for natives, but likewise for travellers.

The depth of the river, like its width and current, also varies. Generally speaking, the Syr-Daria flows through a deep and steep-banked hollow, the depth at about one fathom from the shore being above a man's height, and then progressing from one fathom to five and six fathoms. During low water, shoals occasionally occur in some parts, particularly in the Djaman-Daria, and at the mouths of the Syr.

The Syr-Daria abounds with excellent fish. Sturgeons, dog-fish, carp, bull-heads, (*cottus**), sudaks, (somewhat resembling the perch-pike, or sandre), pike, rudd (*erythrophalmus*), &c., are among the fish caught in it. The appliances of the Kirghizes for catching fish are very rude; while the Russians, with the exception of the Fishery Company of the Sea of Aral, whose operations sometimes extend to the mouth of the Syr-Daria, only aim at supplying their own occasional wants.

The following arms and lakes occur on the right bank of the Syr-Daria:—

I. The Ber-Kazan arm, at the point where it diverges from the Syr, is twenty fathoms wide, and one and a half fathoms deep, and continues its course in a series of polders or expansions, which have local names, and are mostly overgrown with reeds. This branch finally disappears in the Kara-Uziak marshes, after a course extending over about thirty-five miles.

II. The Kara-Uziak branch has no regular bed, but consists of a labyrinth of lakes and fens, interspersed with sheets of clear water, fringed with reeds, and extends from Fort Perovski to Fort No. 2, one hundred versts in length, and from fifteen to thirty versts in breadth. Its channel is interrupted by

* *Cottus Gobio*,—or Miller's Thumb.

morasses at two distinct points—at one for forty, and at another for ten versts; and, owing to this peculiarity, the water at the mouth of this river is perfectly clear, though of a marshy taste.

III. The Kazala arm has, where it first strikes off, a well-defined bed, about twenty fathoms wide, with a depth of two fathoms, and a slight current. Further on, its energy becomes expended in reedy fens and aqueducts, so that, like the Rhine, its bed cannot be traced, and it reaches Tal-Bugut as an insignificant canal, bearing already another name! At the lower course of the Kazala the Ak-Gerik valley spreads in a Northerly direction. At times it becomes flooded, forming, then, either one large lake or a series of small lagoons.

IV. From Tal-Buguta to Aman-Utkul the right bank of the Syr forms a depressed valley, by far the greater part of which is overgrown with reeds, while in the Northern part are formed the lakes Rami, Djalangatch, Koiazdy, and Kamyshlybash, which have no springs of their own, but are fed by canals conducted from the Syr, and are, in fact, nothing more than inundations over a saline, marshy valley; the water in them is consequently brackish, and becomes decomposed, if not refreshed by the flowing stream of the Syr.

The following branches and lakes occur on the left bank of the Syr-Daria:—

I. The river Djany-Daria (in Tartar dialect Yany-Daria, or New River) is a Southern branch of the Syr, disemboguing in the S.E. part of the Sea of Aral. According to the Kirghiz, this branch was formed in the end of the last century, when the Kara-Kalpaks, driven away by the Little Kirghiz-Kaisak Horde from the lower course of the Syr, were forced to migrate elsewhere. A portion of the Kara-Kalpaks advanced up the river, and occupied the lands adjacent to the present embouchure of the Djany-Daria, and betaking themselves to agriculture, excavated a large canal, which ultimately formed a branch of the river Syr. The Kokanians, after the erection of Akmechet fort, dammed up the Djany-Daria, in order to deprive the Kirghizes and Kara-Kalpaks, who had fled from their oppression to the lower course of the river, under the protection of the Khivans, of all possibility of subsisting there and of pursuing agriculture, and to induce them by these means to settle around Ak-Mechet. This compulsory measure displeased the Khivans, and they repeatedly endeavoured to induce the Khan to demolish the dam, but their intercession was not attended with success.

II. The Kar-Bugut dam was constructed by the Kokanians two versts below the point of issue of the Djany-Daria into the Syr, near the ruins of Fort Sandyk-Kurgan, where the breadth of this branch is not more than six fathoms. The pressure of the water often destroyed the dam, in consequence of which the Kokanians made several attempts to arrest the course of the river at points higher up in its course, where the pressure of the water would be less strong. In October, 1853, the old Kokanian dam, near the ruins of Sandyk-Kurgan, which had been demolished by the Kirghiz chief, Bukhar-bai, was repaired by the Russians, with the object of raising the general level of the Syr-Daria, so as to enable steamers to navigate it; the dam, however, was ere long once more destroyed by the pressure of the water.

III. The river Kuvan-Daria flows first Southwards, then bends to the West, and, dividing into three branches, forms a lagoon, which is covered with reeds. This river over a course of fifty-five versts is sufficiently deep, with a width of about thirty fathoms and a current running from one to three knots; its banks are low and bordered with reeds, and in parts with good meadow grass. The lagoon formed by the branches of the Kuvan-Daria extends from E. to W. for seventy versts, and twenty versts in width. At a short distance from its left border, at eighty versts from what was formerly Fort No. 3, are the ruins of the deserted Khivan fort, Khodjanias.

IV. The now dried-up Daria-lyk branch, which at one time connected the Kuvan with the Djaman-Daria, was more than 120 versts in length.

V. The Bish-Aram branch flows out of the Syr at Utch-Urga settlement, its course bearing at first to the S.W. Soon after the branching off from the Syr, it separates into several streams, of which the Bish-Aram loses itself in reeds, and forms marshes. Its course extends altogether over fifty versts, and its waters are sweet.

VI. The Kara-Aryk canal, fifty versts in length, forms the direct connecting link of the river Syr-Daria with the Sea of Aral. In the lower course of the Syr such canals are very numerous, and are modestly termed *aryks* or *ditches* by the natives.

VII. From Talbugut to Aman-Utkul, the left bank of the Syr, like the right, presents a depression, which is flooded and overgown with reeds, and bears the name of Kara-Kul Lake. Its length, measured along the course of the river, is fifteen versts, by six to nine versts in width. At its S. E. part, it forms an open and rather large (Kara-Su) bay, whose depth is as much as seven fathoms.

VIII. Near the Aman-Ulkul ferry, are the two Sary-Kul lakes, whose respective areas do not exceed one verst square.

The character of the ground around the basin of the lower course of the Syr-Daria, depends on the degree in which it is affected by the waters. Thus, wherever the banks of the river or its branches are very low, either lagoons completely overgrown with thick and high reeds, or else ordinary marshes, are formed. The soil consists mostly of an alluvial mud.

The Ber-Kogan, Kara-Uziak, and Kazala branches, the upper courses of the Djany and Kuvan Darias, between what was known as Fort No. 3, and that of Hodjanias, the Bish-Aram and Utlyau branches, as well as the Syr-Daria between Tal-Bugut and Aman-Utkul, are all bordered on both banks by extensive marshes.

Where the banks are not very depressed, and therefore only occasionally submerged, thus becoming enriched with alluvial mud, there frequently occur very valuable meadow patches, but more frequently flats covered with small reeds intermixed with meadow grasses. Such spots occur in belts of varying width along the banks of the Syr and its branches; the banks of the former in particular, above the Djaman, and those of the Djany and Kuvan-Daria being almost exclusively bordered by this description of vegetation.

On these meadow lands, in addition to the description of bushes in which the Southern part of the Kirghiz Steppe abounds,—willows, wild date-trees, and poplars are found growing. Willow trees cover the greater part of the islands of the Syr, and date trees are first met with near Kazala, at some points at and beyond Fort Perovski, where they form whole woods. The poplar is comparatively rare, and is only found between Fort Perovski and Djülek.

The parts which are not exposed to inundation, form saline Steppes, on which nothing grows except bushes of wormwood, saksaùl, tamarisk, djuzgun, chingil, thorn, and many other prickly plants, all of which are usually met with on the sands and meadows. The marshes, meadow lands, and cultivated fields which closely adjoin the right bank of the Syr, from Djülek to the settlement of Ak-Suat, are bordered by saline Steppes, stretching northwards as far as Turgaef, and forming the so-called Barren Steppe. The space between the rivers Syr and Kuvan, likewise consists chiefly of saline Steppe.

Cultivated fields may exist in the meadow-land, as also in the saline Steppe itself, so long as the land is conveniently situated for artificial irrigation, by which it is moistened and fertilized with loam, and experience here has revealed the very unexpected fact that corn grows even better in saline soil than on ordinary alluvial ground! Agriculture is at present actively pursued along the right bank of the Syr from Djülek to the Djaman-Daria; and along both banks of this river below Mailibash, as well as around the deserted Hodjanias Fort, and the Russian forts Nos. 2 and 3. The existing traces of aqueducts testify that cultivation was formerly an important avocation in other parts, and especially along the right shores of the Kara-Uziak lakes, along the upper course of the Djany and Kuvan Darias, &c.

In addition to the tracts already described, considerable plains of sand are found at the lower part of the Syr. The largest of these form the

Kara-Kum sands, which occupy an extent of 225 versts in length, and from 130 to 200 versts in width, and are confined on the North by Lake Chelkar, and the lower course of the Irgiz, which, flowing from the Westward, debouches into that lake; on the West by a saline Steppe, and the Sea of Aral; on the South by the river Syr, from its mouth as far up as Ak-Suat settlement; and on the East by a barren Steppe. This region is for the most part covered with friable sands and hillocks, interspersed occasionally with salines and saline hollows. Not a single river, or fresh lake is found in it, and drinkable water is only to be obtained from wells (*kuduks*), which are generally dug in the small hollows which are found in the midst of friable sandy hillocks. The water in these wells is not always good, and as moreover it soon becomes impure, it is always found necessary to clear the well out before drawing a fresh supply. The vegetation on these sands, though rather better than that of the saline Steppes, is generally poor, but shrubwood is plentiful.

The nature of the soil and the scarcity of fuel and pasturage, render the passage over the Kara-kum sands extremely difficult, and only solitary Kirghiz horsemen can travel from well to well in all directions. All the nomad Kirghizes, as well as Bokharian caravans and Russian transports, proceeding to Orenburg and the Orsk fortress and back, cross the Kara-kum by the only route which has for ages been frequented by Asiatics, and extends from the former Aralsk fortification, or the point of passage over the Syr, to the N.E. extremity of Sary-Chaganak Bay, and thence along the Western edge of the sands to the Uralsk fort or to Mana-Aulié settlement. This route is undeniably the best in every respect for connecting the lower part of the Syr with the Russian line; it runs for the most part through saline valleys, and crosses the sandy ones in a few places, while wells exist at every stage in sufficient numbers for the supply of considerable caravans.

To the East of the Kara-kum sand stretches a broad belt of waterless saline Steppe, called the Barren Steppe, extending as far as Lake Balkhash. It is crossed, though with great difficulty, by Bokarian and Tashkend caravans proceeding to Troitskand and Petropavlovsk, and since 1853 Russian convoys pass through it in the autumn, on their way to Fort Perovski.

With regard to the sands, it must be observed, that although their vegetation is scanty, they yet present greater conveniences as camping-grounds than the saline Steppes. Sweet water may nearly always be procured by digging wells, whereas the Steppe is almost entirely dry, and the wells which do exist in them are either very deep, or their water is of bad quality. Pasturage for horses can also be obtained along the sands, whereas the saline Steppes only contain food for camels. The hillocks and mounds occurring in the former afford protection to horses and cattle during the winter hurricanes. On these accounts the sands are preferred by thè Kirghizes as camping-ground.

Ever since the commencement of last century the Russians have laid themselves out to obtain more reliable information respecting the lower course of the Syr, or in other words, since the establishment of the Orenburg line, and the reception of the Kirghiz-Kaisaks and Karakalpaks under Russian protection in 1730. The course of the Syr was at that time occupied by Karakalpaks. They had their own Khans, who did not exercise much power, but were chiefly swayed by the Hodjas. The chief occupation of the Karakalpaks then, as now, was agriculture. They had but few horses, but like the patriarchs of old, were rich in cattle, which they occasionally sold in the neighbouring country, but principally to the Khivans. For their own protection against the Kirghizes, they manufactured powder, lead, and guns, which they also sold to the former. When invaded, they sought shelter in towns surrounded by walls of earth. In the winter, they camped in the reeds, chiefly around the sea of Aral, which were likewise resorted to at that season by Kirghizes of the Little Horde. Being an agricultural and peaceable people, the Karakalpaks suffered great oppression from their neighbours the Kirghizes, and eagerly sought the protection of other races against them. The Upper Karakalpaks in the beginning of last century owned allegiance to the Dzungars, and the Lower determined to follow the exampie of the Little Kaisak Horde, who through their Khan, Abul-Hair, had, in 1732, intimated their desire to place themselves under the protection of Russia. In 1732 the Interpreter of the College of Foreign Affairs, Murza Tevkelef, who had been despatched to receive the oath of allegiance of the Kirghizes, arrived at the camp of Abul-Hair, at the mouth of the Syr. The Karakalpaks seizing this opportunity, swore fealty to Russia, along with their Khan Kaip. In consequence of this, in the instructions given to Karilof, despatched on the 18th May, 1734, to organize the Orenburg region, he is directed among other things to forward a letter entrusted to him, to the Khan of the Karakalpaks, and to endeavour to establish a harbour and armed vessels in the Sea of Aral. Neither of these two things, however, could be accomplished at that period, owing to the unsettled state of the new region. The "gramota," or Imperial letter, was soon after returned to the Russian Bureau of Foreign Affairs, and it was not till 1847 that forts and vessels of war were established at the mouth of the Syr.

As soon as the relations of the Karakalpaks with Russia were broken off, the former suffered long and severely from the pillaging inroads of Abul-Hair and his sons, who at last drove them away from the Lower Syr, at the same time compelling some of them to settle in Khivan and others in Bokharian territory.

With the retirement of the Karakalpaks, the lower course of the Syr remained entirely in the hands of the Kirghizes. Many of them took to agriculture, and settled down to cultivate the country, while others of the Horde emigrated to these parts every winter with their flocks, migrating to other camping-grounds in spring. It is said that formerly both the stationary and nomad populations were more numerous in these regions than at the present day, and that it is in consequence of the rapacity and cruelty of the Kokanians and Khivans, who acquired an unjust influence over the lower course of the Syr about the commencement of the present century, that the whole country has become depopulated to a considerable extent. This account receives additional confirmation by the many abandoned fields, ruined aqueducts, and neglected dams and reservoirs that everywhere meet the eye.

At the beginning of the present century, the Kokanians had no fixed station on the Lower Syr, and did not exercise any influence over the Kirghizes, who wandered along its banks, but after the capture of the town of Turkestan in 1814, allured by the possibility of extending the limits of their territory still farther to the North-West, they began to interfere in the affairs of the Kirghizes, and to demand tribute from them. The Kirghizes resisted the demands of the Kokanians, and incessant inroads were made on each other by the rival peoples, resulting in great loss of life on both sides. Worn out at last with this incessant struggle, but without abandoning the idea of establishing their power over the Kirghizes, the Kokanians resolved to occupy several points on the Syr below Turkestan, and erected successive fortifications at Djany-Kurgan, Djülek-Ak-Mechet, Kumysh-Kurgan, Chim-Kurgan, Kosh-Kurgan and others. The most important of these, Ak-Mechet, was built, according to Kirghiz accounts, about the year 1817, on the left bank of the Syr, and removed a year after to the right bank. The part of the Lower Syr thus taken possession of by the Kokanians formed an outlying or frontier province of Kokan, and was governed until 1855 by the Beg of Ak-Mechet, who was subject to the ruler of Tashkend, but who, taking advantage of the differences between Tashkend and Kokan, often acted irresponsibly.

By erecting these fortifications the Kokanians attained their object. The Kirghizes, accustomed to repair to the convenient parts of the Syr for passing the winter, were forced to submit to Kokanian rule, and began to pay the Ziaket or tribute demanded of them; the Kokanians, however, not satisfied with this, still plundered and harassed them at every turn. Many Kirghizes in consequence began to go over to the Khivans, but such migrations cost them dear. Placed between two fires, the Kirghizes suffered from the vengeance of both peoples, forcing many of them to seek protection under the Kokan and Khivan forts, and others to scatter in all directions over the Steppe.

Influenced exclusively by rapacity, the Kokanians signalized their rule by ruinous levies, depredatory inroads, robbery from the person, and violence of every description.

"The Kirghiz Tribute," says Mr. Osmolovski, "was collected by the Kokanians under two heads: from cattle—Ziaket—and from corn—Ikhradj. In violation of all Mahometan laws fixing the levy from cattle at one-fortieth, the Kokanians took annually six sheep out of every kibitka or tent, and double that number from rich Kirghizes; and this quite irrespective of the presents made to the Ziaketchik (taxgather) and his assistants."

Of corn, the Kokanians exacted a third of the crop. Under the "Ikhradj" head, they likewise collected a tax in wood, charcoal and hay. Each kibitka was obliged to furnish twenty-four bags annually of charcoal, four oxen loads of saksaùl for fuel, hay, and 1000 sheaves of reeds. The Kirghizes, whose encampment lay at a distance from the fortifications, paid the value of these imposts in cattle and corn.

In addition to the Ziaket and Ikhradj, the Kirghizes were required to render service in labour,—much like the old French *corvée* :—

1. In cultivating the Kokanian gardens and fields, to repair the walls of the forts, &c. For this purpose each kibitka sent a man once a month, and provided him with food. The distant Kirghizes paid in cattle for the hire of substitute labourers.

2. For cleansing the stables, stalls, &c., in the forts, which was done about six times during the year; for this work the Kirghizes, whose camps lay near, were driven into the forts at random.

3. In case of a war or inroad, each able-bodied Kirghiz, at the order of the Kokanians, was obliged to serve as long as required, providing his own horse and provisions.

The weight of these imposts and compulsory service was the more burthensome to the poor *eginiches*, or agriculturists, in consequence of the brutality of the Kokanians, who, leading an idle and dissolute life, often visited the Kirghiz aùls, to violate the women, marrying them also in opposition to the *Shariat*, and without giving the customary kalym, or payment for a wife.

By these barbarous means, the neighbouring

country was held in fear and subjection by the fort of Ak-Mechet up to the year 1853; notwithstanding that its material strength was really inconsiderable.

In 1852 the force of Ak-Mechet consisted of only fifty sepahis, or Kokan soldiers, armed with matchlocks, sabres, and spears, and about 100 Bokharian and Kokanian traders were settled in it; Kumysh-Kurgan was garrisoned by twenty-five men, principally Kirghizes, and Kosh-Kurgan by four. In Djülek, in 1858, there were forty men, and two or three Kokanian soldiers in Djany-Kurgan, a small quadrangular entrenchment of a spear's height. These numbers, of course, varied according to circumstances, but they could only be increased by impressing Kirghizes.

Next in order after the Kokanians, the Khivans made their appearance on the lower course of the Syr-Daria. Khiva commenced to exercise influence over the Kirghizes but very recently, in fact since the reign of Mahomed-Rahim, who died in 1825. The endeavours of the Kokanians to establish their power over the Kirghizes of the Syr-Daria, excited the curiosity of the Khivans, who demanded the demolition of the forts on the Syr, to which the former would not consent. In consequence of this, several Khivan forts were erected on the left bank of the river Kuvan about the year 1830, in the reign of Alla-Kul (the son and suc-

THREE INHABITANTS OF KHIVA.

cessor of Mahomed-Rahim), for the collection of Ziaket from the neighbouring Kirghiz encampment, and of dues from the caravans passing from

Bokhara to the Orenburg line, and returning thence.

Like the Kokanian, the Khivan rule over the Kirghizes of the Syr-Daria was marked by acts of rapine and oppression, which were often repeated between the years 1840-50, out of revenge against Djan-Hodja, who destroyed Bish-Kaly.

The commencement of the advance of Russia in the Steppe, must be dated from 1833, in which year the Novo-Alexandrovski, called subsequently Mangyshlak Fort, 43° 40′ N. 53° 30′ E. was erected on the Eastern shore of the Caspian, for the protection of the Emba fisheries against Turkmen pirates. Although two forts, one on the Emba, the other on the Ak-Bulak, were constructed in the Steppe in 1839, before the expedition to Khiva, they were only temporarily occupied, and were, in fact, abandoned on the termination of the campaign. The occupation of the Steppe, on a permanent footing by the construction of regular forts, was not commenced till 1847, when the Steppe was agitated by the insurrection of Sultan Kanisara-Kassìmof. It was during this year, that the Orenburg Fort on the Turgai, the Ural Fort on the Irgiz, and in 1848 the Karabutak Fort, on the Karabut, were built for protecting the communication between the Steppe forts and the line.

This advance of Russia in the Steppe, had the effect of pacifying the districts adjoining the line, but exercised no influence over the Kirghizes, who roamed beyond the Emba, on the Ust-Urt and Syr-Daria.

In order to make the influence of Russia felt by the Khanats of Central Asia, and for the protection of the Kirghizes subject to Russia, who roamed on the Syr-Daria, as also for the safety of Russian caravans, it was necessary that she should predominate without a rival on the Sea of Aral, and at the mouth of the Syr, where the Kokanians and Khivans had arbitrarily erected a line of forts, with the object of intimidating the Kirghizes, and impoverishing them by heavy exactions. The idea of establishing a stronghold with a Russian settlement on the Syr-Daria, originated as early as 1840, but was not realised until 1847.

In 1846, General Obruchev, then Governor-General of Orenburg, obtained the sanction of his Government, to occupy a point on the shore of the Sea of Aral. With this view, Captain Schultz was despatched to select a convenient spot above the mouth of the Syr-Daria, for the erection of a fort; to gather information respecting the navigation and fisheries of the river; to sound the channel from the point at which it was intended to construct a fort to the mouth of the river; and generally to procure information on the capabilities of the country for colonisation.

At the point selected, was founded in 1847, the Raimsk fortification, which name was subsequently changed to that of Aralsk.

The Khivans could not regard with indifference the encroachment of Russian rule on the Syr-Daria, and from the year 1847, hostile relations sprang up between the two nations. In August, a force of 2000 Khivans having crossed the Syr-Daria, fell on the Russian Kirghizes, and despoiled more than a thousand families. The troops despatched against the Khivans, put the marauders to flight, and the fear they inspired spread as far as Khiva, where the arrival of the detachment was expected; the Russians, however, withdrew after liberating the prisoners.

In the month of November, the Khivans appeared in the Kara-Kum desert, and again commenced pillaging the Kirghizes. On this occasion, they murdered many old men, seized the women, scattered the children in the Steppe, and robbed two trading caravans. Immediately on learning that the Russian troops were in motion, the marauders once more retired beyond the Syr-Daria. In 1848, a body of 1500 Khivans had the temerity to appear on the right bank of the Syr, when they commenced their work of pillage, while three hundred Turkmen horsemen rode boldly past within gun-shot of the Russian fort, and visited the Syr-Daria landing wharf. For nearly twenty-four hours they robbed and slaughtered the Kirghizes, after which they recrossed the Syr. In the course of 1848, the Khivans made repeated inroads, but being each time compelled to fly on meeting the Russian detachments, they became conscious of their own weakness, and limited themselves to demanding the destruction of the Russian forts of Aralsk and Novo-petrovsk.

From the year 1850 a hostile attitude was also assumed by the Kokanians, who, as already mentioned, having built forts on the lower course of the Syr-Daria, oppressed and robbed the Kirghizes subject to Russia. Most of the depredatory incursions were undertaken by the Beg of Ak-Mechet, who ruled over all the Kokanian forts on the Lower Syr. These inroads were always accompanied with wholesale robbery; thus in 1850 they drove away twenty-six thousand head of Kirghiz cattle, and thirty thousand on another occasion. In the following year, 1851, the Kokanians having driven off seventy-five thousand head of cattle, the commander of Fort Aralsk, Major Engmann, pursued them and took their fort, Kosh-Kurgan, by storm; but even this severe lesson failed to put a stop to their depredations. Before proceeding further, however, with the narrative, it is necessary to glance at the Russian proceedings on the Sea of Aral.

The navigation of the Sea of Aral by Russian vessels commences with the erection of the Raimsk fortification. Two two-masted vessels, one a vessel of war, the "Nikolai," the other a merchant ship, the "Mikhail," were constructed at Orenburg early in 1847. The first was intended for surveying purposes, the second for establishing fisheries, with which object a public company, as already mentioned, had been formed during the same year. Both vessels having been constructed in Russia, were taken to pieces, and transported in the spring overland to Raimsk, where they were put together again and launched. The schooner "Nikolai" immediately put to sea, but owing to the lateness of the season she only cruised off the embouchure of the Syr. In the following spring the schooner again stood out to sea, and surveyed the whole

Northern coast line. In the meantime another war vessel, the "Constantine," larger than the first, was built at Orenburg. With this vessel, Lieutenant Butakov commenced, in the autumn of 1848, a thorough survey of the Sea of Aral, which occupied full two years ere it was satisfactorily completed.

In 1850, General Obruchev proposed to construct a steamer of forty-horse power, for the purpose of plying on the Syr-Daria. The navigation of the Syr-Daria promised to afford material assistance in supplying the Raimsk fort with the necessary stores and provisions, from the Kokanian territory, and was intended to supersede the costly, tedious, and uncertain modes then in use for conveying goods to the fort across the sandy and waterless Steppe.

The project received the approbation of the Government, and the Ministry of Marine were directed to prepare plans of the steamer. The preliminary expenses under this head were defrayed out of the sum assigned in 1838 for the organisation of a scientific expedition. In the previous year, 1837, the Asiatic committee decided to despatch a scientific mission to the North-Eastern shores of the Sea of Aral, and up the Syr-Daria. The events that occurred in Central Asia in 1838 made it imperatively necessary to abandon this project for the time. A military force marched in the meantime to Khiva; and subsequently, with the construction of the Orenburg, Uralsk, and Aralsk forts, topographical surveys were made of the shores of the Sea of Aral, and a complete examination of these waters, as well as of the lower course and mouths of the Syr-Daria, set on foot, so that the scientific objects of the contemplated expedition of 1837 were ultimately fully attained.

Captain Butakov, of the Imperial Navy, was commisioned to order the steamer destined for the Sea of Aral, and a screw steam barge of twelve horse-power, to act as a tender to the steamer, was contracted for at the Motala Iron Works in Sweden for the sum of 37,444 roubles (£5,620).

No coal having been discovered along the Aral coasts, General Obruchev was requested by the Minister of War to take into consideration:—

1. Would it not be useful to examine the coal layers on the Mangyshlak peninsula, or between the Caspian and the Sea of Aral?

2. Should the coal prove of the requisite quality for fuelling steamers, would the transport of it across the Ust-Urt, by Kirghizes and Turkmens be attained with great obstacles?

3. As a central depôt on the Western shore of

Russian Steam-Barges, ordinarily Stationed at Fort No. 7, opposite Kungrad on the Syr-Daria.

the sea, and armed convoys for the protection of the coal caravans, would in all probability be required in carrying out the plan, in what manner could these difficulties be subsequently lessened?

4. In case no coal be found in the immediate vicinity of the Aral Sea, will it not be necessary to consider the possibility and cost of transporting Don anthracite to the mouth of the Syr-Daria?

Perovski, who was appointed military Governor-General of Orenburg in 1851, though fully recognizing the advantages to be gained by the introduction of steam on the Aral, was of opinion that the transport of Don anthracite would be too costly, and that the only available fuel in those arenaceous wastes was the saxaùl (*Anabasis saxaùl*). The superiority of this plant as a substitute for coal, over every other description of wood, was practically proved, and its abundance on the shores and islands of the Aral was investigated and ascertained by Captain Butakov.

In June, 1851, Perovski instructed the commander of Fort Aralsk to make the necessary arrangements for forwarding, during the navigation season of that year, as large a supply as possible of the saksaùl to the Aralsk Fort.

The experiment, however, did not succeed. In October of the same year, Perovski reported that the navigation of the steamers on the Sea of Aral and Syr-Daria could not be rendered sufficiently secure and reliable, owing to the use of the saksaùl for fuel. Irrespective of its limited supply, and difficulty of collection, its conversion into faggots of wood presented two serious drawbacks. Firstly, the hard and resinous properties of this tree make it almost proof against the hatchet or saw; and secondly, its crooked and knotty logs are inconvenient for stowage, so that the progress of the steamer would always be retarded by having to tow a vessel loaded with this fuel, occupying space disproportionate to its bulk, and insufficient for any long passage.

Anthracite as fuel, therefore, notwithstanding the great cost involved in its conveyance, presented the sole reliable means of establishing steam navigation on the Aral and the rivers that fall into it, on a secure footing. Reeds and saxaùl wood might be used as auxiliary fuel. It was consequently decided to transport Don anthracite to the Orenburg line, for the consumption for the year 1852, and the cost of a pood of this material would be one rouble, twenty copecks, or about £12 per ton.

In May, 1852, the steamers ordered in Sweden were forwarded in pieces to St. Petersburg, whence they reached Samara by water in July, and were despatched with 4000 poods (65 tons) of anthracite to Orenburg, where the convoy arrived in August. In the beginning of November all the land transports arrived in safety at Fort Aralsk, and the work of putting them together was immediately commenced. On the 10th March, 1853, the steamer "Perovski" was launched on the Syr-Daria, and the steam barge, "Obruchev," on the 16th April following. The total cost of the steamers, including their conveyance to Fort Aralsk, and the salaries of those employed in their erection, was 49,347 roubles silver (£7,402.)

By the 31st May the steamers were completed, and ready to commence operations. The armament of the "Perovski" consisted of a nine-inch howitzer and carriage, on a revolving platform, at the bow, and two howitzers resembling carronades, at the stern. The steam barge "Obruchev" had provision made for mounting a howitzer in case of need, at each end, fore and aft.

During the same year the steamer "Perovski" took part in the Ak-Mechet expedition, 400 miles from its mouth.

CHAPTER IX.

PART II.

Survey of the Syr-Daria above the Aral Fortification.—Inimical bearing of the Kokanians.—Expedition of Colonel Blaramberg.—Demolition of the Kokanian Fortifications.—Expedition to Ak-Mechet.—Taking of Ak-Mechet.—It is renamed Fort Perovski.—Proceedings of the Kokanians.

1852-1854.

It has already been mentioned that General Perovski resolved in 1852 to take decisive measures for curbing the insolence of the Kokanians—a pretext for which they themselves were not long in furnishing.

In the month of April, 1852, a survey corps,

consisting of eighty men, under the direction of the topographer, Ensign Golov, was stopped before reaching the fort of Ak-Mechet, the commandant of which flatly opposed its further progress. The proposed junction of the Orenburg and Siberian lines having then been decided on, and its feasibility from the Orenburg side by a movement up the Syr being evident, it was found indispensable to continue the survey, should it even require armed force for its execution.

Accordingly, in the summer of that year, a division was organized, consisting of one staff officer, eleven superior officers, thirty-one non-commissioned officers, and an "ouriadnik," a band of three musicians, 387 soldiers of the line, and thirty-six irregular troops, accompanied by two 9-pounders. The command of this division was intrusted to Colonel Blaramberg, who received the following instructions:—

1. To accomplish the survey through the valley of the Syr-Daria, from the Aral fortification to the Kokanian fortress, Ak-Mechet, upon the right bank of the Syr.

2. In the event of an encounter with the Kokanians, or in case they should make any uncalled-for demands, to attack them immediately.

3. Without touching at any fortifications lying nearer to Aralsk, to proceed direct towards Ak-Mechet, and there to act as circumstances might require. If Ak-Mechet lies within the Russian limits, to endeavour to rase it; but under all circumstances to notify to the Kokanians that the fort must not remain on its actual site.

Taking with him sufficient provisions to last a month and a half, Colonel Blaramberg, on the 3rd of July, issued from the Aralsk fortification, and was on the 18th already within one stage of Ak-Mechet (thus marching twelve miles a day).

Meanwhile, the Kokanians, probably forewarned of the advance of the Russian division had destroyed the dam which diverted the current of the water of the Syr-Daria into Lake Ber-kazan, and deluged the low level ground in the vicinity of Ak-Mechet. Regardless of this obstacle, the division crossed in safety, though with considerable difficulty, five arms of the river. The guns, ammunition, and other stores, were taken over on cane rafts; while the horses, camels, and the greater portion of the men, swam over without any resistance on the part of the enemy.

As soon as this was accomplished, two envoys from Ak-Mechet appeared before the commander of the division, of whom one was a collector of tribute from the Kirghizes, and the other a Bokhara merchant, both of whom requested to know the reason why the division had violated the Kokanian territory.

Colonel Blaramberg, considering that the Kokanian tax-gatherers had no right to visit the country on that side of the Syr-Daria, and disapproving alike of the constitution and tone of this embassage, detained the tribute-collector with his followers, and despatched the Bokharian back again, directing him to inform the commandant of Ak-Mechet that the Russian division was marching along the Russian bank of the river, on which no Kokanian troops or fortifications could be permitted to remain.

The passage of the troops over the five channels into which the Syr branches at this point, had been exceedingly tedious and exhausting, owing to the inundation and the dense and prickly brushwood through which the men had to make their way along narrow deep footpaths, as well as across the ploughed and muddy soil of the fields. Reaching the fortress at length on the 19th, Colonel Blaramberg encamped under the walls forming its Eastern front. The Cossacks not having brought any canoes along with the division, soon scattered themselves along the Syr, and seized two Kokanian boats, near the right bank,—in which the engineers at once proceeded to reconnoitre the fort.

The Kokanians abstained from showing themselves above the walls; but ere long, the Bokharian, Kasan-Beg, again made his appearance in the camp, with a letter from the commandant of Ak-Mechet. Colonel Blaramberg would not take the letter, but ascertained from Kasan-Beg, that it contained a request for a delay of four days, but some Kirghizes who were in camp alleged that he sought this respite in expectation of a strong reinforcement.

Under these circumstances, an immediate surrender of the stronghold was not to be anticipated; whilst at the same time it was impossible to continue under the walls in the midst of an inundated country, in the by no means improbable event of the elevation of the water. On the other hand, as the division was not supplied with ladders long enough to enable the men to scale the walls,—the fortress could not be taken by storm.

Unwilling, however, to abandon the scheme without inflicting on the Kokanians the punishment which they justly merited for their robberies,

Colonel Blaramberg determined, at least, to burn all that lay between the outer wall and the citadel. In the night of the 19th, some grenades from a 13-pounder were thrown into the fort. These were at once responded to on the part of the Kokanians from some 3-pounder swivel guns planted on the bastions of the citadel, and by musketry from under cover of the walls. At dawn on the 20th, the enemy's swivel guns had been dismounted, and the wooden gate of the outer fortifications battered in. Colonel Blaramberg thereupon formed his handful of men in two columns, and led them to the breach. One of these columns, with the aid of pick-axes and hatchets, scrambled up the side of the moat, and climbed the wall, whilst the other burst into the fortress through the broken gateway. The outer works of the fort were carried by the Russians in less than ten minutes. Elated with this success—the troops with cheers rushed beneath the very walls of the citadel. But their height, which was more than four fathoms, presented an insurmountable barrier, and no effect could be produced on them by shot, as they presented a mass of untempered clay, a fathom and a half thick, in which the balls simply imbedded themselves.

It was now deemed sufficient to have gained the

outer fortifications, and a retreat was accordingly sounded. The killed and wounded,—amounting in the first case to fifteen, in the second to fifty-seven—were carried by their comrades from under the walls of the fort; and a few volunteers remaining in the fortification, set fire to all that was within them. The conflagration lasted throughout the whole night; and such of the Kokanians as descended the walls of the citadel to rescue their property were instantly put to death.

On the 21st, the division commenced its retrograde movement down the course of the river. The troops were frequently forced to wade, waist-deep, through the water, so that the passage over the five branches of the Bish-Aryn, occupied the whole of the next twenty-four hours, during all which the troops were in the water, while the heat never fell below 86° Fahrenheit in the shade. During the return march, Colonel Blaramberg demolished three of the enemy's small forts: Kumysh-Kurgan, Chin-Kurgan, and Kosh-Kurgan.

This enterprise, achieved by a small division, at a distance of 500 versts (334 miles) beyond the most outlying Russian stronghold, and 1500 versts (1000 miles) from the line of settled frontier, is of considerable importance in a military and strategic point of view.

In six weeks time, the division had traversed more than six hundred and fifty miles (1000 versts), successfully encountering extreme difficulties of ground, and sustaining the most relaxing heat; without boats or pontoons it had succeeded in crossing three rivers and several torrents, had demolished three of the enemy's small forts, and destroyed the outer works of Ak-Mechet citadel, their principal frontier stronghold.

But besides this, the expedition decided a variety of speculations as to the measures indispensable for the destruction of the Kokanian fortification on the right bank of the Syr-Daria. It was elicited from inquiries on the subject, that there was considerable meadow land above Ak-Mechet up the course of the Syr, and that the banks were fringed with a dense forest of timber, fit for building purposes as well as probably for the construction of vessels.

The result was that it was recognized that, with a view to the permanent establishment of the Russians on the Syr-Daria, for the protection of the Russian Kirghizes against robbery and the daily increasing exactions of the Kokanians, and finally for the main object of connecting the Orenburg and Siberian lines, it was necessary to occupy in force the tract between that river and the Kara-Uziak stream, by which means navigation of the Syr-Daria would be made secure. The occupation of this tract necessarily involved the destruction of the Kokanian forts along the right bank, and the safe navigation of our steamers demanded also that no fortifications should be suffered anywhere, not even in the vicinity of the left bank.

The Kokanians had at that time organized a distinct district, on the tract lying between the Kara-Uziak and Syr-Daria,—which was defended by small fortifications—of which the Government was centred in Ak-Mechet. Without including Turkmen and Tashkendians, the Kirghizes, who had always frequented this district, were estimated at five thousand huts; and about three thousand huts of Kirghizes who regularly wintered there, after leaving the Russian territories. These were all subjected to the heaviest exactions, not to speak of Oriental robbery and spoliation.

In the following year, 1853, it was determined to occupy Ak-Mechet at any cost,—and accordingly early in the spring the troops left the frontier in two divisions, each composed of infantry, cavalry, and artillery, and companies of sappers and miners, taking with them twelve pieces of cannon. The force numbered in all two thousand one hundred and sixty-eight men including officers, besides two thousand four hundred and forty-two horses, two thousand and thirty-eight camels, and two thousand two hundred and eighty oxen for transport of baggage and commissariat.

For crossing rivers the detachments were provided with three portable pontoons fixed on barrels, two flat praams in piece, and three smaller pontoons consisting of india-rubber bags; besides which regular material a supply of timber was taken for forming bridges over the canals that would present themselves on the route.

Both columns having become united at Fort Karabutakh, they advanced *en echélon* as far as Fort Aralsk.

In order to prevent the Khivans from attacking and plundering the Russian convoys of stores, Perovski intended to occupy, by way of precaution, the Khivan fort of Hodja-Nias; but not being allowed to cross over to the left bank of the Syr, he confined himself to ordering the Sultan rulers roaming at the Western and middle portion of the line of frontier, to retire with their followers into the Steppe, and to sweep with their horsemen the whole extent of country between the proposed route of the Russian convoy, and the country to the South as far as the Ust-Urt.

To preserve at the same time the herbage for the cavalry and waggon-horses, strict orders were given that the Kirghizes should not camp during summer along the road leading from the frontier line to Aralsk.

So punctually were these injunctions carried out, that according to Perovski's statement, the expeditionary columns marched as through a wilderness. Not a single Kirghiz tent was to be seen even in the most secluded valley, nor were horses or sheep anywhere visible. Herds of wild "Saigaks" alone enlivened the desert waste, which, commencing even at the Ilek, presented nothing but saline marshes, sands and oozy mud, overgrown with wormwood. The weather was at first mild, but the heats soon set in, the thermometer rising by the end of May above 104° Fahren: One hundred and nine men belonging to the detachment that first reached Aralsk, showed symptoms of scorbutic disease. From Fort Aralsk to the Syr-Daria lay the most distressing portion of the route, which crosses the Kara-Kum sands. The heat here is very oppressive, the herbage scant, and the water, procured from small pits, is both of bad quality and insufficient in quantity. The corps, however, arrived safely at Fort Aralsk in the middle of June, and instructions were issued that it was to remain there until all the parts of the expedition were finally organized.

All the preparations having been at last completed, the expeditionary force marched out of Aralsk, consisting in all of 750 file of infantry, 400 Cossacks and Bashkir cavalry, besides an escort of 150 Cossacks, and 200 Cossacks to guard the train, 10 pieces of field artillery, varying from three to twenty pounders, three mortars, 1140 camels, and no fewer than 777 waggons, besides ox-trains and baggage horses.

The steamer "Perovski" likewise took part in the expedition; a company of infantry having been placed on board of her at Aralsk. After transporting this additional force, together with some heavy stores to Kosh-Kurgan, its instructions were to proceed up stream as far as Ak-Mechet.

On the 23rd June the force reached the right bank of the Kara-Uziak. The first stage, from Kazaly to Baskara settlement, a distance of about 17 miles, was performed through excellent meadow land, high reeds and even cultivated fields; the remaining portion of the distance to Kara-Uziak, notwithstanding the close proximity of a great river, extended through a saline argillaceous soil, lying in a tract depressed below the usual level of the Steppe, the barrenness of which even exceeds the Kara-Kum sands. Good though small patches of meadow-land occurred at a distance of not less than 12 or 15 miles from each other, and these, the only spots suitable for agricultural pursuits, were used for encampment at night. In the absence of these oases, which were produced by heavy spring rains, it would have been impossible even for a small force to have marched along the banks of the river. In these parts even the Kirghizes and their camels can only exist during the winter in the reeds. The only human traces to be met with here are solitary graves, or large cemeteries of ancient and modern origin. In the absence of more definite physical features, by which to distinguish them, these cemeteries give the names to the surrounding settlements.

Notwithstanding the sterility of the country lying along the Syr-Daria, the expeditionary force reached Kara-Uziak satisfactorily. The sultry heat, tempered as it was in the day-time by cool breezes, could be sustained by both men and beasts without any suffering; fortunately, also, during the last week of the march, there was a fall of rain, and the atmosphere was cleared on three occasions by thunder storms. There were throughout the entire march only seven men suffering from sickness in the three battalions, while not a single horse or camel was lost.

Leaving Kara-Uziak on the 26th June, the troops were met by a swarm of locusts, which continued flying over their heads for a whole day. In some places they were obliged to march over a thick layer of these insects. All the grass and reeds were consumed by these pests along the whole route, and at night, no herbage could be procured for the horses, which were on this occasion fed on dry provender. Happily, the tract of country despoiled by the locusts was soon left behind by the troops, and on the next day grass was again procured.

The force still more fortunately escaped another serious danger of by no means unfrequent occurrence in the Steppe.

Two nights in succession a lurid reflection was seen in the skies, and a black pillar of smoke in the day time, which told of burning reeds and brushwood ahead. And so it proved; between Bergunda settlement and Tura-Tan tomb, scorched tracts of land, with a strong smell of burning reeds in the air, were passed. Had the fire made headway from this point, the safety of the troops would have been seriously jeopardized. Luckily, heavy showers of rain falling for two days had extinguished the smouldering Steppe.

Gad flies and mosquitoes, likewise sorely tried the patience both of men and animals; the water also in the last stages was bad, so that wells had to be excavated at several places. Within three stages of Ak-Mechet the corps had to encounter great fatigue in marching along the narrow track of the road, which is thickly overgrown with prickly shrubs and intersected at frequent intervals by canals, some of which are deep and have strong currents. Every step of the road had to be cleared of prickly obstacles, and frequent stoppages were necessary for filling in the canals and levelling their raised banks. The progress of the corps was only at the average rate of two versts an hour and even less. At length, on the 2nd of July, Perovski arrived before Ak-Mechet with a light detachment, and encamped on the banks of the Syr, within 600 fathoms of the walls of the fortress.

Meanwhile the Kokanians had lost no time in taking advantage of the unsuccessful attempt of the Russians against Ak-Mechet during the previous year. In anticipation of a new Russian expedition, they had made great improvements in the fortifications of their stronghold. The exterior rampart, which would have facilitated approaches to the citadel, was now demolished, and the buildings inside pulled down. Two ditches, which had encircled the citadel, were joined into one, one and a half fathom broad and ten feet deep. The configuration of the citadel had likewise been changed. The interior angles were destroyed; the walls thickened, and the whole place had been made to assume a more regular shape. The citadel consisted of a quadrangular structure, with eight towers situated at the angles and at the centre of the faces. The height of the walls was four fathoms. The summit of the walls was protected at the faces by crenelated battlements five feet in thickness, and by a breastwork on the towers. The embrasures in this breastwork, as also those in the walls, being formed of cemented lumps of clay, were easily concealed. The citadel being likewise constructed of the same materials, could be easily repaired when damaged. The only gates of the citadel, which were on the southern face, were defended by a lofty crenelated wall on their exterior front.

In the interior of the citadel, mud huts, as the Kirghizes said, were erected in regular order and formed narrow lanes. According to information which the Russians received, the garrison consisted at that time of 300 men, of whom 100 had horses, and was provided with provisions and provender calculated to last a month. The citadel was armed with three guns, two of which threw one and a half inch shells. It was ascertained that shot, shell, and gunpowder had been sent to the fortress from Tashkend on sixty camels. The garrison had also prepared pieces of clay and huge blocks of wood on the walls, to hurl down at the assailants, on their reaching the breach.

On receipt of the foregoing information, and after a personal inspection of the place, Perovski arrived at the conclusion that the number and calibre of the guns of his force, and also the supply of shot and shell at his disposal, were insuffficent for making a breach in the clay walls of four fathoms thickness. He also considered it inexpedient to order an assault of the walls, six fathoms high, with fascines and ladders alone, without first making a breach. Perovski resolved therefore not to hurry on the approaches, and decided, in case the horizontal fire failed to make the garrison surrender, that the assault was not to be attempted until the mine under the tower had been sprung.

Messengers were despatched, immediately on the arrival of Perovski, summoning the commander of the fort to surrender. The Kokanians, however, allowed the bearers of the flag of truce to approach close within gun-shot, and then opened on them a fire of musketry, succeeded by discharges from their guns. From this day a regular fire was maintained from the fort. As siege operations could only be undertaken on the arrival of the remaining portion of the troops, pending their arrival the necessary preliminary works were at once commenced. A reconnoissance was made of the neighbourhood of Ak-Mechet, and a survey taken of the whole of Ak-Mechet island. A party of Cossacks was sent to occupy the opposite bank of the river, facing the fort, to observe the enemy's movements, the breadth of the river was measured, and found to be from 308 to 318 fathoms opposite the fort, communication with the left bank was established by a ferry, and lastly fascines were being prepared. On the 4th July the steamer "Perovski," commanded by Captain Butakov, arrived and cast anchor two versts below the fort.

On the 5th July, the first battery was erected at

250 fathoms from the fortress, and on the 6th, on which day a concentration of the whole Russian force took place, another battery was constructed on the left bank.

By the 8th all the five Russian batteries had opened fire on the fort. By the 9th part of the batteries had been advanced to 150 fathoms of the walls. The approaches were commenced on the 10th. On the 13th, a Kirghiz, seized at Kosh-Kurgan as a Kokanian spy, was sent to the fort with a summons for the garrison to surrender. He was at the same time the bearer of the following letter to the Kokanian Commandant :—

"*From the Governor-General of Orenburg to the Commander of the Fortress of Ak-Mechet.*

"By order of my Sovereign, the Emperor of all the Russias, I have come to take Ak-Mechet, erected by the Kokanians on Russian territory for the purpose of oppressing the Kirghizes, subjects of His Imperial Majesty.

"Ak-Mechet is already taken, although you are inside it, and you cannot fail to perceive that without losing any of my men, I am in a position to destroy every one of you.

"The Russians have come hither not for a day, nor yet for a year, but for ever. They will not retire.

"If you wish to live, ask for mercy; should you prefer to die in Ak-Mechet, you can do so; I am not pressed for time, and do not intend to hurry you. I here repeat that I do not come to offer you combat, but to thrash you until you open your gates.

"All this I would have told you on the first day of my arrival, when I approached the walls of your fortress unarmed, had you not traitorously opened fire on me, which is not customary among honourable soldiers."

An answer to this summons was to be returned before evening. The messenger was admitted into the fortress; in the meantime the firing was discontinued on both sides until evening, when the messenger returned with a reply from the Commandant. This was to the effect that the existing Kokanian Government declined to be answerable for the acts of oppression committed in the country by the Kiptchaks; that the Russian detachment had approached the fortress without having declared war, and that it was owing to this that the Kokanians fired at the Russian truce-bearers; that the commander was willing to evacuate the fortress on condition that the Russians allowed him fifteen days for the purpose, and retired from under the walls. The garrison would otherwise resist so long as the gun barrels remained in their stocks, or their sword-blades and spear-handles unbroken, and the supply of Kisiak* unexhausted.

In consequence of this message, the bombardment was renewed on both sides on the following day, and the Russians continued to throw up siege works. From the commencement of the attack, and throughout its duration, the besieged opposed a stern resistance to the Russians in their efforts to take the place, and very expeditiously repaired all damages. By the 14th (26th) July, the approaches were brought to within two fathoms of the ditch. The slow advance of the siege works caused great discontent among the Russian soldiers and Cossacks. On reaching Ak-Mechet they were confident that the fortress would be taken a day or two after their appearance before its walls. Regardless of the breadth and depth of the moat, and the height and steepness of the walls, they impatiently awaited orders for storming the place in preference to the tedium of siege operations.

* Kisiak.—Hard lumps of clay hurled from the walls at the besieged.

The Kirghizes, who stood in great awe of the Kokanians, and had been impoverished by them, were at first afraid that the Russians would retire from before Ak-Mechet. Their apprehensions on this account were so strong that they at first obstinately refused to sell their cattle to the Russian soldiery, fearing the vengeance of the Kokanians. Seeing, however, that the besiegers were making preparations for passing the winter in the district, their apprehensions were pacified, and about 150 of them volunteered their assistance in erecting temporary quarters and magazines.

The siege works continued to advance; the infantry soldiers, Cossacks, and bashkirs were all employed in digging trenches. If the latter could only have been kept silent during the night work, they would have been more serviceable than the other troops. But they were distinguished by a childish simplicity, and unnecessarily exposed themselves to danger. Nearly all those bashkirs who had been wounded, were themselves to blame. Some were either tired of proceeding under cover of the trenches, and would boldly expose themselves to the fire of the Kokanians, or some would stealthily repair to the melon fields under the walls, to slake their thirst with the water-melons and other fruits that grew in abundance there.

The infantry soldiers, Cossacks, and bashkirs displayed great daring. One of the former, called Gregorief, on one occasion spied some bags filled with earth, which had probably fallen down from the breastwork erected by the Kokanians on the top of the tower. He sallied out in the middle of the day, and mounting the breach, seized the bags, and shook the earth out of them, after which he quietly returned to his post, under a straggling fire of the besieged. On being reprimanded for his temerity, he urged in excuse, that his linen was in a dilapidated condition, and that he required the bags for furnishing himself with a fresh stock.

The Kirghizes, in the meantime, seeing that nearly three weeks had already elapsed since the Russian troops first appeared before Ak-Mechet, and that the fortress still held out, began to entertain fears that it would never fall into the hands of the Russians. A rumour had furthermore reached the Kirghizes that a strong force was on its way from Tashkend to relieve Ak-Mechet, and the garrison evidently expected speedy succour from that quarter. Perofski determined, therefore, to reconnoitre the country towards Tashkend, as far as Fort Djulek. This operation was entrusted to Major-General Padurof, who, taking fifty Bashkirs and a light field-piece, marched out on the 21st July (2nd August), and reached Fort Djulek — distant 100 miles from Ak-Mechet — on the evening of the 23rd. When within a few miles of the fort, he ascertained from some Kirghizes that the sixty Kokanians who had occupied it, hearing of the advance of the Russian detachment, had hastily abandoned it, and fled in the direction of Turkestan, leaving their arms behind. General Padurof immediately took possession of the fort, and remained in it until the 25th July. During that time he blew down the walls, and set fire to the buildings inside. By the 27th July (8th August) he returned to the Russian camp, bringing with him twenty guns, falconets, powder, and lead, seized in the fort. These trophies dispelled the fears of the Kirghizes concerning the advance of a relieving force from Tashkend.

The siege works meanwhile approached completion; the fosse of the fortress had already been passed by a covered sap, and the mine-gallery finished. It only now remained to load the two chambers, which was done during the night of the 27th July (8th August). The troops at the same time received full instructions for action. The arrangements for storming were as follows:—

At ten o'clock on the morning of the 27th August, two congreve rockets were to be discharged at the walls. At eleven, a gun was to be fired from one battery, and a second shot made at one o'clock on the morning of the 28th July (9th August) from another battery. At midnight, and at two o'clock, false alarms were to be sounded in the trenches, in order to lead the garrison to suppose that the infantry besieging the fortress was still on the same ground. The shots from the batteries, rockets, and two alarms, were intended to fatigue the Kokanians, and lead them to suppose that the assault would not be made that night. It was, therefore, to be expected that towards dawn all would be asleep in the fortress.

After the first alarm at midnight, the troops were to commence issuing in parties from the trenches, and their gradual withdrawal was to continue until the second alarm. Before dawn, at three in the morning, on the discharge of three rockets, the remaining soldiers were to abandon the works, and a company would occupy the covered trenches. All the other men would then be stationed 300 fathoms from the point where the mine would explode. After this, at half-past three, when three rockets would be discharged in rapid succession, the mine would be sprung, and the storm would immediately commence.

All these arrangements were punctually carried out. At three o'clock, in the grey light of dawn, the earth shook, and a black mass of earth was hurled into the air, falling down in two confused mounds on the ground. Dense clouds of dust enveloped the fortress, and piercing shrieks arose from behind the walls. The mine was sprung most successfully; the part blown up presented an opening more than ten fathoms broad, and fortunately the dam for the covered sap across the ditch, in front of the mine gallery, had been left uninjured.

The breach thus made, even before it had time to become clearly defined through the thick clouds of dust, was kept clear by discharges of grape from the batteries opposite it. The garrison at this critical moment showed great presence of mind and intrepidity. Five minutes had hardly elapsed after the explosion, and the shrieks and cries of the women and children had not yet subsided, when the Kokanians were already at the breach, and though exposed to a severe fire of grape, poured heavy discharges of musketry at the batteries and Russian storming columns.

According to previous arrangements, the storming party was led by the 1st company of the 4th battalion of the line, headed by a party of sharpshooters, the whole force being commanded by Lieutenant Erdeli. Twice the Russians rushed to the assault, but were vigorously repulsed each time, and driven into the ditch ; it was only after the third attempt that the Kokanians were forced to retreat, and the Russians, reinforced by another company, occupied all the walls and opened fire from the guns on the garrison inside. The assault lasted altogether twenty minutes, and by half-past 4 A. M. of the 8th of August,* the fortress was in the hands of the Russians.

The defence of the Kokanians at the breach, and at all points, was most desperate. Notwithstanding that Muhamed-Vali, the commandant, who had upheld the spirit of the garrison, was killed at the commencement of the storm, all his subordinates showed the same determined spirit, and were killed to a man. Two hundred and thirty bodies were counted in the ditch and inside the fort, which proves that the struggle, though short, was exceedingly severe.

The Russian loss consisted of thirteen soldiers killed, twelve mortally, seventeen severely, and twenty-three slightly wounded, and eight officers wounded. The trophies of the victors were two bunchuks, or horse-tail standards, two spear flags, two brass guns, several falconets, sixty-six pieces of artillery, mostly dismantled and shattered, one hundred and fifty sabres, and two suits of chain-armour. In addition to these, there were captured 1000 cannon-balls, a considerable quantity of powder and lead, and one hundred and twenty horses.

The capture of Ak-Mechet must have produced a strong impression on the Kokanians, as in it they possessed a very important position in military and commercial respects. This fortress was considered the strongest bulwark of Kokanian dominion on the Lower Syr, and by several supposed to be impregnable, it having withstood several sieges. This belief in its strength explains to some extent the desperate efforts made in its defence, and its fate was a severe blow to the Kokanians, who, in all probability will yet make several attempts to regain it.

Perovski intended at first to leave Ak-Mechet (named Fort Perovski by the Russians after its capture) in the same condition, only proposing to repair the damages it had sustained by the explosion and cannonade, and to strengthen its lateral defences.

On the march of the expeditionary corps to Ak-Mechet, two forts were erected on the Syr-Daria, according to plans drawn up by Perovski; one at the source of the Kazala, the other at Karmakchi settlement. After the taking of Ak-Mechet, the small Kokanian fort of Kumysh-Kurgan, on the right bank of the Kuvan-Darya, was occupied by the Russians. During the siege of Ak-Mechet this small fort had been abandoned by the Kokanians, who on taking to flight, were attacked and beaten by the Kirghizes, who brought to Perovski the falconets and several pieces of ordnance found by them in the fort.

The fort founded on the head waters of the Kazala was ordered to be named Fort No. 1,* that at Karmakchi Fort No. 2, and lastly Fort Kumysh-Kurgan, Fort No. 3.†

Meanwhile the Kokanians could not look with indifference on the establishment of the Russians on the right bank of the Syr-Daria, and determined at all hazards to recapture Ak-Mechet.

On the 21st August (2nd September) reliable in-

* The Aral Fort was removed hither in 1855.

† Abandoned in 1855.

formation was brought by spies to Fort Perovski, that a considerable force of Kokanians had marched out from Tashkend, headed by the ruler of that town, Sabdan-Hodja; that he had passed by Turkestan, and now occupied the ruined Fort Djülek. Intelligence was shortly after received of the enemy having advanced on Fort Perovski. A detachment of 275 men with three field-pieces, was thereupon sent to reconnoitre and attack the Kokanians who were posted at the old Ber-Kazansk ford, twenty-eight versts (eighteen miles) from the fort, at Kum-Suat settlement. The detachment had only just time to form line of battle, when it was attacked by clouds of Kokanian horsemen, who dashed forward with loud cries. The first charge was repulsed by discharges of grape and musketry, but the Kokanians continued to repeat their attacks from eleven in the morning until it grew dusk. Becoming at last fatigued, and having lost a considerable number in killed and wounded, they kindled fires around the Russian position, and apparently resolved to encamp there for the night.

Surrounded by the enemy, and having already had five men killed and twenty-one wounded, Borodin, the officer in charge of the Russian detachment, despatched messengers to the fort for reinforcements, two Cossacks and three Kirghizes, who swam down the river at night, being the bearers of the demands for succour. An additional force, consisting of 200 foot soldiers and Cossacks, with one gun, accordingly reached the detachment by mid-day of the 25th August (5th September). Their assistance, however, was not required. Already before dawn the Russian outposts heard a movement among the Kokanians, and at daybreak it was discovered that they were already in motion and retreating rapidly out of sight. The Cossacks sent in pursuit could not overtake them. The loss of the Kokanians in this affair amounted to 192 men killed, whose bodies were found on the field; the wounded were carried off, according to some Kirghizes, on ninety-six camels, while the whole numerical strength of the enemy had not exceeded 7000 men.

Information was soon after brought by traders returning from Kokan, and by Kirghizes, that large supplies of provisions, powder, and lead were being brought to Turkestan. It was, moreover, reported that the Khan of Khokan intended to repair to Turkestan in person, and to march against Fort Perovski as soon as the Syr-Daria was frozen.

These rumours did not, however, become confirmed until the end of November. On the 30th of that month (O. S.) and more particularly on the 5th December, Lieutenant-Colonel Ogaref, commanding the left flank of the Syr-Daria line, ascertained that the Khan of Kokan had ordered a large force to assemble at Tashkend, under the command of Yakun-Beg, commander-in-chief of the Khan, with the object of attacking the Russians. This force marched to Turkestan on the 24th November, moved to Yany-Kurgan on the 2nd December, and reached Djulek during the night of the 4th. From Yany-Kurgan, the Kokanians sent addresses to the Begs of the Kiptchak Kirghiz tribe encamped near the Russians. The Kokanians in these addresses endeavoured to conciliate the Kirghizes, declaring that they should not suffer any harm, and that the armed force was directed against the Russians, who were to be driven not only from Fort Perovski, but also out of all the other forts of the Steppe.

The position of the Syr-Daria line at this period was far from being secure, as it was impossible to send reinforcements to Fort Perovski during the winter season. A winter expedition could not be undertaken without special preparations. The garrison of the fort, however, was relatively sufficiently strong; it consisted of 631 infantry soldiers, 287 cavalry, ninety-five artillery-men, and forty-two sailors, making a total of 1055 combatants, with fourteen guns and five mortars. The fort was also supplied with forage and other provisions for a year and a half. Under such circumstances, and considering the repulse sustained by the Kokanians, when they had advanced in superior numbers in the month of August preceding, success could safely be counted on, should they venture on another attack.

The condition of Forts No. 2 and 3, situated at 200 and 60 versts respectively from Fort Perovski, was much more embarrassing. Owing to their isolation, assistance could not be sent to them from the latter place. The defences of Fort No. 3 were very weak, and had only been hurriedly repaired after the Kokanians had abandoned it; while Fort No. 2 was nothing more than a field-work, and did not afford the garrison sufficient shelter from snow-drifts. Although the garrisons of these forts were strong enough in proportion to the size of the works, they were yet numerically weak. In Fort No. 2, in December, there were fifty-five foot soldiers, fifty-four cavalry, seven artillerymen, making in all 116 men and one gun.

Fort No. 3 was manned by fifty-five foot soldiers, twenty-six cavalry, and seven artillerymen, in all eighty-eight men and one gun. These would not have been able to resist a numerous enemy. As to Fort Perovski, that general, foreseeing the possibility of an attack in the winter, made arrangements in the autumn for strengthening the garrison with 100 Cossacks of the Ural from Fort Aralsk.

Such was the condition of the Russian fortifications on the Syr-Daria line, when, on the 14th of December, the Kokanians—numbering from 12,000 to 13,000 men, with a small park of seventeen brass guns, appeared before Fort Perovski. Having formed a camp on the left bank of the Syr, two and a half versts from the fort, they made attempts during the 14th, 15th, 16th, and 17th, to surround the fort on all sides, but were always compelled to retire in disorder. The fire of the Kokanian artillery did not produce any damage to the fort, while that of the Russians did great execution. Lieutenant-Colonel Ogaref, conscious of the disadvantage of being besieged for a long period of time, resolved to try the effect of a sudden sortie on the enemy, notwithstanding the great disparity in numbers. At dawn on the

18th, he sent out a detachment of 550 men, with four field-pieces and two rocket batteries, under command of Major Shkupa, who, under cover of the fog, approached within 400 fathoms of the enemy's camp, and opened a running fire of artillery. The Kokanians replied in the same manner at first, and then made several attacks in front and on the flanks, but all these were repulsed by discharges of grape and musketry. The enemy at last surrounded the Russian detachment on all sides, and pressed hard in the rear and on the flanks. The situation of the Russians was becoming rather critical, but Major Shkupa gave a fortunate turn to the affair. Perceiving that the numbers of the Kokanians attached to the guns and in the camp had considerably diminished, he rushed forward with the greater part of his force, routed the Kokanian sharpshooters, and vigorously attacked the Kokanian artillery. The artillerymen fled in disorder, leaving the guns and baggage in the hands of the Russians. At this critical juncture the rest of the Russian force that had remained in position were sustaining a severe fire, and even engaged in a hand-to-hand conflict, until the Kokanians, alarmed by the flames of their burning camp, and attacked by two fresh detachments consisting of one hundred and sixty men, that had been sent out of the fort, hastily retired in disorder. The engagement was over by twelve o'clock. The loss of the Kokanians amounted to two thousand killed, and the Russians had eighteen killed and forty-nine wounded. The trophies that were captured consisted of four horse-hair standards, seven flags, seventeen guns, and one hundred and thirty puds of gunpowder.

In April, 1854, Perovski was informed that the Kokanians had been making military preparations on a great scale in the latter part of the winter of the preceding year. Troops had been collected in Turkestan, and a gun founder had been sent thither to cast some guns, for which purpose the Beg of Tashkend had forcibly seized all the brass utensils of the inhabitants. An organized army of ten thousand men was expected to arrive at Tashkend, and orders were given there and at Kokan to prepare eight hundred horses for the ensuing spring. The object of these preparations was to act on the defensive in case the Russians should march on Turkestan and Tashkend. Should no warlike preparations be made by the Russians, the Kokanians then intended in the spring to march against the Russian forts on the Syr-Daria, and to pillage the

Kirghizes. It was likewise rumoured that the Khan of Khiva had promised the Kokanians to send men and guns to the Fort of Hodja-Nias, so that this force could either act conjointly with the Kokanians against Fort Perovski, or else attack Fort No. 2, while the Kokanians besieged Fort Perovski. But no reliance could be placed on this report, as no preparations were being made at Khiva for this purpose.

With the view of strengthening Fort Perovski, Perovski determined to abandon Fort No. 2, which was not strong enough to hold out against the attack of a strong force.

After the capture of Ak-Mechet by the Russians, and the defeats of the Kokanian hosts in the latter part of the preceding year, no serious movement could be expected from the Kokanians. The great inundations of the rivers that year, prevented the Russians from reinforcing their garrisons on the Syr-Daria line, and at the same time hindered the erection of fresh fortifications.

CHAPTER X.

PART III.

Events in the Steppe during the Crimean War.—Iset-Kutebarof, the Knight of the Steppe.—Attempt of Perovski to occupy Hodja-Nias.—Occupation of Djulek, and Destruction of Yany-Kurgan.

1854-62.

DURING 1854 rumours of hostile preparations by the Kokanians were repeatedly renewed and confirmed by their demeanour in the Siberian Steppe. Rumours of agitations among the Kirghizes were likewise received from time to time. The Sultan-Ali, son of the former rebellious chief, Kenisar-Kasimov, was said to be collecting together a band of seven thousand men for co-operating with the Kokanians by attacking the Siberian Kirghizes, and forcing them to secede from the Russians. The Kokanians in their endeavours to gain over the Dikokamenni Kirghizes to their side, not only concealed the defeats they had sustained in 1853, but even gave out that they had completely routed the Russians, and declared that, having now joined the Khan of Khiva, the Emir of Bokhara and the Sultan of Turkey, who, they said, had already despatched a strong army against the Russians, they intended to drive these invaders altogether out of the Steppe.

Suffi-Beg, a Kokanian leader, who had been forced to fly with his troops from Fort Perovski, in December, 1853, said to the Kirghizes, "We slaughtered the Kaffirs in such numbers that a horse could not step over their dead bodies."

Nothing of importance occurred until the month of October. This irresolution on the part of the Kokanians was partly owing to the relations then subsisting between Kokan and Bokhara, and partly to their own timidity and weakness. It was currently reported that the month of April had been fixed on for their march on Fort Perovski; but the appearance of Bokharian troops on the

Kokan frontier induced the Khan to delay the departure of his force.

The Emir of Bokhara, taking advantage of the unsettled state of Kokan, collected a large army—most probably with the intention of employing it against Kokan, on the first favourable opportunity. The troops assembled by the Emir, receiving neither pay nor provisions, were marched by his orders to the Bokharian Fortress of Konagatchi, on the borders of Bokhara and Kokan, with the object of sacking the frontier Kokanian forts. It was owing to this circumstance that the Khan of Kokan diverted the expedition against Fort Perovski for the time. On the other hand, these noisy preparations for war might only have been the effect of fear, or from apprehension that the Russians would themselves march on Turkestan and Tashkend. In the month of October, intelligence was brought by a Kazan merchant from Tashkend, of the arrival of a Khivan ambassador and suite at that town, with proposals to the Ruler of Tashkend to make a combined attack on Fort Perovski. But as that ruler was under the control of the Khan of Kokan, without whose sanction he could not accede to the request, the Khivan ambassador had proceeded to Kokan.

During the summer, four considerable levies of money had been raised from the inhabitants of Tashkend, and a force despatched in the direction of the Siberian frontier. At the same time that the Khivan ambassador was making proposals of alliance with the Khan of Kokan, the commander of the Khivan Fort of Hodja-Nias sent messengers to the Russian authorities on the Syr-Daria line, with assurances of friendship, It was also reported that the Khivans intended, with a large force, to invade the Russian Steppe, from the side of the Ust-Urt, in the direction of the Aralsk Fort.

During the whole period of the Crimean war, from 1854 to 1856, nothing of special importance occurred in the Steppe, excepting the increase of inroads of Kirghiz bands, particularly under the leadership of Iset Kutebar. This man, who in 1859, during his visit to St. Petersburg, attracted great attention in public, had for twenty years kept the Steppe in a continual state of alarm and excitement.

Iset was the son of the celebrated robber and baranta leader Kutebar, and the constant companion of his father, on whose death he assumed the leadership of the band. Iset's name first became famous in the Steppe in 1822, for the robbery of a

Bokharian caravan that had started from the Siberian line. It would be too tedious to enumerate all the petty depredations of this bold Kirghiz,

ISET KUTEBAR.

and it will therefore be sufficient to mention his more remarkable exploits only.

In 1834 he drove off 1200 horses belonging to

Kirghizes of the Djikeyef tribe. In 1838 he seized a stud of Cossack horses, and took an officer and six Cossacks prisoners, who were subsequently released. In the same year he waylaid and pillaged a caravan of Orenburg traders, carrying off a valuable booty. He also despoiled the Kirghizes of the Tabynsk tribe of 1500 horses, besides driving away 200 head of cattle from the old fortification on the Emba. In 1840 he again plundered a caravan of Russian and Bokharian traders to the value of 15,000 silver roubles. In a baranta in the year 1842, he "lifted" from Kirghizes of various tribes a great quantity of cattle, and about 2000 horses. Kutebar's robberies were frequently accompanied by murder, and after his acts of violence and spoliation, he always hastily retreated into the heart of the Steppe, or into the Khivan territory. Between the years 1842 and 1844 he remained at Khiva, and, returning from thence to the Horde, tried to gain the favour of the Russian Government. He kept the officers on the frontier acquainted with the plans and movements of the Kirghiz Sultan (Kenisar Kasimof), who was then in open revolt in the Trans-Aral Steppe, and furnished information regarding the affairs of Khiva.

In 1845, he made overtures of submission

to Bai-Muhamed-Aichuvakof, Sultan-ruler of the Western division of the Horde; who, deceived by his apparent sincerity, obtained for him—while on

NAZAR KUTEBAR.

a visit at St. Petersburg—a gold medal from the Russian Government. But before this mark of favour reached Iset, information was received that, joined by 100 Khivans, and a considerable band of Kirghiz adherents, he had commenced pillaging friendly aûls, forbidding them to pay the tent-tax to Russia, and was also intriguing to prevent the erection of Russian forts in the Steppe. His force was soon scattered by a detachment sent against it, and tranquillity again restored. But it did not last long. In 1848, Kutebar again summoned 600 Khivans, and made a sudden onslaught on a convoy of provisions and a relieving detachment proceeding to Fort Aralsk. The attempt was not successful, the Khivans having been repulsed and put to flight. Iset, after this, again addressed a letter to the Sultan-ruler Araslan, with assurances of fidelity and submission. On this occasion, they were to some extent confirmed by his actions. He immediately afterwards made restitution to many Kirghizes whom he had robbed in his "barantas," transmitted a letter from the Khan of Khiva inciting him to rebel against the Russians, restored part of the goods of which he had robbed the Bokharian carevan in 1847, and lastly, in 1849, delivered up at the frontier, the greater part of the cattle he had seized from the Kirghizes at different periods.

By these acts, Iset succeeded in gaining the confidence of the Sultan so completely, that when the latter was commissioned to watch the secret relations carried on between Kutebar and the Khivans, he always represented his conduct in a favourable light to the Russian authorities.

In this condition did Kutebar's relations with Russia continue until 1853, when he again exhibited his treachery by inducing the Kirghizes of his camp to refuse supplying camels for the expedition organized at that time against Ak-Mechet. On the capture of that fortress, a Russian force was sent to punish Kutebar; the search for him proved unsuccessful on account of the lateness of the season, but was again renewed in the spring of 1854, from Fort Aralsk, under Lieutenant-Colonel Baron Von Wrangel. This officer, accompanied by several Cossacks, surprised Kutebar in his "aùl," but could not take him prisoner, having previously promised him a safe passage for a conference. But even on this occasion Kutebar surrendered the malefactors who had sought refuge in his camp, and solemnly swore to appear at Orenburg to seek mercy and forgiveness for his misdeeds.

This promise, like the preceding ones made by him, remained unfulfilled. Early in 1855, it became known that Iset had renewed his relations with Khiva, that he openly received the Khivan tax-gatherers, and was again collecting a band of marauders. On the strength of this, Perovski gave immediate orders to the commander of Fort Aralsk, to watch narrowly the movements of the rebel, and commanded the Sultan-ruler Araslan Djantürin, to take the field immediately with a Cossack detachment and 600 Kirghizes against Kutebar, and to endeavour to capture him. This expedition terminated very unfortunately.

The Sultan-ruler, starting on the 7th July, had hardly proceeded 140 versts from Fort Orsk, when his camp was attacked by Kutebar's force, numbering 1500 men. The 900 Kirghizes who accompanied the Sultan, took to flight, and he, with several other Horde dignitaries, were killed in the conflict. Having pillaged the camp, the rebels retreated with their booty, and the Cossacks, seventy-five in number, fell back to the line, taking with them their killed and wounded.

Kutebar's audacity could not be allowed to remain unpunished, more especially as encouraged by his late success, he had commenced to oppress the Kirghizes, and issued a religious proclamation inciting to a general rising against the Russians.

Although the pursuit of the Kirghiz bands was,

in summer, attended with extreme difficulty, it would have been inexpedient to have abandoned the pursuit of Kutebar. Perovski, therefore, without loss of time, despatched from Orsk, Orenburg, and the Lower Uralsk Steppe, 600 Cossacks of the Orenburg corps, 300 men of the Uralsk and Bashkir regiments, two field-guns, and fifty men of the Orenburg battalion of the line. The command of the whole detachment was entrusted to Lieutenant-Colonel Kuzminski.

Besides this force, the commander of Fort Uralsk received orders to act with the Cossacks at his disposal from the side of the Mugodjar hills, on the flank and in the rear of the rebels. A reserve, consisting of a regiment of Bashkirs, 800 strong, was also stationed in the fortress of Orsk.

In this manner, Iset Kutebar was apparently surrounded on all sides. On the 3rd August Kuzminski came up with Kutebar's band, numbering 2000 men, near the Kum-Cheargan sands, at the confluence of the Temir and Emba, 360 versts from the line. The robbers being out of gun-shot, had time to disperse in all directions. The horsemen sent in pursuit succeeded in killing only a few men, and seizing 600 head of cattle and horses. The greater portion of Kutebar's force had taken the alarm a short time before, and sought safety in the Great Barsuki sands, or fled in the direction of the Ust-Urt.

Kuzminski now divided his detachment into several parts, and despatched them towards these localities, while another flying column was to co-operate from Fort Aralsk.

Kutebar's band, after its dispersion, continued its depredations, principally on the caravan route, flying from place to place with great rapidity. To render the Russian communications secure, as well as for the further pursuit of the marauders, it was absolutely necessary to leave the troops in the Steppe until late in the autumn, or until the capture of the rebel ringleaders and their aùls had been effected. A last alternative remained, which was to keep a force in readiness during the whole winter, feeding the horses on dry fodder, and to renew the pursuit early in March when the steeds of the Kirghizes would be weakened from the scarcity of provender.

When it was ascertained that the marauding Kirghizes were seeking temporary refuge in the Ust-Urt, three detachments were sent to surround them there, and it was thought that they would be soon forced to surrender on account of the scarcity of forage and food. In spite, however, of all these arrangements, this expedition, like the previous one, terminated unsuccessfully.

Although one of Kuzminski's detachments devastated 146 rebellious aüls, the success was counterbalanced by a disaster in another quarter. A party of fifteen Cossacks and seven Kirghizes with the Sultan Tungachin, who had been sent to the Emba for a supply of forage provisions, were surrounded on the Temir by a body of 500 Kirghizes. The Cossacks, dismounting and making their camels kneel down, fired from behind them at their assailants; the Kirghizes, however, retiring to a distance of 150 fathoms, opened fire from their long rifles. Their shots did more execution than those of the Russians, who had only their carbines. The fusilade was kept up for four hours, by which time all the Cossacks were either killed or wounded, Tungachin being among the former. When the fire of the Russians ceased, the Kirghizes fell on the wounded, and killed them with their spears; one Cossack alone remained alive, having concealed himself among the slain. But he was soon discovered by the Kirghizes, and though already wounded in two places, received five spear thrusts, and was then led away prisoner. Taking advantage of the darkness of the night, the Cossack made his escape on horseback, and reached Kuzminski's detachment on the fourth day in a miserable condition.

Frost and bad weather having now set in, all further operations were necessarily suspended, and the troops retired to the line. Three hundred Orenburg Cossacks were left through the winter with instructions to strengthen the defences of Fort Aralsk: and, if necessary, to march into the Steppe early in the spring.

This year's expedition against Kutebar was very fatiguing for the troops. The detachment had been got ready somewhat too expeditiously, and started with light equipments; during three months and a half each soldier had marched 2400 versts over very arid and inhospitable Steppes, and suffered great privations in the scorching heat of the summer and the early frosts in October.

It cannot be said that the expedition was altogether unproductive of good results, but its principal object was not attained. Iset Kutebar was still at large, but the rebellious Kirghizes were severely punished; many of them perished in the pursuit, a great quantity of their cattle was seized by the Russians, and Iset Kutebar, though left with the greater part of his followers, who, however, had become impoverished and discontented, fled by all accounts to the South-Western part of the Ust-Urt, to the Turkmen. His influence among the Kirghizes now gradually diminished. In this state affairs remained until the summer of 1856. In the month of June, although everything was quiet in the Steppe, Perovski, in anticipation of new attempts on the part of Iset, despatched a force of 300 Orenburg Cossacks and one gun, in search of him, under the command of Lieutenant Colonel Plotnikof. This officer was to act in conjunction with Bai-Muhamed, Sultan of the middle division of the Horde. In the beginning of August, Colonel Plotnikof having ascertained that Kutebar lay encamped near the Asmantai-Matai sands, 350 versts from the Emba, proceeded to the Ust-Urt. After traversing 160 versts, he left his heavy baggage under the protection of 200 Cossacks and Kirghizes, and advanced by forced marches to the Matai sands, with the intention of cutting off Kutebar's progress to the shores of the Caspian, where he would have found good pasture. The movement of troops in the open Steppe being difficult to conceal, and as the mutinous Kirghizes exercised great vigilance, they hastily fled to the desert shores of the Sea of Aral, on hearing of the advance of the Russian corps. The detachment pursued them diligently for five days, marching over 200 versts during the last two days, at a temperature of 35° Fahrenheit in the day, and 20° degrees at night. Further pursuit was now found impossible, as the fugitives filled up and polluted the wells in their flight.

In spite, however, of these unfavourable circumstances, Plotnikof succeeded by the rapidity of his advance in overtaking a part of the Kirghizes, and in capturing several relatives of Iset, who had been participators in the destruction of the Sultan Araslan-Djantürin, eighteen months previous; he also wrested from them about 900 head of cattle. Two of the captured Kirghizes found guilty of the murder were condemned to death, and handed over to the Provost-Marshal. The sentence, after receiving the confirmation of Perovski, was carried into effect at Fort Aralsk, in the presence of a large number of Kirghizes and their elders, who had been summoned to witness the execution.

During the whole of the summer of this year the tranquillity of the Steppe was not disturbed and the post not once robbed, as had been so frequently the case in previous years.

Unfortunately, at this juncture, Perovski's death occurred, Kutebar remaining still unsubdued.

In May, 1857, a force consisting of 300 Cossacks, under Lieutenant-Colonel Plotnikof, was again sent in pursuit of Kutebar, who was then camping on the Ust-Urt, near Asmantai-Matai.

Once more, Kutebar succeeded in escaping through the barren localities of the Ust-Urt, along the Western shore of the Sea of Aral, towards the Khivan town of Kungrad. Plotnikof sent a small party in that direction, but it was obliged to return, finding the wells choked up or rendered useless. Seeing that it was impossible to prosecute the search after Kutebar, owing to the scarcity of water and forage, and having already lost several horses by fatigue and want of provender, Plotnikof returned to the Little Barsuki sands.

Plotnikof's corps had but shortly left the Ust-Urt, when Iset, who had been driven into the waterless Steppe on the Western coast of the Sea of Aral, again returned with his aùls to Asmantai. But as he had previously destroyed the wells in these parts, he was forced by necessity to pitch his tents a short distance from a Russian detachment, 300 strong, under Lieutenant-Colonel

Borodin, near the former Emba Fort. Borodin, without loss of time, descended the Emba, and then, entering the Ust-Urt, surprised Kutebar's aùls on the 11th of September. About 600 head of cattle were seized, but Iset again effected his escape with several companions. In order to prevent Kutebar from returning again to Asmantai, and to ensure the safety of the scientific expedition, already mentioned as proceeding to the Syr-Daria with Mr. Severtsof, Plotnikof's detachment again entered the Ust-Urt, where it remained for seventeen days; after which, on the 17th of October, it went into winter quarters at Fort Orsk.

Katenin, who succeeded Perovski, seeing the difficulty and almost impossibility of capturing Kutebar on the Ust-Urt by Russian detachments, considered it expedient to gain the rebellious chief over by conciliatory measures and promises of forgiveness in the event of his complete submission to Russia. Katenin at the same time proclaimed a pardon for all who had taken part in the marauding expeditions of Djan-Hodja. This measure proved successful, as during the summer the former followers of Djan-Hodja encamped in small "aùls" on the Syr-Daria, and testified their submission. In the following year they were followed by Kutebar himself, who appeared with declarations of repentance during the journey of Katenin to the Steppe.

In describing Kutebar's exploits, we have had to skip Perovski's last exploit—the attempt, namely, to establish himself on the left bank of the Syr-Daria, on its arm known as the Kuvan-Daria. This omission we now proceed to rectify.

On this Kuvan channel, westward of Fort Perovski, and 85 versts to the South-west of the Russian Fort No. 2, stood the Khivan Fort of Hodja-Nias, erected in 1846. This was the most distant fortified point on the Northern frontier of Khiva, and served as a barrier against the Russians and Kokanians. But this point was not of such great importance to Khiva in political as in financial respects. It was passed by all the Bokharian caravans proceeding to and from Russia, and considerable transit dues were annually collected at it by the Khivan Government. For this purpose, as well as for collecting tribute from the neighbouring Kirghizes, a garrison of never fewer than 100 men was maintained at Hodja-Nias, and the fort was also provided with several pieces of ordnance. Its first governor was Hodja-Nias, after whom the fort was called, Irdjan, his son, succeeding his father in command of it on the death of the latter.

In 1856, Irdjan, on receipt of some important message from Khiva, hastily marched thither with forty men of his garrison. The Kirghizes who camped in those parts, and had long been dissatisfied with the Khivan administration, expelled the officer left in charge of the fort, plundered the Khivan property, spiked and dismounted the guns, and hacked the carriages to pieces.

The immediate consequence of this event to the Russians was an increase of robberies and larcenies committed by the Hodja-Nias Kirghizes, who had hitherto been kept in check by the Khivan authorities of the fort. To prevent increasing disorders it was deemed necessary to despatch a small force towards Hodja-Nias. Had the Russians not taken steps to occupy the fort it would have been seized either by the Kokanians or Bokharians.

Great disorder prevailed at this time in the Bokharian territory, as several Khans were contending for the supreme power. Tired at last by these dissensions, the Khivans and Karakalpaks had, it was said, desired the Emir of Bokhara to take them under his protection. This would have complicated the relations of Russia with Bokhara, and frequent and serious collisions must have ensued. Immediately southward of the small ruined fort in the direction of Khiva and Bokhara, stretches for several hundred versts an arid waste of sands, which cannot be traversed by large detachments of troops, so that this uninhabited desert was considered to form a most convenient and safe boundary for Russia on the side of the Bokarian and Khivan territories.

Up to that time it was generally considered that Hodja-Nias belonged unconditionally to Khiva. This opinion, however, was merely founded on the fact of possession, for from inquiries made on the spot, when it was proposed to effect a temporary occupation of the fort by a Russian force, it was ascertained that the Kokanians never recognized as of right the occupation of Hodja-Nias claimed by Khiva, and had during the ten years' existence of the fort twice taken it and expelled the Khivan garrison. After the last expulsion, the Khivans had paid the Kokan Beg of Ak-Mechet a large quantity of cattle for permitting them to return. The occupation of Hodja-Nias by the Khivans was therefore only tolerated by the Kokanians. The Russians being the successors of the latter in these parts, and putting aside their other ancient rights to the whole extent of country roamed over by the Kirghizes of the Little Horde, were quite justified in claiming the Hodja-Nias district as their own. Other reasons, however, deterred the Russians from taking possession of this point for the present.

From the observations made by the detachment sent to Hodja-Nias, it was ascertained that the mud walls of the fort, as well as the wooden dwellings inside of it, had been destroyed and burned by the Kirghizes. To repair them was impossible, and it was consequently necessary to construct them anew. The situation of Hodja-Nias, and the sterility of the surrounding country, afforded no facility for maintaining a garrison in it. The fort stood in the middle of morasses, formed by the streams of the Kuvan-Daria. Fresh water could only be procured at a distance of two versts, and fuel was scarce. There was likewise insufficient pasturage, and the communication with Fort Perovski—inconvenient at all times of the year, on account of the various canals—is rendered still more difficult at full water, so that a regular supply of provisions could not be depended upon. The detachment sent for the preliminary occupation of the fort turned back after destroying the remaining works.

Perovski's active service in the Orenburg region terminated with this attempt.

On his death, Katenin—who was appointed his successor—drew up, in 1859, a "Memoir on the Policy of Russia in the Orenburg Region." Among other things, he deemed it necessary to take possession of the small Kokanian fortress of Djulek, in order strategetically to secure Fort Perovski. This was not effected by him, owing to his death, which occurred soon after; but was carried into execution by the present Governor-General of Orenburg (Lieut.-General Bezac), who was also ordered to demolish the Kokanian fortifications of Yany-Kurgan, near Djulek.

A detachment was sent in April, 1861, for the fortification of Djulek; and all the works, together with dwelling-houses for the garrison, were completed by the month of October of the same year. A detachment was likewise despatched to Yany-Kurgan, which was demolished after a cannonade of twenty-three hours.

The Kokanians, in revenge for the destruction of Yany-Kurgan, yet at the same time afraid to attack the Russian forts, commenced pillaging the Kirghizes under Russian protection; but a company of soldiers sent against them from Fort Perovski, compelled them to retreat to Turkestan. According to the most recent accounts, the Kokanians had commenced the erection of a new fort in the place of Yany-Kurgan, to defend Turkestan. The Russian forts now existing on the Syr-Daria are: Fort No. 1, Fort No. 2, and Forts Perovski and Djulek.

It cannot be said that the present condition of the Syr-Daria line is all that is to be desired. There is still much to be done in strengthening and improving it. When first organized, the objects in view were—first, that it should serve as a line of defence against the plundering inroads of the Central Asiatics; and secondly, to protect the Russian trade with the Khanats.

It must be acknowledged that neither of these objects has as yet been fully attained.

The Russian forts, as at present constituted, are not capable of defending the country against hostile incursions. Although their own independence and safety are guaranteed, even in case of an attack by a numerous Khivan or Kokanian force, yet they are not strong enough to prevent the musterings of predatory hordes, to defend the Russian Kirghizes and caravans from plunder and oppression, and to check the temerity of individual marauders, by inspiring fear of instant and condign punishment.

In the intermediate space between the left flank fort, and the advanced Siberian fortified points along the Sará-Su, the independent Kirghizes can easily break into the Siberian and Orenburg Steppes, and despoil the Russian Kirghizes.

The commercial relations of Russia with Khiva and Bokhara are far from being rendered secure by the forts along the Syr-Daria line. All the assistance that they afford the caravans consists in securing their passage in a few shallops over the Syr-Daria; but it is not in their power to escort and defend them on the route. The ruler of Tashkend requires the Bokharian caravans to pass through Tashkend, imposing a high rate of duty on the goods, and in case payment is refused, "extorts a benevolence" from them with impunity.

The communication with the Syr-Daria and Orenburg lines, between the fortress of Orsk and the Aralsk fortification, is facilitated by the establishment of Kirghiz post-stations, but between the Aralsk fortification and the Syr-Daria line occurs the most barren part of the Steppe, where water is only to be procured by digging. The organization of regular communication through the Kara-Kum sands presents great obstacles, as the scanty herbage in these parts will never admit of horses being kept at the post-stations. Camels may possibly be used for this purpose, by means of which intelligence will be regularly though slowly transmitted.

The commissariat arrangements for the troops forming the garrisons of the forts are attended with great difficulty, and result at times in serious irregularities. The character of the country occupied by the forts of the Syr-Daria line, does not afford any facilities for supplying the troops by local means with even the simplest requirements in the way of provisions. Though the Kirghizes turn their attention to agriculture, they confine themselves to raising small crops of millet and barley for their own sole consumption. The land will not be cultivated to any great extent by the Kirghizes, until they become convinced that they can do so without fear of being plundered by Khivan and Kokanian robber bands. The labour attending the pursuit of agriculture is very great in such a soil, the fields requiring constant irrigation. A considerable quantity of vegetables is grown for winter consumption in kitchen-gardens around the forts, but they are often attacked by swarms of locusts, which entirely destroy the vegetation of the fields and gardens.

Grass is mowed in the neighbourhood of the forts, on both banks of the Syr, for a distance of twenty-four or twenty-five versts from the forts. Tracts, at present yielding grass of passable quality, were found overgrown with reeds which had either to be cut down for fuel, or burned where they grew. When the over-flooding of the Syr is not great, a sufficient quantity of hay is obtained as forage for the horses and cattle; but when the water rises high, the meadow-lands are swamped, and the subsequent crop of hay is but small. The horses and cattle have then to be fed on corn and other grain.

As regards the requirements of the officers and civilians, they are supplied with even greater difficulty than the soldiers, as they are not able to buy provisions on the spot or at regular prices. The Russian merchants carry on a profitable trade in cattle with the Kirghizes of the Syr-Daria line, and with caravans from Khiva and Bokhara, but neglect the retail trade within the forts. The shops of those traders in the forts who are allowed to sell goods free of duty, are often empty, and the wares of inferior quality, while the prices are unreasonably high, notwithstanding a fixed tariff and other restrictions.

As there are no forests, wood cannot be procured for the most ordinary domestic purposes, and the material used locally for building purposes is clay. Every thing, even the most trifling articles, are obliged to be brought from the Orenburg line.

The cost of transporting goods from Orenburg to the Syr-Daria line is augmenting with each year, and this increase is owing to three causes; to the rise in the price of cattle, which are exclusively used in the carriage of goods; secondly, to the difficulties attending the transit over the barren sands; and thirdly, from the scarcity of provender in the Kara-Kum sands, and particularly on the transport road between Forts No. 1 and Perovski. But in addition to these drawbacks, the increase in the cost of transport is likewise attributable to the carriers, who, seeing that the Russian Government have no means of conveying supplies along the line, and between Fort No. 1, and Fort Perovski, dictate their own terms.*

Communication between the forts is kept up by Kirghiz postillions, who are sent with Government despatches from fort to fort, and so to the

* Steamers can only proceed up the river at full water.

Orenburg line. The road, which is traversed by transports of goods and provisions, extends from Fort No. 1 to Fort Perovski, along the right bank of the Syr, through a desert, inhospitable and partly barren Steppe. When the inundations of the Syr spread to a great distance, the journey on horseback, from the confluence of the Djaman-Daria, with the Kuvan-Daria, to Fort Perovski, becomes quite impossible. Barges are then towed up the river by lines, and the boatmen engaged in pulling the barges are sometimes obliged to wade up to their knees and even waists in water. This journey, even with constant fresh relays of men, occupies seventeen hours.

The condition of the Syr-Daria line, in sanitary respects, is, on the whole, satisfactory. The number of sick is not great, which is mainly owing to the salubrity of the climate. According to the accounts of local medical men, the immoderate use of fruit and raw vegetables is not, as in most other countries, attended with intestinal disorders; all wounds, moreover, heal rapidly, and diseases but rarely assume a virulent form.

The gadflies and gnats, which abound in such multitudes as to become a positive plague, must not be omitted in describing this region. The

Kirghizes and Cossacks always cover their horses, when riding, with horse-cloths, from the feet to the tails, and with rugs under the stomach. When this precaution is not taken, the horses lie down under their riders, and refuse to move. The horned cattle and Cossack horses, as also the camels, which are in excellent condition in spring, become absolutely emaciated from the irritation and physical exhaustion caused by the stings of the gnats and flies, and die in scores. The Kirghizes, who camp along the banks of the Syr-Daria in summer, leave only a small quantity of cattle here for agricultural purposes, and drive away the rest, for the summer, to the Kara-Kum. On this account carriers are, during the summer, procured with difficulty for transporting goods.

Russia thus occupies an almost barren extent of country along the Syr-Daria, while between Djulek and Fort Vernoe extends the Northern part of the Khanat of Kokan, celebrated for its beautiful climate, fertility of soil, and rich tracts of land.

The historical and geographical future of Russia impels her farther and farther towards the South, in spite of all obstacles; and, yielding to these natural impulses, she has advanced, on one side, from the Irtysh to the upper course of the Syr-Daria, and, on the other, from Orenburg to the Sea of Aral; thus incorporating within her boundaries the greater portion of the Steppes dividing Europe from Asia Proper.

Similar extensions of Russian frontier have always been effected in the same order, by the same laws, and have invariably led to the same results. The pioneers of each onward movement were the Cossacks, who were followed by fixed settlers and agriculturists, with their families and farming stock; and it was in this way that, in some distant and desert region, as on the Don and Ural in former years, and on the Amur and Syr-Daria in the present day, Russian civilization sprang up, and Russian settlements were planted, forming germs for future colonies. A necessity then arose for connecting these settlements firmly together, and with this object roads were constructed, stations erected, steamers introduced, as on the Amur and Syr-Daria, and even telegraphic lines established, as at present from the Chinese frontier to St. Petersburg.

From Orenburg to the Lower Syr-Daria there exists a road along which the post travels, and by which goods can be conveyed in carts. Such important and extensive political interests are concentrated on the rivers Syr and Amu-Darias, that it is absolutely necessary to direct attention to the development and improvement of the routes to these extreme points of Russian territory, and more especially to the establishment of a line of telegraph. Should a line from Orenburg to the Syr-Daria ever be organized, the following antagonistic systems are observable, on glancing at the various telegraphic maps:—On one side the widely-spread net of Russian telegraphs, connected with the whole of Europe and converging on the Sea of Aral; on the other, the network of English wires, extending over the whole continent of India, and terminating, for the present at least, at Peshawur. These two extreme points of English and Russian telegraph lines are separated by a gap of country, the greater part of which is occupied by the course of the Amu-Daria. This intervening space can, of course, be cleared, particularly by the known energy of the English; but here arises the great political question—Who is to supply the existing break, Russia or England?

The establishment of telegraphic communication with India is at the present day a question of primary importance both for English supremacy in India, and particularly for British trade. The expense of such an undertaking will not prove an obstacle for its realization; we have seen an English company sacrifice nearly a million pounds sterling on the Trans-Atlantic cable, and feel convinced that it would not hesitate to lay out as much again if there were any possibility of bringing the scheme to a successful issue. If the English, therefore, were made acquainted with the details proving the feasibility of establishing telegraphic communication with East India through Orenburg and the Sea of Aral, they would most assuredly organize a company without loss of time for realizing the project, regardless of all its difficulties. But would such interference and mediatorship on the part of the English in regions where the influence of Russia is still weak, be consistent with the dignity and political views of Russia?

The country as far as the Syr-Daria and Sea of Aral, belongs *ipso facto* to Russia, so that every means of communication can be freely introduced in it, and a telegraph is certain to be shortly established in these parts. Farther Southward, Russia occupies the mouth of the Amu-Daria, and Russian steamers have already ascended this river. Where is the limit to which these steamers will be confined? Burnes, who descended the Amu-Daria, estimated its navigable length at 2000 versts. It is hardly probable that the Russian settlements destined before long to be permanently established on the Lower Syr-Daria will always be confined to that part of its course, or that the steamers stationed at its mouth will never be permitted to penetrate farther up stream. A similar prohibition would be contrary to the natural order of things, and would indeed be practically disregarded. An instance of this is seen on the Amur, which was secured by treaties and government restrictions, in spite of all which we have seen that Russian settlers in the Trans-Baikal region penetrated into the Amur country during the past hundred years, and traded and hunted in it.

Judging, therefore, by historical precedents, one cannot but forsee that the occupation of the mouth of the Amu-Daria will necessarily be followed by the appropriation of the whole river. The Russian Government may probably not have this in view, and will in all likelihood oppose the encroachment, but nevertheless, sooner or later, it will come to pass of itself. Officially the boundary of Russia will remain unchanged; practically, however, Russian emigrants will ascend the river higher and higher by degrees; they will at first open intercourse with Khiva, the nearest Khanat, and eventually make their way to Bokhara. Examples of this are afforded by the Amur and Syr-Daria. Only the embouchures of these rivers were at first occupied, and strict orders given against advancing up the country; in the lapse of two or three years, however, at most ten or twelve, we find Russian military posts already stationed several hundred versts above the mouths, and the parts of the Amur and Syr-Daria thus occupied beginning to be recognized as Russian territory. In a few years more, Russian settlements had not only spread along the whole course of the Amur, but had occupied its source; the Ussuri, or Russian military posts, had encircled the whole sea coast from the Amur to the Corea, and Russian traders commenced ascending the Dzungari, which will by the same historical sequence lead them to the river Leo, and along it to the shores of the Gulf of Petcheli. The same order of events is observed on the Syr-Daria, of which the lower course alone is held by Russia; yet this river must now be considered more Russian than Kokanian, more especially as the necessity of possessing it for the whole extent of its course is year after year more urgently and clearly felt.

The Amu-Daria is, for many reasons, of greater importance to Russia than even the Syr-Daria. It disembogued at one period into the Caspian, and its bed to that sea still remains. Some are of opinion that the course of the river can be again directed to its ancient bed, while others consider it impossible to do so. It can, however, be positively asserted that the existing information on this point is very superficial and inaccurate, and the question will never be satisfactorily settled, until a scientific expedition be sent by the Government to investigate it in all its bearings. The South-Eastern shores of the Sea of Aral are well adapted for uniting the Syr-Daria with the Amu-Daria, and encourage the hope that the united mass of water of such two great streams may force their way through the old bed to the Caspian. The importance of this connection will readily be understood when it is remembered that a water route, in continuation of the Volga, will be thus created, which will extend for 3000 versts into the interior of Asia, and that the extreme points of this uninterrupted water-way will be St. Petersburg and the Northern slopes of the Hindoo Koosh.

There is an idea generally prevalent that the Syr-Daria will serve as a convenient route for future communication with British India; but the Amu-Daria presents infinitely greater advantages in this respect. Its upper course runs farther to the South than that of the Syr-Daria—in fact, it almost reaches the boundaries of the English possessions, and very closely approaches the Indus. These two rivers are divided by the elevated range of the Hindoo Koosh, across which there are several passes, a few alone of which have been visited by English travellers, and the greater part of this region is still but little known.

Thus we see that the occupation of the mouth of the Amu-Daria will inevitably lead to the navigation of the river by Russians; this will require the occupation of several points on the shores which are uninhabited, and only nominally belong to some barbarous rulers, and the establishments of *points-d'appui* will eventually lead to the occupation of the whole river along either bank.

An outcry will be raised that this is a further increase of territory, an extension of Russian limits, which are already too vast. No! this will be no encroachment or enlargement of Russian boundaries, but simply the establishment of a water-way, and an opening up of new markets for Russian trade and produce. These markets are situated on the upper course of the Amu-Daria, whose mouth is in the possession of Russia; and Russia cannot, and must not relinquish them in favour of England, because she is connected with them by a natural water-way. The English are rapidly advancing to them, Cabul being already virtually in their hands. With regard to India, the navigation of the Amu-Daria must not be considered as a route for the conquest of India; it is time to abandon such an illusion. But it will be advantageous for Russia to meet England on the Indian frontier, to establish a direct and reciprocal trade with her, and in case such a trade be impossible, to endeavour, at least, to procure the transit of Indian goods to Europe by means of Russian iron and water-ways. With respect to a military expedition to India, the Amu-Daria may be used for despatching a small force to its upper course, not with an idea of conquest, but for making a demonstration with the object of alarming the enemy and diverting his attention from other points.' The close proximity of the Anglo-Indian Empire to Russia in these parts need not be feared, as it is no easy matter to penetrate to or from Russia from this quarter.

Since the days of Peter the Great, Russia has diligently advanced, and at great sacrifice, through the Steppes that barred her progress; she has now passed them, and reached the basins of two large rivers—two important water-ways,—whose sources flow through fertile and densely-populated countries. She is fully justified in seeking to be rewarded here for her labours and losses extending over a hundred years, and in endeavouring to secure her frontiers by pushing them forward to that snow-capped summit of the Himalayas—the natural conterminous boundary of England and Russia.

From this stand-point Russia can calmly look on the consolidation and development of British power in India.

These considerations lead one to hope that should a line of telegraph from Europe to India ever pass through these countries, it will be entirely Russian. From the lower course of the Syr-Daria, the most convenient localities for laying down a line of wire to India, extend along the South-Eastern Coast of the Sea of Aral up the Amu-Daria, and from its upper sources, by one of the roads leading to Cabul across the Hindoo Koosh. The distance in this direction, between the extreme point at the mouth of the Amu-Daria and that of the English at Peshawur, is about 2000 versts or 1260 miles.

CHAPTER XI.

Diplomatic Relations between Russia and Bokhara.
By Zalesoff.

1836-1843.

Russia has always maintained amicable relations with Bokhara, and its intercourse with the Khanat has been of long standing.

In addition to its political importance, Bokhara presented great advantages to Russia, as a large consumer of Russian productions, and as a channel through which Russian goods might penetrate into Afghanistan and India. The Bokharians on their side advantageously bartered their own indifferent wares for Russian manufactures of primary necessity, which they were unable to procure from other countries. But there was another circumstance that assisted in cementing friendly feelings between these two countries and served to smooth many difficulties and disagreements.

Bokhara, unlike Khiva and Kokan, did not border on Russian territory; consequently, there was no motive for those petty frontier squabbles and depredations with which Russia was so persistently pestered by the two last-named Khanats. Even later, when the Russians occupied the Syr, and the empire came into close proximity with the States of Central Asia, Bokhara remained separated from it as heretofore by the desert sands of Kyzyl-Kum, and while the wandering tribes subject to Khiva and Kokan were committing depredations on the Russian boundaries, this Khanat still preserved a strict neutrality.

The Bokharians, it is true, could not completely renounce their Asiatic habits; they purchased Russian prisoners through second and third hands, while their Government not infrequently sent envoys to St. Petersburgh with the sole object of receiving presents, and almost invariably demanded an extra rate of duty from Russian merchants; but all these acts, although giving rise to a constant correspondence, never led to a rupture. The Russians, with the prospect of extending their trade to Turan, deemed it politic to sacrifice a few individual interests for this object.

With the extension of Russian dominion southwards from the river Ural, these old relations between Russia and her neighbour acquired a more stable character, and as the roads were rendered more secure across the Steppe, a desire arose to become more acquainted with the Khanat for commercial and political purposes: hence the frequent visits of Russian officials and missions to Bokhara.

The commissioners despatched to Bokhara by the Russian Government during the present century were Lieutenant Poverdovski in 1802, who, however, did not reach his destination; Subhankulof, an officer of the Bashkir force, in 1809; an embassy under Mr. Negri in 1820; an armed caravan under the command of Colonel Tsiolkovski in 1824, and which did not reach its journey's end; Mr. Demaison in 1834; and Ensign Vitkovitch in 1835.

The following letter, addressed to the Emir by General Perovski, military governor of the Orenburg region, in 1836, is a specimen of the style of correspondence conducted with Bokhara after the return of Vitkovitch:—

"To the expounder of wisdom and law, the esteemed, all-perfect, glorious and great Emir, descendant of the benignant Hakan; the centre of learning, order and glory, and the disseminator of happiness, we offer our most sincere respect and warmest devotion. May the all-high and powerful God secure you on the throne of dominion and prosperity, shield you from its tempests, and evil destinies, and grant you a long life.

"Be it further known to your heart, replete with glorious qualities, that, praise be to the Founder of Worlds, we abide in health and happiness.

"Rumours of the measures taken by the Russian Government against the insolence of the Khivans have doubtless long since reached the stronghold of your highly-venerated and mighty Eminence. From respect, therefore, to our famous and gloriously resplendent neighbour, I consider it necessary to say as follows:—

"The Khivans have long behaved as enemies, while calling themselves the friends of Russia.

"Khiva, from its insignificance and weakness, could of course do no great injury to its powerful neighbour, but still it took advantage of every opportunity to exhibit its insolence and senseless temerity against a state that has, until the present, ignored the stratagems and intrigues of a weak and powerless neighbour.

"Khiva, however, did not understand the condescension and endurance of Russia, and instead of being penitent and submissive, her proceedings have grown more audacious from year to year. The piracies on the Caspian multiplied, under the connivance of the Khivan ruler, who shared the plunder with the pirates. The number of Russian prisoners in Khiva have greatly increased, and they are treated barbarously. Russian traders dare not even now appear at Khiva, as they are not received with the customary salaam and greeting, but with the noose, knife, and bonds of slavery. Khiva has commenced to collect tribute from the Kaisaks, our subjects, and from Russian traders who traverse the Steppe; she has set some Khans over the Kaisaks, who have long been subject to Russia, and persecutes them at will. When taking into consideration that the subjects of Khiva have enjoyed in Russia even up to the present time not only all the advantages of freedom, but also profited by all the rights and privileges of free traders, trading and departing at all times without molestation, it must be admitted that the proceedings of the Khivans justly merit chastisement.

"The Emperor has now resolved to detain all the Khivans in Russia, together with their property, and to inform the ruler of Khiva that not a single person will be liberated until all Russians now in slavery be set free by the Khivan Government, and it shall have promised to amend its conduct for the future.

"The orders of the Emperor have been strictly fulfilled, and I have already informed the ruler of Khiva of what had transpired. It depends now on himself to arrange matters amicably, or bring confusion on his head.

"In acquainting your mighty and illustrious person of this, I am convinced that the columns of friendship, and pillars of mutual good-feeling between the Russian Government and that of Bokhara will continue as formerly, fixed and immovable; the Government of Bokhara will doubtless never give Russia similar cause for discontent. I am likewise assured that if there be any Russian prisoners at Bokhara, or such as have escaped from Khiva, your exalted Mightiness will give immediate orders for their release and transmission to their own country.

"To all this I have the pleasure to add, what will probably be pleasing intelligence to your Highness, that your envoy through my mediation has been favoured with a reception by His Imperial

Majesty, and that Bokharian merchants, your subjects, had the felicity of being presented to the Emperor on his passage through Nijni-Novgorod, whilst the Khivans, who were there at the same time, were not granted the same honour."

Such was the language of the chief of the Orenburg region, for conciliating the friendship of the ruler of Bokhara, who did not disregard these advances; from 1836 to 1843, Russia was visited by three of the Emir's representatives, and two Russian agents were in their turn despatched to Bokhara during this period.

It is to the diplomatic relations of these six years that we would now draw attention.

In July, 1836, the Karaul-Begi, Kurban-Beg-Ashurbek, arrived at the fortress of Orsk, in the quality of Bokharian envoy, accompanied by a suite of fifteen men, and with four arghamaks (horses) as gifts for the Imperial Court. On the occasion of their arrival, General Perovski wrote to the Russian Minister for Foreign Affairs. The office of Karaul-Begi, signifying chief of the gate-guards, is not of importance, though each gate in Bokhara has a separate Karaul-Begi. The statement made by the Kush-Begi in Vitkevitch's report, should be borne in mind, which is to the effect that the Bokharian Government does not consider it necessary to select men of high position as envoys to Russia, and even vaunts itself on conferring that dignity on persons of low degree.

But notwithstanding this unfavourable recommendation, the Karaul-Begi was courteously treated, and obtained permission to proceed to St. Petersburg with a suite of four persons; the horses were ordered to be distributed among the breeding stables (horse farms) of the Orenburg region.

On reaching the capital, the envoy presented a letter to the Emperor from the Emir, and others from the Kush-Begi to the Minister for Foreign Affairs, and to the Director of the Asiatic department. The object of this mission,—in addition to its being charged with assurances of friendship, and to express the wishes on the part of the Emir that the commercial and political relations of the two countries should be consolidated,—was to lay the following circumstances before the Russian Government: 1st. That the English had again lately sent agents from India to Bokhara, who were trying to conclude a treaty for supplying the Bokharians with English goods on advantageous terms for the former; and, 2nd. That the ruler of

Cabul, threatened by Runjeet-Sing, had likewise despatched a special agent to the Khan of Bokhara, with proposals for forming a defensive alliance against their common enemies.

The envoy returned to Orenburg on the 28th of March, and took back an Imperial letter to the Emir, and also one from the Vice-Chancellor to the Kush-Begi. The mission left Orenburg on the 24th of August.

As no special benefit was to be derived from similar missions, while the expenses attending their entertainment were considerable, the Russian Government resolved to put a stop to the too frequent visits of their neighbours, by delicate hints, and Count Nesselrode, in his letter to the Kush-Begi, pointing out the great distance of the capital of the empire from its Asiatic boundaries, requested that in all urgent matters, the Bokharian Government should apply to the military governor of Orenburg, who possessed the confidence of the Emperor; the Bokharians, however, did not feel inclined to understand such *finesse*.

Two years had not elapsed since the departure of the Karaul-Begi, when in August, 1838, another envoy appeared before the cordon of the fortress of Orsk; this messenger was Balta-Kuli-Beg-Rahmet-bek, who had already visited Russia in 1830, as representative of Bokhara. He was now the bearer of an autograph letter from the Emir to the Emperor, despatches from his ministers to Nesselrode, Perovski and others, and presents for the Court, consisting of an elephant, arghamaks and Cashmere shawls, and furthermore brought three Russian prisoners with him for liberation; his retinue was composed of twenty men.

Two silver roubles a day, or about six shillings, were allowed him by the Russian authorities for his subsistence; five of the more important members of his suite received fifty copecks a day, or one and sixpence, and the others twenty-five copecks, or ninepence. Balta-Kuli-Beg was well received, and allowed to appear at Court. According to Perovski, he was a man of very limited understanding. What could possibly be the object of the appearance of this new envoy of the Emir? In the absence of the written message of the ruler of Bokhara, we must endeavour to arrive at it from the Emperor's letter written in reply, and from the letters of Count Nesselrode to Ishan-Reis, head dignitary of Bokhara, and to the envoy himself. In them we find the same expressions of thanks for the protestations of friendship on the part of the Bokharians, the same promises to encourage the trade between the two countries, and the same accompaniments of presents, as proofs of friendship. The only novel feature in them appears to be a request on the part of the avaricious Emir, for the Russian Government to send him a mining engineer officer, to explore his territory for gold and precious stones. This want might have been made known without despatching a special embassy.

On the 27th of October, Balta-Kuli-Bek returned to his own country from Orenburg, taking with him many tangible marks of favour, in the shape of brocade, cloth, crystal, &c.

The cost of maintenance and travelling expenses of this last guest, with the presents of money to him and his suite, exclusive of that of his residence at St. Petersburg, amounted to 9000 silver roubles, the transmission of the elephant to St. Petersburg costing 3000 more. If to this total we add the value of the presents for the Emir to the Embassy, we shall find that Nusseer-Ulla's renewal of assurances of friendship were rather high-priced.

It was at all events apparent that the constant despatching of missions served as a novel and exceedingly profitable speculation, in which his Eminence sacrificed nothing but a few elephants and horses, the travelling expenses of the envoy to the frontier being almost invariably defrayed by the merchants whose caravans they happened to accompany.

The Emir's request, however, was complied with, and by order of the Emperor an expedition was organized in April, 1839, under the direction of Captain Kovalevski of the mining Engineers, who was accompanied by Captain Herrngros, an interpreter, a head-miner, two viewers, and four Cossacks. Kovalevski was also furnished with a letter of recommendation to Ishan-Reis, a notification having been previously given of his departure to Balta-Kuli-Beg.

Kovalevski was instructed by the chief of the mining department to collect information respecting the geological formation of the soil of Bokhara, its mineral wealth, trade in precious metals, method of manufacturing the Khorassan steel, &c. &c. By the Minister of Trade and Manufactures, he was charged to direct his attention to the Asiatic trade generally, and the Russian Minister of Foreign Affairs gave him special written instructions, in which, among other things, he was instructed to endeavour to obtain a diminution of the duties imposed on Russian traders, to ascertain the opinion of the Bokharian Government on the subject of permanently establishing a Russian Consul at Bokhara, to gather information regarding the quantity, quality, and value of English merchandize, and the competition they present to Russian productions; to obtain the liberation of Russian prisoners; to form an estimate, while on the spot, of the possibility of extending Russian trade to Afghanistan, and other countries on the left bank of the Amu, and finally to collect statistical and topographical data relating to Bokhara, and the countries adjacent to it on the South.

Kovalevski left Orenburg with the Bokharian envoy, and proceeding through Bish-Tamak, across the Emba and Mugodjar mountains, reached the Great Barsuki Sands by the middle of November.

Almost at the very outset of the expedition, it encountered opposition from evil-disposed Kirghiz bands, who were irritated by the movement of General Perovski's column across the Steppe about this time. The dangers of the caravan were still further increased by meeting an official from Khiva, who had been sent by the Khan of that country, to instigate the Kirghizes against the Russians.

Menaces were added to other insults. The Khivan agent insisted that the caravan should cross the Syr, and proceed through the Khivan fortress. He told the Russian officers that they were his prisoners, and ordered a watch to be placed over their tents during the night-halts. Owing to these circumstances, Kovalevski fled secretly from the caravan, and sought protection in the nearest Russian fortification. During the night of the 21—22 November, in a severe snow-storm, the Russian officers, abandoning their luggage, and half-dressed, mounted their horses and hastened to Chush-Kakul Fort, which they reached on the 24th November,—performing thus 300 versts (or 80 miles English) in 2½ days.

All the things abandoned by Kovalevski reached Bokhara in safety, and were taken care of there until the arrival of a new Russian mission, to the head of which they were subsequently delivered; and the officers of Kovalevski's expedition returned to the Russian frontier line with Perovski's detachment in the middle of March. Thus ended this unsuccessful undertaking, which cost the Government 2700 ducats independent of travelling expenses. The despatch of mining engineers to Bokhara was postponed until a more favourable opportunity. But still the speculation in embassies did not cease. The Emir and his Ministers were not the men to abstain from a profitable and easy stroke of diplomacy, but they were likewise compelled by other circumstances to open negotiations with Russia. It was this therefore that caused the appearance of another Bokharian envoy, Kulli-Bi-Mulla Mukin-Beg Mahommed-Seid, at Orenburg on the 15th of August, 1840, with a suit of thirty-nine persons and the inevitable arghamaks for the Imperial Court.

The Russian Government had by this time become well acquainted with the speculative proclivities of the Emir and his Ministers, and the estimable Mukin-Beg might possibly not have had the good fortune of seeing St. Petersburg, had not events in Central Asia about this time called for closer relations between Russia and Bokhara. The English were at that time playing the comedy in Afghanistan on which the curtain dropped so tragically.

The proceedings of the English placed both themselves and the Russians in a curious predicament. On one side exaggerated rumours of Russian preparations on a large scale for a war in Turan, and of the movement of her troops towards Khiva, spread through Europe, while on the other, England hiding her real intentions under the pretext of espousing the cause of the worthless and vicious Shoojah-Ul-Mulh, triumphantly marched an army of eighteen thousand men through Hyderabad and Kandahar to Cabul, and, calculating on anticipating by these means the advance of the Russians on Afghanistan, stationed their forces at the very gates of India.

It will fall to the share of the future historian of Perovski's expedition to Khiva to recount the interesting relations between these two countries; suffice it to say here that during the mission of Mukin-Beg the Baraksi dynasty had already failed, and that Dost-Mahomed, Khan of Cabul, its most able representative, was a fugitive in Bokhara. The advanced English troops had appeared at Bamian and Sigan, and rumours were rife of their movements to the Amu-Daria, and farther to Samarcand.

"All the members of the English Government," says an historian of the English expedition to Cabul, "during Lord Auckland's administration of India, were particularly apprehensive of the Russians; they daily expected a Russian advance to Hindustan, apprehensions that rose to a ridiculous panic on receipt of the intelligence of the Russian expedition to Khiva. Even Burnes was informed by one of his agents that the Russians had conquered Khiva and were proceeding by forced marches to Bokhara. On another occasion it was reported that the ruler of Bokhara had concluded an offensive and defensive alliance with the Emperor of Russia, and that their united forces were marching to Balkh." *

These rumours and apprehensions induced the English, independent of their march on Cabul, to have recourse to other measures for counteracting the imaginary machinations of Russia, and with this object their diplomatic agents appeared in the Turan. Captains Abbot and Shakespere made their way to Khiva, and unsuccessfully filled the parts of mediators in the dispute between that country and Russia; and the enterprising Conolly penetrated into Kokan, while Bokhara was visited by Colonel Stoddart, whose appearance the Bokharians expected to be followed by an English force.

* "Afghanistan and the English in 1841-42."—Neumann.

It was natural, under such circumstances, that the Emir should seriously reflect on his probable fate, and despatch an embassy, not from motives of cupidity alone, to Russia. The agent chosen to proceed to the court of St. Petersburg was one of the most influential persons of Bokhara, and similar care was shown in the selection of his suite; besides the two sons of the envoy, different diplomatic officials, two pages, a runner, and four musicians accompanied it. Mukin-Beg presented a letter, six shawls, and two arghamaks, or horses, from the Emir to the Emperor, besides gifts to the different Russian authorities.

The visible object of the embassy was to complain against the treacherous acts of Khiva, to obtain protection for the Bokharian merchants, and permission for Bokharian pilgrims to pass through Russia to Mecca.

The envoy arrived at St. Petersburg on the 30th of October, with a suite of seven Bokharians. Exhibiting great distress of mind, both during the journey and on his arrival at the capital, for want of his musicians, who had been left behind at Orenburg, he prevailed on the Russian Government to have two of his artists forwarded to him, saying that it was the wish of the Emir that they should see St. Petersburg.

On the 16th of February, Mukin-Beg proceeded on his way back, but did not reach Orenburg. Old age, the fatiguing journey, and his immoderate mode of living, told on his health, which was already giving way when he left St. Petersburg. He obstinately refused medicine, and it was only at Moscow that he consented to take a medical man with him. By the time he reached Nijni his strength was quite exhausted, and he died of dropsy of the chest on the 11th of March, in spite of all medical assistance. The sons were allowed to transport the body to Bokhara, and the expenses of embalming were defrayed by the Russian Government. An inventory of the deceased envoy's effects was drawn up, and they were subsequently brought to Bokhara on the occasion of Major Butenef's mission.

The imperial letters delivered to the envoy at St. Petersburg, and those entrusted to Major Butenef for delivery to the Emir, only contain assurances of goodwill, and it would be difficult to gather from them alone the real object of Mukin-Beg's visit. Fortunately, this is partly revealed by the note on the subject of his mission, delivered by the envoy to General Gentz and Count Nesselrode. We shall not presume to criticise these documents in detail. We can only say that the Russian Government found it necessary to despatch an embassy to Bokhara, composed according to the Emir's former request, of mining officers, the chief, Major Butenef, receiving at the same time separate diplomatic instructions, in addition to his other commissions.

The despatch of agents to Khiva and Bokhara was decided on during Mukin-Beg's stay at St. Petersburg, and 10,290 ducats were assigned to defray their expenses. Before Butenef's departure, besides receiving verbal directions, and being allowed to make himself acquainted with the documents relating to Central Asia, in the Foreign department, he was furnished with written instructions by the Mining, Industrial, and Foreign departments. The instructions of the Minister for Foreign Affairs, after mentioning Kovalevski's mission to Khiva, and stating that the agent was sent to Bokhara in compliance with the solicitations of the Emir, with the object of exploring the mineral resources of the country, go on as follows: —"You are, moreover, charged with the collection of positive and reliable information concerning the Kahnat of Bokhara and neighbouring countries, and with the arrangement of terms, for regulating the mutual relations between Bokhara and Russia." In order to give greater weight to the negotiations between Butenef and Nusseer-Ulla, it was considered expedient to give the agent the title of envoy, and to furnish him full power from the Russian Government. The geological investigations were to be conducted by the junior officer, under Butenef's superintendence. Proposing also that Butenef should observe the effect produced on Bokhara by the recent events in Afghanistan, the instructions proceeded to say :—" The acquisition of this information will enable you to suggest the best means for strengthening the political influence of Russia, and for developing Russian trade in this part of Asia."

The instructions then sketch out an extensive programme for gathering information regarding the Bokharian trade, and pointed out that Russia had always been friendly disposed to Bokhara, and had protected her merchants, but that the Bokharians had often in return shown great ingratitude by oppressing her traders, slighting her envoys, &c. &c. Butenef is requested to explain to the Khan that his real interests would be furthered by maintaining friendly relations with Russia, and to inspire him with confidence in the sincerity of the Russian Government. In assurance of the latter the agent was to draw the Khan's attention to the disinterested policy of Russia with regard to other Mahometan countries, for instance the assistance she had given to Turkey and Persia, against the rebellious Pasha of Egypt in the first case, and in seating Mahomet-Shah on the throne, in the second; and which was also evidenced by her generous forgiveness of the misdeeds of Alla-Kul, when the latter complied with the principal demands of Russia.

"All these and similar suggestions," said the instructions, "made to the Khan of Bokhara with proper discretion and adduced as your arguments, will assuredly convince him of the advantage of Russian mediation and of the honesty of our policy."

Then passing to the negotiations, the agent is to endeavour to procure the consent of the Khan to the following terms:—

1. Neither openly nor secretly to show hostility against Russia.

2. Not to detain in slavery or by any means obtain Russian prisoners, and to guarantee the personal safety and property of every Russian subject within Bokharian territory.

3. In the event of the death of a Russian subject in Bokhara, his property is not to be seized by the Crown, but returned *intact* to the Russian authorities at the frontier.

4. To prohibit Bokharians from robbing and imposing arbitrary laws on Russians, and to inflict immediate punishment on those guilty of such offences.

5. To impose a single duty on Russian goods brought to Bokhara, which duty is not to exceed 5 per cent. of their real value.

6. That Russian traders should not be annoyed and oppressed within the dominions of Bokhara, and that they should be afforded the same protection as Bokharians enjoy in Russia.

In return for these stipulations, the Russian agent was to guarantee in the name of the Russian Government:—

1. Safety of person and property to Bokharian subjects within the boundaries of the Russian Empire.

2. The extension of the same privileges to Bokharians as are enjoyed by other Asiatics trading to Russia.

3. The right of requiring the punishment of Kirghizes and Turkmens subject to Russia, in case they pillaged Bokharian caravans.

4. Permission to Bokharian pilgrims proceeding to Mecca, to pass through Russian territory on condition that they conform to the existing police regulations in Russia.

No difficulty was anticipated in obtaining the Emir's consent to the clauses relating to the safety of the lives and property of Russian subjects, but the minister was not so sure on the subject of the decrease of duties, though the agent is directed in his instructions to gain the adhesion of the Khan to this point by quoting Persia and Turkey where the tariff on Russian goods was regulated by treaties.

The instructions generally direct the agent to conduct the negotiations with proper dignity, firmness and discretion.

Should the Khan, however, refuse to accede to the proposed terms, the agent was not to fail in acquainting him that the fulfilment of these conditions was guaranteed by the lives and property of the Bokharians existing Russia.

Finally, Butenef was directed to obtain the Khan's assent to the temporary presence at first of a Russian official at Bokhara, so that the same might afterwards, under more favourable circumstances, be replaced by a permanent agent, and to use every exertion to obtain the liberation of all Russian slaves within the dominions of the Khan.

If matters went smoothly, the mission was to remain about a year at Bokhara, and to return with a caravan in the following spring; but in the event of an unfavourable reception, and if all attempts at accommodation proved unsuccessful, the agent was to return to Russia without entering into any negotiations.

From the above it will be observed how complicated were the instructions given to Butenef; besides that they touched on such delicate points as remission of duties, liberation of slaves, the settlement of which under the ignorant prejudices and customs of the Asiatics, would at first sight appear impossible, and could only be carried out by the pressure of any extraordinary circumstances in which Bokhara might find herself placed.

"We hope," said the Chancellor to the Vizier, "that M. Butenef will be as well received by you, as are the Bokharian envoys in Russia, and will in like manner be allowed to depart whenever he wishes to do so." And then again: "It has reached our knowledge that the Emir had intended to have despatched the Englishman Stoddart, who is now among you, with your Envoy Mukin-Beg to Russia, but was deterred alone by the apprehension of an attack by the Khivans. According to the existing mutual relations between the States of Russia and Great Britain, this intention on the part of the Emir was most pleasing to us. Now as the former obstacle no longer exists, we entertain the hope that the will of the Emir will be fulfilled. The best way of forwarding the said Englishman to Russia will be to send him on with a caravan to Orenburg, where the Russian governor will make all further arrangements."

With regard to this latter circumstance, it must be observed that the English Government had applied several times to Russia, to secure her co-operation in procuring the liberation of the unfortunate Stoddart.

Information having been received a short time before the departure of the Russian mission to Bokhara, that Stoddart had refused to take advantage of an opportunity for proceeding to Russia, not wishing to owe his liberation to the intercession of any foreign government, Lord Palmerston again addressed himself to the Russian ambassador in London, soliciting the renewal of Russian efforts in behalf of the English agent.

It is evident from Mukin-Beg's notes, that Khiva did her best to rescue Stoddart. The Russian Government on its part could not remain indifferent to the fate of the unfortunate prisoner, both from a friendly feeling towards England, as well as from other reasons, and the extract cited from the Chancellor's letter proves her lively interest in the matter. Butenef was besides commissioned persistently to demand Stoddart's liberation, and to despatch him to Russia by the first opportunity. In forwarding to Perovski the letters of the Marquis of Clanricarde for Stoddart, which were to be delivered to the latter by Butenef, the Chancellor wrote: "The explanations given by the late Bokharian envoy, lead us to hope that Nusseer-Ulla will not oppose Stoddart's departure for Russia, and Lord Clanricarde's letter will probably induce this officer to waive his feelings of misplaced vanity, and to seize the present opportunity for obtaining his release. I would, therefore, request you to do everything in your power, in case Stoddart should reach the Orenburg line, for securing him a friendly reception, and desire you to furnish him with means for enabling him to proceed to St. Petersburg without interruption."

The Russian mission consisted of Captain Bogoslovski, of the mining engineers; the naturalist Lehmann; M. Khanykof, from the Ministry for Foreign Affairs; the interpreter Kostromitinof; the topographer Yakovlef; three miners; two stuffers of animals; ten Cossacks of the Ural; and five Kirghizes; the mission was also accompanied by the children and suite of the deceased Mukin-Beg.* The gold pieces supplied to the members of the mission were directed to be secreted in their sword cases or in leathern belts, so as not to excite the cupidity of the Bokharians who would examine the luggage, which was to be transported by fifty-five camels.

Lieutenant-Colonel Blaramberg, at the head of a detachment of 400 Ural Cossacks, was to escort the mission to the river Syr, and 17,000 silver roubles were assigned towards the maintenance of these troops. Returning again to the political instructions with which the head of the mission was charged, Perovski recommended that a reduction of the duties on Russian goods to 2½ per cent. should be strenuously insisted on, and that the agent, when speaking about the yearly visit of a

* For the expenses of the journey Butenef received 4936 ducats, &c.

Russian official to Bokhara, should work on the vanity and pride of the Emir, by pointing out to him that such persons are stationed at the courts of all independent rulers.

With regard to Stoddart, rumours of his execution at Bokhara having reached Orenburg, Perovski suggests to Butenef, in the event of the report being correct, that he should urge on the Emir the propriety of communicating the circumstance by letter to the Emperor, through the Kush-Begi.

The mission left Orenburg in the month of May, and under protection of Blaramberg's detachment, proceeded through the settlement of Bish-Tamak, the Morgodjar hills, and reached the ferry over the Syr at Mailibash on the 18th of July. On the 22nd, parting with the escort, it crossed the river in a large boat sent from the Khivan fortress, which stands on the site of the former Djanket fort, and arrived at the Kuvan river, from whence Butenef despatched a letter to the Kush-Begi, informing him of the arrival of the mission.

Leaving the mission now to wend its way across the Kyzyl-Kum waste, let us acquaint the reader with the character of the Emir and his principal ministers.

The Emir, Nusseer-Ula, Bogadur-Khan, belonged

to that class of persons in whom a remarkable pliancy of intellect was combined with all the qualities inherent in all Asiatic rulers. He was revengeful, sensual, and proud, though when forced by circumstances, could skilfully play a humble part, deceiving the most experienced European diplomatist.

His conduct towards Hakim-Bai, the former Kush-Begi, and then towards Stoddart, resembled a cat playing with a mouse. His constant flattery of the Russian Government, and the subsequent bad treatment of Butenef's mission, his overtures to the Khan of Kokan, while he was supporting the rival claimant to those dominions, plainly characterize the domestic and foreign policy of the Emir, who for a period of thirty-four years ruled his Bokharian subjects with a rod of iron.

Without giving at length the biography of Nusseer-Ulla, the interesting details of which are to be found in many works, we think it necessary to quote here some observations made by Butenef's contemporaries, respecting the Emir, in order to see what were the opinions entertained of this ruler between the years 1830-40.

This is what the Russian traveller, Vitkevitch, who visited Bokhara in 1835, writes of him:—" The present Batyr-Khan, who is always simply called the Emir, or ruler, has delegated all sovereign power to the Kush-Begi. The Kush-Begi Hakim-Bai, is an old man of great subtlety, covetous in the extreme, and possessing great wealth; being, in fact, the richest Bokharian, and even richer than the Khan. He will not allow any matter to reach the Khan, and entirely acts as he pleases; the Khan can no longer oppose him. The Khan, also, is self-willed, cruel, and given to every description of sensuality, boys and girls being forcibly taken from their parents to gratify his brutal passions."

General Gentz, another traveller, who passed the greater portion of his life in the collection of information on Central Asia, gives the following account of affairs at Bokhara:—"The Bokharians are dissatisfied with the Emir and his Government. There is no Vizier, and affairs are generally in great confusion. The Custom dues and taxes are collected by two boys; of these, the Emir keeps more than a hundred near him, acquiring new, and sending away the old ones. The Emir does not trouble himself about affairs, and gives himself up entirely to the vilest debauchery. In the event of war, no one will espouse his cause; so that, with a small number of troops, Bokhara may be easily occupied. All his actions prove him to be insane."

This sketch was made during the summer of 1840, a short time previous to the starting of the Russian mission, and Mr. Gentz had every opportunity for forming a correct estimate of the Emir's character.

When Butenef arrived at Bokhara, Ishan-Reis, the head minister and successor of Hakim-Bai, was no longer alive. Although Ishan had merely been chief of the police, yet, from the favour he had received at Court, and the friendly feelings he entertained to Russia, it was on him that the mission must chiefly have depended for success. The Bokharians themselves lamented the death of Ishan, saying that in him Bokhara had lost the only man who was capable of managing State affairs with profit and success to his country.

Thus, in consequence of the death of Ishan, the mission was obliged to carry on the negotiations with the new Vizier, Abdul-Halik, a youth of nineteen, and fosterling of the male harem of the Emir. It is true there was another person who enjoyed consideration, the Naib Abdul-Sarmed, a fugitive from Persia, who was then forming a body of regular troops at Bokhara; but this triple-dyed criminal, condemned to the gallows in Persia and India, and deprived of his ears at Cabul for another act of violence, had but little share in political affairs, and was, moreover, on good terms with Stoddart.

Having safely traversed the Kyzyl-Kum sands, the mission reached on the 15th of August the Karagata wells, where it was met by Myrza Fuzail, an official sent from Bokhara; when within ten miles of the town, it was welcomed by another official; and, close to Bokhara, Butenef was greeted by one of the highest local dignitaries, the chief of the Kalmyks, who, in the name of the Emir, invited the mission to repair at once to the palace. The members of the mission, having dressed themselves for the audience in their uniforms, in one of the private dwellings on the way, they entered Bokhara on the 17th of August, in the midst of a great crowd of people. They were here met by another envoy, who informed them, that in proof of the sincere pleasure felt by the Emir on the arrival of the distant travellers, he permitted them to ride into the palace on horseback,—"a privilege," says Perovski, "only enjoyed at Bokhara by the Vizier alone."

After entering the palace in the manner graciously sanctioned by his High Mightiness, the agent was then ushered, through a row of Bokharian officials, into a large court, in which, wearing a white turban and robes (Khalat), and seated on cushions, was the Emir himself. After saluting the Russians, he attentively surveyed them for a long time; he then ordered the head Vizier to take the Imperial letter out of Butenef's hands, and, having repeated a short prayer, dismissed the mission.

The former palace of the Khan's brother Mir-Hussein, the best residence in Bokhara, was set apart for the mission, and Butenef was informed that he might make any arrangements in it he wished, for the accommodation of his party; that a numerous retinue of servants, under Myrza Zakaria, had been assigned to them; and that 104 tiangis per month would be paid to the mission for its maintenance.

In the evening of the same day, a Karaul-Begi was sent by the Emir to receive the Imperial presents, and on the following morning, Mr. Khanykof delivered to the Vizier the articles and letters destined for him.

On the 21st, the agent had an interview with Abdul-Khalyk, the Vizier, in the Khan's garden, and received presents for himself and the other members of the mission. Soon after, Butenef was invited by the Emir to appear weekly on Fridays for morning prayers at the palace.

On the 23rd, the Emir sent his medical man to confer with the Russian agent on the subject of the intended mineralogical explorations.

It was first arranged that the examination should commence at the Nurata hill, but this plan having been altered, Messrs. Lehmann and Bogoslovski were despatched direct to Samarcand and Karshi, for which place they set out on the 7th of September. Mr. Khanykof was also allowed to follow these gentlemen the next day to these towns with the topographer, for the purpose of giving presents to the governors.

On the 8th of September, Butenef visited the Naib Abdul-Samed, at whose house he met Stoddart, and delivered to the latter Lord Clanricarde's letter, a reply to which he received and forwarded by special messenger the same day.

In describing the reception given to the Russian mission, Perovski adds: "Although Lieutenant Colonel Butenef has thus not yet had an opportunity for opening negotiations, still the favourable reception which he has met with, and the ready permission accorded to the members of the mission for proceeding to the eastern and less known part of Bokhara, prove that Nusseer-Ulla values the goodwill of Russia, and lead one to expect a successful termination to the negotiations."

We shall see how far Perovski's anticipations proved correct; but it is first of all necessary to examine the condition of affairs at the time of Butenef's arrival.

He found that the situation of Bokhara was different to that which dictated the despatch of Mukin-Beg to Russia soliciting aid. The successes of the Khan during the previous year in Kokan, had elated the Bokharians; a fresh expedition, consisting of a numerous force, was already being organized, and the weakness of the enemy promised certain victory. Khiva was on friendly terms with Russia, and the presence of a Russian agent at that court counteracted the intrigues of the English, and brought their movements to a stand-still. The state of things on the last and most dangerous quarter, that of Afghanistan, was no less favourable. The Emir was well acquainted with the position of English affairs in Cabul, and was, of course, informed of the plans of Akbar-Khan, and secretly sympathized with him. Many of the Emir's fears were thus dispelled, and his policy had, at the same time, assumed a different form. In his foreign relations, Nusseer-Ulla was thoroughly Asiatic; his concessions and friendships were governed by fear or cupidity; the danger being now nearly all removed, there was no occasion for displaying any warmth towards Russia, and his cupidity was satisfied with the presents he had received. Beyond this he thought or cared little.

On the 18th of September, the Emir left for Samarcand; he had no time for conferences with the Russian agent, as he was anxious to join his troops at Djzizakh, where they were concentrated for marching against Kokan.

In his report on this circumstance, and on the subject of Stoddart, Butenef wrote from Bokhara:

"Having heard several days beforehand of the Emir's intended departure, I did everything I could to obtain a personal interview with him, but without success.

"On the day he left, the Emir gave orders that Stoddart should be lodged with me; he now lives in the house occupied by the mission, and is, according to his own words, well satisfied with his position."

In another letter, addressed to Nikivorof at Khiva, he says :—"I arrived here on the 17th of August, and enjoy with my subordinates the particular favour of the Emir. . . . . Up to the present time, I have had no verbal explanations with the Emir on the subject of my mission. Nevertheless, from what I hear, I am sure the Emir will, at my request, liberate all the Russian slaves here, as well as Lieutenant-Colonel Stoddart, a very clever, well-educated and agreeable man, and who, to my great pleasure, has by order of the Emir been removed this day to the house we occupy."

The Russian agent was thus confident of succeeding ultimately in obtaining the acquiescence of the Khan to the demands of Russia, and lived quietly in the meantime with Stoddart. On the 29th of September, Mr. Khanykof returned to Bokhara, and was soon followed by the exploring party, which had discovered coal formations, and extended their survey as far as the South-Eastern sources of the Zarafshan.

Nusseer-Ulla was, in the meantime, capturing town after town from the ruler of Kokan, and the unfortunate Medali-Khan, after the loss of the Tashkend district and the loss of Khodjend, was obliged to make every concession and acknowledge himself a vassal of Bokhara. On the 7th of November, the victorious Emir returned to Bokhara, and with the dawn of the new year, affairs of greater importance engaged the attention of his High Mightiness. On one hand, the Khan of Kokan had, with the assistance of his brother, the ruler of Khodjend, regained possession of the towns wrested from him, while, on the other, a rising occurred in Cabul, to which Burnes, M'Naghten, and other Englishmen, fell sacrifices. The ruler of the Bokharian true believers, of course, could not remain a passive spectator of these events. A large force was already collected for marching into Kokan, and was only detained by the frost; the seizure and imprisonment of Stoddart, and of Conolly who had arrived from Tashkend, displayed the Emir's sympathy with the Afghans, and his complete neglect of the Russian agent plainly showed his disinclination to have any dealings with the infidels.

In his report on the events in Kokan and Cabul, Butenef gives the following account of the progress of his own affairs :—

" Colonel Conolly was arrested on his arrival here in October last, and all his effects were sold in public; with him was imprisoned for the second time, Lieutenant-Colonel Stoddart. The Emir, however, before their arrest, promised me that they should be allowed to accompany me back to Russia. . . . . In a conference I had with his Highness, he refused to deliver over to me all the Russian slaves detained here, without receiving indemnification; but I still hope to succeed in gaining the point. With respect to the duties, he verbally promised me that more than 5 per cent. would not be imposed on Russian goods; but, notwithstanding this assurance, a Russian trader was lately obliged to pay 10 per cent., and the Vizier here has, up to the present time, prevented me from having a personal explanation with the Emir on the subject, and generally throws obstacles in the way when I wish to see his Highness."

Acknowledging the receipt of the 900 ducats for ransoming the slaves, the agent again repeats: "I am already preparing to return; the Vizier Abdul-Khalyk still keeps me out of sight of the Emir by all manner of devices."

It would indeed be strange that a mere boy of nineteen could have influence enough to prevent the Russian envoy from seeing the Emir; in a later report the true reasons of his failure are clearly brought to light.

Time passed, and the negotiations did not progress at all. The Emir remained at Bokhara busily preparing for a campaign against Kokan; the members of the mission were received with cool indifference when they appeared at the Palace every Friday with the Bokharian officials.

Spring had arrived. The Cabul massacre was over, the Bokharian army was put in motion in the direction of Kokan, and still all the attempts of the Russian agent settling the terms of a treaty before the departure of the Emir proved fruitless.

"I am at length convinced," he writes, "that it was not the Vizier who kept me back, but that the Emir himself avoided all intercourse with me."

On the 12th of April (N.S.), the Vizier's brother brought presents of Khalats for the mission, and informed the agent that he would be summoned by the Emir the next day for final explanations. Apparently the first of April (13th N. S. 1st O. S.,) is observed as a day of delusions and snares even in Central Asia. The day passed without bringing the expected invitation to the palace, on the next, however, the following unceremonious interview took place:—

"At dawn," writes the agent, "I was roused by Shagaul-Beg, who invited me to the palace to hear *the gracious words of the Emir.* On reaching it, I was stationed in the court-yard, and after waiting an hour, the Emir made his appearance, equipped for his journey; he hurriedly told me that he had instructed his "Dostrakhanshi" to communicate to me every thing that was necessary in addition to what he had told me himself, and greeting me with the words "Hosh amedid," rode out of the Palace gates and left Bokhara.

The Dostrakhanshi or Vizier did not receive me that day, but sent me a request the following morning to furnish him with a note of what I intended to demand at the interview. Strange as this message appeared, I nevertheless sent him the required note, requesting him to acquaint me of the Emir's ultimatum on the following points :—

1. Respecting the conclusion of a treaty with Russia.

2. On the liberation of Russian slaves.

3. Permission for allowing Stoddart and Conolly to return with me in accordance with the promises made by the Emir.

And fourthly, on the reduction of Customs duties levied on the goods of Russian merchants.

This note the Dostrakhanshi despatched after

the Emir by special messenger, and on the morning of the 19th of April the following answer from the Emir arrived:—

With respect to a treaty, the Emir declared that if the Emperor signed and forwarded the same to Bokhara, he, the Emir, would also confirm it.

The Russian slaves in Bokhara would be sent back to Russia on the conclusion of the treaty.

The Customs duties would be reduced as soon as the Russians decreased those imposed on Bokharian merchants.

So far as concerned the Englishmen, the Emir declared that they had presented a letter to him, in which they said that their Queen desires to be on friendly terms with Bokhara, in consequence of which he had himself written to the Queen, and on receiving an answer would despatch them both *direct to England.*

In conclusion the Dostrakhanshi told me by order of his master, that the Emir entertained sincere feelings of friendship and respect towards the Emperor.

Such was the result of Butenef's mission. It is clear that the Emir did not wish to come to any arrangement on the proposed points, and would not bind himself to anything; his haughty answers, and their indelicate communication to the agent, required the adoption of decisive measures on the part of the Russian Government.

After all this, the Emir had yet the assurance to give orders for equipping an embassy to Russia, and on another occasion displayed the same unceremonious behaviour towards the Russian agent.

"During the night of the 19—20 April," writes Butenef, "the mission started on its way back, taking with it three old Russians, two of whom had lost their legs, and as they were perfectly unserviceable we hoped that they would be permitted to follow us. But even this benevolent design was frustrated, as on the 22nd of April, they were taken away from us on approaching the town of Vardanzi."

On the 23rd of May, the mission reached the Syr, where it was received with every respect by the commander of the neighbouring Khivan fortress, and continued its journey on the 26th.

A Bokharian caravan, which was accompanied by Karaùl-Begi, Hudoyar, the newly appointed envoy to Russia, left Bokhara immediately after the departure of the Russian mission. His caravan bivouacked for two days together with the Russians on the banks of the Syr, but the Bokharian envoy did not once condescend to visit the Russian agent.

On the 18th of June the mission arrived safely at Orenburg. The total cost of this expedition to the Russian Government was 6000 gold ducats.

Although the negotiations were unsuccessful, yet great acquisitions were made to science during the eight months' sojourn of the mission at Bokhara. The results obtained in this respect were: a collection of geological and climatological notes by Mr. Butenef, a diary of events by Mr. Lehmann, a statistical description of the Khanat of Bokhara by Khanykof, and what is more important, extensive surveys were made, which supplied us with information completely new on parts of the country of which our former knowledge was very confused. Knowing the suspicious nature of the Asiatics, it is a matter of surprise that Mr. Yakovlef, the topographer, should have succeeded in surveying and portraying such an extensive tract of country so accurately as he did. The portions surveyed were the route of the mission from the Syr, across the Kuvan and Yany-Darias to Bokhara; the road from Bokhara along the Zarafshan to Samarcand, together with plans of the towns of Samarcand and Bokhara and their vicinities. A map of the Bokharian dominions was also constructed by Mr. Yakovlef, and the route of the mission back to Bish-Tamak settlement was traced on it.

It may not be out of place to quote here the words of Mr. Khanykof, who took an active part in the negotiations, from his letter to General Perovski, which he wrote on his return from Bokhara :—

"The results gained by our mission were exactly the same as those obtained by all former missions despatched to Bokhara since the days of Boris Godunof,—that is, we brought back assurances of friendship from the Emir, and a decided refusal to the moderate demands of the Russian Government; but even this refusal was in a measure satisfactory, as it was accompanied by a permission to quit Bokhara, where, towards the latter part of our stay we were apprehensive of sharing the fate of the two Englishmen, on the least suspicion of the Emir."

One would suppose from our knowledge of the Asiatic character, that the last words of Mr. Khanykof betray the cause of failure of the mission, did not the conduct of another Russian agent, Mr. Nikiforof at Khiva, prove that boldness and even audacity were equally unsuccessful.

Four days after Butenef's arrival at Orenburg, the new Bokharian envoy, Hudoyar-Klychbai, arrived at the Rudnikof picket station with a suite of seventeen men. In addition to letters for the Emperor, and other high officers, he brought a bale of shawls and five arghamaks as presents.

As already observed, the despatch of this envoy, after the treatment experienced by the Russian mission, was a piece of effrontery truly Asiatic; the presents of shawls and arghamaks could not efface the sense of injury produced on the Russian Government by the last acts of the Emir. The Chancellor, in his letter to the Governor of Orenburg, says: "In addition to the insignificant rank of the envoy, Hudoyar, permission for proceeding to St. Petersburg cannot be granted him, particularly after the inattention and rudeness shewn by the Bokharian Government towards Colonel Butenef, shortly before his departure from Bokhara. Taking into consideration, however, that the conduct of the Emir was the result of barbarous ignorance, and might partly be attributive to his elation on his recent successes in Kokan, the letters which the envoy brings may be received from him and forwarded to St. Petersburg. The presents are not to be accepted, and the money allowance for the envoy and suite is to be fixed as moderately as possible.

Hudoyar resolutely refused to give up the letters he bore to any person at Orenburg, and declared that he would be compelled to do so by force alone; he at the same time returned the provision money, that had been paid him at the rate of 80 cop. silver, per diem for himself, and 40 and 15 cop. for his suite. Another demand for the letters having been again refused, Hudoyar was desired to leave Orenburg, with a notification of the Emperor's displeasure at the disregard paid to Butenef's demands. He was told: "Assurances of friendship alone, unsupported by corresponding actions, cannot inspire confidence towards the Bokharian Government, which, to regain the good will of the Emperor, should immediately liberate the Russian prisoners in Bokhara and the two Englishmen—Stoddart and Conolly."

But while this was being written, Stoddart and Conolly were no longer among the living; in the month of June they were publicly beheaded in the chief square of Bokhara, and the last Russian prisoners only received their freedom in 1858, on the urgent demands of General Ignatief, the last Russian agent sent to Bokhara.

Thus terminated the six years' almost uninterrupted diplomatic relations between Russia and Bokhara, which were entered into, on the Emir's part, from cupidity and apprehensions for the political existence of his dominions, while on the part of Russia, they were maintained with the object of freeing the Russian slaves, developing Russian trade in Asia on a more secure basis, and thereby increasing the influence of Russia in the Turan, which belongs to her by right of civilization.

The interchange of friendly civilities during the six years, with the entertainment of envoys and transmission of presents, cost the Russian Government 20,000 silver roubles, in addition to which, the expense of sending two agents to Bokhara was 8700 ducats.

CHAPTER XII.

On the Commercial Prospects of Central Asia viewed in connexion with Russia.

THE number of Turkmen, Kirghiz-Kaisaks and other nomad hordes in Central Asia is computed at three millions, and the settled population at more than five millions. The intercourse of the inhabitants of Central Asia with their neighbours on the other side of the mountains is very limited, partly on account of the impassable character of the roads, and partly from a similarity in their productions, which prevent their having anything to exchange with each other.

From China, however, there is some traffic

through Kuldja and Chuguchak, on one side, and Kashgar on the other, principally in tea, the use of which is widely spread in Central Asia, as also in China porcelain ware to a limited extent. Silver, in bars and ingots, used to be formerly imported by this route.

Sugar, indigo, cotton stuffs (to a small extent), and cashmere shawls are imported from India. From Persia the chief item of trade, in addition to an inconsiderable amount of European goods, consists of Persian slaves, captured by the Turkmen.

Of much greater importance is the internal trade of the Central-Asiatic countries, and their dealings with Russia. The Kirghizes and Turkmen are exclusively engaged in cattle-breeding, and, in exchange for the produce of their flocks and herds, procure all their manufactured articles of consumption from the Russians, Kokanians, Bokharians, and Khivans. Since a very distant period, the Asiatics have been supplied with iron, copper and hardware of every description from Russia.

Towards the middle of the last century, when the treasures amassed by Nadir-Shah had become distributed in Asia, gold or silver was the medium of exchange for Russian merchandize. Subsequently, however, as the country to the East of the Volga and Siberia commenced to be populated, the use of the cotton fabrics of Bokhara and Khiva became so general, that the demand for Russian manufactures declined considerably; a large quantity of the precious metals was, therefore, yearly exported into the countries of Central Asia from Russia.

The quantity of gold obtained in the Khanats of Bokhara and Kokan is so small that the inhabitants of the different Central-Asiatic States are compelled to have recourse to Russia for the precious metals of which they stand in need. This being the case, whatever may be the state of trade between Russia and Central Asia, gold and silver must necessarily form one of the items of the Russian export trade to Central Asia.

Now that Russia is endeavouring to develop her manufacturing industry, her commercial interests have become altered. She is endeavouring to find a market for her fabrics, and although she cannot compete with the productions of Western Europe, she can at all events rely on the superiority of her wares over Asiatic goods; and the markets of Central Asia being inaccessible to European goods, must present a surer guarantee for the consumption of Russian manufactures, on account of Russia being the only consumer of Central Asiatic commodities.

Let us examine the present condition of the Russian trade with Central Asia after its existence of a century and a half.

According to the Custom House returns the value of goods exported beyond the Orenburg and Siberian lines was as follows :—

In 1835 ...	Roubles silver ...	1,850,000	(£277,500.)
1845	„	2,000,000	(£300,000.)
1855	„	2,580,000	(£387,000.)
1860	„	4,900,000	(£735,000.)

Imported into Russia :—

In 1835 ...	Roubles silver ...	2,400,000	(£360,000.)
1845	„	2,520,000	(£278,000)
1855	„	4,179,000	(£626,800.)
1860	„	8,000,000	(£1,200,000.)

From two-thirds to three-fourths of the total amount of imports and exports are to carried, according to official accounts, to the Kirghiz Steppe, half of the remainder to Bokhara, and the other to Kokan and Khiva. At present the preponderance is in favour of Bokhara both as regards exports and imports, in consequence of the troubles in Kokan and Khiva, and of these countries being obliged to purchase Russian goods almost exclusively through Bokharian middle men.

Until very lately cotton manufactures constituted

in value little less than one-half of the total of goods exported; in 1860 they had already exceeded that figure. In that year goods of this class were exported to the amount of 2,667,000 roubles (£400,000), of which only 1,650,000 roubles' worth (£247,500) was sent to the Kirghiz Steppe, and 826,000 (£123,900) to Bokhara. The proportion of cotton goods despatched to the Kirghiz Steppe has remained up to the present time unaltered as compared with the total amount of goods sent to Central Asia. A rapid increase is observable in the export of these goods to Bokhara, where, in 1855, their value was only 154,000 S. R., while in 1860 it had attained 826,000 S. R., and as this increase corresponds with the considerable falling off in the exports to Kokan and Khiva, it must be supposed that a portion of the cotton manufactures sent to Bokhara must have afterwards reached the neighbouring Khanats.

The remaining exports to Central Asia, classed according to their total value, are yufta or leather to the amount of 400,000 S. R. (£60,000); corn, 300,000 S. R. (£45,000); cloth, 227,000 S. R. (£34,500); hardware, 200,000 S. R. (£30,000); lump sugar, 90,000 S. R. (£13,500); iron, 70,000 S. R. (£10,500); manufactured leather, 37,000 S.

R. (£5,500); dye stuffs, 65,000 S. R. (£9,750); copper, 58,000 S. R. (£8,700); wooden chests, 25,000 S. R. (£3,750); after which follow silk and woollen goods, &c.

The relation of these several items to the total sum of goods exported has remained almost unaltered during the last thirty years. Corn is exclusively disposed of to the Kirghizes, who are also large purchasers of yufta and of a large proportion of the cloth and hardware.

The condition of the import trade is more remarkable. From 1835 to 1860 its value has increased to 333, while during the same period the exports only rose 260, per cent. Relatively the different items of the import trade have altogether changed, as will appear from the following data:—The value of the cotton goods brought to Russia from Central Asia formed, in 1835, three and six-tenths, and in 1845 one-quarter of the general imports; in 1855 it was only one-tenth, and in 1860 less than one-twelfth.

Silk and woollen goods were never imported in any large quantities. The latter consist chiefly of Kirghiz felt. The total value of silk and woollen fabrics imported in 1835 amounted to 35,000 silver roubles, while in 1860, it reached 135,000 silver roubles (£5250 to £15,750).

The chief increase was on the item of cattle produce, supplied by the Kirghizes, and on that of raw cotton from Bokhara. The value of cattle—particularly sheep—driven to the line in

	1835	was	850,000	silver roubles	(£127.500.)
	1845	„	830,000	„	(£124,500.)
	1855	„	1,600,000	„	(£240,000.)
	1860	„	3,644,000	„	(£546,600.)
Raw hides,	1835	„	38,000	„	(£5,700.)
„	1860	„	750,000	„	(£112,500.)
Wool,	1835	„	7,000	„	(£1,050.)
„	1860	„	86,000	„	(£12,900.)

showing an increase from 37 to 60 per cent.

From 1835 to 1860, the quantity of raw cotton imported rose from 11,929 puds (430,000lbs.) to 174,059 puds (6,266,000 lbs.), and cotton yarn fell from 26,938 puds (970,000 lbs.) to 5,247 puds (31,500 lbs.). Madder, which in 1835 was not imported at all, now figures for 24,523 puds (883,000 lbs.), in 1860.

The importation of fruit has increased tenfold during the last twenty-five years, and amounted in value in 1860 to 190,000 puds (6,840,000 lbs.). Raw silk appears to form a new branch of trade, and 799 puds of it were imported in 1860 from Bokhara. The Baikof and brick teas, which, since the opening of the Russian factories at Kuldja and

Chuguchak, are imported from Chinese Turkestan. The value of the tea brought across the Kirghiz Steppe in 1855, was 450,000 silver roubles, and only 185,000 in 1860.

From this it will appear that the Russian trade with Central Asia is developing itself steadily and rapidly, and assuming an aspect particularly favourable for Russia, for whose manufactures there is an increasing demand in Central Asia, whence she obtains her raw produce in return.

It is very significant, however, that the value of the imports far exceeds that of the exports, and that the proportion in favour of the import trade is constantly rising. But, considering the barbarous and poor condition of the inhabitants of Central Asia, and their commercial relations with India, Persia, and China, from whence they procure indigo, cotton stuffs, and tea, for which, having no suitable commodities to offer their neighbours in return, they are obliged to pay in specie, only obtainable from Russia, it is not surprising, under such circumstances, that there should be a constant drain of Russian gold and silver to Central Asia.

An approximate equalization of the balance of trade cannot even be hoped for, as in civilized countries the wants of a people grow in proportion to their means, and the more barbarous they are the longer is the time required for developing these wants. While the cattle produce of the wandering tribes is yearly becoming of greater importance to Russia, and while (in consequence of the American crisis) the demand for Bokharian cotton is unlimited, even the secondary productions of Central Asia—such as rice and dried fruit—can find a ready sale.

Putting aside the question of Bokharian cotton, the demand for which at present is urgent, though probably only temporary, it must be acknowledged that Khiva, Bokhara, and Kokan are, in commercial respects, much more dependent on Russia than Russia is on them, as these countries have no other sources for procuring iron, copper, gold, hardware, wood-work, yufta, and dyes.

Without Russian gold or other Russian commodities, they cannot pay for the tea, sugar, indigo, &c., sent from China and India. Russia only requires sheep, hides, and wool, which are the productions of the Kirghiz Steppes subject to her, and in these Steppes she disposes of the greater portion of the goods despatched by her to Central Asia.

In the face of such a state of dependence of the Central Asiatic Khanats on Russia, the Government of this country have it always in their power to force the Khanats to yield to their wishes, by threatening an interruption of commercial relations, but it must be observed that every stoppage in the trade would impose a loss on Russian manufacturers. Such a peaceable measure would thus be more prejudicial to the Empire than the employment of military force.

With regard in particular to the Kirghiz-Kaisak encampments, the degree of their productiveness and well-being depends chiefly on the state of order and security in the Steppe, and this cannot be maintained without the assistance of troops and the construction of a large number of forts against the marauding Khivans and Kokanians.

The rapid development of trade with the Kirghizes has been the result of measures recently adopted by the Russian Government for their protection.

However great the benefit which has been reaped from their measures adopted up to the present time, they are still insufficient for the complete pacification of the Kirghizes, owing partly to the fact that between the last posts on the Siberian and Orenburg line, there is an unoccupied extent of 400 versts through which the Tashkendians and

Kokanians freely make irruptions into the Steppe and pillage the Kirghizes, as also to the left bank of the Syr-Daria presenting rich pasturages along which there were formerly irrigated fields, which are now entirely deserted in consequence of the fears inspired by the inroads of the Kokanians. Here, as elsewhere, security is the first element of increasing commerce and its abundant civilizing influences. The more prosperous the condition of the Kirghizes, the greater will be the development of Russian trade with them. The Russian Government, therefore, in the interests of the Kirghizes themselves, whom it has taken under its protection and with whom a trade amounting to more than eight million roubles silver (£1,266,000) is yearly carried on, will find itself forced to follow up the policy it has laid down.

Russian manufactures cannot compete in point of cheapness with the productions of Western Europe, and are driven out of all the markets in which they meet; and hence even on the Southern sea-board of Persia, which is as easy of access to Russia as the communication between Persia and Western Europe is difficult, it is only the raw produce of Russia that finds purchasers.

With the opening of the Chinese ports to all

the European nations, it is to be apprehended that the sale of Russian goods will all but cease in China; the only available market for them in that case will be that of Central Asia, which is closed in on all sides except to the north by insuperable physical obstacles. Similarly placed with regard to Russia are the markets of Chinese Turkestan, or Little Bokhara, which are also shut off from the whole world, as they can only communicate with the distant provinces of China on the East, and with Russia and Kokan on the West and North.

According to the treaty concluded with China, in 1851, Russian traders are allowed to visit two towns of Eastern Turkestan, Kuldja and Chuguchak; but these are situated in a thinly populated country, and serve only as military outposts of the Chinese empire. On this account, like Maimatchen in Mongolia, they are mere transit depôts of tea, and have hardly any independent trade of their own.

To the South of Kuldja, separated from Chinese Turkestan by the Thian-Shan range, is little Bokhara, surrounded on three sides by almost inaccessible mountains, and open only on the East where it merges in the desert of Gobi.

Russian goods may be introduced into Little Bokhara by two routes; by the Northern, from Kuldja to Aksù, and by the Western, from Kokan to Kashgar. Both traverse ridges of snow-clad mountains; but camels it is said can travel along the first road, while the second can only be passed by pack-horses with a burthen of not more than eight puds (about 2½ cwt. English). About 3500 of such caravan horses pass along this road annually.

The road to Kuldja is less frequented by trade-caravans than the Kokanian route, which leads through a country similar to Little Bokhara, in origin, faith and historical traditions, whereas Kuldja is the place of residence of the Chinese authorities, against whom the Mussulmen cherish an antipathy amounting to deep hatred. As already mentioned, caravans travel in eighteen days from Kokan to Kashgar, while the distance between Kuldja to Aksù is reckoned at 100 versts. From Aksù to Pekin, the journey of a caravan occupies from four and a half to five months. The incessant warfare carried on by the Little Bokharians with the Chinese ever since 1825 has desolated an extensive tract of country which was once rich and populous.

The Central Asiatic market can thus be extended across the Celestial Mountains, but to effect this Russian traders must first of all be allowed to penetrate into Little Bokhara, which is closed against them at present.

The total value of Russian goods now annually disposed of in Central Asia does not exceed five million roubles (£750,000), and deducting that of the Kirghiz Steppe, the whole trade will not amount to more than two millions (£300,000). This amount is doubtless very insignificant, but following the example of England, whose commerce encircles the world, and now spares no efforts in discovering new markets for her manufactures, Russia must direct particular attention towards developing her trade with Central Asia, which is almost the only country in which there still exists a demand for Russian manufactures, especially as this demand is yearly increasing.

It is of course impossible to say what limits Russian trade with Central Asia might reach under favourable conditions; it will be sufficient to observe that Persia, with its population of about five millions, receives, by way of Trebisond and Erzerum, European goods to the amount of four million roubles (£600,000) annually; while from

Russia the exports to that country amounted during the same period to only one and a half millions (£237,500), while a considerable quantity of merchandize is sent from India by way of the Persian Gulf. Two-thirds of the goods imported from Europe into Persia consists of cotton fabrics, notwithstanding that cotton is grown and manufactured in almost every part of Persia!

This illustration is a proof of the extent to which the Russian trade with Central Asia might be developed, particularly as Russia presents so extensive a market for the produce of Bokhara, Kokan and Khiva, and furnishes these Khanats with the means of purchasing her goods. Silk being the only commodity that Persia sends to Europe, she experiences great difficulty in paying for the goods she receives, and is extricated therefrom by Russian gold, to which is probably attributable the diplomatic myth of secret relations between Russia and Persia—the one the head of the Greek church, the other that of the great Mahometan schism.

Unfortunately for Russia, even the Bokharians, the most civilized of the Central Asiatics, are far more barbarous than the Persians, and it therefore cannot be expected that there will be the same demand for European goods in Bokhara that there is now in Persia until a considerable time shall have elapsed.

As three-fifths of the inhabitants of the Central Asiatic depression may be said to consist of wandering tribes, who are forced to purchase from their neighbours everything that is not yielded them by their herds, they will as readily have recourse to Russia as to Khiva and Bokhara for these requirements, as long as they can sell their cattle, hides, and wool to the traders of the former country.

Similarly, as soon as the Khivans and Bokharians find it more advantageous to dispose of their raw cotton and silk to Russia, instead of using these articles in a manufactured state, they will purchase every description of fabric from Russia in exchange for the raw material. It is plain therefore, that under such conditions, the Russian trade with Central Asia might be largely developed, but to accomplish this, it is requisite among other things, that the Russian cotton-fabrics should be of a closer texture than they are at present, as the natives of the Khanats pay more regard to durability than to fine finish. But as the price of stout textures depends more particularly on the price of the material out of which they are manufactured, it will be necessary, in order to enable the Russian cotton-goods to compete advantageously with the Bokharian, that the cost of the cotton used by Russian looms should be as little as may be higher than the cost of the material to the Bokharian producer, and this can only be attained by a reduction of the transit duty, facilitation of transport by good roads, &c., and by establishing spinning and weaving manufactories at a short distance from the Bokharian frontier.

Slight cotton fabrics, distinguished merely for their finish and cheapness, are chiefly imported into Persia from England. That these goods meet with a large sale, is due to the circumstance that the Persians are fond of luxury, and that their own coarse manufactures find a demand in the Russian Trans-Caucasian provinces. Were it not for this latter circumstance, the sale of English prints in Persia would be reduced fully one-half.

From the foregoing considerations and statistics, it will appear that the extension of Russian trade in Central Asia, depends mainly on two conditions, on the importation of raw goods from Central Asia into Russia, particularly cotton, and cattle produce, and on the inauguration of a reign of peace, order, and prosperity in these regions.

The demand for the raw productions of Central Asia must increase annually, and the prices, especially on cattle produce, will constantly rise, and that care should only be taken to increase the supply of these products. As regards cotton, as it will have to compete with the American supply, its sale will depend on its quality, price, and local facilities for working.

The large quantities of cotton brought from Bokhara and Khiva yearly since 1855, shows that this cotton can be used for different textures, and that it is capable, to a certain extent, of competing with the American staple; but, of course, it cannot be denied that under present conditions, the Bokharian cotton cannot supersede the American, and that the Bokharians themselves would not now agree to cultivate a greater quantity, at the prices till recently ruling.

In Bokhara and Khiva, the price of cotton per pud, used to range from two to three roubles. The Mazanderan,* which is inferior in quality, sells on the spot at three and three and a half roubles per pud, and the price of cotton per pud in the

* Mazanderan is the name of the Persian province extending along the South shores of the Caspian, of which the important port of Balfrush is the chief city.—[Ed.]

Southern ports of America, was generally from four and a half to five roubles. In England, the Indian cotton used generally to fetch at least forty per cent. lower than the American, and the same difference existed in Moscow in the value of the American and Bokharian cotton. The first was sold at from seven to eight and a half roubles, and the second from five to six roubles. At present it is being sold at from ten to twelve roubles, and the importation of cotton from Bokhara has consequently trebled that of the few years immediately preceding 1861, reaching at present 500,000 puds (about 78,000 bales).

Under the stimulus of such prices, the Bokharian landholders can profitably convert their ploughed land and vegetable plantations into cotton fields, and dispose of their produce, not to local manufacturers, but to Russian spinners.

These high prices are, however, accidental, and cannot long be maintained, and it is therefore to be feared that with their fall, the exportation of cotton from Central Asia will cease.

It is, moreover, of such inferior quality, that hitherto it was only used for wadding, and the coarser sorts of twist, from No. 12 to 16. Some picked consignments, however, were lately brought to Russia, which produced yarns as fine as No. 28. This proves that the same short-stapled cotton, when properly cleaned of seed and dust, and properly ginned and pressed, so that the fibres lie straight and are not tumbled and triturated in transit, at once rises 50 per cent. in value.

If American machines for cleansing the cotton could only be introduced into Central Asia, and proper care were observed in packing the bales by means of hydraulic presses, the Bokharian cotton might in the future even compete in the Russian markets with foreign cotton. But these improvements can scarcely be expected until the establishment of a Russian factory at or near Bokhara, where the native growers might be instructed in the best methods for cultivating the cotton plant, while the factory owner would also exercise the functions of a broker, in condemning all cotton unfit for manufacture in Russia.

Under such an arrangement, the production of cotton might continue to be made self-supporting in Bokhara, even under a decline of price in the market. That the Central Asiatic States are capable by their geographical extent of supplying Russia with the two millions of puds, which her looms at present annually produce, there cannot be the least doubt, as each *desiatina* yields not less than 100 puds of uncleaned cotton, from which at least twenty-five per cent. of clean cotton is obtained. Consequently, for growing these 2,000,000 puds, 80,000 *desiatinas* would be required. According to Khanykof, who visited Bokhara in 1842, this Khanat contains 500 square miles, or 2,000,450 *desiatinas* of cultivated land. Owing to the scarcity of water in Bokhara, which is thickly populated, a greater quantity cannot be made available for fields and gardens; but in the Khanat of Khiva, more irrigatory canals could be conducted over the land from the Amu-Daria, if labouring hands were more plentiful; while in Kokan there is certainly no scarcity in suitable land, with suitable water privileges and facilities.

One of the principal obstacles to the increased importation of Central Asiatic cotton into Russia is presented by the cost and means of transport. For transporting 2,000,000 of puds (32,150 tons) of cotton, not less than 100,000 camels are required, as, for long distances, these animals are not loaded with more than sixteen or eighteen puds; besides which, the caravan journey from Bokhara to Orenburg occupies from two to two and a half months.

Considering, therefore, that the roads at certain seasons—owing, alternately, to heat and cold—are virtually impassable, and that the camels, for this reason, cannot make more than one journey during the year, it is evident that the above quantity of cotton cannot be brought to Russia by existing means. Again, if all the present resources for transporting goods alone be used for carrying cotton, the other items of the export trade of Central Asia would necessarily be neglected. But even if it were possible to bring this vast quantity of cotton to Russia, without raising the cost of transport to a fabulous price, the question arises—in what is Russia to pay the Asiatics for their goods, before the demand for her productions increases among them? If they are to be paid in specie the cost of carriage will be doubled, as the camels would have to return without a freight back. A rapid growth in the demand for Russian goods in Central Asia can, as has already been stated, only be calculated on when tranquillity and order are established in those parts.

Having thus become acquainted with the present state of the commercial relations of Russia with Central Asia, and their future prospects, let us now examine the means which might soonest lead to the realization of these views.

These means must be sought for, while bearing in mind that there is a twofold object to be secured in practice:—First, to make the inhabitants of Central Asia, as far as possible, capable of producing those articles which Russia mostly requires, and willing to accept modern civilization, thus creating at the same time a large demand for Russian goods in return; and, secondly, to lower the cost of the land-carriage of merchandize between Russia and the Central Asiatic States.

To accomplish the first of these objects, it is first of all necessary to establish, as far as it is practicable, a feeling of security and not of tranquillity in these parts.

The "Barantas" or depredatory irruptions into the limits of territory, occupied by Russian troops in the Kirghiz Steppe, have already been almost totally suppressed, but at the head of the Syr-Daria and along the left bank of the river, the Kirghizes still suffer from the robberies and extortions of the Khivans and the Kokanians, to which they are to a certain extent obliged to submit, being forced to purchase their necessary supplies of corn and other articles from them.

The Kirghizes, however, are much more seriously oppressed by the Tashkendians and Kokanians, than the Khivans, and the immediate erection of a few forts on the Syr-Daria, above the last Russian military outpost of Djulek 44° 55′ N., 66° 35′ E. (approximative), appears indispensable. Fort No. 1 is situated 70 versts from the mouth of the river, which is crossed at that point by caravans proceeding from Orenburg to Bokhara. Above this fort, 348 versts higher up the river, stands Fort Perovski, and between the two, is Fort No. 2, which, however, is not of great importance. In the vicinity of Fort Perovski, agriculture was at one time in a flourishing condition, but suffers now from the difficulty of irrigating the fields, which is attributable to the perceptible fall in the level of the river bed of the principal arm of the Syr, the waters having been diverted into a newly established branch, called the Karanzak, which again joins the main stream at Fort No. 2. The bed of the Karanzak is much lower than that of the other branches, and in this way monopolizes the greater portion of the waters. It has but recently been formed out of a canal excavated by the Karakalpaks for the purposes of irrigation, and flows through a sandy tract of country utterly unfit for cultivation. The course of this branch, with its lagoons or overflows, occupies 2000 square versts, and owing to evaporation, it emits a great volume of dense vapour throughout this extent, there is thus a great waste of water, an element of such unspeakable importance in these parts.

Persons who have carefully examined this locality assert that it is absolutely necessary to dam up the Karanzak branch without further delay, by which means alone a sufficient body of water will be preserved in the Syr-Daria, not only for the navigation of vessels, but also for supplying with the requisite quantity of water the Southern or Yany-Daria branch, which at one period reached the Sea of Aral, and whose banks were formerly occupied by a chain of settlements. The bed of this river being more elevated than those of any of the others, is more capable of supplying the artificial water courses. The soil along the left bank of the Syr-Daria is less arid than that on the right.

A hundred versts above Fort Perovski, Fort Djulek has been founded, which fort is about 150 versts distant from the point at which the Syr-Daria approaches nearest to Tashkend, this town standing 50 versts eastward of the Syr-Daria.

From Tashkend, the caravan route is 185 versts to the town of Kokan, situated 30 versts to the Southward of the Syr, which continues to be navigable even for a little distance above this point.

From the extreme Fort at the Chu-Pishnek river, on the Kirghiz-Siberian line to the river Syr, at Fort Djulek, the distance is estimated at 400 versts, along a route stretching Northwards from the town of Turkestan, which is subject to the Khan of Kokan.

Russia must gain a firm footing at the head of the Syr for several reasons: for protecting effectually the Kirghizes from the exactions of the Kokanians and Tashkendians; for securing the navigation along the course of the Syr, as it presents the most convenient channel of communication with Russia, and affords the only guarantee for the safety of the Russian garrisons; and lastly, for supplying both the forts and steamers with fuel, either wood or coals, from the Karataŭ mountains, at the foot of which stand the towns of Turkestan and Tashkend, or from the Ala-taŭ range beyond the town of Kokan.

These mountains are clothed with forests, and formations of coal have been discovered in them. The sand of the rivers descending from them is auriferous, moreover, and the mountains themselves are rich in various descriptions of mineral wealth.

The present condition of the garrisons in the Russian fortifications of the Steppe, deprived of every convenience, and often wanting the necessaries of life, is truly lamentable; and their state can only be ameliorated by maintaining unrestricted communication by means of the Syr-Daria, from its source to its embouchure, as only by water-carriage will it be found possible to supply them with the necessaries they now so much require.

The cost of supporting these garrisons, the supplies for whose use must all be sent from Russia, constitutes a serious item of expense to the Russian Government, which pays 400,000 roubles annually for the transport of the provisions required by the small garrisons of the Syr-Daria posts. This expenditure will be saved as soon as corn is permitted to be purchased for the troops at Tashkend; and in process of time, the other necessaries of life will be produced in the neighbourhood of the forts, by Russian settlers and Kirghizes.

The authorities at Orenburg tried formerly, by every possible means, to prevent the wandering Kirghizes from adopting a settled mode of life, and pursuing agriculture, being afraid that cattle-rearing would be neglected. These apprehensions proved, however, to be ill-founded. First, the quantity of land available for cultivation is very limited when compared to the whole extent of the Steppe, and therefore tilled land will always bear but a small proportion to the whole region; secondly, it is only the poorest Kirghizes that become fixed and stationary, after having lost their cattle; the rich Kirghizes employ workmen to cultivate patches of land near their summer or winter encampments, without abandoning at the same time their roaming habits. In this way the cultivation of the land affords them great assistance, as their families are supplied with corn, which in case of need is also given to the cattle.

The increase of cattle in the Steppe is not prejudicially affected by a scarcity of breeders, as was supposed by the local authorities, but is materially checked by the great mortality among the cattle from snow-storms and frost, and the absence of shelter and fodder for the cattle during the inclement winters of the Steppe.

The spread of agriculture among the Kirghizes would consequently be actually encouraged by the preservation and multiplication of cattle in the Steppe. Besides enriching the Kirghizes and civilizing their nature, it would produce a greater demand for Russian productions, and render those wandering in the southern part of the Steppe more independent of the Khivans, Kokanians, and Bokharians, from whom they are now obliged to procure their supplies of corn.

It does not, however, follow that with the diffusion of agricultural pursuits, the Kirghizes who roam near the confines of the Orenburg region and Siberia, will cease to buy corn from the Russians. On the contrary, as they become more accustomed to the use of bread, the greater will be the demand for it from Russia, as the Kirghizes themselves cannot produce the quantity sufficient for their own daily consumption.

At present the diet of these wandering tribes consists almost entirely of meat, milk, and cheese-curd; bread being very sparingly used, and confined to a few of the wealthiest chiefs. Were the three millions of Kirghizes only to consume a single quarter of corn per head per annum, Russia would export annually into the Steppe, not 100,000 quarters as at present, but thirty times that quantity.

The Russian Government having become convinced of the utility of encouraging the spread of agriculture in the Kirghiz Steppe, and more particularly along the banks of the Syr-Daria, where corn cannot be raised without irrigation, will not fail to perceive the importance of excavating and maintaining artificial water courses in these parts, which indeed are objects of solicitude even in the most unsettled Asiatic countries. By adopting measures for the security of the Kirghizes, and by encouraging agriculture among them, the Russian Government will lay the foundation for the future prosperity of the inhabitants of the Steppe. With regard to the independent territories of Central Asia, it must be observed that in the Khanat of Bokhara social order, to a certain extent, already exists, which may reach the point of development attainable in Asiatic-Mussulman countries, whereupon the turbulence of the neighbouring tribes will be subdued, after which Russian factories can be established at Bokhara.

The Khanat of Kokan is alternately under the sway of one ruler, or is chronically divided into numerous petty territories at enmity with each other. The country of Kokan is richer than that of Bokhara in the gifts of nature, but its population is much more barbarous, and there is consequently greater reason for establishing the civilizing influence of Russia in these parts. With the restoration of peace and order, Kokan is capable of carrying on an extensive trade with Russia. The facility of communication afforded by the Syr-Daria, the navigation of which is suspended only during three or four months in the year, will enable a Russian force to overawe the countries bordering on the river.

The repression of the Khivans will be a more difficult task, but Russia cannot allow them to go on as they do at present without injury to her general relations with Central Asia. The Khanat of Khiva is very thinly populated, and is far from possessing the natural riches with which Kokan is endowed.

This country might, therefore, be altogether ignored, were it not for the circumstance that the whole existence and economy of Khiva is founded on an institution which is the cause of all the robbery and anarchy in the neighbouring States. This cause, so productive of evil, is slavery. All laborious work in Khiva is performed by bondsmen, and their acquisition consequently becomes a necessary condition for the existence of the Khanat.

Formerly there were many Russians among the slaves in Khiva, but at present slaves are almost entirely obtained from Persia, and the sole occupation of the neighbouring Turkmen tribes consists in kidnapping Persians for sale at Khiva. The whole of that portion of Persia laying to the East and South-East of the Caspian, and containing the provinces of Astrabad and Korassan, both abounding in natural productions, is most unfortunately situated, on account of its defenceless condition, against the inroads of the Turkmen.

The tracts of land occupied by the Turkmen lie along the rivers Gurgan and Atrek, localities which, by the ruins of ancient monuments they contain, bear evidence of having been once inhabited by flourishing communities. Now that the Turkmen are deprived of the opportunities for selling their captives, there is every probability that they will revert to peaceful pursuits, and the Khivans being no longer supplied with slaves, would exchange their freebooting occupations for the more lucrative industry of the plough, and their example would be followed by the neighbouring Turkmen encampments, as well as the Kirghizes and Karakalpaks.

The slave traffic in Khiva cannot be suppressed without having recourse to compulsory measures, and these it would be more difficult to enforce here than in the Khanat of Kokan.

The entrance of armed vessels into the Amu-Daria is extremely difficult on account of the shallowness of its mouth, there being only three feet over the bar at high water, besides which, at low water, the shoals in the river above are so numerous that vessels drawing more than two feet cannot possibly ascend it. Were flat-bottomed steamers to be despatched up the river with troops, even during the season of high-water, their retreat, in the event of any miscarriage, would be attended with serious obstacles. The Amu, furthermore, yields no other fuel along its course than the bushes of the Saxaul, which would prevent the vessels making an extended cruize. Notwithstanding these difficulties, it is certain that the Russian Government, if determined to abolish the slave trade of Khiva, might devise the necessary means for this purpose, but it must be owned that any military operations on the part of Russian Central Asia would be attended with great outlay.

If the military picket line of frontier were removed to the new boundary of the empire, the Ural-Orenburg and Siberian lines, extending from Yurief on the Caspian, to Bukhtarminsk, a distance of 3300 versts, would then become useless, and the Cossacks by whom they are maintained, being relieved from that duty, might be removed to the fertile places on the Upper Syr, where the cost of their subsistence would be considerably less.

Overcoming in this manner the obstacles which the barbarous Asiatics place in the way of the development of Russian trade, the natural impediments by which nature has cut Russia off from that rich oasis watered by the Syr and Amu, remain to be considered. The chief obstruction is presented by a vast extent of barren Steppe, traversed however by five principal routes, viz.: 1, from Khiva to Mangyshlak on the Caspian; 2, from Khiva to the Western shore of the Sea of Aral towards Orenburg; 3, from Bokhara Northwards to Orenburg; 4, from Tashkend along the Eastern border of the Kirghiz Steppe to Troitsk; 5, to Petropavlovsk. Of these, the first-named is the shortest, not exceeding 1000 versts, but it passes through waterless regions infested by pillaging Turkmen, and is for these and other reasons unfrequented. The second route, which is 1300 versts long, is open to much the same objections, and is therefore equally neglected. The third road, that in ordinary use, leads from Orenburg to Orsk (225 versts), from thence to Fort No. 1, on the Syr-Daria (721 versts), offering a safe traversable road for vehicles; farther on again to the Yany-Daria river (about 200 versts), and lastly trends southwards through a completely waterless Steppe for 300 versts, from whence to Bokhara there remains a distance of about 200 versts, over sandy but less arid localities. The whole distance from Orenburg to Bokhara is reckoned at 1700 versts. From the fortress of Orsk to Bokhara there are forty stages, and as many from Troitsk to Tashkend. Along this last route, good pasture for cattle is found. Still better, however, is the road from Tashkend to Petropavlovsk, which is throughout the whole distance passable for wheel carriages, and though it extends across a barren Steppe, wells are to be found along it. The length of this road is 1600 versts. It is only lately that certain kinds of goods are transported from Russia into the Steppe, as far even as the banks of the Syr, by means of oxen and carts. The ordinary mode of carrying goods is on camels, which animals are alone capable of supporting the want of water, or of drinking water of bad quality, while they can also subsist on the prickly shrubs of the Steppe. Goods are despatched by caravans, and only at those seasons of the year when snow hurricanes in winter and the sultry heat and aridity of summer do not render the Steppes impassable.

Owing to these circumstances only two caravans pass between Bokhara and Orenburg during the year, and the number of cattle and men forming the caravan is in proportion to the difficulties to be encountered on the journey. The number of beasts of burden in the caravan is also governed by the supply of water and pasture along the road. The route from Khiva to the Caspian has been abandoned on account of the scarcity of water and pasture. Caravans are from two to two and a half months performing the journey from Orenburg to Bokhara and *vice versâ*. The cost of transporting goods is from five to fifteen roubles, or averaging ten roubles (£1 10s.) per camel carrying a load of sixteen puds, or 576lbs. avoirdupois. From Orenburg to Bokhara the price paid is 60 copecks per pud (5s. 8d. the cwt.)

During the year 1860, 25,565 beasts of burthen and 5072 carts arrived at the Orenburg, Troitsk and Petropavlovsk Custom Houses, and 8145 and 4337 respectively were despatched from those places. Waggons or carts are principally used in transporting government stores, or goods destined for the troops stationed in the Steppe. The trade with the Central Asiatic countries is mostly carried on by means of beasts of burthen (pack animals); calculating, therefore, at sixteen puds per camel, the quantity of goods brought into Russia amounted to 400,000 puds, (4160 tons,) and sent from that country to upwards of 130,000 puds, (1972 tons). These figures are very low when it is taken into consideration that a great portion of the heavy bulk is made up of metals.

Naturally, large quantities of goods cannot be transported by the present inadequate means of conveyance, and although the cost of transporting goods to Russia is now lower than formerly, since the pacification of the Steppe to the North of the Syr-Daria, and the exemption of the caravans from Khivan toll-dues, the cost of transporting goods from Bokhara to Moscow is seldom less than two roubles per pud, about £18 10s. per ton. In order to lessen the expense of the land carriage, a more direct route than the present one must be selected, or those in existence made more convenient for the passage of caravans.

The most direct route for sending goods from Khiva to the Volga is undoubtedly that *viâ* Mangyshlak, where stands the Nov Alexandrovski Fort. But unfortunately the whole extent of country between the Amu-Daria and the Caspian is almost totally devoid of water, and infested by marauding Turkmen. But when this route, though only traversable by camels, is cleared of these

CARAVAN-BASHI (KHIVA) AND ATTENDANTS.

robbers, it will acquire greater importance and will always serve as an auxiliary road, should the means of conveyance on the other lines of transit be temporarily cut off, or be found to fall short of commercial requirements.

The conjectures so often hazarded in different works respecting the diversion of the course of the Amu into its ancient bed to the Caspian, are altogether undeserving of serious attention, as the great evaporation in the Steppe would preclude the possibility of the waters of this river reaching the sea, even were the whole stream directed to it by shutting up the irrigating canals which absorb so large a quantity of its volume. This last measure would have the effect of impoverishing the whole population of the Khanat of Khiva, whose very existence depends on a supply of water for their fields and pastures.

The waterless and dangerous character of the route leading from the Amu to the Caspian cannot but be regretted, more particularly as Bokharian goods might easily be conveyed to Khiva along this river, which is only fifty versts from the town of Bokhara. At this part it is navigated by native boats. The river is considered navigable for a distance of 1100 versts, 800 of which are through a populated country. Along this waterway, Russian goods might penetrate to the very base of the Celestial mountains.

At first sight it may appear easy to transport the goods brought down the Amu to the Sea of Aral, and, carrying them up the Syr, the mouth of which is a little deeper than that of the former river and is never shallower than three feet, and so bring them to Fort No. 1, from whence they can be despatched overland to Russia. But considering the small depth of water at the embouchure of the Amu, and that the flat-bottomed boats which may be used in navigating this river cannot be safely used on the stormy and turbulent Sea of Aral, for which reason the goods would have to be transhipped, the difficulties in the way of surmounting this scheme will be found very great.

Acknowledging therefore the unavoidable necessity for the time being of transporting goods between Russia and Bokhara overland, it only remains to render it less perilous and costly.

The extent of 500 versts between the Kuvan-Daria and Bokhara, now traversed by caravans, is scanty in water and forage, and is imperfectly guarded against the marauding Kirghizes owing to the impossibility of maintaining stationary military pickets in these parts. The road can therefore be traversed only by camels and strong caravans, and at the most favourable season of the year.

The road from the Syr-Daria to the Russian frontier can be used by carts drawn by a single animal at all seasons of the year. The communication with Russia would of course be greatly facilitated, were the transport of goods between Bokhara and the Syr capable of being carried on in the same manner; this, however, can only be effected by skirting the wilderness stretching from the left bank of the Amu and the Sea of Aral to the Western slope of the Kara-taù and Ala-taù mountains. The most convenient route, therefore, from Bokhara to Russia should lead to the Syr-Daria through Tashkend or Kokan. Goods despatched from Bokhara to Russia cannot safely pass through the Kokanian territory, until the incessant warfare carried on between Bokhara and Kokan has subsided, and this can only be effected by Russian influence.

The duty collected during 1860 on the goods passed through the Orenburg and Siberian frontier custom-houses yielded 315,000 roubles, of which 97,000 were collected on salt from the Kirghiz Steppes, 90,000 on cotton manufactures, and 23,000 on silk and woollen fabrics.

It appears advisable, therefore, in order that Russia should effectually protect the Kirghizes who have placed themselves under her rule, and to extend the commercial intercourse between Russia and Central Asia, to adopt the following measures :—

1.—To occupy the upper course of the Syr-Daria by a military force, so as to ensure the free navigation of the whole river, by which means the struggle carried on between Kokan and Bokhara would be stopped.

2.—To secure a firm footing on the Amu-Daria, in order to put a stop to the traffic in slaves, and subdue the Turkmen tribes camping on the Eastern shores of the Caspian.

3.—To connect the Syr-Daria and Kirghiz Siberian lines by a series of forts.

4.—To transfer the Orenburg and Siberian frontier lines to the above new military boundaries.

5.—To establish regular steam communication on the Syr-Daria.

6.—To despatch consuls to those Central Asiatic countries with which Russia maintains commercial relations, and to endeavour to establish Russian factories in those places.

7.—To encourage agriculture among the Kirghizes.

APPENDICES.

APPENDIX I.

ITINERARY OF ROUTES IN THE TRANS-ILI AND CHU REGIONS.

(A) *From Fort Vernoé to Pishpek.*

(1) Keskelen river, 28½ versts.

The road trends along level ground, crossing the Great Almatinka, Boraldai, and Aksù rivulets, which issue from the mountains. All these rivulets are diverted into innumerable aryks or canals. The road extends at a distance of five versts and more from the base of the Ala-taù.

(2) Kargaly river, 21 versts.

Numerous gullies formed by the deflux of the waters in spring from the Ala-taù are crossed, and the Chemolgan rivulet, an affluent of the Keskelen, traversed.

(3) **Fort Kastek, 31 versts.**

The ground is more level here than on the preceding stages. Good pasturage is found along the Uzun-Agatch and Kara-Kastek rivulets.

(4) **Bugu-Muyus river, 23 versts.**

Here the road traverses small ravines similar to those occurring on the second stage of the route, and gradually approaches the mountains. The halting-place for the night on the Bugu-Muyus is at the very head of the defile. This portion of the road is intersected by the Djiren-Aigyr and Kara-Archa rivulets.

(5) **Salt Marsh at head of Djamanty river, 16 versts.**

Running through the defile in which rushes the Bish-Mainak torrent, the road continuously ascends the chain, and in some parts crosses spurs of the main range. Occasionally it leads over tedious and dangerous slopes.

(6) **Kara-Kunus river, 28½ versts.**

After attaining the summit of the range, at a

short distance from the head of the Djamanty, and from the Boladjan mountain, the road gradually descends to the valley of the Chu, over numerous spurs which impede the progress. The Kara-Kunus rivulet, where it issues from the mountains, is well supplied with water.

(7) **Former Tokmak Fort, 15 versts.**

On gaining the Valley of the Chu, this river must be crossed; the passage is more easily accomplished above Kekmek-Sengir than immediately opposite Tokmak. In hot weather the fords over the Chu are not deeper than three feet.

(8) **Kagety river, 21 versts.**

From Kara-Kunus, the Northern side of the Chu Valley may be followed. The night-halts will be at the Kara-Su spring, twenty-five versts from Kara-Kunus, and on the banks of the Chu, close to the Chumitch ford, a distance of twenty-three versts. The distance from Chumitch to Pishpek is nine and a half versts.

(9) **Fort Pishpek, 25½ versts.**

The road extends through the Chu Valley, parallel

with the base of the Kirghiz-Alatau, traversing the Shamsi and Naurus rivulets.

On the whole of this extent there are convenient places for night-halts, and sufficient grass and water at all the localities indicated; the water of the Chu is very muddy, and it is therefore preferable to avoid this river.

Total, 209½ versts, or 139⅔ miles.

B. *Another Route from Pishpek to Kastek.*

(1) Argaity river, 25 versts.

The Chu must be crossed at the Chumitch ford, and a northerly direction pursued over even ground. The reeds along the Chu spread to a width of three versts.

(2) Argaity river, 14 versts.

The road leads through the narrow valley of this river, which is also partially overgrown with reeds, and has a slight inclination.

(3) Kurdai river, 30 versts.

A journey across inconsiderable mountains to the northern side of the Alatau, emerging midway on the source of the Kurdai, which, in hot weather, dries up where it leaves the mountains.

(4) **Taldy-Bulak rivulet, 20 versts.**

The road trends close along the base of the Ala-taù, through the perfectly flat Kopa Valley. The Taldy-Bulak is a small stream disappearing altogether in a few aryks that serve to irrigate the Kirghiz pastures.

(5) **Sarymsak spring, 36 versts.**

Journeying still through the Kopa Valley, leaving on one side the Djamanty, Bish-Mainak, and Kara-Archu rivulets, which become completely dry in summer, the ground along this extent is level.

(6) **Fort Kastek, 25 versts.**

The road traverses several hollows and ravines, and crosses the Utch-Bulak stream to Djiren-Aigyr, at which point it emerges on the first route.

The Chumitch ford is worse than the fords above Tokmak; but the Kurdai pass is, on the other hand, more accessible than that of Bishmainak.

Total 151 versts, or 100¾ miles.

(C) *From night-halt on the Kurdai to It-Kichu.*

(1) Uzun-Su rivulet, 17½ versts.

The road stretches along the base of the Ala-taŭ range, which at this part is of inconsiderable height, and past the Iri-Su and Kizyl-Su springs.

(2) Kendyk-Tash rivulet, 15 versts.

The character of the country remains the same. The Kopa valley becomes somewhat narrower, and is bordered by low and rocky mountains on the North and South.

(3) Chokmar-Su rivulet, 24 versts.

The same description of ground. The Kopa valley widens by degrees; at the Chokmar-Su it descends Westward to the Dala-kainar valley.

(4) Dala-kainar river, 20 versts.

The road runs along the rivulet and occasionally over small elevations.

(5) Mai-Bulak rivulet, 24 versts.

As the Dala-kainar becomes exhausted before reaching the Chu, the journey must be continued to the S.W., over undulating ground, to Mai-Bulak spring; this latter, however, contains but little water.

(6) Fort It-Kichu, 25 versts.

The ford here over the Chu is very shallow; the shores are overgrown with reeds.

The grass on this route is poorer in quality than along the other described roads.

Total 122½ English versts, 80¼ English miles.

(D) *From Pishpek to Aulié-Ata, on the Talas.*

(1) Sokuluk river, 27 versts.

The road runs through the valley of the Chu, and is intersected by the rivers Shiraly, Kiunuk, and Djilamys.

(2) Fort Aksu, 24 versts.

Same ground. The Chu valley becomes wider as the bed of the river turns to the North-west.

(3) Upper Kaindy river, 22 versts. Fort Merke, 25 versts.

The road presents similar features. Still the same ground; on nearing Merke ravines are crossed.

(4) Tarty river, 20 versts; Toichi-aryk, 20 versts; Makmal river, 30 versts; Kara-Archa, 25 versts; Aulié-Ata town, 30 versts.

The ground at first is pretty even, and only intersected by small ravines with rivulets; but approaching Aulié-Ata, it is more undulating. Nearer to the Talas it again becomes flat.

Total, 223 versts, or 148⅔ miles.

(E) *From Aulié-Ata to Namangan.*

(1) Utch-Kurgan, 25 versts.

The road extends along the valley of the Talas, along the left bank of this river.

(2) Kara-Bura Pass, 40 versts.

At five versts from Utch-Kurgan along the Talas valley, the road strikes off Southwards into the mountains, and follows the Kara-Bura spring, as far as the culminating point of the pass. The steep descents and rocky ground make this journey very difficult. Caravans traverse it in two days, halting midway for the night.

(3) Chirchik river, 35 versts.

The descent from the mountains follows the Marzashnyn-Choty rivulet, the road presenting the same character as above.

(4) Kurgan-Chanysh, 30 versts.

After fording the Chirchik, the journey is continued along the left bank of this stream, over ground traversable by vehicles.

(5) Chanysh Pass, 25 versts.

The road again runs Southwards, entering the mountains, along the Chanysh rivulet to the summit of the pass.

(6) Ak-Tash locality, 25 versts.

Descent.

(7) Iskı Abat settlement, 13 versts.

The small settlement of Safet-Bulak occurs at five versts from the night halting-place, at the foot of the mountains; beyond, the ground is even.

(8) Namangan town, 20 versts.

The road here stretches over a plain, and the village of Goleshan is passed on the sixteenth verst. Namangan is on a river of the same name which issues out of a snow-capped range. Several canals exist in the neighbourhood of the town, and irrigate the fields of the many settlements that spread here.

Total, 213 versts, or 142 miles.

(F) *From Aulié-Ata to Suzak.*

(1) Asa river, 20 versts; Bel-kul lake, 25 versts.

A level road through the Kara valley.

(2) Djangys-Agatch spring, 16 versts.

A level road down the course of the Asa.

(3) Arba-tash spring, 20 versts.

The road crosses low hills.

(4) Cherbakty river, 15 versts; Chernakty river, 25 versts; Babaty river, 25 versts; Sunduk river, 30 versts; Uzun-Bulak river, 30 versts; Cholak-Kurgan fort, 15 versts; Suzak fort, 55 versts.

Along the whole of this extent of the road, water and grass are procurable at the night halts. The road skirts the Northern foreland of the Boraldai range, at a distance of five versts. The ground is level.

Total, 276 versts, or 184 miles.

(G) *From Aulié-Ata to Tashkend.*

(1) Asa river, 30 versts.

Along the Kara valley.

(2) **Kuyuk hills, 20 versts.**

Passing first through a valley, the road then runs over gentle heights, which may be traversed in carts.

(3) **Ters settlement, 20 versts.**

The road descends from the Kuyuk hills, and extends along the Ters valley—abounding in water and grass.

(4) **Arysh river 25 versts.**

The road crosses mountains, and then separates into three branches: one leading over the Chomkan elevation, passable by carts, another through the Kulan pass—not a very good one—while the third is merely a pathway used by single horsemen.

(5) **Karakchi-Bulak settlement, 14 versts.**

The road descends the valley of the Arysh, the river remaining on the right.

(6) **Mashat town, 20 versts.**

Continuing in the same direction, Westward, the road deflects from the Arysh, leaving on the left the mountains, from whence all the rivulets that occur on this journey take their rise.

The Arysh flows at a distance of five versts to the North of the road.

(7) **Mankent settlement, 13 versts.**

The settlement of Mankent contains about 1500 inhabitants, consisting of husbandmen and petty traffickers.

(8) **Kizyl-Su river, 16 versts.**

The road intersects the Aksù rivulet.

(9) **Saraim town, 20 versts.**

This small town stands on the banks of the Saraim which flows into the Arysh and takes its rise in the Kara-tinbe mountains.

(10) **Badam river, 18 versts. Duvan-Kurgan, 20 versts.**

The road passes over low spurs of the Kyzyr-kurt.

(11) **Ak-Djar settlement, 26 versts.**

Through Sharib-Khan Settlement.

(12) **Djas-Kichu ford, 20 versts.**

This ford is over the Keles river, with which the road runs parallel.

(13) **Kara-Kamysh locality, 25 versts.**

Midway, the road crosses the Uzun-Aryk canal, conducted from the Chirchika rivulet.

(14) **Tashkend 8-10 versts.**

The latter part of this marche-route, from the settlement of Ak-Djar, does not quite agree with that contained in Humboldt's "Asie Centrale," Vol. III, p. 338.

Total, 285 versts, or 190 miles.

(H.) *From Tashkend, to the River Chu.*

(1) **Ak-Djar settlement, 55 versts.**

Back by the same road.

(2) **At-Bulak, 20 versts.**

Turning off from the Keles, the road runs over low hills.

(3) **Chemkend town, 20 versts.**

After descending from the hills, the road emerges into the Badam valley. The wooded summits of the Kyzyrkurt are left on the right.

(4) **Arysh river, 25 versts.**

The journey is continued over gently undulating ground, to the Arysh river, below the mouth of the Chubar-Su, its affluent. The river here is deep and broad, and a ferry exists, at times, over it.

(5) **Bogon river, 20 versts.**

Undulating ground.

(6) **Arslandy river, 30 versts.**

Same ground. The Chayan rivulet occurs half-way.

(7) **Kara-Bash river, 20 versts.**

The base of the Kara-taù mountains is approached at Min-Bulalak settlement.

(8) **Cholak-Kurgan Fort, 36 versts.**

A pass over the Kara-taù mountains. It is generally cleared in two days. The road lies for some distance through a valley after descending from the mountains, and before reaching a settlement.

(9) Kli spring, 20 versts.

Across a level Steppe.

(10) Kara-Kul lake, 15 versts.

Level and partly sandy ground. Reeds in the direction of the lake.

(11) Tum settlement, 30 versts.

A tedious journey across sands; salines and a marsh occur at the night halt.

(12) Chu river, at the Kazangan-Utkul ford, 25 versts.

Similar country. Reeds extend for six versts towards the river.

Beyond this, the road runs past the Tes-Bulak settlement, through a barren Steppe to Semipalatinsk.

Total, 316 versts, or 210⅔ miles.

(I) *From Azret (Turkestan) to the Chu.*

(1) Karsakty, 15 versts.

Over even ground covered with rich grasses.

(2) Babai, 15 versts.

The road reaches the foot of the Kara-taù, clothed with birch woods.

(3) Suzak Fort, 45 versts.

Crosses the mountains through a rocky and well watered defile. This stage is generally passed in two days, halting for the night in the defile. Beyond the descent the road extends for some distance through the valley. The name of the defile is Suùndyk.

(4) Chu river, at the Toitube ford, 80 versts.

The road on this journey stretches over a sandy Steppe, in which, however, there are many wells (at Ak-urpek, Burumbai, &c.) Copses of the Saxaùl are met with. Nearer the Chu, there are salines and reeds.

Total, 155 versts, or 103¼ miles.

(K) *From Aulié-Ata to Lake Balkhash.*

(1) Kara-Archa river, 32 versts; Makmal, 27 versts; Djar-Su, 20 versts; Tarty, 15 versts; Kuragaty, 20 versts; It-Kichu fort, 35 versts; Djidel rivulet, 30 versts. Bata-Burn river, 30 versts; Well in the Steppe, 23 versts; Djir-tashmir river, 22 versts; Lake Alakul, 22 versts; (part of Lake Balkhash).

The ground is mostly even, except during the first stage; the grass is good but becomes scorched in hot weather.

The passage over the Chu is convenient, and the

valley of the river is overgrown with reeds. The greater part of the road runs across an even Steppe.

Pass over the Khan-taù mountains.

Undulating ground badly watered, grass tolerable.

Gently undulating ground. Salines occur.

Total, 276 versts, or 148 miles.

NOTE. This information was collected in 1859, in the Trans-Ili region, from many persons acquainted with the country, and the first three routes are founded on personal knowledge of the region.

APPENDIX II.

Astronomical determinations of points in Eastern Turkestan and Dzungaria were made by European missionaries, members of a learned commission, formed in the reign of the Emperor Tsian-lun, for describing the country, then newly annexed to China on the West. The first commission, which was organized in 1755 for exploring Dzungaria, was under the direction of Hé-ho-tszun; and the second, which explored Turkestan, was headed by Min-hotu. The following figures have been extracted by M. Zakharof from the book of Si-yui-tu-chji, and other sources, and differ in some portions from Klaproth's "Carte de l'Asie Centrale" of 1836:—

FROM THE BOOK OF SI-YUI-TU-CHJI.

	North Latitude.	Longitude East of Greenwich.
On Southern An-Si line:—		
Tszia-yu-huan barrier	39° 45′	98° 41′
Yui-min town	40° 5′	97° 52′
Tszin-ni town	40° 10′	97° 16′
Lu-hou-pu station	40° 25′	96° 39′
Chạn-ma, river source	39° 0′	96° 33′
Dan-chen town	39° 35′	95° 49′
An-si-chjeu	40° 34′	95° 45′
Hua-chjeu, new station	40° 32′	95° 44′
Ma-len-tszin station	41° 50′	95° 37′
Dun-huan town	40° 12′	94° 36′
Has lake	40° 4′	89° 53′
On An-Si Northern line:—		
Ban-chi-tsuan station	42° 37′	95° 34′
Sin-Sin defile	42° 5′	95° 31′
Talnatszin station	43° 31′	95° 23′
Tugurik village	43° 42′	94° 30′
Hara-hot	43° 50′	94° 25′
Sun-shu station	43° 32′	93° 48′
Nan-shan-kéù pass	43° 15′	93° 44′
Hami (Komul) town	42° 53′	93° 40′
Mu-cheu town	43° 53′	93° 34′
Kara-tinbé station	42° 52′	92° 58′
Ha-shun station	44° 0′	92° 21′
Barkul town	43° 39′	92° 12′
Habtak, station at mountain of	45° 0′	91° 48′
Baitak mountain	44° 43′	91° 14′
Ulau-usu station	43° 44′	91° 11′
Murui station	43° 45′	90° 38′
Kitai town	43° 45′	90° 23′
Hu-cheu town	44° 4′	90° 21′

	North Latitude.	Longitude East of Greenwich.
In Urumtsi district:—		
Tszimsa station	44° 9′	89° 22′
Urumtsi town	43° 27′	88° 18′
Foo-kian town	44° 0′	88° 24′
Chau-ki town	43° 45′	87° 47′
Loklon station	44° 3′	87° 45′
Yan-balgasun station	44° 17′	86° 39′
Manas (Sui-lai)	44° 20′	86° 25′
An-tszi-hai station	44° 13′	85° 40′
Northern Thian-shan line:—		
Kur-kara-usu town	44° 24′	85° 19′
Tszin-ho station	44° 33′	83° 43′
Chaban-baisin village	44° 32′	83° 16′
In the Tarbagatai district:—		
At confluence of the two Irtysh sources	47° 10′	87° 48′
Ulan-huchjir village	46° 15′	86° 58′
Ket-hobok village	46° 25′	86° 19′
Narin-hobok village	46° 25′	86° 19′
Nam village	45° 10′	86° 19′
Chuguchak town	46° 48′	82° 51′
Emil village	46° 8′	85° 14′
Chor village	45° 4′	84° 32′
In the Ili region:—		
Kunges, source of river	43° 33′	83° 9′
Kash, "	44° 8′	83° 13′
Yuldus, "	43° 17′	85° 23′
Kuldja (Ili, Hoi-yuan) town	43° 56′	80° 53′
Karatal, point on river	45° 40′	79° 3′
Hongor-olon (Kunur-ulen) point on river	42° 17′	78° 28′
Edemok settlement	42° 10′	76° 13′
Chu river, point on	43° 8′	74° 54′
Talas river, point on	42° 30′	73° 44′

	North Latitude.	Longitude East of Greenwich.
On Southern Thian-Shan line.		
In Pichusan district :—		
Hun village	42° 50′	91° 12′
Toho or Taku station . . .	43° 19′	91° 50′
Pichjan town	42° 52′	90° 28′
Lukchak village	42° 40′	90° 3′
Ilalik village	42° 46′	89° 48′
Turfan town	43° 4′	89° 18′
Chjoha-hoto settlement . .	43° 6′	89° 21′
In Kharashar district :—		
Chuhoi village	42° 17′	87° 36′
Karashahr town	42° 7′	86° 54′
Kurunlé station	41° 46′	86° 15′
Yugur village	41° 44′	84° 5′
In Kuchi district :—		
Tohanai station	41° 20′	83° 26′
Mouth of the Kizyl, at the Ukend	41° 35′	82° 5′
Toibolady village	41° 10′	83° 20′
Shah-yar town	41° 5′	83° 56′
Kuché town	41° 37′	83° 39′
Kuké-puyun	41° 20′	83° 30′
Eshik-bashi station (Ichké-bashi)	42° 9′	83° 12′
In the Sairam district :—		
Kizyl station	41° 45′	81° 48′
Sairam town	41° 41′	81° 33′
Hara-Usu station	41° 45′	81° 1′
Bai town	41° 41′	81° 1′
Yailgan village	40° 45′	80° 42′
In the Aksù district :—		
Ilgatsi	41° 44′	80° 41′
Uchjuma village	40° 0′	79° 28′
Aksù town	41° 9′	78° 58′
Chjaergé (Chjaekdé) village .	40° 52′	78° 35′

	North Latitude.	Longitude East of Greenwich.
In the Ush district:—		
Ush-Turfan town	41° 6′	77° 46′
Seferbai village	41° 1′	77° 21′
Sogon village	39° 50′	75° 4′
In the Kashgar district:—		
Kizyl-bni station . . .	38° 30′	75° 19′
Toprak (Topuluk) station . .	38° 29′	75° 1′
Yanyishahr (Ingashar) town .	38° 47′	74° 23′
Kashgar town	39° 25′	73° 48′
Aragu station	39° 52′	73° 32′
Osh (Haoché)	40° 17′	73° 22′
In the Yarkend district:—		
Duva village	36° 52′	79° 6′
San-chju town	36° 58′	78° 26′
Kuhé-yar (Kok-yar) village .	37° 7′	77° 11′
Barchuk town	39° 15′	76° 38′
Ak-Alyk village	37° 41′	76° 25′
Yarkend town	38° 19′	76° 3′
Saralyk (Serlek) village . .	37° 48′	73° 49′
Karchu town	37° 11′	73° 41′
Serikul (S. extremity) . .	37° 48′	73° 49′
In the Khotan district:—		
In the Kerya, or Keldya, town .	36° 58′	82° 48′
Tak town	36° 13′	82° 28′
Charé or Tsirlé village . .	36° 47′	81° 31′
Yurun-kash village . . .	36° 52′	80° 36′
Khotan town	37° 0′	80° 21′
Kara-kash village	37° 10′	80° 2′

From the Book of Si-yui-shui-das-tszi.

Chan-ma river, source of . .	38° 50′ ?	96° 39′
Dan river, source of	36° 58′	95° 33′
Sarten lake, from 38° 50′ lat., 110° 47′ long., to . . .	39° 5′	93° 10′
Lob-nor lake, from 40° 30′ lat., 105° 57′ long., to . .	40° 45′	89° 4′

	North Latitude.	Longitude East of Greenwich.
Bosten-nor lake	42° 8′	87° 44′
Karatala-ishek lake, or Bulhatzi-nor, from 44° 35′ lat., 100° 42′ long. (?)	44° 46′ ?	83° 33′ ?
Confluence of Kunges and Tenes	43° 45′	81° 53′
Mouth of Kash or Ili . . .	43° 41′	—
Source of Great Yuldus . .	42° 45′	81° 43′
Source of Kizyl-su . . .	42° 20′	81° 3′
Confluence of Kizyl-su and Muzart into the Yarkend-Daria	41° 25′	82° 3′
Source of S. Muzart river . .	42° 20′	79° 53′
Mouth of E. Aksù . . .	40° 4′	81° 8′
Source of Yurun-kash . .	36° 0′	81° 13′
Source of Kara-kash . . .	36° 0′	80° 5′
Kara-kul lake, from 88°21′ long. to	44° 10′	72° 23′
Source of Derbichuk river . .	43° 45′	71° 53′

FROM THE BOOK OF HÉ-YUAN-TSZI-LIS.

At bend of Yellow River to the West . . .	34° 6′	101° 14′
At entrance of Yellow River into China . . .	36° 0′	101° 9′
Huhunor lake, from 36° 6′ lat. 100° 13′ long.	37° 4′	101° 8′
Bulungir river, source of . .	37° 5′	97° 14′
At confluence of Haidu-golo with the Tarim . .	40° 2′	87° 4′
Little Serten lake . . .	39° 4′	—

APPENDIX III.

Marche-route from Turfan to Kashgar in Little Bokhara, from a verbal statement made in 1831 *by a Chinese inhabitant (Ma-tiang-shi) of the first-named town. By Golubef.*[*]

First night-halt: *Turfan.*

Seventy lis from Turfan, a Chinese picket; the military force here consists of forty Chinamen

[*] During the wars of Madali-Khan of Kokan, with the Chinese in 1830, conducted in Little Bokhara to the disadvantage of the latter, several Chinamen were taken captives and detained at Kokan. Many of these arrived at Orenburg with a Khivan caravan, intending to return through Russia to their native country. Every possible assistance was rendered them, and the staff of the Orenburg corps took advantage of their arrival by endeavouring to obtain from them some information concerning the unknown regions of

and fifty Kashgarians. The commander is a Chinese. They all live together in a little stone fort, such as is built at every picket station. The soldiers are relieved every three years, and do not live with their families at the stations. They obtain water from a rivulet issuing from the mountains, and losing itself in the sand not far from this picket.

Second night-halt: *Tugusun.*

Eighty lis from Turfan; the picket or guard consists of Chinese, like at Turfan, and close to it is a settlement of Kashgarians, which does not contain more than 500 or 600 inhabitants. A considerable trade in all goods is carried on here in the shops. The settlement is situated on the same rivulet as the Turfan picket.

Third night-halt: *Subash.*

Eighty lis from Tugusun; a picket and small fort in the hills. Water is obtained from wells.

Central Asia. Unfortunately, only a few of the statements of Ma-tiang-shi must be accepted as deserving of credit; the other accounts being both contradictory and doubtful. These, however, were taken down as being to a certain extent instructive, and the manuscript has since been preserved in the Siberian Archives.

Fourth night-halt: *Okhobula.*

One hundred and thirty lis from Subash; a picket in the mountains. A rivulet runs from here to Subash, where it loses itself in the sand.

Fifth night-halt: *Kumysh.*

One hundred and forty lis from Okhobula; picket. Bread and water brought from the mountains, and sold at three different stages on the road between Okhobula and Kumysh, in houses specially constructed for the purpose. The Kumysh picket obtains water from wells. Between the stations caravans frequently halt for the night at these houses for spring water.

Sixth night-halt: *Yushuku.*

Ninety lis from Kumysh picket; also a picket with settled residents, in five or six houses removed from the town of Aksù. Wells are here dug for water.

Seventh night-halt: *Ushtala.*

One hundred and twenty lis from Yushuku; a picket and six or seven houses adjoining, permanently occupied by traders who have settled here from different parts. A small house is constructed at each of the three different stages on the road between Yushuku and Ushtala, in which are sold bread and a kind of black pea for horses; money is also demanded here for well water. The inhabitants and troops at Ushtala obtain water from springs.

Eighth night-halt: *Ching-Shui-Hoza.*

Sixty lis from Ushtala; a picket and twenty houses with occupants, who are obliged to furnish twenty of the forty men composing the guard: the other twenty are Chinese. This place is situated on a rivulet bearing the name of the station, and flowing to the town of Kara-Shagiar.

Ninth night-halt: *Shu-at-Hoza.*

Seventy lis from the last picket station; a picket and a settlement consisting of thirty houses; wells dug for water. The Ching-shui-Hoza rivulet remains to the left. Within ten lis from Ching-shui-Hoza picket the road traverses this rivulet across a bridge.

Tenth night-halt: *Kara-Shagiar.*

Seventy lis from Shu-at-Hoza; a large town inhabited by Chinese. Kalmyks live in huts about the town under the government of a woman of their own race. The number of troops here amounts to 500 men; there are also 500 shops, an arsenal, and a powder magazine. This town lies between two rivers, the first the Ching-shui-Hoza, a small stream, the second the large and navigable Kei-du-Hoa. The latter is crossed in boats on the road to Kashgar, in the first stage, not far from Kara-Shagiar.

Eleventh night-halt: *Hiu-Chan.*

Eighty lis from the town of Kara-Shagiar. The Kei-du-Hoa river is crossed at one li from the town; the current of the river is towards the left bank. There are thirty-five soldiers at Hiu-chan, of whom fifteen are maintained and billeted by Mussulmen occupying here fifteen houses. Spring water.

Twelfth night-halt: *Kogolé.*

A small town inhabited by Mussulmen, ninety lis from Hiu-Chan, on the Shiui-Dalié rivulet, which issues from the mountains on the right. There are 200 soldiers.

Thirteenth night-halt: *Bugur.*

One hundred lis from Kogolé; a picket and settlement consisting of 200 houses occupied by Mussulmen agriculturists. A rivulet runs by here from the mountains on the right.

Fourteenth night-halt: *Ara-Batai.*

Eighty lis from Bugur; a picket and settlement, consisting of fifty houses occupied by Mussulmen agriculturists. Spring water.

Fifteenth night-halt: *Tokania.*

One hundred and twenty lis from Ara-Batai; a picket and settlement of thirty houses. Mussulmen inhabitants. Spring water.

Sixteenth night-halt: *Kuchia.*

Seventy lis from Tokania; a very large town, composed of 100,000 houses, occupied by Mussulmen; 600 Chinese soldiers. The Hi-shu-Hoa river runs between the town and the fort, which is garrisoned by the Chinese.

Seventeenth night-halt: *Yang-shiui-Ku.*

Seventy lis from the town of Kuchia; a picket and

settlement of thirty houses, occupied by Mussulmen. Spring water.

Eighteenth night-halt: *Yareng-Ku.*

One hundred and thirty lis from Yang-shui-Ku; a picket and settlement of thirty houses, situated on a rivulet.

Nineteenth night-halt: *Biai-Chin.*

Eighty lis from Yareng-Ku; a large town with 60,000 houses, on a rivulet flowing from right to left. The Chinese garrison consists of 400 men.

Twentieth night-halt: *Yar-Dju-Ku.*

Sixty lis from the town of Biai-Chin, a picket and settlement of thirty houses; spring water.

Twenty-first night-halt: *Hala-Yugun.*

Ninety lis from the Yar-Dju-Ku; a picket and settlement of thirty houses; spring water.

Twenty-second night-halt: *Zamyn.*

Ninety lis from the Hala-Yugun picket; a picket and settlement of 100 houses, on a rivulet.

Twenty-third night-halt: ***Aksù.***

Ninety lis from the Zamyn picket; an immense town, taled at 500,000 houses. The Kum-Bash, a large river, runs westwards past the town; it is not crossed on the route here described. There are 700 soldiers in the town.

Twenty-fourth night-halt: ***Yang-Aryk.***

Forty lis from the town of Aksù; a picket and settlement of thirty houses on the banks of the Kizyl-Su river, which flows from Kashgar.

Twenty-fifth night-halt: ***Yan-Ali.***

Seventy lis from Yany-Aryk; a picket and settlement composed of 500 houses on the same river (Kizyl-Su.)

Twenty-sixth night-halt: ***Shisian-Han.***

140 lis from Yau-Ali; a picket and settlement of twenty houses on the same river (Kizyl-Su.)

Twenty-seventh night-halt: ***Shiagiar-Tang.***

Seventy lis from Shisian-Han; a picket and settlement of thirty houses on the same river (Kizyl-Su.)

Twenty-eighth night-halt: *Shiji-Tang* (or Shiai-Tang.)

Eighty lis from Shiagiar-Tang; a picket and settlement of thirty houses on the same river (Kizyl-Su.)

Twenty-ninth night-halt: *Shi-Tang.*

Sixty lis from Shiji-Tang; a picket and settlement of thirty houses on the same river (Kizyl-Su.)

Thirtieth night-halt: *Yany-Djan-Tkhaidze.*

Eighty lis from Shi-Tang; a picket and settlement consisting of 200 houses on the same river (Kizyl-Su), which, in its course from Kashgar, makes a large curve and approaches the road, which is straight. Proceeding from Turfan to Kashgar, the river beyond Yany-Djan-Tkhaidze runs far to the right of the road.

Thirty-first night halt: *Tkhu-Tkhiai.*

Seventy lis from the last place; a picket and settlement of thirty houses. Wells dug for water.

Thirty-second night-halt: *Ur-Tkhiai.*

Seventy lis from Tkhu-Tkhiai; a picket and settlement of thirty houses. Wells dug for water.

Thirty-third night-halt: *San Tkhiai.*

Sixty lis from Ur-Tkhiai; a picket and settlement of thirty houses. Wells dug for water.

Thirty-fourth night-halt: *Sy-Tkhiai.*

Eighty lis from San-Tkhiai; a picket and settlement of thirty houses. Wells are dug for water.

Thirty-fifth night-halt: *U-Tkhiai.*

Ninety lis from Sy-Tkhiai; a picket and settlement of thirty houses. Water from natural springs.

Thirty-sixth night-halt: *Liu Tkhiai.*

Seventy lis from U-Tkhiai; a picket and settlement consisting of 100 houses, on a small river.

Thirty-seventh night-halt: *Chu Tkhiai.*

Ninety lis from Liu-Tkhiai; a picket and settlement consisting of 100 houses, on the same river.

Thirty-eighth night-halt: *Pa Tkhiai.*

Eighty lis from Chu-Tkhiai; a picket and settlement of seventy houses, on the same river.

Thirty-ninth night-halt: *Yarkend.*

Ninety lis from Pa-Tkhiai; an immense town, containing 300,000 (?) houses, situated on the river Sa-Koa, flowing on the left side of the road. The military force in the town consists of 1000 soldiers. Ma-Tiang-Shi considers the town of Yarkend to be five times as large again as Orenburg, where there are 1500 houses.

Fortieth night-halt: *Ta-Lian.*

Seventy lis from the town of Yarkend; a picket and settlement composed of 400 houses, on a small river.

Forty-first night-halt: *Tun-Chan.*

Eighty lis from the Ta-Lian settlement; a picket and settlement of seventy houses, on a small river.

Forty-second night-halt: *Tir-Chan.*

Eighty lis from Tun-Chan; a picket and settlement consisting of 200 houses. Water is here obtained from springs.

Forty-third night-halt. *Tala-Uba.*

Eighty lis from Tir-Chan; a picket and settlement consisting of 400 houses, on a small river.

Forty fourth night-halt: *Yanyshahr.*

Eighty lis from Tala-Uba; a large town on the Ak-Daria River, flowing on the left side of the road. In the town there are 300 soldiers.

Forty-fifth night-halt: *Pian Cho.*

One hundred lis from the town of Yanyshahr; a picket and settlement consisting of 100 houses, on a small river.

Forty-sixth night-halt: *Kashgar.*

Seventy lis from Pian-Cho; an immense town, containing 160,000 houses, situated on the Kizyl-Su river, which runs from here with a large bend to the Yany-Aryk picket, and thence along the above road to Yany-Djan-Tkhaidze. The military force in this town numbers 1500 men.

The night-halts are herein indicated at the pickets and in the settlements; but some of the stages of the road are so long that caravans are sometimes unable to perform them in a single day, and are obliged to halt for the night on the road. For this reason the distance from Turfan to Kashgar is reckoned a passage of fifty-eight days instead of forty-six.

APPENDIX IV.

Notes on the Intercourse of Russia with Khiva. By G. Kühlewein, Secretary to Col. Ignatief's Mission to Central Asia.

[NOTE.—Since the foregoing was in type, attention has been directed to the accompanying paper which is so important, both in itself and from the official position of the writer, that no apology is needed for including it in the Appendix, although its proper position would of course have been after Chapter III.]

KHIVA was in communication with Russia as far back as the 14th century, but the first official intercourse between those countries of which there is any authentic record took place in 1557, in the reign of Ivan the Terrible, after the taking of

Kazan, when Khivan Ambassadors arrived at the Court of the Tsar to ask for liberty to trade with Russia. Similar missions visited Moscow, in 1563, 1566, and 1583. The present political relations between Russia and Khiva may be said to date from the latter part of the 17th century, since when the Khivans have had recourse to frequent missions and been profuse in gifts and promises of allegiance, when sent to appease the displeasure of the Russian Sovereign for ravages committed on their frontiers; but strong in the imagination of their own inaccessibility, the Khivans have always returned to their evil practices, and defied the power of Russia, until recalled to reason by imminent dangers of chastisement.

The Tsars, on the other hand, have alternately used conciliations and threats in the pursuit of their favourite object, that of opening a trade with India through the countries of Turkestan. In the early part of the 17th century the Khivans complained of the inroads of the Ural Cossacks, who to this day retain the traditions of their campaigns against Khiva. In 1602, the Cossacks even took Khiva, but were defeated on their return thence. In 1622, Afghan, the Khan of Khiva, expelled by his relations, sought the protection of Tsar Michael

Fedorovitch, and offered, if restored to his dignity, to become a vassal of Russia.

A Khivan envoy presented to Peter the Great in 1700, a letter from Khan Shamaz, in which the latter asked the Tsar to receive the allegiance of the people subject to him. By a letter of the 30th July, Peter intimated his compliance with that request, confirming it subsequently in 1703 by a letter to the new Khan of Khiva, Arak Ahmet. The *Moscow Journal*, of April, 1703, contained the following notice on this subject :—

"The Khan of Khiva has sent his Ambassadors to our High Lord and King, requesting the High Lord to allow him, the Khan of Khiva, with all those under his dominions, to render for ever allegiance to His Majesty the Tsar, which our Sovereign Lord has graciously granted, and now sends his Ambassador to the Khan of Khiva."

At this time there were reports of gold sand being found on the Amu-Daria (Oxus), the Caspani mouths of which were said to be purposely filled up by the Khivans, and its waters deflected into the Aral; and that it would be easy to destroy the dams erected by the Khivans and to restore the river to its ancient bed. This intelligence was brought to Astrakhan by a Turkman called Hodja-

Nefes. At Astrakhan, Nefes made the acquaintance of Prince Samonof, a native of Ghilian, converted to Christianity, with whom he set out in 1713, for Moscow, to propose to the Emperor that he should seize, with assistance of the Turkmen, the country bordering the Oxus, then in the possession of the Uzbeks. Prince Gagarin, Governor of Siberia, arrived in Moscow the same year with a report to His Majesty on the gold sands of Little Bokhara. Hodja-Nefes and Prince Samonof were presented to the Emperor by Prince Bekovitch-Cherkaski, Captain of the body-guard, and in great favour with the Emperor. Ashur-Bek, the Khivan Envoy then at the Russian Court, confirmed the report about the gold sand of the Oxus; he remained at St. Petersburg, from 1713 to 1715, and enjoyed the favour of Peter the Great. He was also very intimate with Prince Gagarin, voivode of Siberia.

Ashur-Bek suggested that Peter the Great should construct at the old mouth of the Oxus, probably on Krasnovoda spit, a fort capable of containing 1000 men, and told His Majesty, that the Khan would not oppose the destruction of the dams reported to have been constructed, nor the restoration of the Amu to its former bed.

This Envoy was dismissed from St. Petersburg, in 1715, the Emperor giving him among other presents for the Khan six guns with everything complete, and a considerable quantity of powder; but these were taken away and the Envoy temporarily detained at Astrakhan in consequence of a revolution at Khiva. Yadi-ber had died in 1714, and was succeeded by Khan Arang, of the Karakalpak tribe, who was in his turn replaced by Khan Shirgazi of Bokhara.

In a letter of the 5th March, 1715, to Chirikof, the Commandant of Astrakhan, Ashur-Bek, writes that he was commissioned by the Emperor Peter to go to India for the purchase of parrots and panthers.

It is probable that Peter, wishing to ascertain the nearest route to India, and to establish commercial relations with that rich country (as further indicated in the subsequent appointment of Lieutenant Kojin and the Murza Tevkele), sent Ashur-Bek on a mission of that kind, who, after making the necessary purchases in India, was to have returned to St. Petersburg.

In the year 1716, Prince Bekovitch Cherkaski (of Circassia), was sent as envoy to Khiva and Bokhara, to inquire about the gold, the East Indies, the trade of those countries, and other local circumstances. Many officers were sent with him to survey the Caspian and Aral seas, and for other purposes. Prince Samonof and Hodja-Nefes were likewise with him, and the rest of his suite consisted of merchants from Astrakhan and other parts of Russia, Tartars, and Bokharians, numbering about 200 men. On the road, after passing the Emba river, he received an autograph order from the Emperor to send to India, through Persia, a man acquainted with the language of these countries in whom confidence might be placed, and who should collect information about this country, and particularly about the rivers where gold was reported to abound, returning to Russia by way of China and Bokhara. Murza Tevkelef was accordingly sent. The barbarous murder, in 1717, of Prince Bekovitch* at Porsu, a town about seventy miles N.W. of Khiva, in which, however, the Khan of Bokhara was not implicated, put an end to their enterprise.

During the reign of the Empress Anne, in 1731, Colonel Erdberg was sent as envoy to Khiva, but

* His head was stuffed with hay and sent to the Emir of Bokhara, in token of victory. The soldiers forming the expedition were either murdered or reduced to slavery. *Vide* Chap. II., p. 24.

being pillaged on the road, he was obliged to return unsuccessful. Nine years after, in 1740, the Khivans invited Abdul-Kaira, then Chief of the Lesser Horde of Kirghizes, subject to Russia since 1730, to reign over them as Khan, and he was accordingly elected. On assuming the sovereignty of Khiva, Abdul-Haira declared the Khanat to be subject to Russia, thinking by that means to arrest the march of Nadir, Shah of Persia, then on his way to attack him. At that time there were two Russian officers at the Court of the Khan—Lieutenant Gladishef and a topographical engineer of the name of Muravin. They had been sent at the request of Abdul-Haira to build a town at the mouth of the Syr-Daria (Iaxartes). They had orders to make a preliminary survey of the locality, but not finding the Khan at his Horde, they proceeded to Khiva. Muravin was then sent by the Khan to meet Nadir Shah, and ask for mercy, but his intercession was of no avail, and the Shah soon after took Khiva by assault.*

In 1750, during the reign of the Empress Elizabeth, the Khivans proposed, through their

* See account of Gladishef's and Muravin's Journey from Orsk to Khiva and back, in 1740-41. Ed. by Khanikof in 1851.

envoy, Ir-Bek, an intimate alliance with their country. This did not, however, prevent a Russian caravan from being pillaged the following year.

Doctor or Major Blankenagel was sent to Khiva in 1792, by the Empress Catherine II., at the special request of the Khan. Being persecuted by the latter for his inability to cure blindness, he was obliged to flee for his life, and returned to Russia by way of Mangyshlak and Astrakhan.

After Abdul-Haira another subject of Russia was chosen Khan of Khiva, namely Nurali, son of Abdul-Haira. In 1750 Khiva was governed by Kaip, a Kirghiz Sultan, also subject to Russia; and even to the year 1800 the Inekhs or successors, were always elected from among Kirghiz and Karakalpak princes subject to Russia, who to this day are the sole lawful heirs to the throne of Khiva, being of the "white bone," as descendants of Mahommed and Genghis-Khan. When Iltizer, an Uzbek prince, subdued the petty princes at the beginning of the present century, and took the title of Khan of Kharesm, the subjection of Khiva to Russia ceased, and was even replaced by an offensive policy. This is more particularly remarkable in the reign of Mahommed Rahim, brother of Iltizer, between 1801 and 1824. He began by subjecting the Aral territory, now no longer in existence, and oppressed in various ways the Kirghizes tributary to Russia.* He made inroads on the latter, drove away their cattle, and induced whole camps to enter his dominions, so that at last the whole of the Lesser Horde was compelled to pay tribute to the Khan of Khiva. At the time of the death of Mahommed Rahim, in 1824, the Khivan Khanat, says M. Khanikof, possessed already the form of political unity, actually subject to the ruler of Khiva, acquiring thereby a certain amount of political importance. But this reform, although a decided success if compared with the previous state of the Khanat, was nevertheless not sufficient to make the latter important either as an enemy or an ally of Russia.

The insolence of the Khans of Khiva was, however, so great on several occasions, that Russia was more than once on the point of punishing them. Twice, in fact, viz., in 1801 and 1804, the seizure of Khiva had been ordered by the Emperors Paul

* The Aral territory, lying to the South of the Aral, was long independent, but at last became tributary to Khiva in the reign of Mahommed Rahim. The majority of its population was composed of Uzbeks, but there was a considerable number of Karakalpaks and Kirghizes.

and Alexander, but the expeditions were delayed, owing to some disturbances in the Orenburg country, although in 1802 the Khivans disputed the passage of a Russian mission to Bokhara under Lieutenant Gaverdovsky, from Orsk.

Captain (afterwards General) Muravief travelled in 1819 and 1820 from Mangishlak Bay, in the Caspian, to Khiva, having been sent, together with a Bashkir official, to negotiate with the Khan; but they were unsuccessful, and Muravief, after being detained some time a prisoner, narrowly escaped with his life.*

In order to put an end to the depredations of the

* In 1835 the Russian Government, finding that they could not put an end to the intrusions of the Khivans, and the excesses which they committed, resolved on more rigorous measures, and seized a site near Mangishlak on the Eastern shore of the Caspian, opposite Astrakhan, and built a fort which commanded the landing places in the bay.

This gave great offence to Ullah Kuli-Khan, who remonstrated strongly, and failing here threatened to send out plundering parties more numerous than before. He complained to the Khans of Bokhara and Khiva about the division of his country, but they gave him no assistance, while they admitted the justice of his demand. The Russians, shortly after occupying the Eastern bank of the Caspian, sent out a reconnoitring party of about 120 men, under two men of rank. They were all brought to Urgendj and sold as slaves in Bokhara and Kokan, notwithstanding the remonstrances of the Emperor of Russia.—Burnes.

Khivans and to liberate the many prisoners they had made on the Caspian and on the Orenburg line of frontier, the Emperor Nicholas ordered, in 1836, an embargo to be laid on all Khivan traders and their goods, found on the frontier lines of Orenburg and Siberia, in Astrakhan, or within any of the dominions of Russia. In return for these the Khan was called upon to give up his Russian prisoners, numbering several hundred men, and cease all offensive measures towards Russia. The Khivans were not to be released, nor was any trade to be carried on between the two countries, until these conditions had been fulfilled.

The Khivan traders in Russia* were accordingly detained, in August, 1836, on their return from the fair of Nijni-Novgorod. The Governor-General of the Orenburg country then informed Allah-Kul, the Khan of Khiva from 1824 to 1840 (a son of Mahommed Rahim), of the measures which had been adopted by the Emperor, and demanded the restoration of all the Russian prisoners and the immediate suspension of his evil designs against Russia,

* These are said to have been forty-six in number. This summary proceeding gave great offence to the Chiefs of Turkestan, who at once commenced a system of retaliation.—BURNES.

threatening the retention of the Khivan traders with their goods, and the interruption of all commercial intercourse, until these conditions were carried out.* The first effect of these measures was the arrival of a courier with letters, in the month of January, 1837. The Khivan messenger declared that the Khan was ready to deliver his Russian prisoners, if Russia liberated the Khivan traders and destroyed Fort Novo-Alexandrovsk on the Caspian. The Khivans were told that the traders would only be released on the return of the Russians detained in Khiva; and their insolent demand respecting Fort Novo-Alexandrovsk was treated with silence. In the month of November of the same year, Kabul-Bai arrived at Orenburg as envoy from Khiva, bringing twenty five Russian prisoners and considerable presents. His son was amongst the Khivans detained at Orenburg. The Khan, finding

* General Perovsky wrote as follows to the Khan on the 18th September, 1836:—" Your actions are bad, and bad seed produces bad fruit. If you wish to come to your senses in time, return all your Russian prisoners at once, and promise to conduct yourself peacefully and amicably in future; do not countenance rapine and murder, nor interfere with the government of the Kaisak people; give the subjects of the Emperor of Russia the privileges His Majesty gives to yours in his own dominions, and the past will be forgotten."

that his subjects were well treated in Russia, thought he would get out of his difficulty by the exercise of some cunning, and accordingly assured the Russians that he had taken some trouble to collect the prisoners, and that if any still remained they would be liberated. It was ascertained from the Russians who returned that the Khan was afraid of being met with other demands after fulfilling the first conditions, and that he would be made to pay *Kun*, or the price of blood, for the murder of Prince Bekovitch, and give satisfaction for the numerous robberies of caravans, or even Kun for all Russians who had died in captivity. This is why he only sent twenty-five prisoners by Kabul-Bai. The envoy was sent back the same month with the answer that the demands made by Russia would not be modified, that the release of all the prisoners would be insisted on, and that until these demands were complied with, every Khivan subject entering the dominion of Russia would be detained, and kept until a general exchange of prisoners took place. After waiting two years, scarcely 100 men were restored, while in 1839 about 200 and more fishermen had been seized on the Caspian.

It was now evident that the interests of Russia,

the prosperity of her trade, and the well-being of her subjects, could only be secured by more active measures. On the 14th (26th November, 1839, a declaration was published at Orenburg, of the causes and objects of the military operations against Khiva. That document proceeded to say:—"Just and reasonable considerations have induced His Majesty the Emperor to send a military force against Khiva in order to secure by force of arms the rights and interests of Russian subjects, to put an end to pillage and rapine, to liberate prisoners then in Khiva, to inspire the respect due to Russia, and to establish the influence indisputably belonging to her, and which was the only guarantee for the maintenance of peace in that portion of Asia. Such is the object of the intended expedition against Khiva."

The results are well known. Leaving in winter, the forces under General Perovski were obliged to return without reaching Khiva, owing to the severe frost and the depth of the snow. The expedition, which numbered 5000 men, had nevertheless the effect of bringing the Khan to his senses, though temporarily. In the summer of 1840 he released all the Russian prisoners. Shakespere, an English officer who had arrived at Khiva from Cabul in 1839, undertook to conduct the prisoners to Russia. They were about 400, and had been taken at various periods between 1780 and 1839. Some of them occupied high positions in Khiva; thus one of them, William Laurentief, was Chief of the Artillery, while Ann Kostin, the wife of a soldier, acted as housekeeper to Khan Allah-Kul.

On the 18th July, 1840, the Khan of Khiva issued a proclamation or firman abolishing the trade in Russian slaves, and prohibiting inroads into the Russian dominions; this, coupled with the releasing of the prisoners, was considered satisfactory by the Russian Government, and it was determined to renew commercial relations and open negotiations with the Khivans.

Lieutenant Aitof, who had also been detained in Khiva, returned to Orenburg before the arrival of the other prisoners on the 18th (30th) October, 1840. He accompanied to St. Petersburg a Khivan envoy, Athanias, Hodja-Reis' Mufti, who brought a letter addressed to the Emperor, and returned in the spring of 1841. There were three envoys after him from Khiva, but none of them went to St. Petersburg.

In 1841, Captain Nikiforof was despatched with

one of these envoys (Shinar Mahmet-Niaz), as agent, with instructions to re-establish relations with Khiva, and, if possible, to make some kind of treaty; but he returned without success.

Colonel Danilevski, another diplomatic agent, was sent to Khiva in 1842. He succeeded in making the first treaty between Russia and Khiva. During his residence in Khiva, Allah-Kul died, and was succeeded by his son, Rahim-Kul. But treaties and stipulations were of no avail. The Khivans still continued to injure Russia in the Kirghiz Steppe, and endeavoured to strengthen themselves as much as possible on the Syr-Daria (Iaxartes,) where Russia had been for many years past erecting fortifications. The construction of forts on the Syr-Daria frightened the Khivans; they fully appreciate the importance of the occupation of the bank of the river, saying that if the Russians are to drink the waters of the Syr-Daria with them, they can no longer exist. Since the erection of Fort Perovski, Khiva has evidently been afraid of open war with Russia. Thus she has always evaded the invitation of an alliance with Kokan against the Russians. Without openly manifesting any unfriendly disposition towards Russia, Khiva never ceased to avail herself of opportunities to injure

Russia in secret, by continuing to send spies and gatherers of tribute into the Steppe. She urged the thoughtless Kirghizes to a fanatical enmity towards Russia, supported the insurrectionary attempt of Kenisar, Iset Kutebar, Nazar and other Kirghiz rebels, by promises of assistance in case of open rebellion. In addition to her own disposition, she was probably incited by Turkey, which was visited by her envoys in 1853 and 1854.

Since 1856, Khiva is governed by Said Mohammed, son of Khan Mohammed Rahim, and brother of the celebrated Allah-Kul. He was elected to the Khanat in 1856, at the age of thirty. His election was preceded by many disturbances and internecine wars; but these have ceased for the present. In 1857, Said Mohammed sent Fazil-Hodja, the Sheikh-Ul-Islam of the Khanat, to announce his accession and to convey his condolence on the death of the Emperor Nicholas, and his congratulation on the accession of the present Emperor.

THE END.

CPSIA information can be obtained
at www.ICGtesting.com
Printed in the USA
LVHW022023120422
716028LV00006B/149

9 783752 590487